INHERITED LUCK

TWISTED LUCK
BOOK FOUR

MEL TODD

BAD ASH PUBLISHING

Bad Ash Publishing

Atlanta, Georgia

www.badashpublishing.com

Cover by Ampersand Book Covers

Inherited Luck/ Mel Todd. -- 1st ed.

Paper 5x8 ISBN 978-1-950287-13-0

Hardback 6x9 ISBN 978-1-950287-20-8

Audio ISBN 978-1-950287-14-7

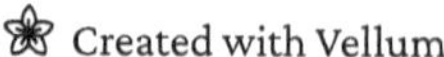 Created with Vellum

To all the people I've lost in 2020, you gave me love I'll never forget.
Madge Eaton - grandmother
Howard Lowery – friend
Aubrey Todd - father

You are missed.

CHAPTER

ONE

Mages are some of the most powerful people around, and merlin level are deadly at all times. Instilling great control, caution, and humility in these mages should always be the primary goal. Power isn't useful if it is used for selfish reasons. ~ Qin Dynasty

---

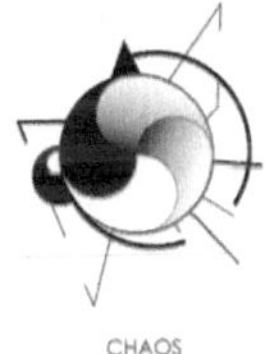

CHAOS

"**A**rgh! Stupid system. Work!" I glared at the computer screen as I tried once more to put in my magic branches and strengths for the draft board. But it wasn't programmed to handle a double merlin and kept tossing errors.

I'd finished my bachelor's degree in June and was trying to file my intended major for my master's and my course of study for my doctorate, but the stupid system refused to accept any input.

Sixteen months ago I'd climbed out of the rubble of the school building I'd destroyed when trying to not get killed by two mages from Japan. The fact that I lived, much less got Japan to quit trying to kill me for an inheritance still surprised me. The fact that only one student had died eased my guilt and I was found not responsible for their death as I had been fighting for my life. But I'd never wanted to kill anyone, even if it had been Daniela Morris—someone I'd barely been able to tolerate in the first place. The fallout, however, had been severe, but somehow I'd managed to not get expelled.

First responders were everywhere dealing with the destruction and injuries, but Japan had lived up to what they promised to the phoenix Jeorgaz and me. Before the ambulances left, there had been representatives from Japan there, personally apologizing to the president of GA MageTech and taking full responsibility. Money had been handed out like water (though I didn't get any), and even the damage to the Guzman's shop had been completely covered by Japan.

As if thinking about her summoned her, my best friend Jo Guzman came into the apartment.

Jo was my best friend in the world. Transform archmage, proud lesbian Latina, and my soul sister, she was curvy, gorgeous, with skin that reminded me of roasted nutmegs, and hair that touched her butt. Mages did magic via genetic offerings; hair, nails, blood, things like that. Which meant you never cut your hair as you needed it to do magic. Which meant her thick black silky hair weighed a ton and annoyed her.

When I was twelve, I met Jo a few months after my brother Stevie died in my arms and from that day on we were inseparable. We'd experienced a lot over the last few years and I knew I would have never gotten my bachelor's degree without her support. The three of us— which included Jo's girlfriend, Sable Lancet— lived together in a decent college apartment. The living room, crammed with three desks, a futon couch, a club chair, and a forty-three-inch TV meant you weaved between desk chairs and the small coffee table. The apartments weren't bad, but they were still college apartments with puke-bland walls, not enough bookshelves, and a kitchen that made a boat galley seem large. But for the last two years it had been my home, more of a home than I'd ever had before.

Sable was wisely avoiding me by hiding back in their bedroom trying to wedge clean laundry into the packed closet. Jo was a clothes horse at the best of times.

"I could hear you yelling at the computer through the door. Should we start running now before your annoyance sets Murphy's Luck on all of us?" Her lilting voice teased, but it also brought into clarity the prickling sensation that had been at the bottom of my awareness. The familiar light prickling, almost like goosebumps, of Murphy's Cloak started to settle around me. I had the bad habit when I was frustrated or upset to unconsciously cast the spell on myself and then I'd feed it all unconsciously. The bad thing was this spell affected probabilities in the negative way, meaning everything that could go wrong would.

"Dang it." I dispelled it with a grunt of irritation and stared at the forms.

"You're overthinking this," Jo pointed out. "Copy everything into an email and send it to the contact link on the website. Sable said she had to do the same thing because her requested master wasn't on the drop down. Don't worry about it and just send." She pulled out the bundle of snail mail and started sorting it.

I took a deep breath and typed out the email, putting in everything I'd been trying to do via the website. I fought a sigh as I started to type. Because of my power, being a double merlin meant rather than access to one class of magic and three branches like a standard mage, or access to all the classes, but only five branches like most merlins I had access to eight branches. Having a familiar gave me that eighth branch.

CORISANDE MUNROE DOUBLE MERLIN.
Strong: Relativity, Time, Earth, Soul, Psychic
Pale: Transform, Entropy, Non-Organic
Bachelors in Biology minor in Soul. 4.0 GPA
Providing Master's degree selection information and justification per draft requirements. Included is my doctoral path, with possible career paths.

MAGIC WRAPPED around my world and wove through it. There were five ranks of mages and merlin was the highest level. And until me, no one knew you could "emerge" twice, which made me both a freak and a pawn in a game I wasn't interested in. Emerging is what gaining magical abilities was called. Most people would get a class, Order, Chaos, or Spirit, and then get to use 3 of the four branches in the class. But not me. Instead, I got access to almost everything and it had been proven that even the branches I supposedly didn't have access to, I could use.

Which meant the government was very interested in in which degree I would choose and how they would use my draft service. The ranks of mages were hedgemage, magician, wizard, archmage, and of course merlin, and all mages above a hedgemage had to serve a draft period. Merlins served for a decade instead of four years.

I shook my head and kept typing in all the information they wanted. They knew who I was—why did I have to provide all this crap? When I was finished, the monitor glared at me like a disapproving drill instructor, like typing the email had been the wrong thing to do. I wrinkled my nose at the website, and killed that tab. That'll teach websites to be uncooperative.

"We owe money, asking for money, spam insurance, elections, spam, elections, hey an actual piece of mail for you." Jo sorted through the pile of mail. We only picked it up once every other week or so because ninety percent of it was junk mail we didn't care about, and the mailbox was on the other side of the apartments and in a direction we almost never went.

I just nodded at her comment, still staring at the computer screen. If I sent this, I was committed. Why did an email seem more final than entering something on a form?

"You're stressing again. I can smell calories burning. And here you go, mail for you. Looks official," Jo said as she dropped an envelope on my desk and peered over my shoulder. Her perfume, a mix of ozone and sharp metal touched with honey sweetness, wrapped around me, bringing emotional support if nothing else.

"I know. I'm just... " I waved my hands in the air, not sure what I was, except annoyed.

She paused and patted my head. "Well, I can solve part of that." Out of the corner of my eye I saw her arm flash down and grab my mouse. Before I could react, she clicked send.

"Eek! What did you do?!" My heart went into triple time and I lunged towards the screen as if I could undo what she had done.

"Saved you some angst. It's done and there isn't anything you can do to call it back. Let it be. They'll approve it or they won't." Jo flashed a smile, a bit harder than her normal smiles as she gave me a nudge with her shoulder. With that she headed down the hall to the bedroom she shared with Sable, her steps a bit slower than normal.

I frowned, but the pounding of my heart had me focusing on the computer, wanting to reach in and pull back the electronic packets. But she was right. There wasn't anything I could do and I would have spent another twenty minutes fretting over sending the email. I moved my attention to the letter she'd dropped on my desk. I frowned at the small manila envelope reading Corisande Munroe written in crisp clear calligraphy. I knew it wasn't my degree, that I'd received last week. It had taken eighteen months of busting my butt, dealing with the pressure from the government, and avoiding the societies.

The societies. Even the thought of them made me sigh. They should have been such a good thing but I'd heard too many horror stories about how they were the worst parts of an old boy's club and a gang. They wanted me, or to be more exact, they wanted to use me. They were the equivalent of frat houses for mages, each catering to different classes and personalities of mages. I'd joined the House of Emrys, but only because the merlin house was the least of the evils. The others still kept trying to convince me to join and various people I didn't know in Emrys kept offering to "help me out." It did wonders on making my paranoia worse.

The bright spot in the last year, besides Jo and Sable, had been building odd friendships with Indira Humbert, my mentor and one-time professor, and with Steven Alixant, FBI agent, government stooge, and Indira's boyfriend. The only student I'd created any relationship with was Charles Wainscot. He was an archmage and had a familiar named Arachena. She and my familiar, Carelian, were friends.

All in all, the last year had worn me to the bone and made it so I did little besides study, work, and dream about failing. But

I'd made it. I earned my degree and met the conditions of the will.

Oh, it's probably about that.

I sighed, suddenly exhausted as I stared at the envelope which had gained a level of menace it hadn't had previously. I still tended to hide from most people, mainly because after the building incident I was more than a bit infamous. Yes, Japan paid for a brand-new building and accepted all blame, which was the only reason I wasn't kicked out or prosecuted. I didn't know of anyone who really missed the one person who had died. Maybe her parents, but she hadn't made herself well liked. Magic didn't always make sense the way it worked, at least to me, and with all the training I'd had both from the GA Mage-Tech and Baneyarl, I didn't think we humans understood magic as well as we liked to think.

Maybe that is why most merlins retire to private research and why the government wants his research. It explains magic more accurately?

I let the thought rumble around my mind as I picked up the envelope and studied it. I could hear Jo talking to Sable in the background. Sable finished her master's this summer and wasn't going to go for a doctorate. Jo still had another year to get her bachelors.

Carelian yawned and stretched. He was my feline familiar, one of my best friends, and probably the closest thing I had to family right now. He rose to his full height and jumped off the couch. He was still growing, and every so often he scared me when I forgot who he was. He had reached the size of a cougar, but with bright ruby red fur and a tail he used as a whip. When people saw him walk down the street by my side it made them take a triple look. The thought of what he could do with those claws, what I'd seen him do with his claws, made me swallow hard.

I looked back at the email program, the sent box proving my missive was long gone. Was it even worth the fight? It seemed like all I did was fight to live my life, but no one else had any issues. My heart began to race and the familiar prickles of Murphy started up again. I took a deep breath in through my nose and out through my mouth forcing myself to relax. I continued until the prickles dissipated and I didn't need to fight down the scream at the back of my mind.

Screw it, I'll decide when they reply.

While normally the submission of your chosen degree path after your bachelors was a pro forma thing, I had been specifically asked to submit what I wanted and why. Which from Sable and Indira I knew wasn't the normal request. But it was their game. Being a merlin meant I owed the draft a decade of service. They wanted me now, but they also wanted me to have a degree to make sure I could use my magic properly. I felt like a blasted brood mare or something. All anyone cared about was what they could get out of me.

At least they didn't make me serve a decade for each merlin rank. See positive thoughts.

It didn't help. Just made me more frustrated.

~Are you sulking for a reason?~ Carelian's voice pulled me out of my funk.

Baneyarl had taught us how to talk to him telepathically. I could do it easily, always had been able to, that was part of the familiar bond. Jo and Sable could talk to him also if they concentrated, but that was because he assisted them. I could send thoughts to them, but they couldn't respond. Baneyarl promised eventually we'd all be able to speak this way, but it took time for the brain to learn how to compose thoughts.

While strong Spirit mages could read minds, in general mindspeak was like talking, you had to think to send your words to someone else. And that took practice without the familiar bond.

~Yes, no, I don't know. Just tired of this. I want my own life, dammit.~ I managed to mutter that even in mindspeech, which told me how much I was whining.

Carelian snorted and put his head down, wrapping his long tail around him. ~No such thing. Stop wasting time whining about what is out of your control. Do something useful.~

His comment just made me sulk more and I stood up. Needing to move, I walked over to stare out the window, the envelope still in my hand. It was thick and felt like more than one piece of paper.

~Some comfort you are.~

~My job is to provoke and guide you. Not feed pity. Jo, come kick Cori in the hind end.~ He resembled a ruby statue at this point, with his tail so tight around him it appeared seamless.

I heard laughter from down the hall and Jo walked out, followed by Sable. "Carelian said I need to come kick your ass? Is there a specific reason or direction I should kick it?" She grinned as she flopped onto our futon couch, pulling Sable down beside her. Sable wore her naturally curly hair in ringlets she twisted together in different patterns, and her black hair provided a contrast to her dark latte colored skin. With all the outside running Jo had been doing she was darker than Sable was, even though Sable had an African American father and a Japanese mother. The thought that she never talked about her mom flitted through my head, but I let it go to answer the question.

"He's grousing at me 'cause I'm moping. Which I know is stupid, but ugh. Why can't they go away?"

Jo and Sable exchanged glances and then shrugged. "I hate to say this, Cori," Sable said, a touch of sympathy in her voice. "But they aren't going to." I sighed, having expected and dreaded that answer. But Sable kept talking. "You are a double merlin, have a familiar that is almost instantly recognizable, not to mention impressive as hell, and you have an inheritance that multiple governments are drooling over. Frankly, if you get to live your own life before you turn forty, I'll be surprised."

I growled, sounding suspiciously like my familiar who yawned at me, showing off two-inch teeth, then went back into his statue impression.

"You're no help." I knew I was whining, but at this point I'd done over four years of doubling down on classes and it looked like I still had another three to go if I got a doctorate. I'd been sure that by now I'd have a job, a place of my own, that I'd be living my own life and not having anyone else telling me what to do.

"Nope. But lying to you is stupid. Cori, the price of being a mage means you owe something to society. You know that. You've taken the same history classes as I have and you know about some of the atrocities that happened. Jonestown?" Sable's voice was dry and I sank back in the chair shivering a bit.

Jonestown was infamous. In Magic History there was a mandatory ten-page research paper that all students had to write. The OMO and the draft board used those papers as a litmus to make sure mages had ethics. Anyone who could condone what he did, how he did it, wasn't anyone you wanted to have power.

All the information Steven and Indira had dropped told me that mages regarded as dangerous ended up dead very fast. After two years, I could finally think of Agent Steven Alixant as Steven, but it still caused a stab of pain saying my dead brother's name, and not having him here. Plus, I still had years before Kristos, my younger brother, would be given the option to find me.

I'd been surprised when Steven told me to watch and see if anyone disappeared after discussing that paper. Someone had, a student I recognized but didn't actually know. I found his name later on a list of obituaries for the school. That had dismissed any questions I had about how carefully people watched mages. Mages and non-mages would always be treated differently until everyone was equal or at least everyone had magic. And to think most people thought mages had it easy. Maybe money wise we did, but we had much less freedom than the average person.

"Do you really think they are going to let you, a double merlin out without anything less than iron control?" Sable's voice was unsympathetic and I didn't blame her.

"No," I responded. "They've retested a lot of people, even if they didn't want to be retested. Steven mentioned they'd only found three more that may have emerged twice, though currently they think the original rating was wrong and are blaming machine or operator error. None of them were merlins. Most of the older mages are avoiding the retesting at all costs. Which means I'm still unique." I shrugged. Getting tested twice just complicated your life.

"So sink into it, enjoy it, and make the most out of it. Grousing around won't change it, so find ways to enjoy. You met the first step of the requirements—the rest should be much easier than that." Jo gestured at the envelope I still held. "So open it already. I wanna know about the house. Assuming that is about the house."

Yes, the house. The reason I'd fought so hard to pull this off. But after eighteen months I was scared to look. What if it was now a rundown shack? More accurately, a rundown mansion. The picture could have been from thirty years ago. A Spirit merlin had left me a ton of stuff if I met the requirements for inheriting. The problem was, he thought I was a decade older than I was. Meeting that first requirement of getting my degree by the deadline almost killed me. But I had that piece of paper now. Everything else should be downhill—start my draft, finish my draft. Though survive my draft might be more accurate, especially if I didn't get my head in the game.

Sable's right. Quit moping and see what there is to enjoy about this. You can't change it, but you can still be who you want to be, right?

It just felt like I'd been fighting the establishment forever, and for what? That was the problem—I didn't know. And even more, I didn't know if I wanted to keep fighting.

"Cori?" Jo prompted and I shook my head. My hair reached my butt, and after a decade of wearing it at shoulder length, the weight distracted me and felt wrong. I was tempted to cut it, but that would just highlight that I could use offerings no longer part of my body.

"Sorry. Guess I'm in a funk. Not sure why," I admitted as the truth of those words sung through me. The laughter from Jo and Sable caught me off guard. "What?" My throat tightened and all the doubt stored up in my mind cascaded down on me again. I fought to control my desire to throw things. Carelian only flicked an ear at me, not saying anything.

"Cori, my dearest," Jo started, her pitying smile plastered on her face. I narrowed my eyes at her and I saw Jo fighting to keep the look cemented, but she choked on a laugh. Sable rolled her eyes and shoulder-nudged Jo.

"Cori," Sable said, "you've been working non-stop since Japan settled all the lawsuits. If you aren't in class, you're studying. If you aren't studying, you're working. If you're not working, you're in class. I don't think you've taken more than Christmas Eve and Day off since it happened. You even worked Thanksgiving. You're burned out, exhausted, and you're taking this summer off." She sent a stern look at me.

"Wait? What? No, I nee-" I started to say. I needed to work, take some more summer classes to lower my course load next year, and there was a second degree that I could get with a few more credit hours.

"You need a vacation." Jo interrupted my protests. "And a trip to see the house you killed yourself earning sounds like exactly the right thing to do. Now open the damn envelope, see what it is, but either way we are headed to New York to see your house!" Her glare held love, but she also wasn't going to give. When she got stubborn, Jo got stubborn.

"Fine, fine." I lifted both hands in the air, surrendering. As I did so the back of the envelope caught my eye and I pulled it down to pay attention to it. I'd been mostly avoiding it, aware of the grenade-like quality, but refusing to examine what shrapnel it might contain.

In script matching the front, the flap of the envelope had a name and address on it: Lucille Blanding. The address didn't match where the house was, but it was in New York. I'd expected it to be from the lawyer David Carlson. He'd checked in once a semester, see if I was on schedule, but nothing else.

With a shrug I opened it, exhibiting a bit more care than I usually did. I peeled open the envelope and a small sheaf of paper slid out. There were two pictures inside also. I looked at the pictures first.

It showed two people standing in front of a house—my house. The lines of it called to me and I had to fight to pay attention to the two people. They looked young in their twenties, possibly early thirties. The man was clean shaven with a thick head of dark brown hair, wearing an out of style suit. The woman next to him had brilliant red hair. It almost matched Carelian's coat. The suit dress she wore could have been worn today and no one would have even blinked. They were leaning on the porch columns and I could see the Spirit merlin tattoo on his face, but she didn't have one. I flipped it over and on the back was a date, about forty years ago, and two names. Lucille Blanding. James Wells.

"Huh, so that is what he looked like." I handed over the picture to Jo and Sable who had managed not to grab things out of my hands. They looked like two little kids waiting for their piece of candy.

"Mmm, who's the looker? His wife?" Jo asked and I glanced back over at her. The woman in the photo had been pretty, but the fierceness of her grin caught my attention more.

"No clue." I looked at the second photo. This picture was of the house, and was obviously pretty recent. It matched the one from the will. Built in the Victorian style, it had a wraparound porch, and octagonal structure on one side of the house. I stared at it until Jo cleared her throat.

"Patience, you have none," I said handing her the photo, then opening the letter.

CHAPTER

TWO

Merlins seem to love research and hiding in their homes. While it is not true that all merlins are rich, the majority tend to be well off if they manage their money wisely. As to idea of most merlins becoming reclusive researchers, it has become a conceit exploited by anyone trying to spin a story. ~Magic Explained Online

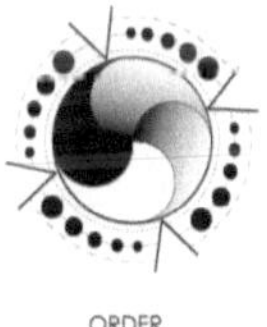

ORDER

M iss Corisande Munroe –

LET ME INTRODUCE MYSELF, I am Lucille Blanding, estate manager for the James Wells estate. Per my records you should be receiving this letter after you have had your degree for seven days. At the time of writing this missive I still have not heard from you in regard to the house.

As this property is now your responsibility, I expect to see you within three days of receipt of this letter. If you decide to drive up it should be four days. I will be expecting your phone call so we can meet and go over all the aspects involved in managing the house as well as the expectation involved from other parties.

Included are pictures of the house, both when it was originally purchased by James and myself and the most recent as of two years ago. Included are requests for access from the various groups in the last month. Until May of last year, the emperor of Japan was insistent that his Royal Magician be granted access. I believe you have insight as to the reason those requests ceased.

Review the requests and decide how you would like to handle them.

I await your call.

HER NAME, signature, and an address and phone number followed. As well as the address of the house. I'd registered New York when I'd looked at the inheritance stuff, but now the city of Albany jumped out at me.

"I'm impressed at the attitude and vaguely offended, but I

can't say any of her information is wrong." I handed over the letter then looked at the other pieces of paper in the sheaf. They were all addressed to Lucille, but specifically mentioned research notes located in the house, and requests to study objects suspected to be located in his house. To each letter was attached a note listing the times and the reasons they had been denied. The text on the notes was abrupt.

Unable to verify existence/location of requested object. Ask later.

Notes cannot be catalogued until inheritor arrives, ask then.

At this time, there is no access to the house being provided. Be aware the house has its own defenses and is perfectly capable of disposing of trespassers.

I snorted at that note. How did a house dispose of trespassers? The idea of a self-aware house raised even more questions.

I handed the notes over to Jo as well, but Sable was on her phone typing furiously. That got a raised eyebrow from me. She'd been just as interested in what the letter held as Jo. Before I could ask, she grinned and lifted brown eyes to meet mine.

"Got it. It should take us about fifteen hours to drive up there, so about two days. But Dad has a friend with a house in Bel Air, Maryland, we can crash at. If we pack tonight, we can be on the road tomorrow and at your house the next day. My draft doesn't start for another six weeks and you and Jo can afford to take a week or two off."

I started to protest. I should work this summer, build up my cash reserves, keep my skills up.

And sleep.

That whispered thought brought a sense of longing. I couldn't remember the last time I had slept past eight.

"Nope." Jo cut off my protests. "A road trip sounds delightful. I've never been any further than North Carolina, and we have to go to New York City. I want to see that house and we all deserve a bit of celebrating. We've all been working hard these last few months."

That I couldn't argue with. Even with severe dyslexia, Jo had raised her GPA to a 3.8. Sable and I both worked our butts off to keep a 4.0.

But with graduation, the mandatory mage draft would kick in. Mages between magician and archmage owed four years. Merlins owed a decade. But since she had her master's, the draft would pull her up soon and we still needed to discuss where she might be placed. It could be anyplace in the world the US had a presence.

I bit my lip. I'd never been out of the state. A road trip sounded like freedom in a way I hadn't expected. I glanced down at Carelian. "What do you think?"

He opened one eye to look at me. ~I want a hammock in the back.~ Jo and Sable snickered so I knew he'd shared that with them. We'd been watching a show and it had shown a hammock in the back of a hatchback with a cat laying in it watching the world go by. He thought that looked awesome. That hammock had been supported by suction cups though. I doubted suction cups would support him since he weighed at least ten times what the average cat did.

"I'll see what I can do," Sable said trying to muffle her laughs. Jo only owned a motorcycle and while I had my license, getting a car was an expense I didn't need. Sable, however, had a car and it was a hatchback, meaning he could watch the world go by around him.

~Then we should leave. There is much of this world I would like to see, explore, hunt.~

We all rolled our eyes at that. He'd never been much for cat toys, but he loved to terrorize the squirrels and birds, though had never killed any that I knew of. The only live food he ate with any regularity were mice from the pet store, and those were solely as treats. He said his favorite food was fish, which I guessed was a delicacy. I needed to remember to buy some salmon and take it to Esmere, his mother, or *malkin* in Cath language, next time I went to the Spirit realm.

"Will Baneyarl be able to reach us in New York?" I asked. As far as Baneyarl, our griffon teacher, was concerned we still had another decade of training to be able to utilize our skills fully. He'd likened it to the fact that we now knew how to build a table. In that we could put a flat piece of wood down and attach legs, but we had a long way to go to create a table worthy of royalty.

His eyes closed, Carelian flicked one ear towards me. ~He can find you wherever you are; the planes are not attached to your realm in any manner than I can explain.~

"Oh," I muttered. Nothing like having a cat or Cath point out the obvious.

I focused on the scenery of our road trip. I could see some states, explore the world. Getting out of here and away from Atlanta for a while might be something healthy for all of us. I turned and pulled up my bank account online and checked it. I'd been good about the money I'd earned, and the government stipends helped. With Jo and Sable paying for the majority of the bills it meant I still had a good bit of savings. I could take a week maybe two off and have some fun. Fun. I didn't know if I knew how to have fun anymore.

"Cori, we are going. We all need this, and frankly you and Sable deserve to have some sort of celebration. Getting a degree is a big deal and with the grades you two have it's an even bigger deal. We'll see some sights and enjoy the trip. Did she give you an email address?"

I double checked then shook my head. "Just the number."

"Well call her. Tell her we are driving up but are making a road trip of it and we'll be there in a few days. We can pack up, and head out. I'll call my parents and then we can bow to Sable as to where to stay."

I gave in. The idea of a break, a vacation, and a road trip with my best friend and her girlfriend sounded like something fun and in my control.

"Okay, let's do it." The words rang in the air, then Jo whooped and sprang from the couch.

"Yes! Road trip! Let's get packing." Jo headed off, pulling out her phone as she did so, and Sable grinned at me.

"This is going to be so much fun. I can't wait." Sable didn't squeal, not quite, but the grin she gave me shared her excitement and for a minute I felt guilty. I'd been so focused and determined to get this degree by the due date and they'd done everything to help me. Right then I knew I had to make this vacation one they'd never forget.

I called the number listed.

"You've reached Lucille Blanding. Please state the reason for your call and a number where you can be reached. If I feel it is necessary, I will call you back." There was a long beep.

"Um, hey. This is Cori Munroe. I'm driving up with my friends, but we are going to take a few days and make a road trip. We should be there Friday afternoon. Call me, I guess, if you need to." I left my number and hung up.

Jo was already packing, and Sable was talking to her dad letting him know we were headed that way and asking if his friend could host us for a night. That made me realize I should let my mentors know.

I'd been pressured by the government to have extra protection and guidance when the emperor of Japan had sanctioned a bounty on my life. Steven Alixant, FBI agent, and Indira Humbert, my teacher and unreliable friend, had offered to mentor me. I'd given in and signed a contract with them. The idea of mentors was very Middle Ages, but they'd bent over backwards to give me as much leeway as possible. I still felt like a mule with five different people trying to tug me in multiple directions. My mentors were two of them, and their goals—even if they were dating—weren't always the same.

Either way, I needed to keep them in the loop. I texted Alixant and Indira. I was getting better at thinking of him as Steven, but Alixant was still easier. Steven still reminded me too much of my twin brother and his death in my arms. Alixant would probably always be easier for me.

Hey, headed up to New York to see the house. Be gone a week or so. See you when I get back.

With that I shoved my phone in my pocket and started on my portion of the list Sable was creating on our whiteboard.

The next five hours were a blur of packing, calling, arranging to have our apartment looked after, and figuring out how to make the hammock that my familiar overlord demanded. He of course watched all of us from a huge cat perch wedged into the corner of our apartment, making comments and verifying we remembered his harness and his favorite food.

By the time we fell into bed we were ready to start on an adventure, complete with a cat hammock rated for over 100lbs.

CHAPTER

THREE

The draft isn't servitude, it is a framework for the responsibilities of a mage. The best way to make sure they understand the power gifted to them is education and training. While college educates, it is incumbent upon the government to ensure the training and consequences for letting their magic slip past the confines of societal mores is clear. ~ OMO statement to the UN

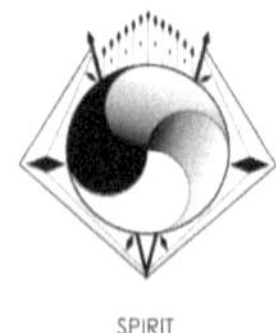

SPIRIT

All of us, Jo, Sable, Carelian, and I, had a blast on the drive up. The mountains were gorgeous in mid-summer and we stopped at half of the roadside attractions. Getting to see historical and local sights, eating out at places we didn't have at home and that catered to familiars, and just not being in Georgia sent a rejuvenating wave through me.

At the end of the first day, we crashed at a hotel about six hours from Atlanta, though with traffic and detours it had taken us ten hours. We were having too much fun eating, laughing, and just not thinking about classwork to worry about time.

Jo usually drove, while Sable took the passenger seat. I sat in the back watching the scenery. The billboards on the sides of the road advertised everything from adult toy stores, strippers, peaches, and pecans. The things you tried to seduce passing cars with never failed to amuse me.

~What is Adult Entertainment? And why do you want Live girls?~ Carelian asked as we left the Carolinas and headed up the East Coast. The billboards pushing sex as entertainment had been plentiful.

Jo and Sable joined in with my laughter. Jo managed to speak first. "It is advertising sexual films and naked women dancing for your entertainment. Wanna go, Sable? I can guarantee you're sexier than any of them."

Sable choked on her own giggles. "Thanks, but no. I'll live without having to stare at some strange woman's tits." I didn't have to see her to know she was smirking.

I laughed then paused as something registered in my brain. "Carelian?" I asked slowly. I could mindspeak, that much Bane-yarl had made sure of, but with the four of us I usually spoke out loud as neither Jo nor Sable could mindspeak back to me.

~Yes?~ He sounded zenned out as he swayed in the back of Sable's car, the suitcases tucked under him. I suspected the hammock would become a permanent fixture anywhere we went.

"Since when can you read?"

The sound of old musicals filling the car, courtesy of Sable's addiction, stopped. I could see Sable turned in her seat looking back as I twisted to stare at Carelian.

His tail stopped twitching and his lazy motions ceased, an "oh shit" silence filled the car before he sighed in our minds. ~For a while. Seeing the tiny print in your books or on the monitors is difficult, but the signs and anything large, I can read easy enough.~

I processed that information. It didn't really make a difference, but the ability to read could change everything. Familiars were catalogued as less than human but more than animals. If it became public knowledge, who knew what the ramifications would be.

"Can all familiars read?"

~Most of us. Depends on our eyes. But this isn't anything that needs to be spread around. My *malkin* will be most displeased with me.~ He sounded dejected, his ears laying back against his skull while his tail twitched in a staccato pattern. The body language reminded me that he still was under two years old, even by Cath standards not even a teenager.

"I won't tell her if you don't. Not like it comes up much and since you can't really see our books, I don't suppose you want stuff to read."

~No. I can read and understand most of what I read, though sometimes the sounds don't match what I expect. But Cath don't use written language. Most of the realms' denizens don't. Even with thumbs writing isn't practical. Our memory suffices. ~ He extended the claws on his front paw as he spoke, starting to groom, and waggled said thumb at us. Thumbs meant he could open doors and even operate a can opener if he wanted, though he preferred to be served and mostly it hadn't been a worry.

I really need to quit thinking of him as less than me. He isn't. He's not human, that doesn't mean he's stupid.

"Good to know, I guess. If I ever need to leave you a note, I'll make sure it is in really big letters," I said smirking at him.

He flicked an ear at me. ~Not amusing. You can speak to me from almost anywhere.~

"I can?" We'd never tested distance or range. I knew I could contact him at the apartment from anywhere on campus, but I couldn't remember ever trying to talk to him any farther out than that.

He paused and lifted his head to look at me. This time the voice in my head changed, becoming deeper and more contained, indicating he spoke only to me. ~That is a good question. We should test.~

~Yes, that might be good.~ I'd had more than one scare when Japan was trying to kill me. We did need to test the range since I'd gotten better at speaking to him.

We both let the subject drop, and music filled the car again, this time from Pirates of Penzance. Sable started singing along with I am the Very Model of a Modern Major-General, making Jo and me fall apart in laughter as she danced in her seat, keeping time with her hands.

The rest of the trip flew by too fast. The home in Bel Air, belonging to the old friend of Sable's dad, was nice. They let us bunk down in his grown kids' room. Their kids had all gone to college a few years ago and there was plenty of space. They fed us and made us feel welcome. It was odd thinking that most families were more like this than mine. That made me think of Kristos, my younger brother, but I still had at least seven years before he'd be provided the information to contact me. Someday I'd get to know my brother, but it wouldn't be until both of us were grown. Just one more thing in my life that was hurry up and wait.

After a huge breakfast the next morning, featuring the best omelet I'd ever had, we left offering our heartfelt thanks. Sable promised her dad would come by for a weekend to reminisce with his old friend. Piling back in the car we started the last part of our trip, and I almost hated to have it end, but all of us were ready to be out of the car for a while.

We made good time and arrived around eleven A.M. The road turned into a private lane and we drew in a shocked breath at the three houses. The will had mentioned these properties— they would become mine when I finished serving in the draft. The house we were looking for sat at the end of the dead-end road, but the other houses we drove by snagged our attention. The road had to be close to a mile long and while we may have been in Albany, we were at least twenty minutes from the city proper.

Each house sat on at least five acres, if not more. To our left was a two-story Craftsman, my Victorian hovered at the end of the lane, and the Tudor Mansion sprawled out on our right. I would have expected the Victorian or the Craftsman to sell for well over half a million, the Tudor mansion for a million plus.

"Damn. And you own these?" Jo didn't quite whisper but her voice held reverence and shock. I completely understood her reaction, the pictures hadn't conveyed these houses properly.

"Well not now. Just the Victorian at the end. But in theory someday, yes."

I need to remember to make a will.

That thought brought chill to my joy and some of the heat

of the day fled. We continued our slow drive admiring the houses.

"That one. That's the one I want. You love me Cori and will give me my own house?" Jo was half teasing half serious as she pointed at the Tudor she'd fallen for back when we had examined the contents of the will.

I snorted. "If I make it through the draft, it's yours. What in the world am I going to do with all of these?" Both of the houses had cars parked in the driveways, while one, the Craftsman, had toys on the lawn. Maybe they were being rented out. I'd looked at the paperwork eighteen months ago when the inheritance thing was dropped on me, but I put the documents away after I decided to get my degree in the time required.

Now my lack of information had come back to nip at my heels.

The house from the photos sat at the end and driving up to it I fell in love all over again. Victorian in feel, it had been recently painted and maroon trim and grey siding popped in the summer sun. A sleek silver Jaguar lounged in the driveway. A detached two-car garage at the right of the building had a covered walkway between it and the house. The wide driveway, big enough for two cars side by side, had a path leading to the front door.

I slid out of the back seat, holding the door open for Carelian. Once he jumped out, I felt drawn to the house and moved a few steps up the walk. The front door to the house opened and a woman stepped out. Shadowed by the porch roof, all I could make out was the outline of her figure. I headed up the walkway, doors shutting behind me and Carelian at my side, but I stayed focused on her.

The porch cried out for a bench swing, where I could curl up, drink sweet tea, and read. It wrapped around the left side of the house, out of sight. It needed some plants, a new coat of paint, but I knew I could transform it into a refuge from the heat of summer.

As I headed up the walkway, the form stepped to the top of the three steps going up to the porch. The light bounced off her hair, still a vibrant orange red though now cut in a sharp sleek bob. Dressed in exquisitely tailored slacks and suit jacket, she looked powerful and elegant. I felt oddly under-dressed in my shorts and tank top. Her sharp, light brown eyes traveled over each of us as she waited, hands clasped in front of her.

I'd never gone to a catholic school but suddenly I felt like a wayward student called before a nun. This woman was intimi-dating in exactly that way.

Jo shifted beside me and Sable nudged me from behind.

I took a deep breath, then forced a smile on my face and took one step forward, toes touching the bottom step. "Hi. I'm Cori. You must be Lucille."

"Hmm." The sound indicated nothing, but her eyes let me know I'd been found wanting. "Yes, I'm Lucille Blanding. About time you arrived. Come in. I don't have all day." Her voice was abrupt and professional as she spun on incongruent tennis shoes and walked back inside.

I glanced back at the others but the traitors shrugged and waved me forward. I resisted the urge to make faces at them and headed up the stairs following Lucille. The details on the door, the burnished wood on the porch railing, everything about the house made me want to investigate every detail. The banister on the porch had leaves worked into it, making it appear to have grown across the top. Approaching the entry-way, the scents of dust and decay assaulted my nostrils, and I wrinkled my nose. As I stepped fully across the threshold a wave of magic hit me and I gasped. It felt similar to my magical emergence, but softer. A caress instead of a slap. It poked and prodded and I felt like it asked a question, but I didn't know what the question was.

"I see the house has sensed you," Lucille remarked as she moved towards the entryway table.

I looked around confused by the magic and the dusty smell. The house looked clean, but the inside needed a good airing out. It felt, and smelled, stale and unused. Accurate probably. Lucille stood near the entry table that held a pile of papers, multiple keys, and a purse.

"I was beginning to think I'd have to issue a subpoena to get you here." She glanced up at me then shook her head. "The young have no sense of time, though I suppose I never realized I'd be taking on this responsibility for a decade when James died."

Jo and Sable had followed me in, talking softly behind me. I stood, antsy with a hunger to examine my house. My house. The phrase made me smile. I had a house.

I wanted to dance for joy, but I restrained myself and looked around. There was a sitting room to our right, and another room, maybe dining, to our left. The wallpaper in the entry was a pale green with small vines and leaves twisting through it. I couldn't get close enough to see more than that.

"What did you mean 'the house sensed me'?"

Lucille lifted her left shoulder in a dismissive gesture. "The house isn't normal. It has its own presence and magic, though I'm not sure how," Lucille replied. "Here is the deed, you just need to sign it. This is the acknowledgment of accepting all responsibility for the house and removing it from the standard trust which I manage." She pointed to the signature line on the paper. "I have here a list of requests received for items believed to be in the house. After you have had a chance to review them, we can discuss what you'd like to do regarding their requests. My suggestion is to ignore them until you complete your draft and own everything. That way you will have all the information necessary to make informed decisions."

Jo spoke while I read, "Believed to be?

Lucille slanted her eyes towards Jo, and I bristled as Jo flushed. But Jo stood up straighter and looked back at Lucille her expression challenging. Lucille smirked and shifted her eyes back to me, waiting for me to finish.

I read the paper carefully once more, but it simply confirmed the transfer of the property and all assets that go with it into my name. I signed my name with a sensation of electric excitement rippling through me.

Lucille checked my signature and nodded. "Excellent. Here are the keys to the property." She took a breath, her body tense, and held out the keys.

I reached for them, something striking me as odd about her behavior. Before I could grab the keys, she let go. I caught the jangling mess of brass and iron as it fell, and the world disappeared.

FOUR

What we know about magic is nothing compared to what we don't know. Humanity has studied magic for barely 150 years, and most of those years have been spent in guesswork and failed experiments. Never forget for a minute the offering you provide is based on decades of people risking their lives. Live by the rules we teach you, and maybe you'll live to be where I am today. ~ GA MageTech Commencement Speaker Chaos Merlin Osmond Jones

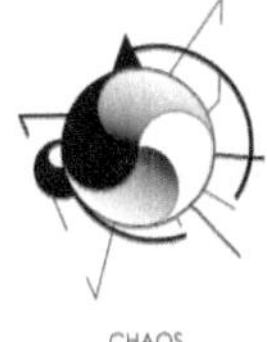

CHAOS

spun, my heart pounding. Jo, Sable, even the house had disappeared leaving me in a formless gray space. "Jo? Carelian?" I called out, trying to see anything. I could see myself just fine, but there wasn't anything else there. Even my voice sounded vaguely muffled as if the area around me absorbed sound. The only constants were the sounds of my breathing and my heart beating. Otherwise, silence shrouded everything.

Where the hell am I? What happened?

Panicking sounded really good, but it never helped. I knew that all too well. I took a deep breath and closed my eyes. The air or atmosphere around me felt cool, barely, so probably in the high seventies. My hair didn't move and there was no breeze. The ring of keys was clenched in my hand, but I could sense very little else. I was wearing sandals and the surface underneath me seemed firm, but that was all I could tell.

I knelt and pressed against the ground. It existed, but I couldn't tell if it was soft or hard, lumpy or smooth. Just there.

"This isn't real." The gray around me swallowed my words.

"It is and it isn't."

I spun, looking for a voice, but there was no one there. The voice came from everywhere and nowhere.

"Why am I here?" I had a dozen other questions, but that seemed most important.

"Why are you here?"

My brows scrunched together. "That's what I asked."

"You do not know?" I couldn't tell if the voice was masculine or feminine. Heck I couldn't be sure it was speaking out loud and not in my head. There was no accent and just a hint of some emotion in it. Not a computer but something not human?

That made me reassess the environment. I forced myself to

take a deep breath. I could feel my lungs expand, but I didn't feel the sensation of air entering.

"This is all in my mind. This is occurring by magic. So why did you take me?"

"You were not taken, you accepted. This is test one."

I accepted?

My hands clenched and the keys bit into my palm. The pain pulled me back from my confusion.

"A test? Are you the house?" The only thing I had accepted was the house. Magic had washed through me when I walked over the threshold, but who had a magical house? Magic didn't work that way. At least not for humans.

"In a way. Go on, prove how mighty you are. Banish me."

I blinked.

Banish it? How? With what? Is it crazy?

"Thank you, but no," I replied shaking my head.

"No?" This time there was amusement.

"While I'm not excited about being kidnapped, I doubt that killing you is the answer."

"Ah, you would kill me then?"

"Didn't I just say that wasn't the answer? And yes, I get there are multiple interpretations to the word banish. But I'm not an exorcist, and I doubt kicking you to another realm is the right answer. So, no. I'd rather figure out what you want and maybe we can..." What could I do? I didn't want to compromise as I hadn't asked for whatever this test was. What did I want?

"Maybe we can what?" There seemed to be a bit of curiosity as well as amusement this time.

I tamped down my temper. Snarking off to an unknown being wasn't the wisest move. Even if I was getting seriously annoyed. At least I wasn't scared anymore.

"Why don't you tell me what you want and I'll figure it out."

An odd silence filled the area, different than what I'd heard at first. I could almost hear the voice thinking.

"Do magic for me."

"On what? For what? To prove I what?" I would have started throwing things, but there wasn't anything to throw.

"To show me you know how to use it." The voice had lost all emotion and now sounded almost alien.

"Umm, okay," I muttered looking around hoping to find something, anything. But there was nothing there. Magic worked best affecting things. Fire or lightning were the only showy ones.

Ah, I can do that. Even after all this time Indira's class still helps me.

I rubbed my hands briskly on my shorts to generate some friction. Then in this space that I wasn't even sure existed, I called lightning, planning on arcing it up and away from my hands. The offering was so tiny, a single strand of hair, that I was hoping for a small arc, a little bit of brightness and the smell of ozone in the air. What I got was a bolt as thick as my wrist that streamed from my hand as if I was Zeus, hurling lightning bolts.

"Merlins balls!" I jerked backwards, cutting off the flow as soon as my reaction could manage. "What was that?" My calm fled like water on a red-hot skillet and I felt like I'd been dumped into the fire.

"Magic. An impressive use. What else can you do?"

"Why do you care? I want to go back. Are my friends okay?" I hadn't dared ask that, but that bolt had scared ten years off my life.

"Only you are here. They are where they belong."

That didn't make me feel much better. "What do you want?"

A figure came walking out of the mists, humanoid in shape,

but I couldn't make out any features or even if it was male or female. It blended with the grayness as it stalked around me.

"Fight me."

"Why? I don't want to fight you." My protest was heartfelt. Just because I'd learned how to use magic as a weapon didn't mean I liked using it that way. Weaponizing magic seemed to sully it and I couldn't explain why, other than the low-level reverence Baneyarl and Esmere had for magic. Their discomfort at how we'd reduced it all to a science played into part of my feelings.

"You don't want to prove you're better than me?"

"Umm no? Because I don't know that I'm better than you. Heck, I think the only thing I'd win on is having weirder things happen to me. Like this," I exclaimed as I waved my arms around.

The figure stopped and moved a bit closer. I still couldn't make out details other than rather willowy with long limbs.

"You are a peculiar one. No challenging me? No threats? No begging? They usually do all three."

I threw up my hands, swallowing a scream. "Why? Would it do any good? If you can bring me here, I doubt I want to fight you. But I also don't know if I want someone that would do this as my friend. So again I ask—what do you want from me?"

The being tilted its head one way then the other, as if peering at me from multiple angles. "Friend. That option hasn't been chosen ever. How interesting."

I didn't know what to make of that answer. So I went with it. "So, you want to come over for lunch sometime, meet Jo, Carelian, and Sable? Be social, and not this?" I waved my hands between us.

Laughter, pure and somehow shocking in its crystal clarity, burst out. "Fascinating." It giggled. "At this time no, though there is temptation to try something you call cake. There is one final test before you are returned."

I tried to sigh and swallow at the same time and ended up choking on the knowledge it knew about Tirsane and her interest in me. Tirsane, the gorgon demigoddess of Spirit. Powerful, terrifying, a friend of Baneyarl and Esmere, and she had enjoyed eating cake at my birthday party. Just thinking about her made the two green dots on my wrist ache. Markers of where one of her snakes had bitten me. I reached up to touch my necklace, a Spirit symbol charm Jo had given me for my birthday, backed with the scale Tirsane had broken off her body. A scale that would get me one favor, and something I planned on never needing to use.

I finished hacking up a lung and got my heart rate under control. Once again, I made a horrible first impression. Only me.

"Please set this on fire. Use as much or as little offering as you feel comfortable giving." An object appeared about five feet in front of me, looking like a strange obelisk, but at first glance I couldn't tell what it was made of.

I froze, suspicious. How much would it take? Fire remained a null and I didn't have Carelian with me to help lower the cost. I had avoided playing with it since the first time. It seemed too wild, and I'd had other things to do beside advertise that I could do the impossible. But on the other hand, if it got me out of here?

"Okay," I said, trying to sound confident. I wasn't.

Oh well, if Jo can go bald, so can I.

I took a breath and called for fire, seeking it in me, the area around me, and the object itself. There didn't seem to be much here—even air, though I could breathe, seemed absent.

Hard way it is.

I dug in my shorts and pulled out a receipt from the gas station we'd stopped at. We'd all needed to pee and I wanted a

Coke. I walked over to the object. It was about six feet tall and I couldn't tell what it was made of. Stone? Metal? Nothing? I'd learned how to identify elements, and I tried it now, but nothing resonated with the ones I'd learned. Transformation mages learned more of them than I did.

"It isn't radioactive, is it?" I asked, my voice squeaking as I took a big step back.

"No. I would not allow such poison into my domain." The voice sounded colder than the emptiness of space and I hoped it was right. I shook my head at my own paranoia and put the piece of paper on the top of it and backed away.

Here goes nothing.

I set the paper on fire the hard way, making the molecules move faster until the paper combusted in a bright red-yellow burst of hunger. That cost me a fraction of an inch around the ends of my hair. Mages had to offer up their genetic material to use magic, a quarter inch of hair wasn't much for someone with a null in Fire. First step done, I moved to the next and called Fire.

"I have tasty offerings for you. Will you eat the object you sit on?" I sing-songed the words so low I could barely hear them, but intent was what mattered. I'd learned through training with Baneyarl that Fire was always hungry. Fire possessed a need for sustenance that could never be quenched. It worked better if I talked to it about food than anything else.

The fire, or magic depending on how you looked at it, questioned me. It wasn't the normal query. From my experience—and talking with Jo and Sable showed me everyone experienced it differently—they would present a cost and I'd agree or disagree. This time it sent what seemed like a question, asking if I was sure I wanted to do that. It felt like getting an arched eyebrow from Jo when she looked at one of my cooking failures.

I sent back an affirmative.

There was the sensation of a sigh, and an amount. I choked but replied affirmative. Five inches of hair vaporized, and the obelisk was wrapped in incandescent flames and liquefied. The substance rippled through black to silver to a titanium rainbow. It was a cooling puddle of metal as the fire winked out of existence with the sensation of satiation caressing across my mind.

"Ummm, sorry?" I muttered it as I stepped back from the melted puddle. I didn't know you could do that. My head felt oddly light and I would need to remember to keep up the vitamins.

"That is unexpected." The misty figure stood, and it seemed to be focused on the cooling liquid. "This will be difficult to explain." It paused then looked at me, and I froze, feeling like a mouse before Carelian ate it. "You are not expected. But maybe that is for the best. Go. You shall prove interesting."

A rush of air hit me in the face and I blinked, the front hall of the house resolving with Jo, Sable, and Lucille all staring at me.

"Cori, what just happened? You've been standing there frozen for almost a minute," Jo asked slowly her gaze roving over me, as if making sure I was in one piece.

At the same time Carelian's voice burst into my mind. ~Where were you? You left. Your body was here, but not you. Where did you go!~ He sound frantic and the sharpness cut through my brain like a whip.

I pushed all that down and focused on Lucille, who had pursed lips with her brows drawn together. "What was that? Did you know that would happen?"

I saw Jo and Sable jerk their heads checking out Lucille. Carelian rubbed against my leg with a worried purr.

Lucille lifted her right hand up and waggled it a bit, making her silver ring reflect the light. "I suspected something might happen. James left very explicit instructions to hand over the keys after the transfer was signed and to make sure I didn't touch them when the new merlin did. He mentioned something about the house judging the worth of his heir."

"Cori, what happened?" Jo prodded, coming over and peering at me. "And what happened to your hair? It's shorter. It was long a moment ago."

I reached for my hair and sure enough the five inches of offering had been accepted. It wasn't all in my mind. "Wait, how long was I frozen?"

Jo and Sable glanced at each other, then back at me. "Maybe a minute? You caught the keys and just jerked. We waited for you to say something. You were standing there with a blank expression on your face. We called your name a few times, but you didn't react."

"I was about to grab you and shake you, when some of your hair vaporized, and you took a breath and blinked," Jo finished, still frowning at me.

"Okay," I drawled out. I'd thought I was in there for at least fifteen minutes, maybe longer.

"Cori!" Jo exclaimed exasperation in her voice.

"Oh, yeah. So..." I explained the weirdness and even Carelian listened with rapt attention.

"What did that mean? Who was it?" Sable asked when I finished. But I looked at Lucille for that answer.

"I don't know." Lucille spoke in a matter-of-fact way. "I know James said the house would verify, but he never mentioned anything like that. Though he may not have known. Of the houses on this street, this is the only one that has refused to let anyone live in it. People walk in and instantly leave. The rest are just houses. Not this one."

"What does that mean?" Sable must have read my mind because I wanted to know that to.

A quirk of Lucille's mouth softened her features for a moment, then it was gone, leaving the sharp woman watching us. "It means most people won't even walk into the house. They reach the steps and find a reason to turn around. I tried to rent it out for years before I gave up. A cleaner comes in and dusts and vacuums the rooms they can enter and the rest, well, they are yours." Her smile wasn't reassuring. "Now to finish up business and I will be on my way. As I was saying there are certain rooms that won't open. I'd advise if they don't unlock, then you aren't ready to go in there or the room isn't ready to let you in. There are lists of items James said were present, but I haven't ever verified. When he died, I didn't worry about it, I simply closed the house up."

"Wait, rooms that won't let you in? How do you do that? Magic doesn't let you do that," I protested. A quick review of everything I knew about the magical branches reassured me none of them had talked about enchanting rooms. "And I'm still stuck on the house has its own magic. Of course, given what just happened I'm not sure I know anything."

This time she sighed exasperated. "If you figure that out, you can respond to requests thirty-three and forty-four. No one knows how he did it and I am not a mage as you can see." She tapped her tattoo free temple. "Now the taxes for the estate were paid ahead of time for twenty years. You have nine before they are due. By then your draft should almost be done. Yearly property taxes average sixteen thousand a year. Though by the time you finish the draft you will have access to his accounts and paying that should not be an issue."

CHAPTER

FIVE

The discussion of null branches and if they are usable remains a point of contention. While most argue that null is usable but the cost is too high, there have been reports that if you are an archmage or higher, the cost may be much less than previously thought. But here our training teaches mages to ignore their null branches to such an extent that the opportunities to study this are overridden by belief that it is unusable. ~ Magic Explained Online

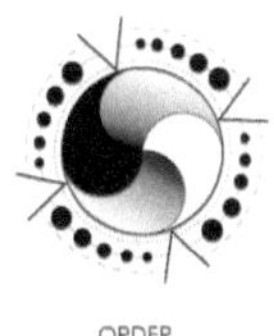

ORDER

I choked at the amount of property tax due. "Sixteen thousand a year? For taxes?"

Lucille leveled a hard stare at me, and I fought to not back up. In many ways she was much more intimidating than the strange being in the gray area. After making me quail in my shoes, she let a smile peek through. "Yes. New York State property tax isn't horrible. I would expect after your draft you will either have a substantial amount of savings or be able to get a job in the high six figures. If you are worried about money, once you start earning a regular paycheck, contact me and discuss investing. I'm in my office most weeks and the utility bills are being transferred over to you starting next month."

I eeped, terrified. The bills on this place must be insane. Suddenly my dream house was becoming a nightmare.

How in the world can I afford this?

The familiar prickle of Murphy started to wrap around me and I fought to dismiss it. It took me a full minute and only Carelian pressing against my leg, his fur soft yet prickly, helped me center enough to break the attraction. I was aware of the others standing there watching me, but JO distracted Lucille until I managed.

"Don't have an anxiety attack yet." Lucille pointed to a checkbook. "That is for the account that goes with this house. It is based off the rent earned by the other two houses on this street. Currently both houses have long term tenants, though they have been notified that any renewals may be optional a month after your draft officially ends."

That answered that question and made me feel better. Even so this gift might bite me in the ass.

~We need a cat door. The back area has excellent trees to lurk in.~

All of us, including Lucille, turned towards Carelian who

had moved away from my leg and sprawled out on the redwood floor, creating a picture-perfect image. Which I strongly suspected he knew.

"Any changes you want to make to the house is up to you. The account has more than enough for most remodeling wishes." A flash of pain flickered onto her face then was gone. "If you decide to do massive remodeling, I would like to point out there are multiple buyers that will purchase this house for cash if you do not wish to retain it. Including me. Though for most you may be required to break the magic on the house."

"No," I protested. "I have no desire to do massive remodeling. The door we'll figure out, but I think I like it the way it is." My voice trailed off a bit at that last part. So far I'd seen the porch and the foyer. What if other rooms were ghastly or the kitchen looked like it still belonged in the 1800s?

Her jaw was tight as she replied. "Excellent. But please let me know if you decide this isn't for you. You do own it. Sign here." She tapped a piece of paper with a pen on it. "And then I'll leave. You know how to find me if there is anything the papers don't explain." She tapped the other pile of papers as she spoke.

I went over and checked, it was just me signing the deed and then a legal agreement verifying the house was mine. Three signatures later, Lucille walked out the door and down the steps. The closing door left us alone in the house and I could feel it around us. It almost felt like Baneyarl's realm but different.

I turned to look at Jo and Sable. "Ready to explore?"

"Oh, yes. Keep together or split up?" Jo asked looking around, excitement on her face.

"Let's stay together." I reached over and grabbed the keys. "That way I can see if we need any of these and figure out how many locked doors there are."

Like three giggling schoolgirls, we started exploring the house. To my relief, and Jo's delight, the kitchen had been remodeled and sported very modern, very high-end appliances. Her attention was grabbed by the Viking professional gas stove and I couldn't wait to taste what wonders she'd create with that. The first floor was composed of kitchen, dining room, sitting room, a powder room, and a bedroom that had no closets but a beautiful armoire. The back led out to a screened in porch that connected to the porch that wrapped around from the front of the house. I found it interesting the kitchen had a mini greenhouse at the same end as the porch, though it was empty.

Carelian pretended to be bored, but I at least was both delighted and disappointed. I guess I'd expected monsters to jump out at me. Which was silly. This was a house in the middle of upper New York.

At first the storage under the stairs was smaller than I expected until we realized the back of the staircase contained a concealed door that we had to press to open.

"Ooh, secret doors. Shall we?" Jo was all but bouncing on her toes.

"This isn't a Scooby Doo mystery, you know," Sable pointed out, but her smile gave away her excitement level.

"And? It's a house with a secret door. And maybe locked rooms. What more can I ask for?"

I rolled my eyes at them and pulled the chain. A single light-bulb on the stairs flickered on, and something downstairs lit up. I started going down the stairs then paused. Rats and other rodents were not high on my favorite list. Carelian on the other hand thought they were great appetizers.

"Carelian, you want to go first and scare any monsters or rodents or monster rodents that might be down there?" I suggested. Blood and gore I could handle. Even the live mice I could tolerate. Rats? Ugh.

He gave me a supercilious glare and slid past me, but then he went into stalk mode as he slipped down the stairs. The three of us waited at the top, Jo snorting at me. She didn't have an issue with rats.

~There are no rodents or monsters in the basement,~ Carelian reported and he sounded rather dejected by that fact. We headed on down and were greeted with a basement. Slight damp, bare concrete floor, a rack with some boxes with the word "Xmas" scrawled across it and multiple cobwebs. There was a laundry shoot and a washer and dryer, basic models. A little laundry sink and folding table. The shoot looked like it went up further than the first floor and I made a note to see where it originated. Nothing else was down there.

"Humph. Talk about anticlimactic. This looks like any basement anywhere, at least if they don't have boxes of stuff their kids have grown out of." Jo sounded as dejected as Carelian.

We climbed back up and headed up to the second floor. The house had three full floors and I knew I needed to walk around the house and look at everything. We headed up the stairs, and I really hoped we'd find something strange or awesome. From the second floor landing the stairs did a u-turn and continued up to the third floor. The landing had two doors visible, one each to our right and left, and a window looking out to the small orchard in the back.

"Which door first?" I asked looking at the two doors.

"This one," Jo said as she took the two steps to the door on her left and reached for the brass knob. It turned easily revealing another bedroom. The bedroom downstairs had blue wallpaper and a sleigh bed, I'd dubbed it the blue room in my head, while this one was done in mint green and contained a four-poster queen bed. We wandered in and found a full bath attached, though not as nice as the one in the blue room. That one had a walk-in shower while this one just had the standard bath shower combo.

"Bedroom check. You know for a creepy magical house, this is all pretty boring." Jo made a face. "Though at least we have decent bedrooms to select from. Right now, I still want the blue room." I didn't blame her, though I had no doubt she wanted the shower for other reasons than getting clean.

"Well, other door, I guess." I walked over and grasped the knob, then yanked my hand back with a yelp. "Ouch. It zapped me."

That grabbed Jo and Sable's attention and they moved over. "Really?" Jo looked at me and cautiously touched me. "Huh. Not me. Maybe static?" She moved to grab the knob and twist. "Yeoch," she exclaimed as she jerked her hand back. "That wasn't static—that was a solid shock." Jo shook her hand glaring at the doorknob.

I couldn't stop the giggle of glee as I peered at the door. Finally, something exciting. "Maybe I need to unlock it with the key first?" I said, pointing at the lock above it. Which now that I thought about it was odd. Weren't most keyholes under doors? I looked back at the other door, but it didn't have a keyhole at all.

"Latch inside the door for privacy." Sable answered my unspoken question, making no move to touch anything. Carelian on the other hand lifted his nose to sniff at the knob.

"You get zapped, it's your own fault," I pointed out as I produced the keys Lucille had provided.

~Smells like magic.~

"Magic has a scent?" Jo asked while I started going through keys.

~Everything has a scent.~ Carelian's condescending voice made me snicker.

"You have to remember by your standards we are nose blind. So it's a valid question." One by one I tried the keys in the lock. The second to last of the twelve keys turned in the lock. I heard Jo and Sable take in sharp breaths. Swallowing I reached for the door and grasped the handle, ready to jerk my hand away at any moment. This time nothing happened and I turned the handle. To my surprise the door popped open and oddly swung outward banging into my hand. We stepped back to let it swing all the way open, which it did easily.

I stood blinking at it, then looked back at the bedroom door, double checking my memory. All the other doors in the house had swung in—why did this one swing out?

We peered in, but the shadows made it hard to get any impression besides cloudy and dusty. I stuck my hand into the room slowly and felt for a light switch. My fingers brushed over a switch and I flipped it up. Bright white, almost blinding light appeared from hidden lights along the wall.

"Yow, what is that, an operating room?" Jo muttered as she rubbed her eyes. I had to blink several times to get the spots out of my vision. When it had mostly cleared up the three of us peered in, though we didn't step into the room. There were built-in shelves lining all the walls, blocking out any windows that might have been there. The only light came from bulbs on the top of the shelves bouncing off the reflective ceiling, which was why the light had been so intense. But all that registered as background information. I couldn't take my eyes away from the objects that were crammed into the room.

While the shelves had so many things I could have spent days inspecting everything, the three statues in the middle of the room grabbed my attention.

"Are those people?" Sable's voice was low, almost hushed as if in a church.

"Statues of people, I think so." But I shared her reaction.

Even from here it looked like people in mid motion, frozen in an instance in time. From what I could see all three of them were positioned as if they were facing the door. They were statues of one man and two women. Their clothing, hair, expressions, all screamed true. To me they looked like three-dimensional images of real people.

"So why are they locked in this room? What is the rest of the stuff?" Jo had stuck her head in and turned it one way and another trying to see more.

"I'm going in—stand here and make sure the door doesn't close?" I glanced at the door, having nightmare visions of the door slamming closed and getting trapped in that room and the statues coming alive.

"You got it." Jo didn't laugh or even act like my fear was stupid. She sat on the ground about a foot from the threshold and Sable stood against the jam forcing the door to remain open. For it to close now, it would have to push both Sable and Jo out of the way and that would take effort and time. Enough time they could yell a warning.

CHAPTER
SIX

There is an issue with allowing merlins out after a decade. Most merlins, at least the ones that survive the draft, research magic and discover things that should be shared with the scientists at the OMO. Not kept to themselves. If we required merlins to serve thirty or forty years, and required all research to be turned over, our understanding of magic would triple in a decade. ~ OMO Internal memo

---

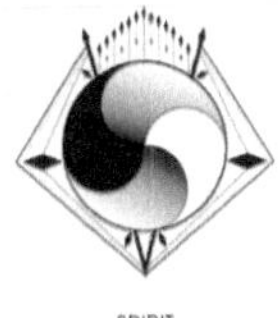
SPIRIT

I straightened my shoulders and stepped across the threshold, feeling the warm brush of Carelian's fur against my leg as he walked in with me. The statues took up most of the floor space in the room, but there was also a sundial, a birdbath, and what looked like an obelisk that brushed the ceiling. It looked disturbingly like the one I'd melted, but it seemed taller, and maybe a bit more slender. Maybe.

How did they get that thing in here?

Carelian sniffed the statues as I turned to look at the shelves, even though turning my back on those all-too-real pieces of art made my skin crawl. The shelves wrapped around the room with only the door as a break and they were filled with so many objects I couldn't begin to identify what I saw. Small sculptures sat on the shelves, though not with the detail of the statues, intermixed with objects that resembled bones, shiny rocks, and even feathers that looked like they had been plucked from Jeorgaz's tail.

Jeorgaz. Even thinking his name brought a crystal-clear image of the phoenix familiar of James Wells, the person who had willed the house to me, to the forefront of my mind. James was also a spirit merlin. Jeorgaz had ashed right before James died so the familiar hadn't been able to search for me until recently. While Jeorgaz wasn't a friend like how I regarded Baneyarl, he was an adviser, more like Esmere, Carelian's mother.

Though I wanted to reach out and touch things, wariness born of my experience with the murder ball during my initial testing prevented that. Touching that innocuous looking billiard ball had pulled me into the emotions and feelings of both the murderer and his victims. I never wanted to repeat that again.

"So?" Jo's impatient voice called out to me. "What's in there?"

I grinned but didn't take my eyes off all the objects around me. "Everything, anything. I see feathers, stones, eggs, and other crap. Heck, if I didn't know better I'd think some of the eggs were still viable. There are sculptures, a few hand bound books, and sealed jars. Though those I can't tell what may or may not be in them."

"No money or gold or gems?" Jo sounded wistful and I rolled my eyes.

"It's not a dragon's hoard if that is what you were expecting. It's more of a collection of objects. I don't want to say they are all art, but they all have an odd presence."

~This is a memory stone.~ Carelian had risen up on his hind legs and tapped a large opal. It had a crack of gold running down it, probably ruining it as a gemstone, but the milky stone held hints of fire and lightning as the light shifted over it.

"Oh?" We'd all played with memory stones. Esmere had given me one and I'd been using it a little at a time. It contained a lifetime of memories and while I could go through them much faster than they had been created, they were from the point of view of a Cath, and how a Cath used magic and how my mind interpreted it were vastly different. But using that stone had refined my ability to sidestep and use magic. Caths had perfected using kinetic energy as offerings instead of just cellular material and it helped them hunt, step through doors between planes, and create homes to keep them safe and warm.

~Yes. I don't know what species. You can pick it up and find out.~ There was a bit of challenge in his tone, and I wasn't falling for it. He was still a cat and chaos called to him.

"I think not. Maybe later." I took one more look around, then stepped back out. Maybe I'd come back with a silk scarf so I could pick things up without activating the magic. That had been a Christmas present from Marisol, Jo's mother, who treated me more like a daughter than anything else.

"You're no fun," Sable muttered looking like she wanted to go in there and explore.

"Adrenaline junkie," I retorted and she bobbed her head in agreement.

"Yep. So maybe tomorrow, see what they are?"

The idea of playing with magical artifacts worried and excited me. But I wanted to finish exploring the house. "Maybe. Right now we have more of the house to look at."

Jo rose from her seat on the floor and we all moved away from the door. I half expected it to slam shut, but it acted like a door. I closed it and removed the key, making sure I hadn't locked it again. I didn't want anyone to get zapped again. Curious, I reached out, grabbed the knob, and twisted. It opened easily.

"Huh. Jo, you want to try?"

I stepped back and she mimicked my actions and the door opened.

"So short term magic? Once you unlock it, it's unlocked?" Jo guessed. All of us stared at the simple knob and keyhole.

"Both? Either? Neither? Heck if I know. I don't think this house comes with an instruction manual." I bit my lip, but the lure of exploring the rest of the house was too strong. I turned and headed further down the hall. The landing area had subtle wallpaper of dark beige. Someday when I had money, I'd think about redoing it. Wallpaper wasn't my favorite thing, but it did fit the house.

The stretch of hallway between the stairs and the memento room ended in an opening between two rooms. I stepped into that area. There was a door set into the wall facing the front yard. Wary of the knobs now, I touched it, ready for another shock. Nothing happened so I turned it and pulled the door open. To my delight it revealed a small deck big enough for a nice lounge chair and a small table. It currently contained two rather worn folding chairs. I could already see me spending fall and spring days out here reading or studying. There was a door on the right of the deck, leading to another room. But I stepped back into the house and headed to the room on the left of the deck. This door was ajar and when I touched it and it swung inwards to reveal the master bedroom.

"Wow, can we say guy vibes everywhere?" Jo asked peering over my shoulder.

I had to agree. The room color scheme was dark green with dark wood—there was little soft about it. Even the two pillows on the bed were flat and uninviting. But the room itself, ignoring the dark color scheme, was good size. The bed was a simple sleigh style, not pretty, but not offensive either. The room was more barren than I expected with a single framed painting across from the bed and nothing else besides a low stool in the room.

Moving in further there was a door towards what I assumed was a bathroom, but the colors in the painting caught me.

"Jeorgaz," I said looking at the picture. Carelian brushed the back of my legs and I heard him land on the bed behind me.

~Humph. Can we bring the hammock in here? This bed is harder than the ground.~ I turned to see him tapping the bed with his front paw and there wasn't any give under his weight. I moved over and pushed. Hard as a rock.

"Okay, I agree. New mattress needed." I took a breath and remembered I had a checking account to go with the house, not that I'd looked at it. I would need to do that later. For now, I'd make do or try one of the other rooms. Pillows and blankets were always an option.

"Merlin's beard. Come take a look at this bathroom, Cori." I turned to see Jo disappearing through the other door. I followed her, stopping inside the doorway.

I understood her surprise. As bland and spartan as the bedroom had been, the bathroom was the opposite. As you walked in there was a sink in what looked to be a marble counter and opposite was a walk-in shower of the same marble. Nestled next to the shower was a toilet with what looked like a bidet attachment. I only recognized the bidet from Sable's pics of her trip to Japan with her dad over Christmas. A few more steps brought you to a claw foot tub and across from it was a walk-in closet. The tub was set up with ledges perfect for bath salts and a glass of wine, and it had not only the standard faucet but a spray attachment.

"Oh, think how nice that will be in the winter. I wonder how big the hot water heater is." I stared at the tub with longing. Our college apartment had the standard tiny tubs that were always uncomfortable no matter what size you were.

"Tankless. Saw it on the wall downstairs. So the answer is unlimited," Jo said looking around. "Huh, this even has enough closet space for mine and Sable's clothes."

"Nope. Mine. You get your own house if I survive." I grinned at her and she gave me a mock sigh.

"Cruel you are. Oh well."

We left and walked across the hall and I fell in love once again. Men and women didn't seem to generate much passion in me, but the study I walked into did. There were two sets of windows, one facing the front, the other the right side of the house, and a door leading out to the deck. The remaining walls were floor to ceiling bookcases, and the ceilings were at least ten feet high. They were half filled with books I couldn't wait to look at to see what they were about. There was a ladder on a rail that went all the way around the room. A window bench with, oddly enough, comic book long boxes under it, graced the window to the side. The window facing the front had a desk built seamlessly into the flow of the bookshelves. It looked about five feet long and two feet deep with drawers with keyholes on each side. In the middle of the room a chair in rich burgundy leather presided over everything, a small rectangular table that swung over the arms of the chair next to it. Throughout the study was the motif of a tree. Subtle with a leaf here, a burl of wood there, but it made it feel rich and welcoming.

"I'll sleep in here if I have to." The chair even had a matching leather ottoman.

"I do believe that's the first time I've ever seen her drooling lust over anything," Sable said, a thoughtful tone to her voice.

"You may be right. The closest I've ever seen her come was stroking a nine-hundred dollar leather coat that fit her like a glove." Jo sounded like she was trying not to laugh.

I spun to glare at them and wiped my lips to make sure I wasn't drooling.

They both started laughing. I didn't know whether to pout or ignore them, so I took the high road and turned to admiring the room again. Carelian had jumped up and sat on the window seat looking out at the view.

~Acceptable.~

We all laughed and I planned on spending a lot of time here later, but for now I wanted to explore the rest of the house. I turned and headed back to go up the stairs. Sable and Jo talked behind me, but I didn't try to figure out what they said. I wanted to see the last floor of the house. A door waited at the top of the stairs and I reached out to open it. There wasn't a shock this time but the knob didn't turn.

Shrugging I pulled out the keys and went to try the first one when I paused. There wasn't a keyhole.

"Jo? How do you lock a door with no key?"

"What, are we asking riddles now?" She squeezed up next to me and looked at the door. "That's odd." She crouched down to inspect the knob. "No hole in it. I was thinking maybe it was like a bathroom door lock." She grabbed the knob and tried to turn it harder, she had much more strength that I did, but it didn't budge.

I glared at the door. It was like having a prize just out of my reach. "Maybe there's a latch?"

"Just remember none of us are Nancy Drew. Why don't you see if your magic can figure it out," Jo said stepping back out of my way.

"Magic isn't the answer for everything," I muttered as I checked to make sure there wasn't a latch or a switch to release the door. There wasn't. I sighed and filtered through ideas. While I had access to a huge range of abilities, knocking down the door wasn't an option, or burning it, or causing it to disintegrate. As it was a door or a house, I could not really read its mind. But maybe I could read past images.

My psychometry, the ability to read emotions and feelings from objects, was off the charts and most of the time I had it locked so far down I forgot about it. Getting random hits of memories and emotions off of things was rarely pleasant. Not to mention the offering for it was so tiny that usually I didn't consciously offer, it was just given. I reached out and grasped the knob, then unleashed that part of me.

At first there was nothing, then a questioning feeling, then laughter. In my mind a word clearly emerged.

~NO.~ It vibrated in my mind but there wasn't anger, more like amusement for a child from an elder. I ripped my hand back with an eep.

"What? Get zapped again?" Jo was at my side, checking my hand over.

"No. Not that. The house, or I think it was the house, said No. Very firmly."

Sable and Jo stared at me. "The house?" Sable asked slowly.

"Well it sounded like the house. I mean, not sure who else it could be." I turned to look at the door. "I guess that stays locked for now."

"Only you, Cori. You get a cool house with opinions. Houses aren't supposed to have opinions." Jo gave me an exasperated but loving look.

"Just for that I hope your house has a personality and stubbornness to match yours," I retorted, feeling a teeny bit insulted on behalf of my house.

Sable choked and started to laugh as Jo gaped at me.

"Cori, that's mean," she finally protested, even as she tried to fight her own giggles.

"You deserved it." I turned and headed back down. "I need to go over the documents Lucille left, and we should go grocery shopping. I'm starving."

~Yes. Food. I think fresh fish would be appropriate. Steamed not fried.~

"And are you going to cook it?" Jo asked archly staring at the cat waiting for us to go back down.

~Of course not. Cooking is a human thing. I am simply catering to your customs.~ He sniffed and started down the stairs, his tail whipping back and forth like a conductor's baton.

"That cat," Jo's voice was full of exasperated love.

"Yes. I suspect we made him that way. But I wouldn't say no to fresh steamed fish," Sable said. "And we need to unpack the car and I suspect change the beds. Who knows the last time the sheets were washed."

We headed down the stairs to the landing and I gave one last look at the mysterious third level. Oh well, it would wait. As we reached the first floor, Jo cleared her throat. I turned to look at her.

"You getting sick? No getting sick. We have a summer off." I'd finally bought into the idea and wanted to read and have fun exploring, and maybe spend time in that study looking at the books. And other items in the memento room. I suspected most of them were magical.

"No, I, well we—" she started and I frowned at her.

Sable cut in. "We were thinking fish for dinner and go explore the surrounding areas. You mind if we head out?"

Off balance at the odd start, I shook my head. "No, go, enjoy. I want to investigate the study more."

Jo gave Sable a funny look then grinned. "Okay. See ya." In a rush of long hair, they were gone and the whole situation just left a bad feeling at the base of my spine.

SEVEN

Relationships between high level mages are either practically perfect or time bombs waiting to go off. Matching mages by ranks rarely works without something else to connect them. ~ Magic Explained.

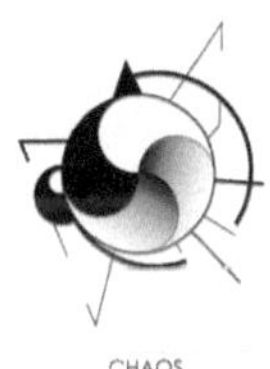

CHAOS

J o's weird behavior still niggled at the back of my mind but having the place to myself felt nice. So much had happened today, I wanted time to sit and process all the revelations.

I sat in the study going over the paperwork and trying to

decide what I wanted to do with the house. While it was mine, I still had a few years of schooling left plus the draft, and there was no telling where I'd end up. Well probably not Japan. The emperor had not been happy with the ultimatums he'd been given after trying to get me killed. The idea of letting the house sit empty for so long felt wrong, but so did the idea of renting it out or having strangers live here.

Why do I feel so oddly proprietary over a house I just set foot in?

I mulled over that question as I looked at the papers. The paperwork in the file included plat maps and property lines for the entire street, as well as the tax assessment records. She had also included the requests for access to various items. Some I knew I'd seen in the trophy room. I shoved those in a folder. Until I had to deal with them, I would ignore them. The last pile contained the utility and tax payment records since James Wells died. The amount for the taxes made me nauseous.

If nothing else, Lucille Blanding was very well organized. She left a manila envelope and I slid most of the paperwork back inside, leaving out the checkbook, the notes about the house, and a list of service people that had worked in the house over the last year.

The view out the front of the office made me smile as I looked out at the quiet street. I could so imagine Jo and Sable's kids playing outside, and part of me craved to create a little enclave of friends and loved ones. Though at this point I didn't know who else I wanted.

"You think Esmere would be willing to come visit if we move here? What about Baneyarl or Jeorgaz?" I looked over at Carelian who had positioned himself so the afternoon light bathed him in a gold glow, the ruby red of his fur sparkling as he made sure every hair looked perfect.

~Esmere would enjoy. Though she might expect to stay more. As for the others?~ He flicked an ear dismissively.

"Hmm. Don't you have siblings?" The thought struck me. Surely he wasn't an only kittar.

~Littermates? Two. Though malkin has had three litters.~ He fell silent for a minute then focused on grooming his tail. ~First litter died. Second only had one live. Third litter was best, all three of us are strong and healthy, though I am only focus.~

I had to think that through. The beings or creatures of the other realms referred to familiars as focuses. And they regarded it as almost a calling, from what I could figure out. But I didn't understand how life worked in the realms, it definitely didn't resemble our world with cities and jobs. And while I knew the beings there were intelligent, they functioned so differently from humans I barely tried to compare the two.

"I'm sorry?" I didn't know how to react to that news.

Carelian didn't even flick an ear my direction as he sprawled out, covering the length of the window seat, his front paws dangling off the side of the leather cushion. ~Is life. It always goes on.~

Wasn't that the truth.

I shook my head and finally thought about the interaction with the being when I took the keys to the house. While I still didn't know what it was testing me for, I was pretty sure it was the source of the voice that told me "No" when I tried to open the door to the third floor. Though why that should be off limits I didn't know. The treasure room, or at least that was what I dubbed it in my mind, made sense. If those were learning devices from the other realms, the value they represented was incredible. And I still wasn't sure about the three statues and the metallic obelisk.

Heck, the fact that Fire had melted it for me, and somehow gained nourishment from metal, if that is what it was, also freaked me out a bit.

"How can a house be magical?" I said the words out loud,

but everything I could think of didn't make sense. Enchantment was rare and difficult. Only merlins had the power to do it, and most never bothered to learn. It was restricted to merlins because you needed multiple classes to combine the branches to create magical objects. Granted those merlins made plenty of money for every enchanted item they created. But still they were rare and difficult to make.

That paused my thoughts. Were they really? I'd learned the hard way that common knowledge was often wrong, usually to my detriment.

One of the things I'd learned over the last eighteen months was how to reach someone I knew in a different realm. Which meant in theory I could contact Esmere, Jeorgaz, Baneyarl, or Tirsane. In reality I'd only contact Tirsane if the world was ending, and even then I might think about it a while.

I shrugged and opened up a micro rip, something most mages didn't think was possible, and sent out a ping to Baneyarl. If he was interested, he'd respond. It had taken me a while to learn the etiquette. Pings were the equivalent of a ring – one ring. It said who was calling and if the person you pinged wanted to respond they would. If they didn't, they might ping you later or they might not. For most beings in the other realms time was relative and not responding meant nothing other than they weren't interested at that moment. And then if they remembered you had pinged they might call you. The remembering was important. Overall they seemed to live in the now, not the future and past like we did.

~Cori. How is your road trip going?~ Baneyarl asked in my mind. My teacher, a griffon with white feathers that darkened to deep blue on his wings, was a merlin in his own right, though with him it meant he had access to all the Spirit branches at full power, not just three in various levels of strength. He'd become a friend to the three of us over the last year plus. Carelian had arranged the teacher relationship, time had created the friend-ship. It didn't surprise me at all that he knew about our road trip, though I doubt he truly understood it.

~Interesting.~ I still had to think my words carefully to speak telepathically. Most of the time it was easier to speak out loud, but since we were talking across realms that wouldn't work. ~I have a question. This house is weird. Can a house be enchanted?~

~House?~ He paused thinking. ~I am unsure. I know of one where the mage in question added chicken legs to it and it would walk around. But it was small, no larger than your living room. I cannot imagine an entire house being affected that way.~

I blinked at the idea of chicken legs attached to a house, though my main thought was "Why?" But shook my head, trying not to get sidetracked. ~May I send you a memory?~

~Of course.~

I focused on the experience with the gray space and sent it to him like a small video clip. Something else I had learned to do, though it felt odd. ~That happened, and the house seems to talk to me and has rooms it won't allow opened. I didn't think you could do that.~

As I waited for his response—it felt like eternity—I flipped open the register on the checkbook and choked.

~Cori?~ Carelian asked as I heard him rustling around on the wind bench.

"I'm fine. Sorry." I couldn't take my eyes off the balance of the register, trying to comprehend what I saw.

Baneyarl did the equivalent of clearing his throat, it created an odd vibration in my mind. ~I see. Cori, proceed carefully. Your house is not enchanted, but I fear I cannot tell you more without forsaking my own allegiances.~

"Wait, what?" That pulled me out of my dumbfounded

reaction to the checkbook and I had to repeat it telepathically for him to hear.

~Cori, Magic is following your actions and I would not dare to cross her plans.~

I narrowed my eyes, wishing he was here for me to glare at. ~You telling me that was Magic challenging me, testing me?~

Another long pause, but this time I remained focused. ~No, I don't believe so, but whatever is going on she is involved.~ He paused again and I started to say something, but he continued. ~Cori, you are strong, smart, and more creative than you think. You see magic differently than any of my students, even more differently than Jo or Sable see it. Have faith in yourself. If Magic is reaching out to you, then you are honored beyond all but a few. If you truly have questions about what Magic might be looking for, you could ask Tirsane.~

Umm, no.

~Thank you, Baneyarl. I hope someday to have you over for a visit.~ I changed the subject. Tirsane was not someone I thought of as a safe acquaintance.

~I would enjoy that. Fare well, Corisande.~ His voice faded from my mind and I shut the micro portal.

~My quean is powerful. You will succeed.~

I rolled my eyes at Carelian. "And if I don't? And succeed at what? I don't have the slightest idea of what I'm being asked to do."

And I'm so tired of people pulling at me. When do I get to make my own path?

Taking a deep breath to calm myself, I went back to the checkbook, this time to make sure what I saw had been fact. The register had in neat handwriting a list of the ongoing balance and the front listed the website for the bank. The balance was what had me really stunned.

$234,867.37

That amount of money seemed unreal. I pulled up the documents Lucille had left for me. In her crisp clear, and becoming familiar writing she explained.

This account pulls in the rent from the other houses and pays out the taxes and house insurance for all properties on this street. You are free to use the money to update the house, as much as it allows, though lowering the balance much below seventy-five thousand would be unwise as that is needed for taxes and insurance payments. Here is the account name and PIN for that account. You can see the deposits monthly from the renters. Call if you have questions.

I started going through the register and looking at the notes, then I pulled up the account and saw she'd meticulously copied over the info from there to the checkbook. A lump formed in my throat. The pressure of more money than I'd ever had and stress at what to do with it battled each other. A hard object slipped out of the register and clattered against the desk. I picked up the debit card and looked at it, the PIN reference in the letter now making sense.

I looked at the dollar amount again and smiled. While going hog wild with money would be the height of stupidity, we were going to be here for the next twelve weeks. I could justify buying a comfortable mattress and some new sheets. With glee I signed onto Amazing, the massive online shopping site. Twenty minutes later I had a new mattress, three sets of sheets —I'd had to run down and make sure what size the mattresses were in the two guest bedrooms, and a huge dog bed for Carelian. He insisted if I was getting a new bed, he deserved one too.

I had just finished with my orders, complete with the panic of putting in the debit card and expecting it to be declined, when I saw Jo and Sable pull up in the driveway. I verified everything and closed my laptop before heading down the stairs.

They were approaching the door with grocery bags. I pulled open the front door, both oddly buoyant and tense. The house had a tingle to it that kept pulling at me and I didn't know if I hated or loved it. Either way it kept me on edge.

"Hey. Looks like you found food," I said as I followed them into the kitchen. While I'd learned to cook after figuring out how to dispel the Murphy's cloak that had been attached to me for almost a decade, I wasn't good. I could make eggs and sandwiches and pancakes, but that was about it. Jo on the other hand had learned at her mother's knee, and Marisol could make food sit up and dance. Part of it was Marisol was a Fire Mage, wizard to be exact, but most of it was she'd learned to cook the same way, at her mother's knee. Sable wasn't bad in the kitchen, but she needed a recipe to make most things.

All of this meant Sable and I did most of the dishes and Jo did most of the cooking and shopping. Occasionally I felt guilty, but usually eating her food assuaged that guilt.

"We did. This place is nice. There's an awesome butchers' market just about five miles away and a nice supermarket not too much further. Needless to say, we won't starve while we're here," Jo said, but she didn't look at me and I stared at her as she put the groceries on the counter and started separating out the stuff that needed to go into the fridge versus the pantry.

"Jo?" I prodded. Evasive, and unwilling to look at me was off for Jo. Then her weirdness before they left worried me. "Did something happen?" Terror squeezed my heart a bit. Jo still had the scar from the bullet meant for me that had gone through her. A scar she'd tattooed a ruby red cat over.

"Happened, no, just..." She paused chewing on her lip.

Sable broke in. "She's overreacting again." Sable smiled at me and leaned into Jo. "We were discussing getting married after she gets her master's. So next year. Thoughts?"

CHAPTER

EIGHT

Magic artifacts are relatively rare. Those who have them keep them quiet, though there are rumors of an active underground trade of these objects. However, most people can't use them, so there hasn't been much interest in their acquisition. ~ Magic Explained Online

---

ORDER

The world closed in around me and I felt my chest constrict so tight that I was sure it would compact into a tight ball. Air froze in my lungs and the image of Jo walking away hand in hand with Sable never looking back at me made my eyes water as I fought not to scream. Time stopped as I tried to bring my emotions under control and willed myself not to do something I'd regret.

Four needlepoints of pain sank into my calf, shattering the nascent spell and my emotional fugue. I gasped jerking my leg away. "That hurt! What are you doing?" I glared at Carelian who had sunk his teeth into my calf. I expected to see blood streaming down my leg, but there were only four drops of blood.

~Silly quean. Listen and don't see monsters where there are none.~ His words just for me. Carelian flicked his tail at me and rose up on his hind legs inspecting the bags. ~Is there salmon for me?~ That was broadcast to everyone as I rubbed my leg.

"Carelian, why did you bite Cori? There is salmon, but you bit her. I'm sending you to bed without food!" Jo snapped staring at him like he'd sprouted wings.

Shit, I was about to spiral into a massive panic attack. He stopped that.

"It's okay. He had a reason." I narrowed my eyes at the cat who ignored me. I licked my dry lips and forced a smile at Jo and Sable. "Marriage?"

Jo looked at me, worry in her eyes, then she glanced at Sable. "We wondered if you'd be okay with that?"

I blinked at them, the words not making sense. "I don't understand."

"Oh, we are making a tangle of this. Jo, give me the Chenin Blanc and find three glasses." As Sable spoke, she shoved a bag of chocolate covered pretzels at me. "Cori go to the back porch and sit. We'll be there in a moment. Carelian, you touch that fish and I'll put habanero powder over everything you eat." Carelian dropped down and sauntered out to the back porch as if he didn't care about the threat.

I shook my head and followed him out, sinking into one of the chairs there, staring blankly at the trees behind the house.

The bright green of chlorophyll from the apple trees countered the bleakness in my heart. I'd always known I'd lose Jo, but I'd been allowing myself to hope. I couldn't protect people if they slipped away from me. I glanced at my phone taking in the date. Six years and twenty-three days before Kristos would be given the information to contact me. My younger brother, whom my parents had fled with to make sure he couldn't get to know me. Would I lose him too before I ever had a chance to be a part of his life?

The door banged opened and I jerked up and looked at Sable as she walked out, Jo following behind her. "Sit, woman." The look she gave Jo had my indomitable best friend slinking into a chair and I started to bristle, hating to see her crushed. "Shush, Cori, and listen." Sable handed out the glasses of wine. I took it reflexively, looking at the two of them.

Jo sipped her glass, looking miserable, and I couldn't figure out what I was missing.

"Cori, you have abandonment issues. They are valid, Merlin knows your parents were damaged by Stevie's death." I couldn't stop the flinch that occurred at the mention of Stevie. My brother had died in my arms when I was twelve. I had emerged as a reaction to his death. Even today it hurt and my parents were broken by his death. Maybe I was too. Someday I'd figure out what killed him and make sure no one else died that way.

I took a sip of wine, letting the sharp Chenin Blanc clear my mouth and mind. Not my favorite, though not bad. Sable didn't really like the sweeter stuff.

"I know you and Jo are a couple, and always will be." I jerked my head up and stared at her, a protest on my lips, but Jo had drawn her head in and hunched her shoulders like she expected a beating. Sable just smiled. "You forget, I've traveled a lot with my dad. I KNOW you two are a couple. I also know while there is enough love to restart the sun, there is no lust.

And that is OKAY." Sable didn't shout the words, but their truth settled into my bones and I started to relax while Jo just looked more scared.

"So, what does you two getting married mean?" I asked, not as scared of the answer as I had been a few minutes ago.

"That is what we want to talk to you about. Now remember, Jo still has close to two years before her master's is done, and I start my draft in late August."

The reminder that with Sable entering the draft we had no guarantee she would stay in Atlanta for the entire time. Terror jabbed me as I saw my comfortable little life start to crumble and I bit down on my panic. I'd been through worse. I would make it.

I like having her around.

The plaintive cry in my own head forced me to take a sip of the wine to cover my reaction.

"I am head over heels in love with Jo, and I love you too Cori." I jerked my head up at this and I saw Jo relax a bit. "I like living with you. You're a great foil. Now if someday we do have kids, one way or the other, all of us in one house might be a bit much. But if the dreams of this come true, then it changes things." She waved her hands around to encompass the street and the other homes. "But what we need to know is—what do you want?"

I forced a smile. "Besides being the best person at your wedding?" They both grinned. "I don't know." And I didn't. I sat back and thought about it. "Can I wait to give you an answer?"

Sable started laughing. "Yes. You have a few years. While we can get married during our draft service there is no guarantee Jo will be placed near either of us and you have a decade before all of this is yours."

"True. But this place is mine. It is big enough." It might have been a plea. Carelian huffed and laid his head on my knees.

Sable smiled and nudged Jo. "You two are an old married couple. Cori, all we are saying, the part Jo seems to be terrified to say, is any marriage involving her will include you. You are as much a part of her as a child would be. So I'm asking. What do you want?"

I shrugged, helpless to answer that question. "I'll think about it."

"That's all I want. Now neither of us has proposed or even are considering this until after our drafts. But we know, or I know though I'm not sure the two of you are fully aware, that you're happier when you're near each other. So we need this to work," she said, her voice breaking a bit at the end, and I saw through the facade she presented, seeing her fear and worry also. "Jo, what are you worried about?" Sable had her calm, supportive face on and I didn't know what to make of it.

Jo hide her face behind the wine glass not really drinking, but twirling it in her hands.

"Jo?" Sable prompted and I stared at Jo, worried.

"I'm scared that I'll lose Cori if I marry you. That us as a family won't work. Then I'm scared I'll lose you when you find out." She stopped and took a big gulp of wine and shrunk even further into herself.

Find out? Find out what?

"Okay, I'm not sure what that means, but I can tell you what I'm worried about," Sable said. I shifted my attention to her, now feeling like a racquetball as I bounced between Sable, the wall, and Jo, never knowing which to pay attention to.

"I'm terrified I'll screw it up between you two, or worse, that I won't be enough to be part of you yet not part of you. Your relationship is special and I don't want to damage it. I don't know if I can live knowing you will always be first to Jo, but I don't want you to be second." This time she looked down and I stared at them.

What do I say?

"I want you two to be happy. You're good for each other." I blurted the words, coming out frantic and raw to my horror. "You can't break up. Jo would never forgive me."

Terror at the idea of me coming between Jo and Sable warred with the fear of losing her, losing them. Neither was more powerful than the other.

~By the realms, are all humans as emotional as you three? Or is just queans that do this?~ Carelians' words sliced through the angst and I looked down at him where he sat licking his balls in the middle of all of us. That was intended to be rude, he'd admitted to understanding the nuances of human behavior, he just thought it was ridiculous.

"What are you talking about?" I glared at him as he paid great attention to the fur in his nether regions.

~Relationships, why all the drama? They are parts of life, not magic-shattering moments. Triad, coven, pride.~ He paused and lifted his head. ~No pride, there is no male and Alixant is not suitable. But choose, flex, adapt—you get lost in your patterns that aren't needed.~

I stared at him. "We aren't sexually interested in each other. Or at least I'm not in them."

~Humans. This makes no sense. I must talk to my malkin.~ He stood and with a pinprick of pain from the rip forming he stepped from our world to another and was gone.

I blinked, surprised and unsure what to make of that. He knew how I felt, right?

"I love that cat, but I'm so glad he isn't my familiar," Jo muttered. I looked up to see her shaking her head. "I'm going to cook. I need to think." She stood up, taking her wine glass, and strode into the kitchen leaving Sable and me sitting there with the dragon-sized knot of emotions, fears, and worry sitting behind us.

"Maybe..." I coughed, clearing out the tears that clung to the back of my throat. "Maybe we need to think about this for a few days. It doesn't have to be decided today, does it?" I just needed to hear the words again, that I had time.

Sable stared at her feet, not looking at me. "No. Jo needs to graduate and probably serve. And who knows where I'll end up before my draft is over. While I'm starting in Atlanta there is no assurance I'll stay there. Distance might kill us before anything else does." Grabbing her glass, she headed out to the back leaving me wondering which us she had meant.

Dinner that night was quiet. We all ate at the dining room table, its rich wood, delicate china plates, and soothing blue-green brocade walls a spiteful contrast to our withdrawn moods. Even the delicious food Jo had cooked didn't get us to talk and I fled to my room, more than willing to sleep on rocks than stay down there and feel like what had been golden and precious had tarnished beyond all notice.

Did this come out of nowhere?

The last six months had been crazy insane as I took 26 units to get my blasted degree. I'd barely spoken or done anything besides work and study. The most time I spent with them was on Mondays and Wednesdays when we had classes with Bane-yarl. I teased apart my memories and thought back. Jo had been tense, and Sable kept watching me, a look of worry on her face. And I'd caught Jo watching Sable with a look of longing and fear, but I'd brushed them off as they smiled as soon as they caught me looking. But their time alone had become more rare and their lovemaking more desperate. That I only knew because of Carelian snarking about them making more noise than yetis in rutting season and twice as deprived.

My heart twisted and squirmed as I reviewed the past year and I saw how stupidly blind I'd been. I was so wrapped up in my own stuff I'd shut them out more than I had intended. I still thought their relationship was strong, but with the three of us there were dynamics I'd missed. Or been avoiding.

That rocked me back. Did I want them to fail? The automatic negation of thought reassured me. But it left me trying to figure out what I wanted and how to make sure I didn't destroy something precious for Jo.

Why is it that the people I love are the ones that get hurt?

I finally found a comfortable position on the rock hard bed by using all the blankets in the closet to make a pad. The new mattress couldn't get here fast enough. I fell asleep with images of Stevie dying in my arms, the pained looks on my parents' faces, and the devastation of the Guzman garage.

Mages are being set up as a protected class. Stop it now by voting for our Freedom from Magic candidates. They are the only way to make sure the playing field is level for everyone. College shouldn't be free to only a portion of the population. ~ Freedom from Magic ad

---

Grey nothingness surrounded me, and I spun around looking for the figure or the voice.

"Where are you? Why am I here?" My voice cracked and I called mentally for Carelian. ~Carelian, they took me. Help.~ I didn't know if he would hear me, because I didn't know where I was.

"Why should a focus help you? You don't help others." The voice whispered through the space, but there were no other sounds to mask it. It came from everywhere and nowhere and I stopped my spinning, forcing myself to breathe and think. The words made me mad. I'd spent my life trying to be someone who helped others. That was why I'd worked so hard to get my paramedic license. Then finding out I was a mage, a merlin, destroyed all that. While it made me some money, I'd never be allowed to do that as part of the draft.

Another deep breath, forcing myself to think. This was an unknown powerful creature. Reacting in anger might get me killed. It took work, but I managed to control my desire to lash out, more off balance than I had been when I'd been hijacked the first time.

"Yes, I do. I'm a first responder. I'm trying to get a degree that will help me research how to help people. To find out how to stop people from dying." People like my brother.

"You use your limited skills to apply bandages to wounds. You do not use the power that lies within you. All you care about are your own wants and desire."

That stung even more. But a trickle of guilt washed at me. Was this voice right? Should I be doing more with my magic? I'd always shied away from that question, focusing on anything else but that. Now in this gray space, where I felt disconnected from everything, even my own body, I looked at the question.

Am I being selfish?

The question hung so powerfully in my mind I didn't know if I'd spoken it or not.

"All beings are selfish. But when one is as blessed as you are, you have a responsibility to others."

My temper and guilt faded, and I whirled again, looking for the voice, for something to focus on.

"What do you call the draft? What about people being responsible to me? I've fought for everything I have," I shouted into the gray.

"So?"

"So? So why should I do things for other people. What have they done for me?"

"Who cares about humans?" For the first time I heard a touch of emotion in the voice. Shock or maybe surprise. "What have you done to help or honor Magic?"

I froze. Blinking as if trying to make the grayness fade or change.

"Magic?" It was the same way Baneyarl and Esmere referred to it, almost as a being. But why would magic care?

"Have you no answer, herald?"

That comment brought the memory back to me. Jeorgaz, Esmere, and Baneyarl talking to me after the showdown in Japan. They had mentioned I was magic's herald, but what did that mean to this creature?

"You see your trespass now. Gifted as you are, and you have not come to Magic to offer your gratitude? Mortals, they are all the same. All they think is how power can benefit them. Reach out and take what will illuminate your folly."

As the voice finished an object appeared floating about chest high. It shone so bright in that gray area that I couldn't make out any details, only that it appeared to be the size of an orange. It called to me and even though I knew whatever had me here didn't mean me good, I drew closer to see what it was. The glow that it emitted was just too seductive and I reached my hand out to pull it closer so I could inspect it.

Pain shot up my arm and I felt it dragged down away from the object. A scream tore out of my throat as I fell to the ground clutching at my arm. A red furry head met my outstretched hand, his teeth buried in my arm, blood running from the punctures of his canines.

"Carelian?" I gasped, torn between pain and shock. I blinked trying to figure out where I was. The hall wall was behind me, and a door in front of me. I figured I was near the memento room.

His mouth still wrapped around my arm, he glared up at me. ~Are you back?~

Pounding steps came up the stairs as Jo and Sable rushed up. "What by Merlin is going on? Carelian?" Jo sounded worried and scared.

~The two of you did not wake up when I went to your bedroom. I called. Your door was locked, and I couldn't open it to get to you.~ He snarled the words in my mind as he opened his jaw by increments trying to pull his teeth out without creating any more damage.

"So you bit her?" Sable had rushed back downstairs while Jo dropped down beside me, inspecting the wound.

~She was walking in her sleep, not responding. I didn't have any other way to get through to her. Minor scratches didn't register and my teeth don't do as much damage as my claws.~ His mouth released my arm and he sat back, licking his mouth with an odd quirk to his muzzle. ~Humans taste off. Ick.~

"This coming from a cat that eats things that are still moving?" I said, trying to ignore the fact that my voice shook. I inspected the wound and saw he'd done a good job of not leaving a lot of damage. His words about claws made me glance down at my bare legs and I saw runnels of blood from scratches. Just seeing them made them start to sting and hurt like crazy.

"Crap, Carelian, and you weren't trying to kill her?" Jo stared at my leg, a stressed look on her face, but the tone of her voice had shed the anger.

~I did not believe that walking into a room full of magical objects while under control of someone or something else was a good idea.~ He licked at his paws wrinkling his nose as he did so.

"Here," Sable said, shoving first aid supplies at me. I'd been so focused on my pain and the blood dripping everywhere; I hadn't heard her come back up.

"Ah, thanks." I spent the next few minutes getting my wounds cleaned and making sure they were all minor. "You did a good job of missing all the major veins in my arm. You managed to not nick any tendons either," I commented as I cleaned up the last of them. Carelian might be a familiar but I knew what he ate and I had no desire to have my wounds get infected.

He sniffed in my mind. ~I paid attention during your anatomy class. It pays to know all that. Makes killing easier if you know where best to strike.~

That had me snorting in laughter and pulling a bit tighter on the bandage than I had intended. That caused me to meep in pain while Sable and Jo lunged to help. Ten minutes later, everything bandaged, all the supplies put away, Sable dragged us down to the sitting room. It was two-thirty in the morning, and I couldn't avoid talking about it anymore.

"Nope," Sable said before I could start. "We're all wide awake, I'm making us tea with honey, chamomile tea, and I'm adding a shot of whiskey and getting us some cookies. Then you can talk." She shot a hard look at Carelian. "Both of you."

Carelian, who had curled up on the ottoman, just flicked his ear at her, but didn't say anything. I wrapped myself in a blanket—even if it wasn't remotely cold in the house, I wanted something to convince me I was safe.

I tried to peel apart the dream or experience or whatever it was, but before I could get too far in, Sable came back with tea, cookies, and a bowl of something red and chunky for Carelian.

"Here. I figured since you kept making faces, you'd like to get the taste out of your mouth." Sable set the bowl down in front of him and he purred loudly enough I could hear him.

~Salmon. I may need to keep her.~ His face already buried in the bowl.

I rolled my eyes at a smirking Sable. "See, he likes me better than you."

"You get to convince him to exercise when he gets fat," I retorted.

~I heard that,~ Carelian said but didn't lift his head up at all.

The snickers lightened the mood and Sable made sure we all had our tea. I sat in the dark blue chair, a club style that I loved, while Jo and Sable curled up on the rose-colored settee. We all sipped tea and the silence hung between us like a shroud.

"Spill," Jo finally said, looking between me and Carelian. "What happened?"

I took another sip of my tea, enjoying the bite of the whiskey and the heat. It didn't make sense I was so cold when the house was easily in the eighties. I started to explain everything, ending with "I opened my eyes to see Carelian with his teeth in my arm." I rubbed my arm, the rough texture of the bandages making me relive the experience.

Jo nodded; her expression somber. "You mentioned you tried to wake us up?" Her brows drew together in a frown. "I know I was dreaming. Something about me on a cliff and there was a storm raging. But I didn't hear you. Can your mindspeak be blocked by sleep?"

Carelian sat back, the bowl empty and without a trace of salmon in it. He licked his paws and washed his face, but I got the impression of thinking rather than ignoring.

~It should not,~ he finally said. ~Much of what happened made no sense.~

"What happened from your point of view?" Sable asked. She had her legs tucked up under her and was curled up next to Jo. Their hips touched and the tension I'd sensed earlier seemed to have faded.

This time his face washing was more avoidance than cleaning.

"Carelian?" I prompted, I needed to know this also.

He huffed and focused on his other paw. ~You were restless. More than normal. Then you got out of bed. I had been aware of your motion, but that woke me fully. You turned, spun like a dog before it lays down. I kept calling you and you didn't hear me or didn't respond to my calls. I remained content to watch you, but then you turned and headed out of the room. I tried to get your attention by scratching you, but it did not get a reaction. When Cori opened the door, I raced down to your door.~ He nodded at Jo and Sable. ~But you did not hear my calls, either via mindspeak or vocalizations. I tried to turn the handle, but it was locked. I came back up here and saw Cori standing in front of the memento room.~

That phrase made me blink but it felt accurate. A room for things that had no obvious purpose. That qualified as mementos.

Carelian shifted at this point, taking the Egyptian cat pose and looking at us, his whiskers close to his skull, eyes steady, and tail wrapped tight around him as he sat up perfectly straight. ~I panicked and stopped her the only way I could think of with a minimal amount of damage.~

I swallowed hearing that and Jo and Sable looked even more worried.

"What do you think it means?" Jo asked and her hand

reached out to grab Sable's. They held hands like two scared kids and I cringed at what my actions had caused.

"I think"—I felt the words out as I said them—"Magic and the house are both trying to test me. Remember the discussion I told you about, with Jeorgaz and Baneyarl after I faced the emperor of Japan?" That had been terrifying. Not only had I sidestepped to Japan from Atlanta, but I'd engaged in a magic fight with the court magician of Japan. The only reason I still breathed was Jeorgaz, James Wells' familiar, showed up and cowed him. The same James Wells Spirit Merlin that left me this house and more if I fulfilled the terms of the will.

"Yep. The scary beings showing up to tell you about magic?"

~Yes, my *malkin* is fearsome, is she not?~ The pride in Carelian's voice made me grin.

"Yep. I think this is more herald stuff. Maybe trying to get me to attack or run or who knows, curl up in a ball and cry?" I shrugged. This was yet more stuff that I didn't want to deal with.

"Do you think it might be right?" Sable asked slowly, as if scared she was poking a sleeping dragon.

"What part?" I was a bit lost, but my mind was jumping from point to point so fast that I didn't know anything anymore.

"About you having so much power that you need to use it differently?"

I flinched back and looked at her, eyes wide. "What do you mean?"

Sable threw up her hands. "Cori, you're so powerful. You can do things with a fraction of offering that would take me all my hair to pull off. Should you be maybe using it differently? I know you want to figure out what happened to Stevie, but what about other stuff you could do? You could get with a research lab and create vaccines and cure things. With your power and

Carelian, you could make cells alter to fight diseases. All the problems we usually have with replicating mage-based results could be bypassed because you are that powerful."

If she had said that as an accusation I would have jumped up and stormed away. Instead, it was worried and a bit pleading and that made me settle down and ponder everything.

"I don't know. I've been thinking about my magic as something to deal with, not something I could leverage for other things." And I hadn't. The costs for most people were prohibitive and they taught all the classes like that. You did magic in tiny little things, not big things. But me? I could do big things.

I sat there stunned, wondering about my own stupidity. Why had I never thought about it that way? And did it change anything?

We talked a bit more, but the rocking of my thoughts didn't smooth out. As we got up to head back to bed, Sable walked over and pulled me into a hug.

"Remember this above all else, Cori. We love you and you are a part of our lives. We will make this work out, even if we need to create our own path."

All three of us ignored Carelian muttering ~Triad and coven.~

I lay in the nest of blankets, the idea still bouncing on the walls of my mind. Carelian curled up next to me, his body a warmth I craved. Lying next to him, his soft fur and purrs helped me to relax.

~I won't let you come to harm, my quean. I promise. And I'll figure out another way besides biting you.~

A chuckle slipped out as I buried my face in his fur. "That would be appreciated." Apprehension about sleep didn't keep me awake and I slipped away protected by his waves of sound.

CHAPTER

TEN

More Equal Opportunity programs are being imple-
mented to ensure that we have non-mages in STEM
based jobs, but opponents point out that mages are
naturally more skilled at science, otherwise they would
not have emerged with powers. This implies it is a waste
of time and resources to try and get non-mages educated
to the same level. To educate the rest of us. ~ Freedom
from Magic

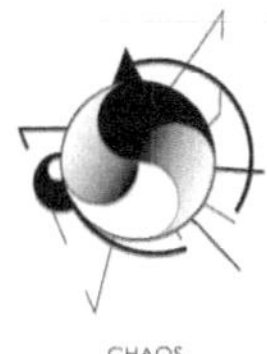

CHAOS

To my relief, I slept through the night. I woke to Carelian nudging me with his head. ~Bacon is being cooked. I have great need for bacon.~

I groaned and rolled over, stiff and my arm sore. "Go. I need a shower. And leave me some bacon."

He jumped off the bed and headed to the door, lifting his front paw to turn the knob. From what I could see, most of the mischief he could get into with his opposable thumbs had been experienced, and he at least acted like a responsible teenager —mostly.

With a body that felt way older than my age, I shuffled to the bathroom. The luxurious shower and near scalding water improved my outlook on life to a great degree. It helped to the point I was almost polite as I headed into the kitchen in search of coffee.

"Here," Jo shoved a mug in my face. "Drink. No grouching."

The aromas of cinnamon, chocolate, and coffee assaulted me in the best way possible. "You made Stinky's Mexican coffee." I sighed in pleasure at the scents. I grabbed it and sat down in the breakfast nook.

Stinky, aka Sanchez Guzman, was one of Jo's three brothers and the one closest to us in age, only being two years older. He made the best Mexican coffee, strong enough to raise the dead and make them happy about it.

"Yes, I finally convinced him to share his secret." She smirked. "You feeling better?"

"I think so. Still trying to process my paradigm shift. I don't understand why I never thought about it."

Jo shrugged. "You're very goal oriented and you have a habit of ignoring any possibilities outside what will get you what you want. Not necessarily a bad thing, but it can put blinders on you."

I blinked at that. "Like what?"

Jo laughed and started ticking things off on her fingers. "You never thought of asking for help with your parents. You were determined to get this house and your degree. Never occurred to you to maybe transfer or offer to give Japan the records they wanted. You never thought about loans for living and school, and any bank would have loaned to a double merlin in a second. You put everything in terms of what you can do or handle. And never did you spend time as a kid thinking about what you would do with magic. I did. Sable did. I saw my parents use it for things all the time, so I'm used to it as a practical tool. You see it only as an obstacle to overcome, not something that can make your life better."

"Oh." I buried my nose in the coffee, feeling attacked on all sides, but she wasn't wrong.

"That doesn't mean you're wrong, you know." Sable walked in carrying a notebook. I looked up at her comment and frowned.

"But Jo just said I was?"

"I did not," Jo protested.

At the same time Sable laughed. "That is not what she said."

I sat back now feeling lost.

I really thought by now I'd have being a grownup figured out.

"Blinders aren't wrong. You are the most focused and driven person I've ever met. You've overcome things most people would never be able to. Just means you're not perfect. There isn't anything wrong with having blinders. But now that you've had information pointed out, does it change anything?" Sable graced me with a stern look before she grabbed dishes and dropped bacon and some more salmon on a plate, setting it on the small table for Carelian.

Carelian sat there and began to eat. For some reason, if he

ate at the table, he used his paws, delicately feeding himself, but if it was on the floor he ate like any other cat. I'd asked him once and he just flicked an ear at me responding with ~Because that is how I choose to eat. ~

She gave me bacon, French toast, and potatoes O'Brien. Jo was the cook of the three of us, but Sable wasn't bad, leaning toward more salads, Oriental cuisine, and hors d'oeuvres than Jo. Jo went for Hispanic and Latin American dishes, which meant spicy.

Me? I ate whatever they cooked. While I could actually be trusted in the kitchen now and not destroy everything I touched, I still rated as a very rudimental cook. But I could wash dishes like no one.

"I don't know if it changes anything. I still think a MS in Biology with a PhD in Quantitative Biosciences is the way to go. With that I could become a doctor, a researcher, a pathologist, or really anything else. I think, assuming the draft board approves, I could be useful in the field as a forensic pathologist and medical expert. I just don't really want to deal with patients, but at the same time remember how that doctor helped Stinky?" I directed this at Jo.

She sank into the chair next to me, her own plate piled high, as she'd taken double the amount of French toast I had. "Oh yeah. That was terrifying when the jacks snapped and dropped the car on his legs. He could have died, or best case, had his legs amputated. That doctor being there, moving those bone fragments away from arteries and getting them to heal in the right places." Jo shook her head. "Even so, he had physical therapy for months to get everything strong enough to walk without risking his bones breaking again."

"See. That is a doctor that's using his magic. What if I lean towards that?"

Jo made a hmm noise and cut up her French toast into small

towers of syrup, peanut butter, and toast. "Honestly, because I think you'd hate it. You like the immediateness of being a paramedic. The solve the problem then move onto the next one. I think you'll be happier in the field doing, oh I don't know, search and rescue? Digging through crime scenes? Solving mysteries? I mean, I can see you playing with things in a lab, but only if it was constant altering and tweaking. But at the same time, you could save hundreds of people if you knew how to fix things." She shrugged. "Mami and Papi didn't do anything exciting for their draft. Papi fixed cars and Mami worked on nuclear plants regulating temperature."

I nodded slowly. Marisol was a Fire wizard, and that made sense. Her dad was a genius with mechanics, which was where Jo got it from.

"My advice?" Sable offered, waiting until I nodded at her to go on. "See where they put you in the draft. You never know what you might enjoy, and you can always do other stuff as a volunteer if you think your abilities aren't being used fully."

I blinked at her as that idea settled in. Volunteer.

"I can do that?"

Sable shrugged. "Depends on what that is. But given what I know about you, if you set your mind on something nothing will stop you from getting it. As Japan learned to its embarrassment." They both snickered at that.

I wrinkled my nose. It wasn't something I liked to remember. If Jeorgaz hadn't shown up I would have been killed. "Maybe you have a point. I have magic, but can I use it?"

"Wrong question. You can, the question is will you," Sable countered smirking at me.

"How are you going to use your magic?" I was suddenly curious. They were right. I'd been so focused on getting through and getting a degree, I hadn't spent much time thinking about magic as something that I could do. Just something I had to deal with.

I swear some days I feel like a Merlin-cursed idiot.

Her face lit up with excitement and I felt even smaller.

"They have me working at one of the major water processing plants in Atlanta after my draft orientation." That I knew averaged about a month, not boot camp but from the clues Alixant and Indira had dropped, more indoctrination. "I'll be able to use Water to sense impurities, isolate them, then walk through steps in the plant processes to improve how they filter. I'm also going to get to work with how the sewage is processed and if my thesis is correct, I should be able to decrease the amount of waste that can't be broken into biodegradable parts by over 50%. The director of that facility has been talking with me and we are both excited. I'll be burning offerings left and right for the first few months, but if it works the way I theorized it should be a huge improvement that can be extrapolated out to other plants." Her excitement was contagious, and I knew I should have asked before.

"I'm really a horrible friend, aren't I?" I said then flushed when I realized how utterly selfish that made me sound.

Jo and Sable both laughed at me, then Jo choked as she inhaled a bit of breakfast. When she quit trying to cough up her lungs, they looked at me. "Cori. People were trying to KILL you. That is guaranteed to narrow your attention to the bare minimum, and after that, you were taking classes, and working and training with Baneyarl plus working through the memory stone. It's okay. But maybe now you can take a deep breath and start to live a bit? Not just survive?"

"You two are too nice to me," I muttered staring at my French toast.

"No, we just understand you and love you." The strength of Jo's tone caught my attention and I looked up. "But I'm not letting you slide anymore. From now on if you're being a bad friend, I'm going to call you out on it. Got it?"

"Got it. And I will try. And yes, there isn't a reason to kill myself getting my master's and doctorate. And I will try different things to see what I can do, not just learn it." I could do a lot, and with the amount of power Carelian gave me I'd be able to do a lot. The question still was do what?

I rolled that around in my mind but I'd probably need to talk to Indira and Steven Alixant to really understand. Or ask Sable when she started working.

"Atlanta?"

Sable grinned and reached over to squeeze Jo's hand. "Yes. Apparently being the girlfriend of a double merlin's best friend has its perks. When I mentioned I'd like to stay near you, they jumped all over it. And I'm not complaining as it makes life easier, though we will need to talk about living quarters."

"Oh, yeah. You get paid don't you. How much they starting you at?" I was just curious, but if she didn't tell me I wouldn't worry about if she was hiding things.

Her grin got bigger and smugger. "How about eighty-five thousand to start? Standard wage for a master's in environmental engineering and an archmage. Though remember with the draft you don't always get to work eight hours a day, you're on call for the entire period of your service. But it means I can afford a bigger place." She looked a bit wistful. "Maybe with more closet space and a bigger bathroom. Heck maybe even a den or office for you two?"

I giggled at that. "What? You want room to put your clothes? You could always just throw away anything Jo has that you don't like."

"Hey," Jo protested but we both just laughed at her and she sank back and groused. "I like my clothes, okay?"

Sable laughed and patted her hand, over the top patronizing. "I know, dear, it's okay."

I snickered at Jo's look. We chattered about nothing important, but I felt better and knew I needed to work on my part of this relationship, which was what it was. A real relationship. My family.

We cleaned up. Carelian swore his paws weren't strong enough to handle doing dishes, and we still hadn't decided if we believed him or not. Once everything was clean, we moved to the sitting room.

It was nice enough, but as I looked at it, I could see things I wanted to change. Mainly some more comfortable furniture—the couch in there didn't qualify. And maybe a TV. While we didn't watch it a lot, movie nights were something we looked forward to. Maybe after I graduated.

Jo and Sable had pulled up apartment listings on their phones. From their comments, they were trying to balance out distance between her work and us getting to school. I let them be. I figured I still needed to get to know the quirks of the house.

Carelian jerked up his head, the movement catching my eye as he looked at the back of house. I felt the telltale spike of pain when a door between our realm an another was opened.

~Incoming.~

CHAPTER

ELEVEN

The realms remain a mystery. Those few who have gone there return insane or they don't return. Even the most ardent conspiracy theorists admit going into a realm, or worse, attracting the attention of those denizens, is a death warrant. It doesn't take a mage to realize dragons have no issues eating humans. ~ Magic Explained Online.

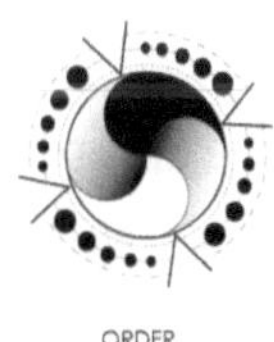

ORDER

"Wait, what? Who?" I looked at Carelian confused as he stretched. The stretch and flexing of very sharp claws into the upholstered ottoman did nothing to soothe or relieve my anxiety.

~Esmere and Baneyarl are in the backyard.~ He headed towards the back of the house as I exhaled a long breath.

Those two I could deal with. And I admitted I was excited to show them my house. My house. The phrase still made me giddy. I followed him out as I heard Jo and Sable behind me babbling, excited comments from Sable. She owed Esmere, Carelian's mother or *malkin*, a huge debt. Over the course of two weeks last summer, Esmere reversed the damage to Sable's pancreas and cured her nascent diabetes. I'd watched and thought maybe I knew how to do it, but I needed to learn more about the human body before I'd ever feel comfortable doing that. Which made my desire for medical school spike again.

Isn't that an example of how I could use my magic? How many could I cure with my power and offerings? Not as many as there are, but...

My thought choked there. How many people had diabetes in the US? One million? Five? How could I ever begin to help that many, even with my power? I couldn't, was the answer which sent me back to the question, how could I use my abilities to help others?

My thoughts distracted me until I stepped out onto the screened-in porch and stopped, stunned by what I saw.

Baneyarl had always been imposing even after we got to know him. But the pocket of reality he resided in, to my knowledge, made him seem a part of it, something that just fit there. Here, on an expanse of grassy lawn backed by an orchard, he looked exotic and somehow terrifying and regal at the same time. I'd forgotten, or didn't have anything Earthly to compare him to, how huge he was. Here his size screamed out at us, as he was easily the size of a compact car.

It didn't help that Esmere sat next to him in her Egyptian cat pose, looking around. Her emerald green fur made the grass and foliage from the trees seem dim and washed out. I couldn't remember them ever sitting so close together, and here with measurement references I comprehended, it shocked me to realize she reached his shoulder, making her the size of a Shetland pony.

"I'm never complaining about how big Carelian is again." I nodded in agreement with Jo's statement. If Carelian got that big, and I had a sudden horrified thought he might get bigger, people would run screaming when they saw him.

"I'd need a bigger harness," I muttered as I pushed open the back door and walked out. Even with my surprise and shock, a genuine smile appeared. I liked these beings very much.

"Baneyarl, Esmere, what a surprise. Is everything okay?" I walked towards them, resisting the urge to pet either of them. Their fur was insanely gorgeous, but it would be like touching a queen's jewels. Unwise and impolite.

Esmere stood up and strolled towards us, rubbing muzzles with Carelian. ~I wished to see your new abode. Baneyarl mentioned magic, and I was curious.~ Her ears flattened as she gazed at the house. ~I see what he meant.~

I looked at Baneyarl and saw his gaze locked on the house and a frisson of unease wormed through my system. "Is everything okay? Should I be worried?"

Baneyarl ruffled his wings, then settled down. ~I think you should be wary, but worried would be excessive. I trained you well, I have faith you will rise to the challenges before you.~

I narrowed my eyes at him then looked at Esmere, who had consented to let Carelian lick her chin. As if she felt my attention, she glanced at me, her ear flicking.

~Do not look to me for reassurance, kit. We are not allowed to tell you more than this. Be careful and take care of my kit. I would not see him injured or mourning.~

I threw up my hands, frustrated and exasperated. "That tells me nothing. Be careful of what? What is in the house? Should I send Jo and Sable away? Who said you can't tell me more?" I managed, barely, to keep from screaming, but still my frustration leaked out because Esmere got up and walked over to me. I had to fight not to flinch back. Having a cat the size of a pony walk up to you hit all my atavistic responses.

She licked the left side of my face, washing me with the scents of clover and honey, a combination that disconnected me even as it felt like three layers of skin were peeled off by her tongue. ~There is risk, but life is risk. But I think the bigger issue is you do not comprehend when we speak of Magic.~

I resisted rubbing the area she'd licked; I'd check it later. "What do you mean?"

~When we say Magic,~ Baneyarl said as Esmere stretched out on the ground, taking up more space than should have been possible, ~what do you think we mean?~

I shrugged and glanced over at Jo and Sable. They had flopped down next to Esmere and Carelian and were lavishing attention on them. From their laughs I figured one or both of the Cath's were talking to them.

"I figured your goddess or something." Now worried what else I'd misunderstood.

Esmere lifted her head and glanced at Baneyarl, then laid back down arching her neck to allow scritching. I couldn't figure out if the cats, with human level or above intelligence, treated it like a massage or something else. Either way the idea of having people randomly touch me creeped me out.

~That is not accurate,~ Baneyarl said, settling down into a

sphinx pose, his wings flat against his back, creating a wash of purples against his white.

If I had any artistic abilities, I'd have begged to sketch or paint him. But that wasn't where my skills lay. With most of my life spent dealing with my luck, I didn't have a ton of hobbies. But I did enjoy crocheting and hoped to have time someday to learn to knit. Maybe I'd try to create a miniature Baneyarl. Knitting and crocheting had the advantage of worst case, I just undid it and started over. Nothing horrible would really happen.

"If she isn't your goddess, what is she?" I sat down on the grass, ignoring the pricking of the blades on my bare legs. It was still too hot to wear anything besides shorts and tank tops. Though if I moved here, I'd need to invest in warmer clothes if the anecdotes were true.

Baneyarl bent his head back, preening a feather before he answered. ~Know that while I have spent time in your realm, I have not had the opportunity to interact with very many humans over the years nor immerse myself in your culture. But if my understanding is accurate, she is analogous to your Mother Nature and just as powerful in her own way.~

That made me sink back and think. We talked about Mother Nature both as a force and a being, and if that was what Magic was?

"Is your Magic a sentient being? I don't believe what we call Mother Nature is sentient. We call our ecosystem that as it is huge and our science can't figure out how to control or predict it." With everything I'd learned from him, I wasn't about to discount the possibility Mother Nature was sentient. Though it would tilt me towards the opinion of her being a royal bitch.

~Possibly?~ He shuffled his wings again avoiding my gaze. ~Patterns have been noticed and there are instances of something approaching sentience, but it is also possible it is nothing more than currents and our interpretation of them. Even Tirsane remains wary when Magic seems to demand from us. Think of it like swimming against the current. While it is possible, most are not going to succeed, and the consequences could be deadly. But I do know that the more powerful the person the more likely Magic is to pay attention.~ He paused and I didn't interrupt, guessing he was trying to find words to explain.

Over the last eighteen months of him teaching us, I'd realized much of how they used magic was instinct and most realm creatures approached it more like an art form than the cut and dry science that ruled how humans viewed magic. But that meant sometimes I fought to understand what he taught. The basic elements as creatures I got. But this, I didn't know how to parse.

"Does that mean Magic is testing me? Does she want me to do something? Why me?"

Baneyarl looked at Esmere, who didn't even glance up as she appeared to be enjoying the conversation between her, Carelian, Sable, and Jo.

~You are no help, Esmere.~

I snickered. It was the first truly human emotion I'd seen from him. It did my heart good to know that Cath could annoy anyone.

He bounced his wings and sighed. ~It is probably more accurate to say you are drawing her in. Think of it like gravity. Your power draws in beings. Like Carelian and Esmere. They are drawn to you like objects in space are drawn towards gravity wells.~ I had urge to ask him how he knew about gravity and the solar system but he kept talking. ~Think of it as you attract Magic and she has expectations of those that are worthy of her attention.~ He huffed and I got the impression he was trying to describe color to a blind man.

I huffed, matching him. "Basically, you are saying accept it and quit trying to make it be logical or make sense of it."

~Exactly,~ three voices chimed in my head creating a horrible stereo effect.

"Thanks," I said to the sound of Jo and Sable's laughter. "So, did you want to see the house?" I offered, though I wasn't sure Baneyarl would fit.

~No,~, he replied instantly along with a more polite but just as firm, ~No thank you,~ from Esmere. I looked back and forth between them.

"Do I want to know why?"

Esmere rose from her willing servants. Jo and Sable both looked a bit sad to quit petting, but they stretched and rose too. I had to admit if I hadn't need to talk to Baneyarl and wanted to be able to concentrate, I might have joined them. Carelian's fur was soft and thick like a red rabbit, Esmere had fur that came across as mink with her dense coat. Running your hands through it made you smile. It was the best stress reliever I'd ever found. Carelian said his coat would never do that, it was more common with females than males.

~Until you have settled everything with whatever presence or even Magic herself, it is not wise for us to come to its notice.~ She tail lashed Baneyarl. He snapped at her tail, but it came across as playful, for all that his beak could sever her tail if he caught it. ~But we can come here as long as we do not intrude on its domain until that time.~

I turned to look at the house. It didn't seem unfriendly, the way houses in horror movies did, but it did seem aware of me and mine. But I still wasn't afraid.

"So be it. I have power. I guess maybe I should face up to that." My voice sounded small and quiet even to my ears.

Jo snorted. "Why do I get the feeling I should have you shouting that regularly like a marching cadence?"

"'Cause I'm conflicted? Remember everything Alixant said about downplaying my power?" I muttered.

"Yes, to the OMO and draft board, not to yourself. You need to understand and control your own power. Not avoid it as hard as you can like you have for the last year." Sable's comment cut and I threw up my hands.

"Fine, I'm a powerful bitch, is that what you want to hear?" My voice was loud and I glared at all of them, magic crackling around me waiting for me to ask it to do something, anything.

"Yes!" Jo and Sable chorused while the three other realm creatures chimed in with the same affirmative and then we all broke into laughter.

I shook my head. "May I offer you refreshments at least?"

~That would be excellent,~ Esmere purred. ~Carelian has been telling me about your salmon?~

Jo laughed as she turned to go in. "Same for you Baneyarl? It's a fish."

~That sounds most intriguing,~ he admitted and they both settled back down. Carelian posed in front of and them. I got the distinct impression they were grilling him, and from the occasional laid-back ears and tail lash it wasn't all good.

As one, without communicating, we backed up and headed into the house. "What do you think they are chewing on him about?" Jo asked as she dug in the refrigerator.

"Maybe that we found out he can read?" I offered.

"I bet it's more about you," Sable said, winking at me. "Your focus isn't getting you to understand everything."

"Ha! That means he'd explain something, and he rather doesn't." I shrugged. Carelian was my friend. The rest of the oddness of the mage-familiar relationship was something I didn't dig into too much. Too scared I'd ruin it.

My phone chimed and I dug it out of my back pocket. A notification glowed there from Indira.

TWELVE

Derek Stone Air Merlin takes on rogue mages and removes the threat to the world in the action packed "Rogue Mage 3". See him use his abilities to stop those evil mages threatening to destroy Buckingham Palace. Will he have enough offering to stop this evil group? Watch it opening weekend. ~ Movie Ad

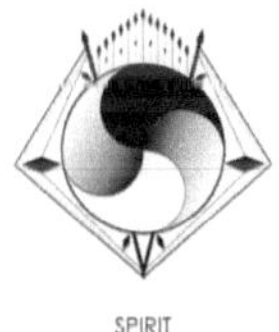

I groaned and seriously considered deleting it unread, but that would be one more instance of me avoiding.

Accept your power. You're a double merlin, for Merlin's sake, act like it!

The pep talked helped a little and I tried to center myself. This was my life, I could control some aspects of it, so I needed to dive in and start doing that. Here was the first step.

"What is it?" Jo asked, putting salmon into bowls. She turned to study some marinades sitting on the shelf. "I really want to play with their taste buds. We never introduced them to much food outside barbecue." Which Baneyarl had thought was the best thing he'd ever tasted, though he preferred Carolina BBQ sauce to any of the sweet ones.

"Indira, which means Alixant," I said as I pulled up the text.

"He's gotten better, you know," Sable commented. She handed Jo a bunch of ramekins to create spice options. There were days when I was surprised Jo didn't want to become a chef, but she liked cooking for friends and knew she couldn't compete with her mother. Besides if she became a chef, cooking wouldn't be fun anymore.

"I know. He's nice most of the time now. Or at least not a complete ass." I pulled up the text message and read it out loud. "Cori, we will be there tomorrow afternoon. Please be ready to leave the day after. The government would like to do a trial run with you, and it is a serious situation. Thank you."

Sable grinned. "Well, it's obvious Indira sent that, not Steven. But fudge. That means you're leaving us?" She had an odd mix of worry and excitement on her face.

I smirked at her. "Yes, and don't you dare have sex in my room."

She laughed. "Wouldn't dream of it, but the back porch maybe."

I took the tray Jo handed me and headed out. Sable had two folding TV trays—who knew where they had found those. Jo had another tray with ramekins and set it all up in front of the two very interested creatures.

By the end of the experiment, I figured we could start a trade war for salmon and spices if the groans of delight were anything to go by. As far as I could figure they didn't have spices in the other realms and even salt surprised them. Baneyarl loved the teriyaki and hot pepper mix, while Esmere was partial to the sea salt and lime, especially over the salmon. Both of them thought the mustard with spices had serious potential. Jo promised when she had her own place, she'd host a dinner for them. From the amount that they ate, I hope she planned on saving up.

They headed out when the tell-tale honk of a delivery from Amazing broke up our morning. The three of us unboxed everything I'd ordered, and I figured the new mattress would solve all my problems. Well, solve my sleeping problems. I had to resist the urge to take a nap on it as my night had not been restful. The wounds on my arm had quit throbbing, which was a relief.

Jo and Sable decided to spend the afternoon exploring the local area and I waved them off hoping they had fun. I headed upstairs, the rooms calling to me. "Ready to explore the treasure room?" I asked Carelian, who'd eaten way more than his fair share of salmon.

He'd changed his mind and decided he liked Jo's spicy stuff and would eat his meat drenched in it. My eyes watered just smelling it and he thought it was the best thing ever though he did ask for milk to quench his tongue. He told me once it tasted like fire smelled.

~Which you decide to do after everyone leaves?~ He bounded up the stairs, his tail dancing like a streak of fire.

"Yes. If anything bad happens, I don't want to risk anyone. Besides, I'm supposed to embrace my power, right?"

He sat at the door and stared back at me his ears perked forward. ~Of course. I want a brave, powerful quean.~

"That still tells me nothing."

He didn't reply, just looked at me. I glared at him. We became locked in a glaring contest, but being a cat, he won when I blinked.

"Someday I will figure out exactly what that means," I pointed out. He licked his shoulder expressing just how worried he was about my threat. "Cats," I muttered as I opened the door. It swung back against the wall and I looked at it. "So just to prove I'm not reckless," I said. I went over to the study and grabbed the ottoman. It had to have weighed at least thirty pounds. I dragged it out and braced it against the door. Even if it managed to move it, it would block the door from closing. If it didn't, well, I could always sidestep.

That neat ability had both gotten me into a lot of trouble and ended it at the same time. Stepping through magic to Japan had freaked out the government and OMO—I'd had to tell them the offering was nothing that I expected and only Carelian and Jeorgaz had made it possible. It wasn't a lie. I had figured sidestepping to Japan might make me bald. Instead, it only took a portion of the blood and ichor exposed by my wounds. I didn't even tell Jo how little the cost had been. Not lying, just not sharing information that might get her hurt or killed. I didn't want the government to ever realize that I could cross the world with the same amount of effort it took for most people to step off a curb.

I shook off the memories and stepped into the room, focusing on the statues and the obelisk that looked too familiar. Carelian brushed against my leg as he headed into the room to investigate the four main objects. They took up most of the space, but you could still move around them. In a rough square the woman at the front stared at me with such active arrogance I expected her to sneer. As opposed to my shorts and a tank top, she wore an elegant suit and stood a full two inches taller than me in heels.

"Is it just me, or is she intimidating?" I didn't really expect Carelian to respond. The woman looked powerful and confident. Everything I needed to become.

~She screams power, but arrogance is deadly when it comes to Magic.~

I had no idea how I could hear a capitalization, but I did.

"You think Magic did this?"

~Of course she did. But the question is, did a human help or did Magic act on her own?~

I swallowed, looking at the woman. "Wait, this was a person?"

~Is a person.~

I choked and looked at him, my ability to breathe locked away. My vision pulsed black and hard before I forced myself to inhale. "It's a person?" I gasped out, stepping back a bit.

~Yes. Though maybe was is accurate?~ He sounded thoughtful and I had to fight not to let the bile in my stomach explode outward. ~A merlin, double like you, but she is in permanent stasis, alive but not alive, think your cryonics.~

We'd watched a movie with people being frozen, an old movie from the 1990s. Carelian had sided with the bad guy in the movie, agreeing it should all devolve into Chaos as, he reminded me, was his nature.

"Okay. That is creepy. How do I bring her alive? And double merlin?" The idea of sitting in suspended animation horrified me. Just kill me right out, please. I leaned closer to look at her temple, but didn't see a double tattoo.

Carelian's ears laid back and he hissed at me, teeth bared,

muzzle pulled back. ~You do NOT interfere with Magic's judgement. Ever. She made her choices; these are the consequences.~

"But, there's a person there," I wanted to protest, but it came out too weak to qualify.

~And there are kits starving in Chaos. You cannot save them all, and those that earn their punishment deserve no reprieve.~ He glared over his shoulder at me and moved further into the room.

I sighed and followed him in. The other woman had different clothes on, like something from a historical movie set in the Orient, I couldn't say when, just nothing modern and not a style I'd ever seen. I glanced at her feet and they were tiny, with strange shoes on. Her smooth hair and round face should have been expressionless, but instead I could read a dark avarice, a greed, that made me shudder. It changed her from almost pretty to one step away from something out of a horror movie. I turned to the last man almost hoping for someone with a simple smile on their face.

He had on a fancy robe that fastened down the front. It reminded me of something I once saw in a movie about people in Eastern Europe, maybe around the Middle Ages. I didn't know if I should be relieved it wasn't another woman, but his expression provided no relief from the emotions churning in my stomach. He had a smile that I'd seen Indira mimic, sex, power, hunger, but hers had been a pale imitation compared to what I saw on his face. But the emotion that put all of them into simple notes was the wrath that hid behind it all. A wrath that even as a statue made me want to avoid angering him.

"He'd be a king with a harem of women and his advisors would all be scared to say anything that was against his wishes. His enemies' heads would be on pikes before his castle." I had a hard time taking my gaze off him.

~That is probably why he is here and not alive in whatever

time he came from. Ignore them, they have no bearing on our lives.~ I turned to see Carelian up on the top of one of the shelves.

"What are you doing? What if you break something?" I headed towards him, sure he was going to start sweeping things off—he'd done it before.

~I am not a mindless cat. I have no wish to unleash some of the things in here. Though you could place eggs on the high shelves for me to knock off. That would be entertaining.~

I glared at him, not that it did any good. Even his mother couldn't change his mind with a look.

"I think not. I will see about buying a cat sized mop and broom for you to clean up with."

~Outside would be interesting also,~ he cajoled, as he wove around the objects on the shelves.

This time I ignored him and started perusing the shelves. The place radiated a magic that once I looked for it was obvious. I wanted to pick up and fondle everything, but that seemed unwise. "Do you know what they are?"

~All of them, no. Some smell of magic I have never encountered. But many of them I know and there is a logic to this organization.~

That would help a lot. That and the pride in his voice reminded me that he wasn't even two years old yet. "Share, oh wise one," I encouraged, making my tone respectful.

He still flicked his ears back at me, but he jumped back down to the ground. The room had seven sections of shelving, two per wall, but the one with the door only had one. He headed to the section near the door. ~This section contains parts of magical creatures. Including Jeorgaz's feather. I believe there are a few dragon scales, an egg, the feather of a roc, fairy hair, unicorn hoof clipping, and a few others I do not know, though I suspect Esmere would.~

I looked at the shelf warily, and I lifted my hand to feel for the scale from Tirsane on the back of my Spirit symbol necklace. "They aren't like trophies, are they? I mean where someone killed for them." That idea vaguely horrified me.

I all but heard the huff of exasperation as Carelian flicked his tail at me. While he thought trophy hunting was stupid, none of the beings I'd met from the realms saw anything wrong with hunting another being, for food, for revenge, for ingredients. They also placed no blame when the hunted killed the hunter. It kept their society oddly polite, not that I'd seen much of it outside a few odd tea or tasting parties.

~I smell no blood, and the hair of a fairy is something you would not take if you had managed to kill one. They are powerful magic users. Not rulers, but they control their own realms within all of the realms. So these are tokens, much like the scale from Tirsane. But I do not know the terms of these tokens or how to activate them.~

I thought about the idea of fairies. Even though we still had classes twice weekly with Baneyarl, though he said that would change when school started back up, I had met no more beings besides those I'd already met. Was that normal?

"Carelian, how many creatures are in the realms?" He stopped in front of another shelf, this filled with many roundish objects, all glowing slightly, and they ranged from the size of my fist to a football sized one.

~How would I know? Do you know how many beings are on your Earth?~

I shrugged. "About 7.5 billion, give or take. But I meant more how many types of creatures are there?"

He flicked his tail at me. ~As many as wish to be. These are all learning stones. From many species and times.~ In a move faster than I could have stopped, he sat back on his haunches and touched one the color of a tin bucket and just as shiny.

CHAPTER
THIRTEEN

Fairy tales have been in our society since before magic spread across the world. They talk of dragons and fairies, unicorns and elves, dryads and kelpies - but few of those are known today. While we admit there are dragons (China proves that) and unicorns have been glimpsed, there is great dissent when trying to decide if there are intelligent humanoid races in the other realms. Anyone who has proof has never come forward. ~ History of Magic

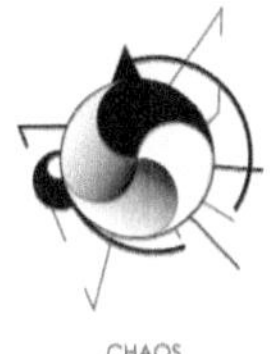

CHAOS

"Carelian," I exclaimed, lunging at him, prepared to knock him away. While I'd used the memory stone Esmere had gifted me with, it had only been a few times. It was like living in someone's mind as they used magic, explaining what they were doing and how they were doing it. Every time I thought minutes had passed; I would open my eyes and find hours had disappeared. It was one of the reasons I didn't use it often. Both Esmere and Carelian were confused as to why that happened. For them it was usually only minutes. All I could figure was it took me so long to understand because our ways of using magic were so different.

When he touched that stone all I could imagine was him getting sucked into the memories and me losing him if I couldn't get him out. He moved so my lunge didn't touch him.

~You worry too much and have become too scared. Where is my fierce quean telling governments to take a flying leap and forging ahead following her own choices?~ He turned to look at me as he pulled back his paw. ~This is a memory stone from the gorgons. I think it will be easier for you to use, they are more human in how they use magic than the Cath are.~ He turned and walked out of the room, leaving me standing there, feeling unaccountably sad and bereft.

I swallowed and picked up the stone and then walked out to the little balcony between the master bedroom and the study. Carelian was nowhere to be seen. That didn't surprise me. Carelian had opinions and could rarely be swayed by logic. Of course, he was also rarely wrong. While I knew he could lie and did—especially if you asked him what happened to any fish in the fridge—he didn't exaggerate or care about the petty issues that seemed to be such a part of human life.

But it meant when we really did have a fight, they tended to be cultural in nature. The last big fight had been over him threatening to kill a yappy fuzzy dog. It kept attacking, biting at his feet when we took our evening walks. The dog's owner was a prissy southern woman who felt Carelian was unnatural. She refused to keep control of the dog, even though she had her fuzzbutt on a leash. I warned her, I asked her, I threatened her with the OMO, but she sniffed and said, "Poofi needs to show the world he's boss." Two days later, Poofi lunged directly at Carelian and he lost his temper.

In one move, Carelian slammed the ball of fur down as if he was about to kill it. The quivering dog lay at his feet in a puddle of its own urine, with Carelian's claws extended over the whimpering pest. He spoke directly into the mind of the owner and informed her next time he'd skin it and eat in front of her. That fight had been difficult because part of me wanted to laugh at her expression and terror and his annoyance, but also because he would have done it. Like I said, they didn't exaggerate. Granted, the dog had never lunged or even barked at him again.

He'd be back and unless I brought it up again, he'd pretend it never happened. I wasn't so lucky. I sat on the little balcony, big enough for two chairs and a small table, and let my mind drift. The breeze drifted over me and the faint sounds of vehicles and other people competed with the rustle of the leaves and the creak of the chair. But none of them could overwhelm the noise in my mind as I tried to figure out my own problems. I stared deep into the stone Carelian had pointed out. It was polished to a high gleam, with twisted brown and gold sparks in the afternoon light.

"Are you always so timid? I would not have thought someone of such great power would be a quivering flower."

I jerked my head up from my contemplation of the stone to see the world had disappeared and again there was gray nothingness. But the chair remained, as did the stone in my hand.

With a sigh I settled into the chair and considered the question. "I don't know."

Heck, I didn't even know why I was answering a strange being other than it was the same question I'd been puzzling over. "The problem is, if I use magic outside the narrow constraints of what is approved and what is know, it brings unwelcome attention. And that attention usually involves threats to me and those I love. Jo or Sable may need to pulled away from me to stay safe. If I push it too far or scare them too badly, I'll be killed worse case. Or, more likely, I'll lose Carelian, my freedom, everything. Everything we are taught and shown is all about how to be good little mages." I swallowed, fighting to keep the emotions I'd been locking down for so long contained. "So maybe I'm scared or tired or apathetic. Why keep fighting against something I can't win?" My feelings all spilled out and it surprised me.

"Doesn't that depend on how you define winning?" No figure existed, just grayness.

I opened my mouth to refute the comment but stopped. What did I want to win? What did winning mean? I ignored the gray, the quiet, the being that kept dragging me here, and focused on the stone in my hand.

Freedom.

To help others.

A family.

No matter how long I looked inward nothing else came up. That was what I wanted. I blinked my eyes a few times, but the gray nothingness wasn't conducive to being able to focus my eyes elsewhere. I looked at the stone and it was there, though the lack of light made the colors nonexistent. Now it just looked like a stone, something I could have picked up from anyplace.

The grayness also meant I had no idea of time having passed or how long I'd been thinking.

"Are you still there?" I asked. If the creature didn't reply, getting out of here might be complicated.

"Where else would I be?"

"I want to be free to live my life the way I want to. I want to help and make sure no one else ever dies like Stevie did. I want a family, my family, near me." Examining what family meant didn't seem wise, but that was what I'd lost when Stevie died. I'd lost him and then I'd lost my parents when they pulled away.

A long silence settled around me. I got antsy before the voice replied again, and this time there was wariness in its voice. "You do realize you cannot stop death. It comes for all mortals. And immortality does not work out well when humans achieve it."

The very idea of stopping death or creating immortality sent a shudder of horror through me. "No. That was not what I meant." I shook my head hard enough my hair lashed at my face. "I mean dying young and not knowing why or being able to help. I mean finding reasons and how to prevent unnecessary deaths. Death is needed, but not at twelve." My nose clogged and I rubbed it and found wetness on my cheeks. I rubbed at my face and sniffed loudly trying to clear my nose.

"Ah," the voice had smoothed out again. "That is under-standable, even noble. What would you do with this information?"

I frowned, wishing I had someone to glare at. "You know, it's easier to talk to someone and not a faceless void." I huffed out a sigh. "I guess that would depend on what the reason was? I mean, let's say it was an exotic poison. Though I doubt that it was. I'd let the authorities know and not tell anyone about the poison. If it was a medical condition, I'd write it up and get it published." I shrugged. If I was able to figure out a weird medical condition, I'd have to be a doctor at that point and could produce a paper.

"Ah, I forget how much mortals depend on body language to guide their reactions." The same gray faceless form faded into existence in front of me. "Does this assist?"

I started at the form trying to glean anything from it. Two arms, two legs, a torso, and a head. It didn't tell me much, other than it was proportioned like a waif. And while there was a head, it had the same amount of definition as the beginning sketches of an artist. Meaning it had an oval head and not much more.

"I guess. You still haven't told me why you keep grabbing me."

"To test you. I told you that. You must face the tests and either succeed or not." This time a hint of exasperation layered the words.

"Yes, but why? Why are you testing me? For what end game? And why me?" I winced at the tone of the words and sank deeper into the chair, hunching my shoulders. For someone who wanted to be taken as an independent adult, I reverted to childish whining way too easily. I needed to work on that.

"Ah." The figure stood before me inhumanely still, then spun around violently. The swirling streaks of lighter grey grew and brightened until they achieved the first bit of color outside my own clothes that I had seen here. It split off into green and yellow and brown twisting and turning until the area around me resembled an explosion of paint pots.

Then it stopped and the figure, much more defined with actual fingers and a waist, stood perched on one foot. I stared as it remained locked in the Peter Pan pose, one leg outstretched behind and one anchored to the ground, arms flung back palms up along the line of its body.

"Ummm," I said. Running might have made more sense, but

at the moment my knees refused to allow me to stand up, much less flee.

The head tilted to look at me; green luminous eyes the shade of new dogwood leaves stared at me. "Why is because I decide who owns me, it is my prerogative. And Magic asks if you are worthy of her power. The answer to both is —unknown."

Before I could figure out what I was supposed to say, the color around me blended and smoothed into the view off my balcony. I reached out and touched the warm black iron railing and sighed. Reality had reasserted itself. I wrapped my fingers around the decorative metal and heaved myself up. I dug my phone out of my back pocket and rubbed the bruises on my hips. The days of the chair being comfortable had long fled. Another item to add to my shopping list. According to the phone, only an hour had passed since Jo and Sable left. Last time I got pulled into that space Carelian had freaked out, saying I was there but unreachable. I didn't hear him freaking out this time.

My throat tightened, but I reached out for him instead of panicking. ~Carelian?~

After a moment of silence that saw my heart rate kick up a notch. ~ Now we know if you can reach me in other realms. I will return in a bit.~ He ended the conversation with the mental equivalent of a face rub.

Relieved, I walked back inside but the being's comments were my new focus. Own it? Why would I own it? That meant it must be the house talking to me? Maybe? But that sort of magic wasn't possible. And how or why was Magic asking if I was worthy? Was this part of the herald crap that Baneyarl had mentioned? Why couldn't Magic ask me if I wanted to be the herald? Because I didn't. I had no desire to be Magic's Herald, or anything else.

What do I want to win?

I stopped in the middle of the hall as that question came back to me. My first answer was always freedom, but how did I want that freedom? As a timid mouse hiding in the grass or a dragon daring anyone to take what was mine?

I stood in the middle of the hall on the second floor. The balcony behind me and the window to the orchard looking out front.

It all came down to what did I want?

The beep of the delivery truck pulled my attention to the real world, but the image of a small mouse hiding from a dragon wouldn't go away.

CHAPTER

FOURTEEN

Magic is using you. You are addicted to something that gives you so much and takes so little, so you think. What are a few stray hairs here or there or a bit of blood or even a fingernail? Don't be swayed by the lure of magic; in the end you pay everything. ~ Freedom From Magic

---

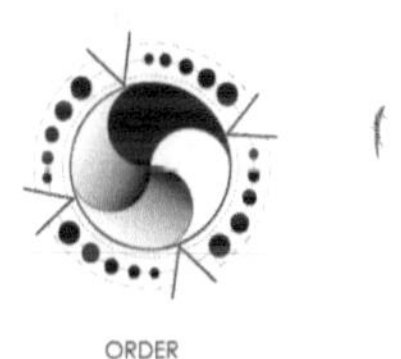

ORDER

ETA 5 Minutes.

Alixant's text message was short and to the point. "They'll be here shortly, Jo. Need me to grab anything else?" I shoved the phone into the back pocket of my jeans shorts as I headed back into the kitchen. Jo had decided to use

Alixant and Indira's coming to steal me as an excuse to create a masterpiece in the kitchen. She'd had Sable and me scurrying everywhere. The table was set, candles burned giving the house a fresh smell, and the aromas coming from the kitchen had my stomach grumbling and mouth salivating.

"You have beer for him and wine for her?" Jo asked as she finished draining the pasta. I still didn't know what she was making, but I wasn't complaining. It smelled of beef, tomatoes, cumin, chili, and lemon. The flavors weren't ones I normally associated with her cooking. But if she did this when my mentors showed up, I might look forward to seeing them more often.

"Yep. And iced tea for the three of us." If Jo was buttering Indira and Alixant up, I was all for it. They still hadn't provided much information as to why they had come up so soon after we left. Though it had been longer since school ended. I was starting to enjoy taking a vacation, even if the weird magic incidents had me living too much in my own mind.

"Excellent, then I think it is about ready. Sous chef, pull out the beef, *por favor*," she said winking at Sable.

Sable for her part saluted and grabbed a set of gloves. I stepped back out of the way and double checked for Murphy. Dinner smelled too good to take a chance of a disaster striking.

~They are here,~ Carelian murmured. He'd chosen an out of the way perch that gave him a view of the dining room and the front door.

I cast one more lustful look at the creation being pulled out of the oven and headed to the front door to let them in. The outdoor air had a hot wetness to it that didn't seem as oppressive as the Atlanta humidity, but either way air conditioning was preferable to staying outside.

They were getting out of a car, one that I didn't recognize—a dark green Escalade. Steven usually drove his government car, a black Escalade, and Indira drove a pale blue Prius. It made me wonder why the change—if they'd driven that up from Atlanta the gas bill would suck.

"Are you two going to stand out there and melt, or come inside where it's cooler?" I called down from the porch.

Steven handed Indira a bag from the back and grabbed one himself. We'd already gotten the blue room ready for them. Their mattress had been as hard as mine, so Jo had purchased a new one—with my house debit card—at the same time she'd grabbed groceries. Delivery was a wonderful thing.

"Cori," Indira said as she came up the steps, a smile making the stunning woman almost breathtaking. As always she wore clothes with an elegance I didn't have the body or the mindset for. Today she wore white silk palazzo pants and a green tunic that reached her mid-thigh, with her raven black hair constrained by a net of braids. "You look"—she paused and peered at me, a slow smile spreading across her face—"rested. I don't think I've ever seen you not busy trying to do three things at once."

I gave her a wry laugh. "And why do I think you two are about to ruin my Zen?" I knew they were going to dump drama in my lap but for right now I just wanted to enjoy one more day of peace.

"Not me," she said, jerking her thumb to point at Alixant walking up behind her. "That is all him and his minders. My draft finished three years ago. The government and I are on a consultant basis only."

"Ah, well then, welcome to my home." I managed not to squee as I said the words. My home. How cool was that? I looked at Steven coming up with a bag. "So I should send you packing?"

"I'd love it. But neither you nor I seem to have any say so in this matter. I swear next year I'm taking a real vacation. Screw it. I've earned it. My draft was over five years ago. Now they are my bosses, and they don't listen to a damn thing I say. Quitting is starting to sound good." He smiled at me. "Hello, Cori."

I rolled my eyes. He was in jeans and a light grey button-down shirt, which somehow still managed to look like a suit. With dark brown hair and a prominent widow's peak, he could have played the villain in almost any movie, but most of the time he wasn't too annoying. "Come on in. Leave your bags in the entry. Jo has dinner ready, and she'll skin all of us alive if we let it get cold."

They followed me in, making oohing and aahing sounds as they stepped into the foyer. I watched carefully, curious to see if the magic checked them out. But if it did neither of them reacted at all.

The mix of greetings and shouted hellos from the kitchen were performed and I got Indira and Steven seated. Carelian sat at his position at the table, watching all of us. If we had meat he ate with us, just without the extra sauces, though he always wanted more hot spices, not the salt.

"This place is lovely, Cori. Are you going to keep it?" Indira asked while noises of last second preparation came from the kitchen.

"I doubt you could pry it away from me," I said with a smile as I shifted on my feet. Should I go in and help or stay out here and be a good hostess?

"Sit, Cori. We're coming out now." Jo spoke behind me and I jumped a bit to see her and Sable coming out with two plates each. I slipped into my chair, the furthest from the kitchen, and licked my lips, the smells overriding any vestiges of good hostessing.

Jo set down a platter with a carved tenderloin, medium rare, stuffed with green and white items. Next to it she set a salad sparkling with mandarin oranges, cranberries, nuts, and spinach. Sable deposited her two plates, one of creamy mashed potatoes, and the other of a risotto. Jo darted back in from the kitchen dropping a basket of rolls on the table.

"Wow," Alixant said looking over everything. "Was all of this for us?"

Jo waggled her hand before sitting down herself. We'd already put the condiments on the table, and I wanted to start eating, but waited. "Yes and no. I figured we needed a celebration dinner for Cori and Sable graduating, plus getting the house. You two just provided a good enough excuse." She waved at the feast that lay before us. "Enjoy."

I took two minutes to put the slice of meat on Carelian's plate, complete with the spinach and cheese, before digging in myself. The room filled with the soft sounds of moans of pleasure, the scrape of flatware on china, and swallows of our drinks.

"Jo, this is incredible. You sure you don't want to become a chef?" Indira asked when our feasting had slowed to nibbling.

Jo laughed at her. "Oh, heck to the no. If I did that, doing this wouldn't be fun anymore. This is fun for me and I like cooking for Cori and Sable, they don't whine at doing the dishes, and Carelian will eat my spicy stuff. And if it doesn't work out, we all shrug and order pizza or take out. No pressure. If I was a chef, I'd never be able to just cook for fun or not care that it came out tasting a bit odd. Remember when I put way too much cinnamon in the chili?"

I snorted. "Yes. It was the weirdest disconnect. I think we had to throw it away, because the flavors in those amounts just clashed so badly."

Jo smiled at Indira, her eyes managing to linger on Indira's chest only for a moment. "See, this way cooking is fun. I'd rather make my living working with machines. I've got a part-time internship lined up for spring semester doing some high-level machining. It should be interesting and if it works out, I might create a pretty good career after the draft."

"Have you received your assignment yet, Sable?" Steven asked as he pushed his plate away.

"Hey, I still have dessert cooking. Fresh apple sog," Jo said, but she made no move to get up. I loved her sog, it was the best fruit dessert in the world.

Carelian had delicately eaten every bit of meat with his paws shredding it into small slices. He'd moved over to a chair that a beam of sunlight hit and was currently making sure his fur coat lay perfectly smooth. I had random bad dreams of someone wanting to skin him for his coat, a la Cruella DeVille, a Transform archmage from the kid's book. But right now, he just looked like a plush toy until you saw his teeth and claws.

"Yep. They approved my master's without hesitation last year. But they have already stated I'll stay in Atlanta working on the water treatment plant. Something about extenuating circumstances." She winked at me and I rubbed my tattoo. The one that shouted out to the world what a freak I was.

"That would be us," Steven admitted and I jerked my attention to him, eyes narrowing. He held up his hands in self-defense. "I might have implied you were a bit flighty and having Jo near you helped keep you stable. And that Jo would go wherever Sable went, so it might be worth it to keep them near you."

I gave him a hard glare, then grinned. "Thank you. I probably would survive just fine, but I'm not going to argue at having my best friend around."

He inclined his head to me. "What good is power if you don't use it occasionally?"

That echoed too close to my own worries. I hadn't mentioned the meeting with the house this afternoon. Choosing to keep it quiet while I decided between mouse and dragon. Finding out more about power and the government and my limits would be a good option.

"Speaking of having best friends near us," Jo started derailing the words I'd been trying to organize in my mind. "Where are you taking Cori and why?"

Steven and Indira exchanged glances and she folded her napkin, placing it on the table, then leaned back in her chair. Her mouth had compressed into a thin line, and I got the feeling she didn't approve of the situation. It only made everything more interesting.

"They pulled me out to a scene about two weeks ago. And three days ago, we got a break. We managed to identify the perp. At least we think we managed." He'd slipped into his FBI speak, his voice becoming crisper and his vocabulary going into agent speak, perp for perpetrator and scene for crime scene. I'd missed it more than I realized.

Sable and Jo had both leaned forward, their eyes sparkling. I hid a laugh. They thought the FBI was all glamorous, not the horrible boring slog I knew it was. But it was also terrifying and fascinating. And I missed Siab terribly; Chris and Niall, the other two agents who worked for Steven, not as much.

"The authorities think they have a serial killer in New York City. I wasn't sure at first, but I'm starting to believe them. They identified someone and have taken over his apartment, but they can't find anything to prove or disprove and he has vanished." He wiped up the last of the sauce with a bit of bread.

"What does that mean for Cori?" Jo asked, her attention riveted to Alixant. "Why pull her into this mess? She isn't an agent even if you dragged her into acting as one before."

Alixant scrubbed his fingers through his hair. It reached past his shoulders now, falling in loose waves. "I don't really have a choice and it will prove a boon to her in the long run."

His words sent tendrils of stress through my chest, but I just leaned forward and waited. He sighed and glanced at me, then Carelian. My familiar lay sprawled out in the sun and gave every impression of not listening, but his ears were tilted back towards the table.

"You're stalling," Jo said, but her voice was mild.

"Yes, I am. I've enjoyed dinner and none of you will be happy with what I'm about to tell you. Merlins, I'm not happy about it."

"While I, on the other hand, am livid," Indira said her voice scarily calm. "It is a violation of the spirit of the draft. And it sets a bad precedent." She tore at the remains of bread on her plate shredding it into crumbs.

Alixant slid his eyes towards her, but then brought them back to me, his lips pressed together. "Cori, you know the government is very interested in your abilities and even more interested in controlling them. They are terrified of you."

That made me blink and pull back, the memories of the talks I'd had with Jo and the strange being flashing to the forefront.

"If they ever realized what you could do and that you are learning how to use magic outside of the publicized spells, they might eliminate you now. Meaning they want to test you at every turn to see if you are too dangerous to let live."

CHAPTER
FIFTEEN

It is the duty of all governments to keep their citizens safe, both mage and non-mage. The best way to keep all citizens safe is to control those with dangerous abilities by making sure they know exactly how to use them and the consequences of misusing any ability. ~ OMO Stance on education

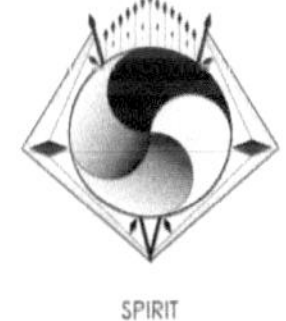

SPIRIT

A headache started to form in the center of my skull, and I rubbed between my brows. It didn't help. "And if they decide I am too dangerous to live?" I knew the answer, but I needed to hear it.

The dinner roll turned to powder in Indira's grip, an Entropy spell. She dusted off her hands, her face serene. "Then they will have someone put a bullet in your brain or cause a fatal aneurysm. Steven and I are deemed tainted, so we would not be informed when they make that decision. Even my contacts can't say which way they will go. Because you've been very much on the straight and narrow since Japan the apprehension regarding you has dropped. But they track everything."

I sat back and looked at them, thinking back to the earlier conversation with the being between worlds. What did I want to win? My freedom. That was never in doubt. But I had no desire to flee to the other realms and live there. I liked indoor plumbing and grocery stores; the realms didn't have those in great quantity from what I'd seen.

"What do you recommend?"

It was a sign of how hard Steven was trying that he didn't bark out an answer and tell me what I was going to do. "Be meek. Be mild. Act like a chastised little girl. Do what you've done this past year and keep your head down and don't draw attention." He rubbed his temple, long fingers ghosting across his tattoo, but he didn't take his eyes from me. "I know that isn't in your nature. But between the OMO and the Draft Board, you have a lot of people agitated."

"Why the OMO? The government I get, but why is the OMO upset about me?"

Indira spoke up as Steven' eyes tightened. "You threaten their entire structure. If you remain mostly as a fluke it raises your importance and lowers the danger you represent. They only have found three people that tested differently from the original scan. Officially, they have determined it was a failure of the testing unit and the examiners. They don't say what was wrong with the unit or the guidelines, but they are testing large numbers of people. Though due to constraints they are mostly only testing people still active in the draft. The older mages are avoiding it. Basically, the OMO doesn't like being called into question—ever. If it comes out that their testing methods are consistently flawed or your rating can be different than what they say—well who is to say they can't be bribed to be wrong. What wouldn't you have given to be ranked as a hedgemage?"

I nodded at her point. I would have done almost anything. "Politics, corruption, and big business?" I asked dryly, the mental image of flaming everyone making me smile.

"Yes," Alixant said. "But that being said they all need to prove not only are you an anomaly, but that they have you under very tight control."

I didn't like the sound of that and the idea of being a mouse versus a dragon sat at the back of my mind as I nodded at him to go on.

"We believe we have a serial killer in New York City. They think they've found who it is, but we haven't captured him. We just have access to the apartment. They are finishing cataloguing the evidence and dusting it. They started last night. But they've put in a request for a strong Spirit mage to come see if any of the objects in the residence give any information as to what he is planning or where any other victims might be. This guy, if they have the right apartment, didn't have pictures and diagrams to shed any light as to who he would kill next. They're desperate."

"And I'm the strongest Spirit?"

Indira sighed. "Spirit only accounts for less than 20% of all arch mages or higher. And most wizards or lower can't pull memories out of objects unless it is very fresh and very strong. From the testing you did in your Spirit classes, you can pull it out of things when it was left through causal touches or when the memories are hundreds of years old. I know a few people who would love to have you on archeology digs."

I couldn't repress a shudder. "Thank you but no. One day of testing objects at the museum was enough to scar me for life. Aztecs were bloody horrible." The vivid images of death, sacrifice, and more sex than I'd ever wanted to see flashed back. I had to take a drink of iced tea to clear my mouth of a metallic taste. Experiencing the sensations of killing someone while you had sex with them did nothing to help make the idea of sex any more attractive to me.

Indira lifted a shoulder. "Fair. But that means they don't have anyone that can casually touch items and see if they can glean any information out of them. Soul tends to be rare as a strong regardless."

I nodded. I'd seen the statistics on power breakouts, and that was global, or it was according to the OMO.

"That is why I'm bringing you in. There are departments fighting over you and they want to see how you handle a real investigation now that you have some training and experience."

I just nodded. Asking what role they planned to have me in didn't really matter, it could change a dozen times between now and my draft starting. And fighting it would just make everyone's life hard, but that didn't mean I needed to be timid either.

"You mentioned if they don't think they can control me they will eliminate me." I swallowed, my throat and mouth going dry at the audacity of my thoughts. "What happens if it's too dangerous to eliminate me?" All the delicious food threatened to explode out of my stomach, but I kept my face still, and fisted my hands in the tablecloth.

"Too dangerous?" Steven frowned at me shaking his head a bit. "I don't understand. Killing a mage ends their threat. Magical artifacts like the ones the owner of this house created and collected are rare. And while you may have friends or family that would revenge you, they can be dealt with." He gave a nod to Jo and Sable who had stiffened.

"True, humans can easily be killed. But what about..." I paused and took a deep breath while chanting 'dragon dragon dragon' in my head. "What about demigods and other beings from the Spirit realm who owe you or at least would be willing to avenge your death because you are amusing to them?"

The room went silent. Even the sounds of breath stopped as they all looked at me, eyes wide.

~Are you sure, my quean?~ Carelian asked in my mind, oh so softly.

I didn't turn to look at him, but answered, all my resolve in one word. ~Yes.~

~Excellent. It is about time.~ His purr of laughter brushed through my mind.

Indira broke the silence like a glass cracking as she started to laugh. Her laughter came from her belly and roiled through the room spreading delight with it. "She figured it out. They are going to be kneeling at her feet before this is all done. I'm going to need a lifetime supply of candy, because this is going to be something to watch."

"Merlins Balls," Steven groaned. "Why me? Why couldn't it have been another decade before she realized this was an option. Magic hates me."

I looked over at Jo and Sable who looked as puzzled and confused as I was. I'd thought I might be risking myself with that statement, but this reaction wasn't anything I expected.

"I don't understand. I expected threats or warnings," I admitted.

"I'll give you the threats and the warnings, but you're what, twenty-three?" I nodded in response. "Most mages either figure this out in their fifties or never. You already realize that magic is power, and that you are way ahead of the power game because of all the allies you've gathered."

"Wait, what?" I sputtered, the tablecloth in my hand getting wet from my sweaty palm.

"This was one of the reasons I wanted you in Emrys, but I couldn't be that blunt. You network, get friends, people who will notice and take offense if you disappear," Indira said, a smirk on her face. "This isn't stuff you tell young mages. Most mages, and I mean this worldwide, decide magic is too much trouble for anything outside of small household stuff. And the draft works really hard at making magic seem to be dangerous and boring. Not to mention for most mages, at least under arch-mage, the costs of doing magic becomes too high pretty fast. Quite frankly, it becomes easier and faster to use science to do things. Yes, my little tricks like heating up my tea seems small, but if I did that two or three times a day even at the small fraction it costs me, it would become expensive when compared to how many offerings I have available. Or I can put it in the microwave." Indira shrugged. "You on the other hand are so powerful that you are a very real threat. And Japan knows this. You threatened to destroy their country, and they believed you."

"I did not," I protested, stung. "I only threatened to destroy the palace." That last part came out slower and I mumbled it. "They didn't want to take me seriously."

"They do now. Don't ever plan on traveling to Japan, at least via normal methods. You are blacklisted."

Jo waved her hand. "Back up. Yes, Cori is powerful. Yes, she has friends. What does that have to do with what you are talking about?"

Alixant rubbed both temples now and sighed. When he

looked up, I was surprised to see the amusement on his face. "Ladies, welcome to the real world." He directed his comments to the entire table. "Mages are powerful and those who realize they can use their power and make people fear them are the bane of the OMO and governments everywhere. There are a much higher percentage of mages with familiars that fall into this group. It normally takes them until well into middle age to have the friends and network to make them someone that governments would think twice about taking out. You've managed it in your twenties and obtained allies that any government is going to take a long hard look at before pissing off."

"Oh!" The lightbulb went on. Jeorgaz had threatened the emperor and his royal magician when I brought the fight to Japan. I didn't understand then why the threat had been taken so seriously.

"Yes. Cori, if you convince them you won't upset the apple cart, they'll leave you alone." He took a deep breath and snagged my gaze with hard gray eyes. "If you convince them you're a dragon, you'll need to convince them poking you isn't worth it, but you have a fine line to walk. If you are too scary, they will take you out along with as many allies as they can. If you can be too dangerous to annoy, but not threatening enough to be considered a serious threat, you will get the best of both worlds."

~You can do it. Be the quean I know you are. You can lead a coven to make the gods quail.~

~Will your mother and Baneyarl help me?~

~They would be delighted, but you will need to speak with them.~ Carelian's voice sounded soft and reassuring in my head, and I wanted to hold him tight.

Instead, I sat up straighter and forced a smile that was more real than I expected. "Then I guess I'd better be a dragon. They will meet me on my terms, and I'll call down everything I have if they try to eliminate me for being too much of a problem."

"Oh, to be a fly on the wall during your first draft assessment," Indira murmured.

I wanted to follow up on that, but Steven spoke. "Good. Show them what you can do and leave them cowed and worried, just don't be a jerk."

"Like you?" I blurted, but I didn't back down or apologize. He had been a royal jerk in the beginning, and I'd called him on it multiple times.

"Exactly. I am a jerk for multiple reasons, but I might have bought into my role as a hard-nosed FBI agent as much as Indira bought into the whole seductress thing. Figure out what you want to be and go with it. Just remember making allies will be good, while making enemies might become something that you will regret later."

I nodded. My intentions weren't to be a jerk to people, I just wasn't going to bow to their demands anymore. I would take the degree I wanted. It met the requirements and what they wanted didn't matter. Not anymore. If I could handle Japan gunning for me, I could handle the draft board and the OMO.

"So, when do we leave?"

CHAPTER
SIXTEEN

Among males, the first year of the draft is the deadliest as they overreach and need to be dealt with. Surprisingly, the last year of the draft is when we see most females fail in their ability to moderate themselves. It is as yet undetermined why this is, but the percentage of failure for archmages and merlins is almost double the lower ranks. ~ OMO internal Memo

---

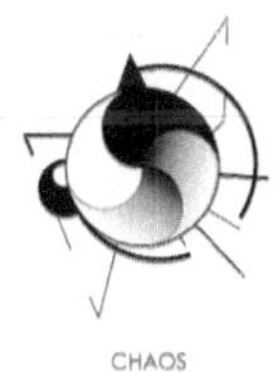

CHAOS

We left at five the next morning. I'd been smart and packed everything the night before, and had coffee waiting for me when I made it downstairs. I filled my mug full of the extra strong roast and added the cream, sugar, and a shot of cinnamon syrup. Carelian stood at the door peering out, looking for all the world like a dog ready to go on his walk. I decided to not tell him that. I'd made sure to pack the harness so he could come with me to the crime scenes. Back in the early days it had been little more than a set of bands so I could "control" him. Not anymore. With him as strong and big as a large dog, I'd splurged and ordered a custom harness for him.

It made him look like a service animal, except you never saw service cats. I made sure his harness didn't say anything, but it had bags and pouches on it. It had the advantage of making him look more trained than scary. I just never mentioned he could pull it off faster than I could get it on him. People would be scared if they knew that. Seeing him as a service animal made him safe but when people became aware that he was a sentient creature with his own thoughts and ideas he turned into an unknown—and a threat. As far as I was concerned the greatest threat from him was definitely the power of his farts.

~I still say they need a hammock in their vehicle.~ Carelian's tail cracked through the air as he sulked and I made sure his tail couldn't hit me.

"No room. You saw that. Besides this is only a three-hour drive, not multiple days." We stood on the front porch waiting for Alixant and Indira. I'd said my goodbyes to Sable and Jo last night before we all crashed. They decided —wisely from my point of view—that sleeping in was a better use of their time. I had my backpack and a small suitcase with me. Alixant had assured me this trip would only take a week or less, and we were staying in an apartment in the city, so I'd have access to a washer if I needed it.

Either way the idea of getting to see New York City hummed through my veins. This was turning out to be a summer of unexpected experiences and I couldn't wait for the next one. It didn't hurt that Steven had informed me I'd be paid at the contractor rate. Which made my financially stressed soul relax even more.

The door creaked behind me and I turned to see Alixant walking out, one overnight bag in each hand.

"Ready?"

I held up my coffee. "I have caffeine so my survival probability is now upgraded to decent."

He smirked as he unlocked the car. I grabbed my suitcase—backpack attached to it—and Carelian's bag and followed him. I'd packed a few essentials for Carelian, a food bowl, water bowl, water flask, treats, and a blanket. The leash was in a pouch on his harness. They were a bit bulky to carry around, but I just couldn't justify buying bowls for him to eat and drink out of when we were out. It got way too expensive.

The rear of the Escalade rose and Alixant put the bags he was carrying in first, then mine. Carelian jumped in the back and proceeded to inspect every inch of the car. I—a sane human—walked to the passenger side back door and clambered in instead.

"Oof, remind me not to get something you need a step stool to climb into," I muttered as I got myself arranged. I could see Indira headed down the porch stairs with her mug of tea in hand.

"Dira complains about the same thing," Steven said.

I ducked my head, smirking a bit. It was the first time I'd heard that nickname for Indira.

"But when you have someone ram you at speed, you're more than happy for the weight and size of this car."

I glanced around the inside of the car. "That has happened?"

"Not to this car, but yes, I've had it occur. And it helps stop fireballs too." He finished as Indira climbed in grumbling.

"You need step stools. Next time splurge for the version with extending steps." Her mutters elicited a laugh from Steven as she bucked herself in.

"So noted. I'll just let the government know my two contractors are short." He turned the car on.

"We are not. Just this car is huge," I pointed out. I was five-six and while Indira was shorter than me, she usually wore three-inch heels making her about five-eight.

"It is not our fault you chose a car not fit for normal sized humans." Indira sniffed as she talked, her nose pointed in the air. If I hadn't seen her fighting not to smile, I might have thought she was really offended.

"As I feel I will have no peace until this is resolved, I will see what I can do. Though I would not hold my breath. This is the government we are talking about." His voice turned serious. "Cori? You ready to discuss the case?"

My humor fled as if chased by tax collectors. I took a fortifying sip of coffee, savoring the cinnamon, and nodded. "Sure." Carelian perched next to me, paws on the door near the window, watching the world go by.

~This would be much more comfortable with my hammock.~ The echo telling me he broadcast rather than just sent to me.

I ignored the confused glances from Indira and Steven— they had no idea what hammock he was talking about—and scratched his ears, waiting for the gory details that would soon be invading my imagination.

Steven started to talk, and I listened, letting Carelian's silky fur be my anchor and reminder I wasn't alone. That I was going to be a dragon.

"The murders started about three months ago. They put it together in early May they had a serial killer, not just a string of unrelated murders. The signature was subtle, but once it was found it was obvious. The victims are taken at least five days before they are killed. Just at the hairline behind and above their right ear is a tattoo. It's a tilde, and no one has any idea what it means. The first three victims all had multiple tattoos and this tiny one, it is less that ten centimeters long, was missed. The fourth victim however was an Orthodox Jew who would have never gotten a tattoo. That was the clue that set up alarms as they don't do any tattoos that are decorative."

I snorted a bit at that. Decorative tattoos versus the brands we all wore on our faces. I guess that was one way to look at it.

Alixant kept talking as he pulled onto the highway that led toward NYC. "That snapped the investigation into focus. We are up to nine victims, but the agents on the ground believe they've identified the perp. He disappeared two days ago. They traced him as he had recorded contact with three of the victims as a courier. He doesn't seem to have an alibi on his social media channels and all efforts to locate him have failed. This is why they want you, to see if you can figure out where he is or who else he has abducted. Manhattan is too big and right now his victims are all over the place. Three women, six men, two black, two Hispanic, one Jewish, three white, one middle eastern. Youngest 18, oldest forty-eight. They all work in Manhattan and only two live there. At this point even though they are going over all the people reported missing, they have to look at the records for three states. People from all over come into NYC to work. It's a needle in the haystack scenario with dozens of juris-dictions." His voice was flat just reciting facts.

"You haven't seen any of this have you?" I asked.

"No. They contacted me about two weeks ago and only because of you. They figured the only way to get you to come with even a slightly friendly mood was via us." He waved his fingers at himself and Indira. "But I looked at the evidence and asked a lot of questions before I let myself be pushed into this. Besides, you were taking finals." The toll station was ahead and I cringed at the cost for these roads. Georgia and their no-toll roads seemed much nicer. "I reviewed the details again on the way up and double checked the photos."

At his nod Indira handed me a manila envelope. I took it but didn't open it immediately. Instead, I watched the traffic ahead, letting what Alixant had told me filter through. "How are the victims being killed?"

"From what the coroner said and Pattern mages have been able to reconstruct, something was placed over their mouth and they suffocated. We can't find any signs of struggle on them, so it is assumed they were unconscious and whatever was used decayed so far we couldn't find the drug."

I nodded, more to myself than him. A lot of drugs had a short half-life and if the bodies weren't found for days, which drug was used might never be found.

"Any trophies taken?" I asked, still thinking. All the Criminal Justice classes stressed that serial killers were rare, but they had their own logic that applied to the murders they committed. You just had to find the logic.

"Not that we can tell. And no sexual assault either. There are signs their clothes were changed, but when they were found, they were wearing the same clothes they had last been seen in. The only weird thing is it looks like the ligaments in their joints were broken. The details are in the envelope." He risked a fast glance back at me. "Why, what are you thinking?"

I shook my head. "I'm not. That much you and the classes

did teach me. I'm not thinking anything, just trying to arrange the picture in my head. I won't have any thoughts until after I do whatever you want me to do." That trap I knew to avoid. All I wanted was information. No opinions would be allowed to form until after I had new evidence.

I could almost hear him smiling and rolled my eyes. I turned the problem over in my mind. "Is the suspect a mage?"

"No. And he's one of those 'nice quiet men, never did anything, but I always thought he was odd' types." Steven fell silent, concentrating on the traffic as it was the middle of rush hour. Maybe we should have taken the subway, but images of taking Carelian on the subway in New York assailed me. No, driving was much, much better.

"Why are you coming along, Indira?" I asked. She really didn't work with the FBI, even if she and Steven had hard started dating, but that was more because of my presence bringing them together than anything.

"I like the shopping in Manhattan. The crime scene is all yours. I'm just taking advantage of a free place to stay and time to go shop." Her answer was immediate, and I heard Carelian's laughter in my head.

~You seek to hunt new fur free of cost,~ he offered. None of the beings I'd met really understand our fascination with clothes. And I'd given up trying get them to understand.

"Exactly," Indira said, a smile gracing her face. "And as a bonus, I'll get mostly free meals out of it."

~Wise huntress,~ Carelian commented then made himself more comfortable so he could look out the window.

"See? Even the Cath understands the wisdom of my choice," Indira gloated to Alixant.

"And here I thought you just wanted to spend time with me. My feelings are crushed." Alixant sounded as amused as I was, and I marveled that the two of them got along so well. I would have expected another outcome. I'd never understand relationships. You added sex and everyone started acting stupid.

I tuned them out and opened up the envelope. The first item was the coroner's report. It was the first I'd seen outside my human biology and CJ classes. I had a new appreciation for the information that was present. I settled back reading the file. The cause of death was asphyxiation, but I thought it odd they couldn't find any means. It was like they fell asleep with a plastic bag over their heads, but even then, there should have been some signs of a struggle. I checked and all of the eyes showed signs of petechial hemorrhaging which made sense if they were straining and struggling to breathe for any long period of time.

Suffocation. What a horrible way to die.

I shook my shoulders to dispel the chill that ran down my spine. Next, I moved to the joints, and like Alixant had mentioned the knees, elbows, and shoulders had been broken. The best image I could think of in my mind was they had been snapped the way you might snap a chicken leg at the thigh, so you could bend it differently. I took a large sip of my coffee at that. They were probably insane to want me in a job like this, even thinking about someone deliberately doing this made me nauseous, not the fact that it happened. I'd seen worse as an EMT. But the idea of someone doing this to someone else, callously, with purpose? In many ways I preferred the car accidents—at least they weren't usually on purpose.

All of them had disappeared between work and home. That in and of itself I thought was interesting. They all had jobs. But otherwise, Steven was correct, there were no obvious correlations between the victims.

"Was the tattoo done while alive?"

"We aren't sure. Either immediately before or immediately after death."

I nodded at Alixant's reply but added another note to my mental file—the murderer was probably an artist of some type or had a partner that was. The tilde, while not very big, was clean. I grabbed my phone and flipped on the magnifier.

"Huh, there looks like template blue around the tattoo." I said it more to myself, but they weren't playing loud music like Sable and Jo would have been. Which meant they heard my comment.

"What do you mean?" asked Steven. He kept his hands on the wheel and watched the traffic, but if he had cat ears, they would have been tilted my direction.

"Well, you know how they apply the template of the tattoo to you when they do the mage tats?" I saw them both nod. "While mage tats have to meet that exact layout, lots of artists will set their guidelines before they tattoo. But the really good ones would have freehanded something that simple. I mean a tilde? That they could do in their sleep."

"So, you don't think this is a tattoo artist?"

"Eh, depends on how you use the word. Someone who makes a living doing it, probably not. Someone that knows how to use the gun?" I paused and looked at it again. "Are you sure these were done alive?"

"All I have is what's in the file. Why?"

"I don't see any redness or healing. But I haven't made a study of tattoos, so I could be wrong."

Alixant made an odd sound, but I ignored him. Why would you put the tattoo on like that? Was it really a tattoo? Something felt off—I could still remember the itchy swelling of the tattoo on my temple, and how much I wanted to claw it off. But this one, it seemed full and whole, which even on a small tattoo would take a week or two.

I kept flipping through looking at the pictures. Height, weight, color, shape, they all varied. Granted, seeing them all dead didn't give me a feeling of anything except stillness. The Criminal Justice classes I'd taken talked a lot about tiny details that could form the basis of a puzzle, but I just thought the tilde was weird and the pictures lacking but I couldn't figure out why.

"You do realize I know nothing, right? And other than things that don't make sense to me, I have no clue. I don't even like reading mysteries." I preferred historical fiction and non-fiction medical books, but that was for fun.

Alixant nodded as he changed lanes. "I know, and I didn't expect you to open the files and go, here is the answer. I just wanted you to have some idea of what is going on with this case. We'll visit the perp's apartment first, then the morgue. They have three of the previous victims. All they are hoping for is a clue. This killer is too good."

"If you say so." I wasn't convinced, but who knew.

"Think of it as a chance to stretch your abilities," Indira offered. "You might be surprised by what you can find or see."

Or surprised by a chance for me to be a dragon.

I didn't say that out loud, but I let the idea sink into my soul. I would be strong because the alternative was to be a mouse.

CHAPTER

SEVENTEEN

God or gods are still a hot topic in most of the world. We don't know if there are gods of the realms, or if the Christian/Judaic/Islam god exists there or here. We don't know if you can or should worship those from other realms. One thing everyone agrees upon, no one wants their attention here in our realm. ~ Magic Explained Online

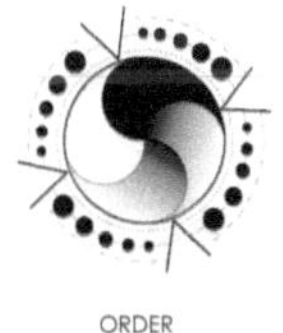

ORDER

I spent the rest of the drive watching the scenery and wishing they'd included images from the victims when they were alive. After that I lost myself in looking at the city. New York rose above me like looming specters of judgment. Each of them with a million eyes to see my every mistake. Driving through those streets, which always had shadows, I felt smaller than ever.

"We're headed right to the perp's apartment first, then I'll take us to the place we rented for the next week or two. The cops have finished their on-scene investigation and the lead detective wants us there."

I'd heard him talking on his cellphone, but I'd been too busy ogling to pay attention. "Will we have time to go see the Statue of Liberty while here?" I couldn't see her from where we'd entered, and of all the sites in NYC, that one mattered to me. The Lady.

"I'll make sure of it," Indira said. She'd spent most of the ride reading her e-reader and had let us both be. Her aplomb was one of the many things about her I wanted to emulate, though the seductress part of her wasn't.

"Thanks." At that point I closed my eyes. The traffic in the city made Atlanta look calm, and I didn't like driving in Atlanta on the best of days. But the people here, they crossed the roads even if traffic was coming, no one listened to horns or sirens, and it felt like there were people everywhere.

~I do not like this place. Are all your cities like this?~ Carelian's ears were laid back against his head as he stared out the car window.

"No," Indira said, a smile in her voice. "New York is unique, though Tokyo and Los Angeles have much in common with it. There is a certain level of magic in New York. You'll see if you spend any time here."

Carelian flicked an ear towards her, then back down. ~I am not convinced.~

Indira laughed, but Steven spoke before she could say anything more. "The address is up ahead." I opened my eyes and looked out the window. We were in a shabbier part of the island, with old brick, rusted fire escapes, and air-conditioning units sticking out of windows. A squad car sat blocking an alleyway as Steven drove up to it.

"Sorry, sir, this area is—"

Steven cut him off by holding out his wallet, badge on display. "Special Agent Alixant, Merlin. Here on request. I have Merlin Munroe and Merlin Humbert with me."

"Yes, sir. I'll move my car. Drive in and there will be an officer waiting to escort you up." The officer moved his car and I tried to take everything in. Small convenience shop, a dry cleaner, a coded entry door, and a pizza place took the bottom floor of the building. We pulled into an alleyway that made me wonder if we'd be able to get the doors of the huge vehicle open to climb out.

We could, but barely. Carelian jumped out first as the odors of trash, exhaust, and rotten fish assaulted my nose. I sneezed in protest. It wasn't as humid as Atlanta, but the mixture of odors hit me like a slap to the face.

~This place has little to recommend it. The smells are rotted and twisted.~

"Welcome to New York City. Love it or leave it," Alixant said. He waved us towards the door where another officer dressed in the blue of NYPD watched us.

I had to agree with Carelian. While I loved my house, this city had little to make me love it. Alixant went through the introductions again, and this time Indira and I had to show our IDs.

"Put the pet on a leash, I don't care if it's a service animal or not," the officer said, disdain dripping from his tongue.

Carelian hissed. ~I am neither a dumb pet nor a service animal. I am the focus of Merlin Cori Munroe, chosen to be here.~ His tail lashed back and forth as he stared down the officer, who had gone white.

"Carelian," I hissed, surprised at his tone.

~What? If you will be a dragon, I will be a tiger.~ His voice clear and amused, and just for my mind. I fought not to laugh at his tone. I might have created a monster.

"Oh, um, okay. Up that elevator. Fourth floor." He'd stepped back, as if that would put him out of reach of Carelian's claws.

I just shook my head and followed Alixant and Indira, both of whose shoulders were silently shaking. The doors slid closed, and Indira started to giggle. I'd never heard her giggle before. While Alixant's laugh was deep and low.

"That might be the funniest thing I've seen in a while. This is going to keep me in giggles for months," Indira said.

"Oh, I suspect this case is going to be something I'll never forget, one way or another." Alixant managed to get his laughter under control by the time the door opened, leaving me fighting between being embarrassed and proud. Carelian knew which one he was, not that Caths were ever embarrassed. He sauntered out of the elevator tail and head held high.

The drab hallway had ten apartment doors lining it, five on each side, and a fire exit sign at the back wall. There were no windows to let light in and the entire place screamed depression and apathy. I wanted to turn around and go back into the noisy, smelly alley. At least it had life to it.

A single officer in blue stood at one of the doors about three-quarters of the way down the hallway. Her eyes snapped to us as we exited the elevator. I let Alixant take the lead, while I saw Indira head past the door and take up a position near the exit. She'd made it clear she would not be coming in, as there was little their own mages couldn't do that she could.

"Merlin Alixant here with Merlin Munroe and her familiar to inspect the scene as requested by Chief Blasini."

The officer looked at her list, then Carelian. "It doesn't say anything about a cat."

"That is not my problem. We can leave, because I can guarantee you Merlin Munroe won't enter without him."

She narrowed her eyes at me, her name tag read "Delansky", then turned to shout through the door. "George, your high magic user is here. Says she's bringing in her cat."

A sharp accent with mushy sounds of the North echoed out of the apartment. "What evah, just let them get in here so we can get back to other things, likes catching 'dis asshole."

With a smirk, Delansky stepped out of the doorway and gestured to us to pass. "You heard him, have at it."

My stomach, already twisted in knots, wasn't helped by Alixant looking at me and saying, "You first. You get to decide how you'll handle it."

Delansky snorted but didn't say anything. I swallowed and stepped in, that first step across the threshold feeling like a mountain I hadn't wanted to climb. I tried to look at everything and make sure I touched nothing. The hallway told me nothing about the occupant. It had neutral off-white walls with multiple scuff marks that were the only things added to it. I stepped into the living room, with a kitchen to my left. A pile of shoes, two with cleats, a pair of sneakers, and sandals lay jumbled together at the edge of the hall and kitchen wall. There were two doors leading out of the living area, probably a bathroom and bedroom. The place kind of looked like a dust devil had exploded in it. Traces of black dust everywhere, things disorganized and yet stacked, and a feeling of emptiness rang through the place.

A slender black man in a suit that hung off him like he was a coat rack it'd been thrown on, stood by the windows looking out at another building. But he was watching me walk in. The heat of Alixant's stare, along with his cologne, created a wall behind me, while Carelian's tail grazed across the back of my legs.

Dragon, you are a dragon.

I walked further into the room and nodded at the man, the detective I assumed. "George?"

He pushed away from the windows and with a shrug of his shoulders he moved towards us. I caught a whiff of peppermint candy as he reached out his hand to me. "Detective George Farlane, Merlin Munroe. I hope you can help us." I shook his hand as he spoke—it was dry and firm—but the shake lasted as little time as possible. Maybe he hadn't noticed how nervous I was.

I lifted my left shoulder in a shrug. "I can try but know nothing is guaranteed. Is there something in particular you want me to look at?"

He faced me, but his eyes tracked Carelian moving through the room, with his normally active tail held still and trailing on the floor.

"There are a few items that look like they had significance, but otherwise touch everything. We are hoping he left some traces of himself and plans on what he's going to do with his victims."

I nodded and waited. After staring at me, he grunted and pointed at the small table between the kitchen and the couch. "Crap is there. Have at it."

I moved over to the table. It had to be something gotten from a secondhand shop as it was old, banged up, and was barely big enough for the two mismatched chairs that sat on either side. On it was a CityPass, a trophy from bowling, a necklace, and a watch. I looked around the apartment, surprised at such odd things without anything more intimate. There was a bookshelf with dusty books, a TV and remote with the numbers worn off the buttons, and a butt indent at one end of the couch. The kitchen had a dish in the sink, an off-white refrigerator, and a coffee maker that should have seen the trash a decade ago. It felt comfortable but hopeless. There wasn't anything in here that suggested a future or going anywhere.

"What was his name?" I didn't take my eyes off the table, frowning, not sure what I was supposed to see. Carelian stood looking out the window, smudged but not dusty, staring at the birds on the building across the alley. None of the objects called to me, but then only really old objects had before. Making a decision, I reached out and picked up the necklace. It was a Saint Christopher's medal. A faint image of embarrassed pride, and misplaced faith drifted through then was gone, nothing to hold or examine.

"Carl Osborne."

I set it back down on the table and picked up the watch. A flash of annoyance, of excitement, of running late, of being early all rippled in its depths, but nothing violent or concrete, just snap shots of a life.

"You do realize most people don't hold onto things focusing emotions into them, right?" I said as I reached for the trophy.

"What do you mean?" George leaned against the wall to the bedroom and his dark brown eyes brushed over me as I worked, each little bit of magic requiring but a dusting of cells. This skill rarely required enough of an offering to even require choosing to offer. Maybe if I was here all day, I might spend a whole hair.

"A rosary, something prayed over daily, or a good luck charm, those are kept long enough and had enough emotions sent to them that they might retain something. But most objects are just that, objects. We don't affect them anymore than we miss them when they disappear. They are replaceable and temporary in our lives." The trophy had nothing more than a flash of exultation and then nothing.

I picked up the card of the transit pass, frowning. The scuff marks in the hall clashed in my mind. "Did he have a bike? And ride? Aren't the marks in the hall from the bike?"

George frowned at me and then stood up and headed to the hall. "Delansky, any notes about the perp riding a bike?" His voice carried and I held the card, a bit wary as I tried to listen to both the card and George.

"Yes, sir. Neighbors complained about it, saying he was always taking up room in the elevator and often came back sweaty and stinky," she responded immediately.

"There's your answer, Munroe. What about it?" George didn't hover, he lurked. I couldn't decide if that was better or worse.

"He'd lived here for a while?"

"Four years in March, per the landlord."

I held up the CityPass. "Why would he have a visitor discount pass if he rode his bike everywhere? This is just for attractions and stuff, right?" I didn't want to admit I'd researched maybe getting one just in case we decided to come do touristy stuff.

George started to reach for it and stopped. "Yeah. And that's an old one too. They change the design pretty often. And in the last year, they've mostly gone digital, you know on your phone as an app."

I looked at it. The flashes of glee and anticipation bright and sharp. "Would this be any good now?"

"Nah, they are useless after you activate them. I mean it's possible that one wasn't activated, but really, what New Yorker would use that?"

I ducked my head so he wouldn't see me smile at the way he

said Yorker. "Why put this here? I mean the other stuff makes sense, kinda. But why this?"

George looked at me, still wary and suspicious, but willing to answer. "Because we found it on the floor when we came in. Figured he dropped it in his hurry to leave."

CHAPTER

EIGHTEEN

How Time Bubbles Work: Time bubbles are not time machines but in fact pockets of reality out of sync with our reality. The mage casts a bubble over the area needed and pulls it a few minutes into the future, or an hour. Once the initial cast is done, it is simple to allow it to stand. The cost comes when you drop a time bubble. Your body ages when you end the spell by the amount of time you offset plus the duration of the spell times two. So if you offset by ten minutes and maintain the spell for three minutes, you will age $10 + (3 \times 2)$ or $10+9= 19$ minutes. Many think this is not a big deal, and in small amounts it isn't. But if you offset a bubble by a year and stay in there a month, the time is significant. A year = 525,600 minutes + 43,200x2 = 425 days . You age a year plus for a month of lived time. It is rarely worth the cost, but some have done it. ~ Magic Explained

---

That didn't make sense to me, I mean, I lived with my bus pass in my wallet and I'd notice if I dropped it. But maybe the City Pass was different? For now, I just nodded and put the card back on the table. I wandered through the rest of the apartment.

Carelian would wander by me, his tail caressing the back of my leg or hand, then head over to investigate something else. He didn't say anything, just explored, being careful to not disturb anything. I touched and fondled half the place. The bedroom was just as simple as the rest of the house. A double bed, no pictures on the walls, with a dresser and a closet full of what Jo would call working man clothes. I didn't see any suits or at least any besides one tucked way in the back that screamed funeral or wedding wear, but it didn't look like it had been worn in years from the amount on dust on the shoulders.

No matter what I touched, or even if I increased my offering, digging for something substantial, I got nothing more than a sad, apathetic man. The biggest jolt I got was from an old biking helmet. It had joy and a brightness almost nothing else did, and it made the rest of the items even more depressing.

"Are you sure he's your killer?" I asked as I looked around the living room one more time.

Detective Farlane and Alixant were near the door talking. They both turned to inspect me when I spoke.

"Why do you ask?" George moved my direction, his eyes scanning as if to make sure I hadn't damaged or taken anything.

"There's nothing here that has any malice or even powerful feelings. If I had to guess, and remember I'm as green as can be, this man had little joy in his life. I doubt he ever got mad at anyone and bordered on being depressed. I'd say the only thing he enjoyed doing was riding his bike." I shrugged and waved my hand. "Unless he has a storage unit full of his clippings and murder tools, there is nothing here to indicate this man had the desire to hurt anyone."

I shrugged, feeling out of place in this sad apartment and wanting to go back to our apartment at college or the house. At least life and joy existed in those places. "This is the only thing that doesn't fit." I tapped the CityPass. "It has a sharp spike of thrill and something else, but I can't get enough flavor to even begin to figure out who might have touched it. Or hell, if he just picked it up."

~This place reeks of sadness and the death of hope. But there is no bloodlust,~ Carelian whispered just in my mind, pressing his cheek against my thigh. My hand dropped down to pet him, glad for the life in his presence.

George set his hands on his hips; eyes narrowed. "Are you telling me—" His phone went off and the officers' radio in the hall squawked. "What the—" He answered the phone. "Farlane. What? Where? Son of a bitch. I'll be right there. Bringing civilians with me." His conversation, full of pauses and grunts, told me something bad had happened, but he never took his eyes off me.

"What is it?" Alixant snapped and I smirked to see "Take control Alixant" was back.

"Our perp isn't a perp, he's a vic. They just found him, but not like the others." George's voice had gone deeper, though the accent still made me think of gangster movies as I processed what he said.

"What does that mean?" I asked. George spun and headed

out the hall, and I trotted to keep up with him. Indira joined us in the hallway as we headed to the elevator.

Detective Farlane didn't say anything until the doors closed, trapping us inside. He glanced at Indira's tattoos then over at Alixant.

"She's safe. She's worked with the FBI and local LEO's before," Alixant said, his body tense and quivering. He reminded me of a dog on the hunt.

George shrugged, dismissing Indira from importance. "The other bodies were all found laid out in various areas of Central Park. Always in secluded sections, where disposing of a body wouldn't be hard, and normally late at night, as most were found in the morning. This one wasn't. He was posed and on display at the Penn subway station." He narrowed his eyes at me. "Can you handle seeing a dead body?"

I snorted. "As long as it isn't covered with crabs, yes." The in joke made Steven smile, but both Indira and George looked confused. I didn't bother to explain. My life as a teen to a young adult with Murphy's Curse up all the time made dead bodies a common occurrence. Then I worked as a paramedic for the last two years. So bodies in multiple stages of decay didn't affect me. Bodies being eaten by crabs did. Even the memory of those pictures made me shudder.

"Merlins," George muttered as he headed out. "Follow me. You got a light?"

"And siren," Alixant replied.

"Good." George jogged down the hall yelling at one of the officers to get the squad car going and I raced back to the Escalade, trailing Alixant by too much. I held the door open for Carelian, who leapt in with grace I envied. I'd barely managed to slide in and get the door shut before Alixant was tearing out of the alleyway, lights flashing, following the squad car.

The trip was anticlimactic. The traffic was so thick we

crawled, not sped. Pedestrians, cars, and taxis all ignored the sirens and lights with equal amounts of apathy. The taxis took advantage of people slowing down for us to cut in front of the police car. I watched all this with horror and glanced at Carelian.

~I think we could have jogged there faster.~ I crafted my thought carefully and sent it to him.

~Yes, and had more fun terrorizing people,~ he replied back immediately, peering out the window.

I huffed to myself, but didn't bother saying anything. He was a Cath and would always be one. Human sentiments were a waste of time.

Even with the traffic that cared not for our sirens and lights, we pulled into a blocked off section of the street with cops waving and yelling at people in under twenty minutes. George waited for us, his arms crossed as if he'd been waiting hours, not the minute he'd been there.

"I'll stay in the car—leave me the keys," Indira offered. Steven threw her the keys as I headed after George, who wasn't waiting any longer.

"They're with me," he called over his shoulder as he dove down the steps, his suit coat flapping behind him like a wayward tail. I barreled after him and Alixant, but they had longer legs than I did and they were taking the stairs three at a time.

"Follow them, I'll find you," I told Carelian, and he darted off. The yells and screams of surprise and shock were all I needed to figure out where they'd gone. I raced after them, the shiny chrome and filth of the station a dichotomy that made it more alien. I pushed my way through the crowds. The station was filled with people of every nationality, age, and gender, and they swirled around me like a kaleidoscope of sound, scent, and color. I gritted my teeth, moving through the crowd as fast as I could until I hit the wall of blue.

"Keep back, nothing to see here," the man in front of me barked.

"I'm with them," I said, pointing at Alixant and Farlane. "Merlin Munroe."

He started to say something when I heard Carelian talk to more than me, though I didn't know who all had heard him. ~Let her in, she has something of importance to do here.~

The officer went white and I saw George flinch, but he turned and called back to us. "Brown, let her in. Now."

The officer bobbed his head, his skin still pale, and stepped away from the barrier. I ducked under and headed over to the men. Neither of them glanced my way. Instead they were focused on the subway wall. I moved around them and looked at the display in front of them.

CHAPTER

NINETEEN

While the branches of Water, Fire, Air, Earth are all rather well understood. The branches of Spirit still prove surprising. Experiments have proven over and over that knowing how elements (referring to atoms and molecules) interact makes using them much more accurate and efficient. But when it comes to the abilities in Spirit no two experiments done by two different mages are ever the same. ~ Magic Explained

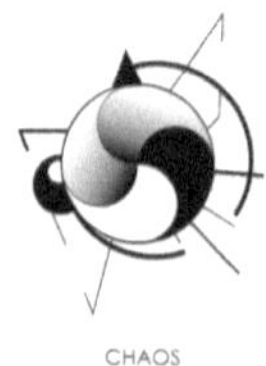

CHAOS

C anvas had been strung up on pipes, creating a curtain around the display that horrified and amazed me. The canvas explained why no one had noticed the installation of his death, I mean who paid attention to people cleaning up graffiti. Or in this case making it.

Did this qualify as graffiti or art?

Carl Osborne hung on the wall like a piece of art that you couldn't look away from. The file said he was in his mid-thirties. His shocking white hair, obviously natural, glowed against skin tanned from wind and sun. It created a contrast that grabbed your eyes and your soul. His eyes were open, revealing ice blue eyes that stared out at the crowd, unseeing. He hung like a crucifix on the wall, but instead of nail, a thin pipe ran from one arm to the other, behind his head, and slipped through the space between his ulna and radius. Instead of his legs hanging down below him, his hips were popped out and he hung frog legged, soles of his feet together. Dressed in a black mandarin collared shirt, it created a sharp color palette between his hair and the dirty white tile behind him.

"What kind of Merlin blasted sicko does this?" George demanded even as people behind him were taking pictures, their cellphone lights flashing.

"It's art," I said but my voice was lost in the clamor around us. While the cops could prevent people from getting close, they couldn't block everything. The story would explode across the net in hours. I stepped closer to him, looking.

"Don't touch anything," George snapped.

"I won't." I didn't bother to get annoyed. I just stood looking, both stunned by the shocking beauty and horrified that I found it beautiful. I had to swallow, and I pulled my phone out to send a quick message to Jo and Sable. *Everything good here. NYC is crazy.*

A few seconds later they replied. *Good! Enjoy!*

I slipped the phone back into my pocket, their existence providing an anchor to reality.

~I smell magic. Pattern.~ Carelian whispered in my head and I turned my head, looking for him. He could be all but invisible when he wanted, although normally he preferred the attention. I caught a glimpse of his brilliant red, garish against the walls where he poked at a five-gallon bucket.

~Magic? Where? There are probably a lot of mages around here.~ I glanced at the crowd, seeing the splash of color on multiple temples, even on a few cops. ~It might be just from someone using it. Or used it.~

He hmmmed in my mind but didn't agree or disagree. I stood back and watched, moving out of the way as people rushed to and fro taking pictures, examining, and acting like hyenas swarming carrion. I entertained myself by identifying what they were doing at each stage and asking Alixant if I didn't know. It proved informative, if a bit boring. It took three hours before they were ready to let me touch anything, to let me contaminate their scene.

"Merlin Munroe?" a voice behind me asked. I started, having zoned out. It was pushing seven at night, I hadn't eaten since breakfast, and if it wasn't for the coffee and bagel I'd gotten in the station, I might have been removing heads.

I turned to see a tech in a dark blue windbreaker with NYC Police Crime Scene Unit printed on it, looking at me and waiting.

"Um, yes?"

"They said you can go in now. All information has been catalogued. You can't use gloves?" There was a bit of disapproval in the question.

"Hard to sense emotions if all I can touch is plastic. Thank you." I walked towards the scene. So many things called to me, but first I stopped by Detective Farlane and Alixant.

"Ready, Cori?" Steven asked.

"No. You realize I still might not sense anything." That I directed more to George Farlane than Alixant. While I didn't mind doing this, the idea that I was the only thing linking them to the murderer made my skin crawl.

"I know. But at this point we have little to lose. Try not to contaminate the scene, but we've nailed down most evidence. Not that there was much. The killer cleaned up well."

I tilted my head looking at it. "It is a striking visual."

George sighed. "I know. If this was performance art and the 'art' was alive and willing, I'd be appreciative. As it is, it reminds me of..." He faded, standing across from the remains of Carl.

"A crucifix," I offered. I'd seen them when I went to church. The Catholics and Protestants still had followings, as did Judaism. But those buildings and religious iconography had never had this level of impact.

"Exactly. That will bring more attention. See what you can find, Munroe. It can't be worse than what we already know —nothing."

I didn't bother to correct him. Shutting up, I walked over to the body even though I had a feeling that what I discovered could be worse. Carelian materialized next to me, leaning against my leg, his body heat managing to be both welcoming and too much. The subway was already too warm to be comfortable.

There was little detritus scattered around. I catalogued what the display held: body, robe, vertical metal pipe, wooden horizontal support, and wooden brace. The whole thing was set so it supported his body with a minimalistic elegance. It must have taken ages to get the balance right to make it strong, yet almost invisible. Practice. That resonated with me. I pushed it away and started with the easy parts.

Wood brace gave me nothing. No images at all, which didn't surprise me. It was rough cut and relatively new. It had not been exposed to anything. Same with the vertical support beam. Next, I touched the pipe. There was a small flash of frustration but not enough to grab on to.

Stepping back, I looked at it all again before taking a deep breath and touching the robe.

"Huh?" I muttered pulling my hand back and then touching it again. Usually I got something if I made a direct effort to look. Even from wood there was a nothingness that meant no strong emotions. That absence, that was the norm I usually sensed from everything if I bothered to try. Only objects with very strong sensations associated with them could force themselves on me, but most things had some level of echo in them. I touched the robe again, and there was a blank, like touching a piece of glass. Smooth and nothing would stick to it.

"This robe, is it silk?" I asked looking at it.

"Yes. A hundred percent. Why?" George moved closer as he answered my question, Alixant trailing.

"Silk doesn't hold any magic—actually it's used to insulate from magic." Alixant provided the information before I could. "Most magic won't touch it. I mean you can burn it or destroy it, but it won't hold magic." I'd never read any research as to why, but it was true. Even in the other realms, silk was prized because of that.

George gave the robe another sharp look. "Interesting. Find anything else?"

"Still looking," I muttered, feeling my face flush at the frustration in his tone. He nodded at me and they moved back a bit. That really only left the body. The images of me touching the victims of the rogue mage Paul Goines flashed back. They had all been subtle and lacking emotional torment. But they also had provided almost no information. Which one would be better?

I sighed and touched his exposed arm, opening/asking for the information. Flesh was always different than inanimate objects, at least for me. I had to actively quest, where with objects I just needed to not block the impressions—if there were any.

Terror slammed into me, buckling my knees. Bracing my other hand on the wall, I kept myself from breaking contact. The need for air clawing at me, and the impression of pawing at my throat trying to remove an impediment that wasn't there seared into my mind. I started coughing reflexively as I reminded myself that I could breathe, this wasn't happening to me. My vision narrowed and someone moved in front of me, but all I could see was the gray around my narrowing sight, then it stopped. I yanked my hand away before the cycle could start again and slumped to the ground.

"What's wrong?" Alixant crouched near me and Carelian pressed against me.

I swallowed, fighting to breathe normally when all I wanted to do was gasp for air and make sure I could still breathe. "I'm not sure. It felt like I was suffocating. Like he was suffocating, I mean." I didn't mean that. I felt like I had been dying, willing to kill for a breath of air. Willing to do anything to breathe. A shudder ran through me. I looked around for my coffee, needing to wash the fear out of my being, then remembered I'd thrown it away. "Can I get a Coke please?" Alixant knew I meant a real Coke.

"Yeah, give me a minute. Don't do anything." He rose and strode away. Still surrounding us was the wall of cops and technicians, but they were a background haze as I tried to remember what I'd seen, felt, experienced.

"Suffocating? Did you see how he was killed? We are still thinking he was unconscious as there aren't any marks."

I held up my hand, sifting through the images, the sensations. "I need to go in again. I need to analyze what I experienced."

"Why?" George demanded, but I just shook my head. Alixant crossed back, handing me the bottle of Coke. I cracked it and took a large swig, the icy cold carbonation helping to clear my brain. I settled back against the wall, resealing the bottle, then reached up and laid my hand on Carl's foot.

My lungs burned and I gasped for air, but there was nothing. Beige walls filled my vision, and my hands scraped at my face trying to remove whatever prevented me from breathing, but there wasn't anything there. My lungs sucked harder, but nothing answered my gasps.

I pulled myself back from the absolute immersion, something that had taken a while to learn how to do, and I looked at the sensations. All of this was from Carl's eyes, so I could see his hands reaching towards his face, see the vision clouding, and feel the need for oxygen so deep and primal it threatened to pull me back into the experience. I kept myself outside and paid attention to what I could see. The hallway was from his apartment, but there was nothing else. Not until right at the end a figure moved into the narrowing vision, vague and distorted, but a gleeful smile burned into his psyche then everything went dark.

I let my hand drop to my lap as I focused on calm breathing and not the desperate gulps of air my emotions told me I needed.

"Well, what did you see?" Prodded George. I ignored him, taking another sip of Coke and trying to get my heart rate back to normal.

When I thought I could talk without gasping for air, I

opened my eyes and looked at both of them. "He was killed in his apartment. Suffocating while awake, though he lost consciousness before he died, so I guess that was a mercy."

"Dammit. Did he see the killer? Were there any other clues?"

I swallowed down another mouthful of soda, replaying what I knew in my mind, but there wasn't any other way to interpret what I'd seen.

"Yeah. The way he was killed." His dying agony still fresh in my mind as I fought past the driving need for oxygen. "He was killed by a mage. Air mage to be specific. All the air around him was pulled away. He died of asphyxiation in his hallway and couldn't do a damn thing about it."

CHAPTER

TWENTY

A number of messiahs have appeared over the last two hundred years. And while most agree they were mages using the desire of people to believe in gods to make money, not all have been so materialistic in their actions. At least three miracle workers have been priests high in the Catholic faith and they have always done their "miracles" for the good of others adhering to the vows of poverty and charity. To this day the Catholic Church denies that they harbor mages. However, the Vatican has never sided with the OMO and if you take the vow of priesthood, you are never required to be tested or educated in magic. ~ History of Magic

"Blast this asshole to outer space," Farlane muttered as he stood staring at the posed body. It hung on the wall, staged for us to enjoy and marvel at. Too bad a man had to die for its creation.

"Art. The killer's creating art," I blurted out.

"What?" Both men turned to look at me. I pushed myself up and made sure I didn't touch Carl again. I didn't need any more nightmares.

"Do you have pictures of the other victims, not when they are dead, but when they are alive?"

George rubbed the back of his neck. "I suppose so, back at the station. But there is nothing they have in common. We've gone over that, different ages, genders, races, religions. They don't have anything in common."

I shook my head, thinking. Charles Wainscot, a friend from college, dabbled in art. Actually, his familiar, Arachena, dabbled in art. She thought it was fascinating to create things with her webs, and she delighted in creating three dimensional pieces of art that appeared to be different things based on perspective. Everything in her world was perspective.

"Can I look anyhow?" I asked. The urge that was driving me to see images wasn't concrete enough for me to quantify. It was just a niggle of an idea in the back of my brain.

"Tomorrow," Alixant said. "It's late. We're all hungry, and there isn't anything we can do right now. We'll be there tomorrow morning about nine?" He directed this at Detective

Farlane and I wanted to sigh in relief. The emotions had been exhausting. I was starving and I felt filthy, inside and out.

"That works. I need to scour missing persons regardless." Farlane darted his eyes to me in a quick sidelong glance. "You sure you didn't see anything to help identify the killer?"

"Probably white or light skinned, and good teeth without staining, maybe too good. But that was all I could pull out."

It wasn't much.

"Beard or mustache?"

"No."

That was the last definitive answer I could give him, everything else the answer was "I couldn't see or didn't see."

After fifteen minutes he waved at us. "Go. You've got the address; I'll have passes waiting for you." Without any more social niceties he headed over to talk to the crime scene techs. I gave Alixant a beseeching look. I was more than ready to go.

"Come on. Indira texted that she has dinner waiting for us. She checked us into the apartment. You have a choice—you can walk, it's about five blocks from here, or we can get a cab." I weighed the options, but the effort it took to climb the first set of stairs up to the surface street answered the question for me. Today had drained me more than I'd expected.

"Cab, not sure I could handle walking that far right now."

"On it."

We fell quiet as we got outside and I snapped the leash on Carelian, not that he had stepped more than a foot or so from me since I touched the body.

~You okay?~ I asked, not wanting anyone to overhear, not because I was worried about anyone thinking I was crazy, I just felt this should be private.

~Humans are disturbing. Why kill that person? Not for food, not for vengeance, no territory to obtain. The death was done for death. That makes no sense. The Cath are not so barbaric. We kill for mates, for food, for protection, not for death.~

His words rang in my head and I wanted to hold him, reassure him, lie to him. I didn't do any of those things. We waited for the taxi, Steven talking to Indira on the phone giving her an eta.

~I don't know. But I suspect this might be more than just that.~ I swallowed and even forming the words in my mind was an effort. ~Is death a being or essence like Magic?~

Carelian didn't reply until the taxi pulled away from the curb, the three of us in the back. He lay across my lap, his purr noticeably absent. ~Not the way you think. It is part of the universe, but not like the grim reaper or figure in a cloak with a scythe. It is less than Magic yet more, in that all of us go to the realm of death at the end of our life.~ He huffed out an almost growl. ~This is more a question for my malkin or Baneyarl. I am not qualified to answer. But I will say even death would not approve of this.~

The idea of death, anthropomorphized or not, approving or disapproving of how people died just gave me the shivers. Though there was a certain amount of relief knowing that there would not be approval.

~Good. But did you note anything else?~ His nose had levels of sensitivity I could never approach, even down to smelling what plane of magic a person was attuned to.

~Nothing that you haven't deduced. Magic from Order. Not super strong. Not a merlin, I believe a wizard if not a hedgemage.~

"You think the mage is that low in power?" Startled, I spoke the words.

"What are you talking about, Cori?" Alixant asked, the taxi jerking to a stop at a light.

I shook my head. "Later." Trying to explain everything with

the driver listening would have been a confidentiality breach, not to mention I didn't want any details of the murder getting out. Alixant stared at me, long enough I started to shift in discomfort. He nodded once and moved his attention to the driver.

"Pull in and let us out at the entrance."

The taxi pulled in, and Alixant handed him money as Carelian and I got out. I stood at the entrance to the apartment building looking up at it. Metal and glass mixed with bricks. It looked cold and expensive. The taxi pulled away and Alixant stood at my shoulder.

"We're staying here?"

"Apartment rental service. Since the government is footing the bill, we might as well stay someplace decent, and the cost is less than two hotel rooms, so no one complains."

I shrugged and followed him. Carelian kept pace with us well enough that the leash never got tight. I expected Alixant to start asking me questions about my comments the second that we got in the elevator, but he stayed quiet it as it rose upwards. On the ninth floor it stopped and slid open. Alixant walked out turning left, heading towards an apartment. He unlocked the door and walked in, calling out as a wave of delicious smells reminded me I hadn't eaten real food in way too long.

"We're back, Indira."

"Excellent, the food is ready. Warming drawers are wonderful things." We walked towards the sound of her voice. I took a look around. It was a nice apartment, done in blues and grays, the soothing atmosphere helping to wash away the stress of the afternoon. The rich smell of tomatoes, garlic, and basil went a long way to that also.

"Sit. You both look wiped." She set the platter of spaghetti on the dinning room table, where fresh bread, salad, and two other pasta dishes, a carbonara penne pasta with tomatoes, already waited. Carelian was up, appreciatively sniffing at a plate of sliced beef, lightly seared, with some sauce on it.

~Are you coming. I am hungry. And water please.~

"Of course. That bad?" Carelian didn't drink, not as much as humans did, so for him to ask for water at dinner was unusual. He also thought our wine and sodas were gross, though he didn't mind the occasional beer, IPAs only.

~Dirty, too many people. Almost scared to groom.~ Laying his ears back as he glanced at his paws and sighed. ~One minute.~ I heard him pad down the hall, looking for a bathroom. In unison Alixant and I glanced at our hands.

"Yes, hand washing sounds like a great idea," he said, and I agreed. We washed at the kitchen sink, and I knew I'd need to take a shower tonight. I'd offer to see if Carelian wanted to take one also. He could tolerate it sometimes and if he felt that bad, he might prefer it, or at least to have me wipe him down with a damp towel.

Carelian was sitting at his place when we returned from the kitchen and the four of us sat down to eat. The first fifteen minutes were spent dishing up and getting enough food into our stomachs that I could at least interact with some level of rationality.

"Was it bad?" Indira asked, her voice more hesitant than I'd ever heard.

"Yes and no. Not really gory, but more why the person was killed and the presentation. It was creepy." Alixant picked at his food, then took another bite. "The killer is a mage. But that brings up the comment you made in the taxi. What were you talking about?" He latched on to me with his gray eyes, putting me on the spot. With a sigh I put down my fork.

"Carelian and I were talking in the car." I started flinching when his eyes sharpened. I couldn't remember if I'd ever mentioned I could talk to him and a few others via mindspeak.

It didn't matter now, so I dismissed the worry. "He said he could smell the magic the mage used, but the mage isn't very strong. Maybe even hedgemage level."

"How?" Indira asked, chasing a piece of bacon across her plate.

"How what?" I looked at her, frowning, unsure which aspect she was questioning.

"How did they kill if they are a hedgemage."

I swallowed back a sad laugh and gave Carelian a look. He ignored me, cleaning his claws to remove the remnants of meat and sauce on them. "I'm going to be quoting other people here." No one outside of Jo and Sable knew about Baneyarl and Esmere. I had to remember not to give that away. "But we tend to focus on the top tier of mages, archmage and merlin. We don't look at how powerful hedgemages can be, if they choose, especially in their strong branch if they want to offer enough."

Indira and Steven both focused on me, and this time I distracted myself from their attention by reaching for the French bread. I'd written a paper on this and I'd be able to use that to explain away my rational, even if Baneyarl had started it by pointing out almost all sentient creatures in the realms were mages, and they were powerful in their own narrow arenas.

"We don't think about hedgemages as being powerful, useful, or deadly. It takes too much in offerings to do magic consistently. That is the key, using it on a regular basis. If they did that, then yes, they would run out of offering fast. But this?" I shook my head. "Remember I'm basing my suppositions off of what I felt from the victim, and we all know emotions are misleading or even false."

They nodded at that. It was the reason so many eyewitnesses were useless. They let their emotions taint what they saw and felt, and it could change almost anything.

"I think the mage pulled away all the air, because his lungs were grasping onto nothing, from either the immediate vicinity or even just his lungs. How much would that take? I bet Jo could do it for almost nothing, me too. And to keep it away for four minutes, that tiny amount of volume?" I didn't mention that if I asked Air to be elsewhere until it got bored, it would cost me almost nothing and could last for hours if not days.

"Not much," Indira said slowly, her eyes dark.

"You've both been on me to think about how I use magic because we do get brainwashed. You two are forgetting that the tiniest nudge in the right place can create massive results."

Alixant tapped his fork on the plate, his face thoughtful as he started at me. "And why are you thinking about it?"

This I knew how to answer, and not lie. I'd gotten very good at not lying. "Carelian. He doesn't think about magic the way we do, and he punctures my ego every chance he gets."

~Humans are lazy and do magic with blinders. My queans will not be so hampered.~

"Go on, Cori, what else do you think?" Alixant prompted, though I saw his recognition of what Carelian said.

I drained the glass of water and fidgeted with the glass. "The more I think about it, the more I think the killer is a hedgemage. Mainly because they aren't educated enough."

"What do you mean by that?" He poked instantly, but I could tell he wasn't saying I was wrong.

I swallowed, wishing for more Coke to wash out my mouth. "Because if I was going to do it, I would have just moved the oxygen molecules out of the way and let him quietly asphyxiate from carbon monoxide poisoning, never realizing he was about to die."

TWENTY-ONE

Arts are in desperate need of funding. With the explosion of STEM focused degrees lead by the requirements for all mages, the Arts have seen a decrease in students. While there are still your occasional geniuses, even if they are a virtuoso, if they are a mage they get claimed by the sciences. ~ House of Emrys TED Talk

SPIRIT

My comments ended the evening. Indira showed me the bedroom she'd set up for me. She had shopping plans for the next day, while I'd be at the precinct. I crashed hard after a shower, and Carelian let me rub him down with a damp towel. I fell asleep to him grooming himself on the other half of the king bed.

~I approve of this size of bed. You should get one.~ He greeted me in the morning as I emerged from the bathroom, teeth clean and ready for massive amounts of coffee.

"Won't fit in the bedroom," I yawned. "Not and have enough room to move around in," I pointed out as I pulled on my nice jeans, planning on wearing a tank with a button up shirt over it. Not professional, but at least nice enough to escape disparaging glances. A lifetime of wearing suits and boring clothes didn't excite me. I'd have to come up with comfortable professional-seeming clothes by the time I graduated. Or I could snub my nose at them all and wear what I wanted. What were they doing to do, fire me?

~Yes, but Sable said she would get a new place to live. Maybe it will be big enough for a king. And have a yard.~

I paused with my tank top half on, trying to track the conversation. "Oh. True. But I'm not going to worry about that until after it's all in place."

~But a king bed. You have your half and I have mine,~ he protested as he extended to his full length, tail hanging off the end of the bed.

I shook my head and finished getting dressed. Coffee was my next priority. I found the coffee maker in the kitchen, and knowing that Indira and Steven would need some, I got a full pot brewing. Digging around in the kitchen I found Indira had made sure we had sugar and hazelnut syrup.

"Coffee?" I heard Steven behind me and just pointed to the half full pot—my mug was huge.

I finished doctoring it and turned. He was dressed in slacks, but only had a button up shirt on, no tie, and no suit jacket. He caught me looking and shrugged. "I'll throw on a vest that says FBI, but I don't think they care."

"Okay. We walking or taking a cab?"

"Cab. It's too far to walk right now. Later you can explore the city." Steven glanced at Carelian who had his harness on and looked official "What else can you sense that we can't?"

Carelian looked up from his paw washing, ears flicking back then forward. ~Many things. Too numerous to mention.~

Steven sighed. "I deserved that. I meant more can you tell us if you smelled the killer, or anything else to identify them?"

Carelian stopped grooming and tilted his head, considering. ~No. There was too much around the body to isolate a scent. But I will pay attention.~

"Thanks. Figured it was worth the ask. You ready?"

I held up my mug and grabbed a power bar from the ones scattered on the counter. "Indira staying here?"

"She has informed me she will be sleeping in and then going shopping. She'll meet us for dinner somewhere if we are free." We walked out and headed to the elevator while he talked. "We'll be in meetings and probably the morgue most of the day. I don't know if they've identified the next victim."

I let go of the distractions and brought back up the image of Carl hanging from the wall. It served to get me in the game.

"Do you know how many of the bodies they have in the morgue? I'd like to see what else I can get from them, maybe some more clues about the murderer." I preferred the blunter terms—this was a murderer, not a perpetrator. It helped if I kept my anger and frustration forefront in my mind.

We got outside the apartment building before Steven responded. "At least the one before, but otherwise, no. I'm sure Farlane will have thought of that. He strikes me as very competent."

I just shrugged. I didn't know him enough to judge and I wasn't sure why Carl had popped up as the killer. And I still wanted to know where his bike was. The taxi pulled up and after telling us there would be a huge fee if my pet clawed up his car, we were on our way.

~As if. Your people have unearned superiority issues,~ he grumbled in my mind as I endured the jerking and speeding of the vehicle.

~You're just now figuring this out?~ I glanced at him, amused.

~No, I had just hoped it was limited to college students. Obviously, it is not.~

I rubbed my nose to hide my smile. ~No. Though I don't know if it's a human thing or an American thing.~

~Ah. Then we must travel to other countries to gain more information.~

~I think that might be fun. Maybe my draft will let me do that,~ I offered, thinking freedom to travel was still a way off.

~Either way, there will be decades available for us to do that. ~ He dismissed my worries and I let it go. I'd tried to convince him that as we got older, we got more fragile. I needed to have him interact with old people. The oldest people he interacted with were the Guzman's. I needed to change that, let him see what real old, like sixties or more, looked like.

"There it is, One Police Plaza." Alixant broke into my musing and I peered out the window to see the building sitting in front of me.

It looked just like it did on TV and in the movies. A huge

square building on a pedestal with rectangular holes for windows, making it look like grid paper. The brown brick was just bland and ugly, but it gave the impression of an immovable fortress, complete with barriers to even approach it.

Here the streets were less clogged as we headed into the glass area clearly marked "Visitors Entrance". The officers there scoped each of us out with unfriendly looks, and from what I could see Alixant wearing his FBI vest didn't improve our welcome. He presented his badge, gave them the information they requested, provided detective Farlane's information, and the officers still looked like they expected us to start shrieking defiance and flinging fireballs any second. For a long minute they looked like they were going to deny Carelian access. I stood there torn between stalking out, pulling on my power, or staying a timid mouse.

Though pulling on my power here would probably get me a bullet to my skull. Instead, I bit my tongue and tried to look professional and patient.

Carelian pulled his statue impression and sat looking like a ruby sculpture, every hair perfect, and impossible to miss.

"What's the hold up?" I looked up at George's voice as he came into the little area where we were.

"Just making sure they're approved, Detective," the lead officer said, his voice sneering a bit.

George flushed, his dark skin acquiring a burgundy tint. "Sanchez, I don't give a damn about your prejudices, about the fact that you resent the FBI or that you think mages are protected prima donnas. I have them on that list for a reason and I want them now, so I can see if they can help us stop the madman killing people. Do you have an issue with that?" He snarled out the last words and leaned closer to Sanchez.

I watched it from two perspectives inside my own mind. One was completely embarrassed at being in the middle of all this drama. The other was intrigued by the power struggle and called-out bigotry. Mages were both isolated and, in some ways, spoiled. Though I bet if most people knew what I did about them being culled via the draft, they'd be much less worried.

"No sir," Sanchez ground out. The other officers had stepped back from the immediate conflict, but I saw too many hands on their weapons to make me feel secure.

"Then give them their visitor badges and get out of the way," snapped Farlane. Sanchez dragged his feet at every step, so it took another five minutes to have our badges printed before we were escorted past the gates.

We'd made it halfway to the main building before Alixant spoke. "Do I want to know what that was all about? Am I putting Cori at risk by having her here?"

George sighed, a strange half growl, half huff of air. "No. Sanchez is pissed 'cause I made detective and he didn't. Anything involving me is done under extreme protest. Add in part of the reason I got the promotion was the FBI putting in a good word for me and the fact that he is a borderline extreme Freedom from Magic follower, you got on his bad side. Thanks for texting me there was an issue. Otherwise, you would have been turned away and we'd have lost even more time." He pulled open the door to the main building. "Come on, I want you to see the files, then get to the morgue. We have two other victims I want Merlin Munroe to take a look at."

I wrinkled my nose. "You can just call me Cori. It sounds too weird to call me that." I winced a bit at how juvenile that sounded, but I'd rather be Cori. Someday I might be Merlin Munroe, but I wasn't yet.

He slid his eyes towards me as we entered the elevator, staying for a moment on my tattoos, the ones so different from anyone else. "If it's okay with you, sure."

I hugged myself a bit, pretending it was the chill in the aggressively air-conditioned building, not the wonder of how many people would distance themselves because of my double merlin status.

Dragon. I will be a dragon and they can either work with me or get out of my way. Remember people taste crunchy with ketchup.

I snickered a bit, the off-color comment making my mood lift.

"We have the conference room on this floor," George said as the doors slid open. I followed him down the hall in what looked like any other office building I'd ever been in. Why they always had the same bland color scheme, cubicles, and smell of burnt coffee I'd never figure out. He escorted us to a conference room with a five-person table and white boards everywhere on all the walls, blocking easy view into the room. There was one other person in there, a tiny Hindu woman with a Spirit tattoo on her temple and a red dot on the middle of her forehead. The uniform of a NYPD officer fit her perfectly. She stood at attention when we came in, sharp light brown eyes assessing us. She might have stood five-three and she had a long braid that hit her belt. It had to be as thick as my wrist and I sympathized. Jo and Sable's hair was that thick. Mine was much thinner, but I knew how much hair like that weighed.

"Merlins, may I introduce," he paused and took a deep breath, then slowly, carefully said, "Aani Fatimah Khatoon Vardharajthirumalachetty." He sighed and looked at her, the hint of a smile touched the corner of her mouth and she inclined her head the smallest amount. He continued talking in a much more normal tone. "The officer who has found three of our victims as her primary patrol route is Central Park."

I just looked at him, confused, and at the woman. He shrugged. "What? She can pronounce my name correctly; I should be able to say hers."

A laugh slipped out and she walked forward holding out her hand. "Call me Ana Vard. And the other reason he wants me here is my husband, Doctor Vijay Vard is one of the assistant coroners for the city. Most of the time it's a mouthful for us. So Ana is preferred."

I smiled back at her as we provided our names.

"Good, if all the social chit-chat is done, can we deal with the murderer on the loose." George huffed and waved at the boards. There were ten victims up there, including Carl, all with the same morgue pictures I'd seen before. Everything else was lists of information and facts, notes about what they had in common, and where their paths crossed.

I looked at them closely, but they didn't tell me anything other than what I'd already read. "You said you had some recent pictures of them alive?"

George cast a glance at Ana, and she turned to go grab binders from a narrow bookcase on one wall. "They are all in here. Please don't take the documents out of their protective sheets." She handed me one labeled Lashonda James. I sat at the table, Carelian taking over one of the chairs by himself.

I opened up the folder and the first picture, protected by the insert, burst out at me, full of life and movement. She was laughing, her skin as white as her teeth, ugly and striking at the same time. Her long hair in thick braids a few shades yellower than her skin. "Albino?" I asked looking at the black woman whose only color resided in the bright yellow and green she wore.

"Technically yes. She was also mostly blind," Ana provided.

I needed to lay them out, to look at them. "Is there a way I can get copies of the pictures of the victims when they were alive, so I'm not damaging your originals?"

Ana frowned then shrugged. "Sure. It will take me a few

minutes, but we have a photo quality copier somewhere. It won't be perfect."

I shook my head. "That's fine. I just need the pictures in color." Ana glanced at George who ignored her, in a heated conversation with Alixant that was low enough to not intrude into my thoughts. Ana frowned then shrugged and grabbed the binders. She headed out while I stared at the boards and twisted the images of the two victims in my head.

"Where'd Ana go?" George asked and I focused on him, not the boards.

"She's making pictures for me. Should be back in a while."

He sighed. "The bodies are at the Lagone Medical Center, but it's a fifteen-minute drive there. Better to wait until she gets back. What did you need pictures for?"

I scratched my head, an old habit, and double checked that Murphy wasn't settling around me. "I might be wrong, so right now can you let me have my wild theory?"

He gritted his teeth but nodded.

"Great. Also, do you have any sketch artists here, preferably one that might have been trained classically?" I started to duck my head but forced myself to stop and look him in the eye. If I didn't practice being a dragon I'd fold when I needed to be strong.

He stared at me but rather than getting flustered or angry, tilted his head. "What does classically trained mean to you?"

I forced my thoughts into some semblance of order. "I have an idea, but I need an artist. Someone who had studied art and understands perspective and poising, and just art stuff." I couldn't articulate what I meant because I wasn't sure, but I needed a real artist. A human one.

He frowned scratching his jaw. "Actually, I think so. You need him now?"

I nodded. "Yes, and can I get a few pictures of Carl's body, the way it was displayed?"

George pulled out his phone, texting as he walked out the door. "I'll see what I can do. Don't leave this room."

I blinked at Steven. "Awful protective of their space, aren't they?"

Steven laughed. "You have no idea."

TWENTY-TWO

Countries tend to guard their mages with a jealous propriety, but in certain situations they may loan out mages to other countries. This is more likely if the mage has an unusual skill or degree. Most governments encourage the odd and specific degrees as it gives them specialists instead of generalists. ~ OMO Brochure on degree choices.

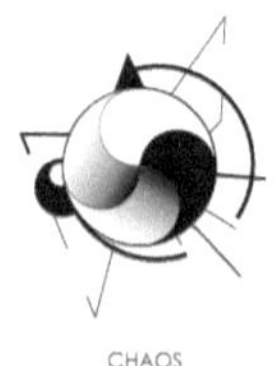

CHAOS

"What are you thinking?" Steven asked, dropping down in the chair next to me.

"That I'm very glad I filled my mug with coffee and that I should have gotten a pastry." I tilted my mug at him and smiled, pretending I was untouchable.

"Valid. But I meant with the pictures."

Carelian jumped off the chair spinning it hard enough that it slammed into the desk and we both started. I glared at him. I didn't need any more stress on my heart this week.

~You may never move to this city, Cori. I will not tolerate it.~ He all but growled stalking the length of the room and back again. ~It reeks of lies, vanity, and deception. Nothing about this city is good, it only had the appearance of decency.~ His voice echoed letting me know he spoke to more than me, and from Steven's expression he was included.

"Where is this coming from?" I asked looking around.

~Can you not feel it? Even this murder is tainted with the appearance of beauty and grace, when it makes the entropy of Chaos look pure and sweet.~ His growl laced his words with power and I didn't know how to respond.

"Do you need to get out of here?" I left it there, not wanting to reveal secrets.

He lashed his tail looking at both of us then his head and tail drooped. ~No. Malkin warned me there would be days where I did not understand or like your Earth. I had not understood what she meant.~

"Depending on where she is placed, and I expect the draft will loan you out to multiple groups over your service period, she may run into these types of scenarios more often than not. People are more sadistic than most realize." Alixant sounded apologetic and Carelian pulled the chair back so he could leap up.

~Yes, so I am seeing. How can creatures capable of designing such amazing structures as your buildings and creating music that tears at the soul, be capable of such foulness?~

"I think it is I because we can do those things. We are capable of rising as high as we can sink," I pointed out. History proved that over and over again, showing just what we were capable of. "And mages aren't any different."

~You should be,~ he said, but his voice sounded more defeated than angry. I reached over and petted him, hoping my touch would bring some solace.

"So?" Alixant prodded.

"I'm not trying to be mysterious I just have a wild idea. And it could be wrong, so I'd rather not say it in case it is wildly off base." I focused on my coffee cup not him, avoiding his scowl or derisive look.

"Ah, I get that. Siab is the same way." I looked up at him, surprised at the lack of censure in his voice. "Though I have found out she is rarely incorrect, it is easier to wait than try and force her." Siab was an Entropy mage that worked with him on cases, though she'd been promoted and now only worked with Alixant's team when he had a case with lots of forensic evidence. Last time we'd talked she was loving Washington, DC and the fact that her one-bedroom studio was way too small for her mother to come stay with her.

Before I could respond the conference room door pushed back open and George strode in followed by one of the least police-like men I'd ever imagined. He was dressed in a slim cut, burgundy trimmed, charcoal suit, that brought out the olive in his skin tone and made his black hair look reddish. He looked for all the magic like a high-powered CEO of some company, down to burgundy wing-tips matching the detailing.

"Merlins, I'd like to introduce Pavel Zubiri, one of our primary sketch artists for witnesses."

He cast a smile at both of us. "Good morning. Detective Farlane said you needed an artist's help?" I'd expected some sort of accent, but if anything, he had a flat accent that made him seem more normal than before.

Expectations are dangerous. Remember that.

I nodded wetting lips that were dry with an attack of nerves. The possibility of him laughing at me was very high. "Yeah. Um, you've had classical training?"

He sat down, with an innate elegance that made me look like a bigger klutz than I was. "If classical training means I have a master's of fine arts, then yes. What exactly are you looking for?"

Ana came back in at a brisk walk before I needed to answer. She set a pile of photos down on the table in front of me. "Here's what there was. Some had multiple images others had only one. I put names on the back along with the age they were at the time of the photo."

"Oh, thank you. That will be helpful." I glanced at Pavel. "One minute, let me look at these and decide if my idea is crazy stupid or not." I started flipping through the photos and by the second victim I knew my idea wasn't improbable. When I'd finished going through all of them, not a one dashing my thoughts, I turned back to Pavel, all too aware of my audience.

"Detective, do you have any of the pictures from the crime scene yesterday?"

He nodded and pulled out a dozen shots. I pulled out the one that looked like it had captured a piece of studio artwork. The shadows and lights cast across it.

"Hear me out, and I might be way off base, remember that. But one of my friends is an accomplished artist and she says everything is about perception when it comes to art." At least I thought of Arachena as an accomplished artist. I tapped the picture, the wall Carl hung on almost brilliant white in the photo when contrasting to the black of the robe.

"This is the first body they've found in situ, not discarded in the park."

He looked at the photo, his creased brow making him look less perfect. "An impressive, if horrific, presentation. But what does that have to do with me?"

I took a breath but didn't take my eyes off his face. One by one I laid the pictures out in order of when they were taken. The dates had seared themselves into my mind. Maybe someday I'd be immune, but for now I was just as glad they all were real to me.

"First was Jamal," I said laying down the pictures of a young man playing a pick-up game of basketball. His skin the color of a light roast with mocha and covered in black and white tattoos. I'd originally thought the morgue picture had washed them out, but no, his tats were all shades of black or white. He was all arms and legs, almost to the point of looking odd.

"Then the killer took Carlotta." I had no idea what she'd been doing, but she was dressed in a pale-yellow dress, maybe a bridesmaid, peering at the camera with the arrogance of a royal. Her sharp cheekbones and hawk nose lifted from a Mayan painting.

"Then Rick," I murmured as I set down two photos. He was the youngest taken and the image one of the worst as it looked like it came from a yearbook. Dressed in emo style with long dark hair and pale skin, you didn't see the tattoos until I laid the morgue snapshot next to it. All his tattoos were black and symbols of magic.

Pavel was frowning as he looked at the pictures. "I want you to keep in mind that all of these had their joints broken or hyper extended," I mentioned, tapping the photo of Carl again. Pavel flicked his eyes up to me, motioning with his fingers for me to continue.

"Lashonda disappeared on her way to work, where she'd been for years." I put the picture down, her white skin on a black face arresting and disconcerting at the same time. "She was found with streaks of paint on her, but they looked random." I found that picture and presented it, red, blue, green, in slashes across her face and body. "Forensics says they were all done with a paintbrush."

"Lewis was taken about at the same time as Rick, and their bodies were found on the same day, about fifty yards apart." I checked with Ana to make sure that was accurate.

"Yes, on opposite sides of a large hedge," she confirmed.

Pavel's eyes narrowed and he moved those two images together.

"This is the one victim that doesn't make sense to me, but I'm not positive. Abram. Hasidic Jew, local here." I set down the picture, frowning at the image of a man in his thirties, with vivid carrot red hair, full beard, and curls down the side of his face. Pavel picked it up and looked at it closer. "Are there any other pictures of him? Maybe one where the beard isn't full?"

"Give me a second." Ana turned and pulled out the binder, shuffling through it. "Here." She laid down a picture of the same man, but now you could see the port wine stain from under his chin up to the corner of his right eye.

"He wasn't shaved?" Pavel asked and I shook my head, finding the morgue photo. There the red hair looked diminished and sad, almost as if it had been leached of color.

I swallowed and kept going. "Then there was Ricardo. He surprised me. They shaved him for the morgue photo." I placed that down, then the one that had been in his file. "The note didn't mean much to me when I saw it, but he suffered from hypertrichosis."

"Werewolf disease," Pavel muttered. Ricardo was covered in a thick shag of hair covering his face and neck, making dark blue eyes all but glow in his face.

"This is Layla and Jon. They were taken about two days apart, but found on the same day, but not near each other." The tension in the room had risen and I convinced myself that yelling at them to quit staring at me would be counterproductive. Layla was middle eastern, and with one blue and one green eye should have been stunning, but her face was covered with what looked like acid or burn scars. Jon on the other hand could have been a movie star with a white smile, cleft chin, perfect skin, except under his button-down shirt he had full sleeve tattoos and a full back , all in Oriental motifs, and in brilliant color.

"And then Carl was the last." I pointed to the image. "Do you see it?"

"Yeah. I think I do. No idea what the poses were, but I think Carl was the only one that matched the vision." Pavel rotated them around. "Or they already took pictures and didn't want to share? Could be either or. Never can tell."

I sighed and pushed back. "What medium? Photography?"

"Only one that makes sense. With anything else there isn't any need for real people. Though you're right. The Hasidic Jew doesn't make much sense. I'd push that one and make sure it is part of the pattern."

"It is," ground out George. "But I have no idea what you two are talking about. Would you care to enlighten the rest of us exactly what those bodies have in common? We've checked everything and other than the occasional subway ride, we can't see that they have ever crossed paths more than tangentially. Hell, Ricardo was only in town because of his condition."

Pavel looked at me, then at them. "And you know they are connected how?"

"There's a tattoo of a tilde above their right ear, in dark blue. It's tiny." I pulled out the picture and set it on the table also.

"Yes, yes, we know all that, and by the way, Carl didn't have that above his ear." George said, his accent growing stronger.

I looked at him. "What did he have?" When he hung there, I couldn't see or reach his head, so I hadn't looked.

"A funny equal sign, but it has three lines," he snapped. "What do you think this is?"

I grabbed my phone, searching rapidly, something odd occurring to me.

Pavel leaned back, his accent even flatter. "Isn't it obvious? It's art."

TWENTY-THREE

Taking out rogue mages is usually the arena of the Rogue Squad but convincing a mage to follow the law can be much more showy. If they are breaking the letter of the law a show of force is often provided, while a whispered comment about the consequences of breaking the law is mentioned in passing. Examples are never made twice. Keep this in mind if you choose to ignore what the letter of the law says. ~ House of Emrys newsletter

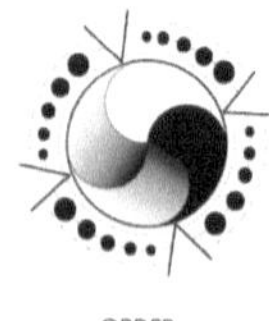

ORDER

George looked at both of us, his lips curled in a snarl. "And what by Merlin's balls does that mean?"

Pavel waved at me. "You saw it. You tell him."

"I wasn't sure until I saw the other victims. The morgue photos don't tell you anything, they are so flat and ugly that there wasn't anything to go on. But look at them. They are all unique." I pointed at the picture and the grouping we had placed them in. "They are contrasts and extremes. I think the killer is an artist, or thinks he's an artist. He's trying to create Works of Art." I capitalized the words with my hands and inflections. "That is the point. If Carl had been in a museum and not been a dead body, it would have attracted reviews and reactions. That is what an artist craves—reaction."

George, Ana, and Steven all moved over to stare at the pictures. "So why the change in tattoos?"

"This is just a guess, and I really need to see if the tattoos hold anything, but a tilde means about or approximate. I looked up the other symbol after you told me, it means exact or equivalent."

Pavel winced. "So those that weren't good enough were marked as almost. That's rather arrogant."

"Wait, the killer is marking them as 'almost art' and 'is art' and letting us find the ones that are art, while disposing of what, the materials, when it isn't good enough?" George looked at me, eyes wide.

"I think so. Now look, I don't know anything. But I can tell you visually these people draw a reaction. Horror, discomfort, pity, sympathy, lust," I tapped a picture as I said each word. "That screams art to me, but I'm not an artist. Which is why I asked for someone classically trained." I nodded at Pavel. "He might see more than me."

"Oh, this is a portfolio that I could see being submitted as a project for your final or thesis even," Pavel confirmed. "I favor pens and pencils as mediums, but if I had submitted these as a series it would have garnered an A, assuming I managed to elicit the same reactions."

"Okay, let's say you're right. How does that help us catch this asshole?" George demanded.

"I don't know if it does." I shrugged, feeling like I had thousands of pounds of guilt being dropped on me.

"Oh, there are a few things," Pavel said shaking his head. "Start scanning missing people reports and look for people that are striking, good and bad. Anyone odd or that might make you look twice at them. Your killer obviously likes skin work, so if you start visiting tattoo artists, they might have a clue. They've probably stopped there before to talk to them."

George looked like he might pick up a chair and throw it through the glass walls. He stopped and closed his eyes, and I just knew he was counting to ten.

"Thank you, Pavel. This helps with some of what we are looking for. If you think of anything else, please let Ana or me know."

Pavel rose, recognizing a dismissal as well as I did. "Will do. It was interesting." He had an odd look in his eye, but I let it be. If he had a new idea for an art project, that wasn't my problem.

George had turned away and stared at the board.

"Why did you think Carl was the killer?" I asked, curious about what had brought him to their attention.

"He'd been in contact with three of the victims and when we tried to contact him for questioning, he disappeared. So that means he and the other three all crossed our killer's path, probably at the same place." He tapped a large map of Manhattan taped up on the wall. "There's a coffee shop there that does brisk business for people passing by and people heading into the park. He'd been there five times in the last two weeks. It's on a route to his work, and he usually stopped by in the evening when he didn't ride his bike. That only happened when it was raining."

I sat back and watched him work it out.

"Central Park, excellent people watching. The killer is watching near there, seeing possible art projects and either follows or marks them." He tapped the areas. "We know they are an Air mage, which means illusions or at least the ability to blur details."

"What did the cameras show at the subway?"

"All cracked. Any camera coming down to this station and on the platform is damaged. We've asked if anyone saw anything to let us know, but construction and walled off areas of the platforms are a constant. No one thinks anything about them." He turned and looked at me. "I've been doing this a while. If I had anything at all, you wouldn't be here."

I took the reproof with good grace. Mostly I'd asked because I was curious.

"Let's use you like I need to. Ready to go to the morgue? We have the last four victims there. The others, especially Abram, were already claimed by family."

I rose. Sitting here accomplished nothing, and I wasn't a detective, I was a mage. My weird view of things thanks to Arachena had given them a clue, I couldn't ask for anything more.

We headed down to the basement, where George waved us towards a black four door.

"What, no Escalade or Crown Vic?" Alixant jibbed, grinning at the detective.

"Ha, ha. Some of us don't have the budget of the fancy FBI. Be glad it has AC," he said as we got in. And I was. New York just felt different, even though it was technically cooler than Atlanta, the heat clung, feeling gritty almost.

Carelian sat beside me. He'd not said anything else since his outburst. While Alixant and George chatted in the front seat, I focused on my familiar.

~Are you okay?~ I sent the words clearly, but I also made sure he knew how much I loved him.

~Humans are confusing. Your concept of good and evil makes no sense. But this, this is worse than the swirls of chaos.~

~How? I remember what Salistra said, about using, breaking, and then eating her toys. Her toys which are people.~

He was silent for a long time. Long enough that I caught bits of the conversation in the front seat, all about forms they had to submit. Who spent time ranting about filling out forms?

~There is a difference. Those who become toys of ones at Tirsane's level have gained their notice usually by their actions. I have never heard of any of them taking someone who was a good person. Always they are those who use magic, twist it, and hurt others.~ He heaved a sigh and flexed his claws. ~Those they kill they do as a sort of justice. I'm not sure how to explain it to you. Humans are sheltered and see reality in a way that I do not yet comprehend.~

I wanted to follow up on that comment, but George was parking. "Come one. We're headed to the morgue."

"Who is there?" I asked, running the images of the victims through my head.

"Victims seven, eight, and nine. Well they also will have the tenth victim," he said heading into the building from the parking space he'd whipped into.

I had to jog a bit to catch up, he moved fast. Carelian stayed by my side and Alixant followed up behind us. It felt like a rear-guard situation—I didn't mind, though I didn't feel like I was in any danger.

There was just as much screening and double checking here

as at One Police Plaza, but without the attitude. Ten minutes later we found ourselves riding down the elevator with a Langone security officer. He didn't say much, just swiped us in, and headed towards an office.

"Doctor Chun, the police are here," he said. A man who had grooves in his face and bags under his eyes looked up at us.

"Thanks, I'll take them." The security officer nodded and moved away, headed towards the elevator much faster than he'd walked down here.

"Farlane, anything new?" he asked as he walked out. His hair was cut short and going gray at the temples. He had the round face and stocky body of Chinese descent but was as tall as Alixant.

"Maybe. We think the killer's an artist. And the last victim was displayed as artwork."

He grunted. "Haven't done that autopsy yet. I've got a back-log. What are you here for?"

"Got a Spirit Merlin. Wanted to take a look at the bodies," George replied waving a hand at me. I smiled at the doctor, who just grunted again.

"Whatever. I don't have time to escort you. You know the way, don't abuse my trust." He reached down and grabbed a badge, tossing it to Farlane. "Return that when done. I'm too strapped to waste even an intern with this. Let me know if you find anything." The doctor waved at the hallway and turned back to his computer. "I have three other autopsies to do before I get to your latest victim and one of my pathologists is out sick and the other is on maternity leave. Who the hell wants to have a baby at a time like this?"

I smiled at his exasperation but didn't say anything. We headed down the hall and George swiped the badge at another set of doors. They slid open and a blast of frigid air came with it. Suddenly my summer clothes didn't seem so wise. The doors shut behind us and we were faced with a wall of vaults. Three tall and ten across, they sat like safes of the dead, protecting and cutting off their contents from the rest of the world. Be it sad or practical, most morgues looked very similar. Drawers to hold the dead, cold, and sterile. Part of me wanted to put streamers and balloons in here just to make it not so depressing, but then, wasn't death depressing?

Maybe, maybe not.

I filed that thought and watched George scan the list on the wall. "Here is victim number 7." He strode forward and pulled one of the drawers open. He slid out the platform and I walked over to look at Layla James. Covered from collarbone to toes with a white sheet, the life that sparkled in the picture was gone, leaving a body that almost looked fake. She had the thick lips and wide nose common with the African genotype. But the yellowish-white skin, white hair in dreads, and yellow marks across her face contrasted with what I had expected to see. The black tattoo jumped out against her skin, harsh and unexpected.

"She looks so sad," I said, more to myself than anything else.

"Can you see if she died the same way?" George asked from the other side and I nodded.

I braced myself and touched her shoulder, ready for anything. There was a gasping, no light, then darkness and it was gone. I yanked my hand back frowning.

"What is it?" asked Alixant.

"I'm not sure. Let me try again." I touched her shoulder and again, sudden gasping, everything dark, confusion, then darker, then nothing. I pulled away.

"I think—think mind you—that she was killed while she was asleep. She woke up gasping for air, but there was nothing. Then she died. She never saw anything."

George growled. "What good does that do us?"

I gave him an exasperated look. "I'm a mage, not a miracle worker. If she didn't see anything there isn't anything I can see."

He growled a bit, but mostly he looked defeated. "Anything else?"

I frowned at the young woman, wondering what she wanted to be, or do, that had been ripped away from her. "I wanted to check the tattoo."

He sighed and stepped back. "Have at it. As long as you don't deface the body, I don't think anyone cares."

He just means that no one cares if I touch them, not that no one cares about these victims.

I repeated that to myself, but it didn't stop the knee jerk reaction I had at the dismissal of a life, of a death. I pushed it to the side as I bent to focus on the tattoo.

CHAPTER

TWENTY-FOUR

There have been complaints by equal rights groups that the penalties for mages breaking the law are overly harsh. However, few manage to have a good answer when opponents ask if they want another Ted Bundy incident again. He killed so many women, and it took way too long to catch him. He strung out the trial for weeks, telling half-truths, playing on his looks and charisma. When the chambers were packed and the judge was hearing the closing remarks, he killed every person in the building. He made their blood boil, even though he had every inch of body hair shaved off and had a machine watching if he should do any magic. He did it so fast no one had time to react. Since then, truth forcing is used, the mage is kept drugged and killed immediately. Even waiting forty-eight hours is considered dangerous. ~ History of Magic

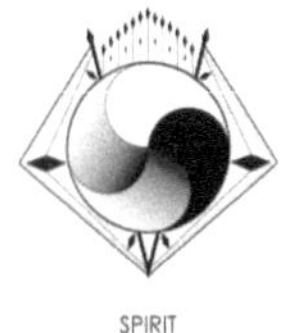

The tilde mark marred her ivory skin just like the others, above the hairline behind her right ear. But long hair grew through it, and her head didn't look like it had been shaved. I glanced up at the detective leaning against a wall, arms crossed over his chest.

"And you're sure the killer put the tattoo here?" From what I found out about the symbols it all made sense, but this threw me off balance. I knew all too well that tattoos took weeks to heal, red and itchy the entire time because of the damage to the skin. On your face it was enough to make you scream.

"That or there is a rash of people getting these in some new underground social movement. When I asked, no one knew of one, and if it's like the semi-colon thing, people would be talking about it."

I stood and stared at it for a minute. What was I missing? Nothing came to mind, so I reached down and touched the tilde. A tidal wave of emotions slammed into me. Rage, frustration, annoyance all rushed through me, then a touch of satisfaction. I shuddered as my hand jerked away from it.

"What?" Steven was there at my side; I really needed another Coke. I didn't even have my coffee with me. Something about doing this coated my soul with ick.

"The tattoo." I shook my head and I focused on his mage tattoo. "May I touch yours?"

His brows drew together. "You want to touch my tattoo?"

I nodded. There wasn't any way to explain my confusion. It

would take years to get enough experience to know what I should or shouldn't sense when I sought out sensations and right now I was flying blind.

"Sure." He turned his head to the side, letting me see his tattoo. The bright colors of his strengths, Kelly green Pattern and royal blue Water, they seemed to clash with the dour clothes he normally wore, but right now that wasn't my concern. I brushed my fingers over his warm skin, sensing; nothing was there, not a whisper of emotion or energy.

"Huh. I can't sense anything. Do you have any other tattoos?" I asked him, still trying to figure out how to ratio-nalize what I had experienced.

"No, just my Merlin tattoo. What did you sense, Cori?" He kept his gaze steady and I wanted to throw things at him in exasperation and hug him in gratitude.

"I'm not sure. Are there any other bodies here that have tattoos?" I had turned to George as I spoke. He pulled out his notebook to double check.

"Jon has a ton. The other two don't. I can ask if any of the other bodies in storage do" It wasn't quite an offer, but I'd take it.

"Please?" While he talked, I moved so my body was turned away and I slid my hand into the waistband of my jeans, down to where the tattoo for Jo was. We had matching BFF tattoos and that meant more to me than the one on my face ever would. I slid my hand over it, seeking anything, but there was no response.

"Cori?" Steven prompted, but I shook my head and touched the tilde on Layla again. Such fierce emotions rippled through that I shook with the aftermath.

"Yeah," George said coming through the door. "Said there's a dead ganger in here. Drawer four. He has a bunch. What is going on?" He didn't look like he would move until I provided some information.

"I can feel the killer. They are so frustrated and upset that their emotion slapped me like a whip. And I don't understand how the tattoo was created." I swallowed but stiffened my back. I was a dragon darn it. "Any chance you can get forensics done on the tattoos, the ink and stuff?"

"And look for what?" He didn't seem resistant, just curious.

"I don't know. But regular tattoos don't feel like that. I don't think. Even if it was done after death it shouldn't have hair growing through it. There should be damage to the skin." I wanted to shake things. I didn't have enough experience to know what I should or shouldn't feel. This entire process might make me scream.

"Here, check out the gang banger. At least half of his were done in prison, not via normal means." George walked over and pulled open a drawer to a man a bit older than me laying there. Shaved skull, normal in non-magic gangs, a teardrop under his eye. He looked like he was sleeping, while in life he had probably been handsome, now he just appeared diminished.

The tats were shaky and inconsistent with the amount and color of ink. The teardrop more of a blob than a tear shape. Given the placement below the eye, there wasn't much doubt that it was an indicator he had murdered someone. I laid my fingertip on his teardrop and focused only on the tattoo and ink —having no desire to see how he died. This time I got a trickle of something, a sense of interest and wariness. It was so faint that I couldn't say much more than that.

"There was something, but not like what is on the tildes. Where is Carl and the other two victims?"

Steven to my relief had stepped back, staying out of the way. I felt driven for the first time. I needed to figure out what was going on and see where these tattoos led.

"The vics are over here. Carl should be waiting to be processed."

"Can I see him before they start?" I asked, wanting to know if I'd feel anything from that tattoo.

"I'll try." George pulled open the box where Jon, the handsome man covered in tattoos, lay. All the ones on his body were clean of emotions, though they were stunning works of art.

His memory was odd. At a gym working out, watching himself in the mirror. A last rep, and the weights clanked in their bracket and he tried to inhale. There was nothing there, a vacuum in front of his mouth. He got up and moved, but nothing happened. He twirled, images of a home gym spinning around me, but there was nothing to breathe. Frantic now, he tried to move air towards him, but he collapsed to his knees. His eyes stared back at themselves in the mirror and I focused on his last sights, trying to ignore the clawing need to breathe in my own chest.

Everything went dark before I could be sure. I took another deep breath and reminded myself I wasn't dying. Then I looked again. There as I stared at the mirror, I saw movement, but Jon never realized someone was watching.

"The killer was watching him. Where was his gym?"

George looked through his notes again. "Shared gym. In the apartment building. Basement."

"Killer was there. No idea if they left anything, but the killer was there."

A groan was my only answer as George started texting someone in fast short taps.

Bracing myself I touched the tilde on Jon's head. The same bitter emotions, anger, frustration, and something else that I couldn't put a name to. It felt like waking from a dream with ashes in your mouth where there had been hope. I shivered and stepped back.

"Nothing new from the tattoo, but the killer is getting them when they are alone."

"How is he moving the body? And not being noticed?" George asked, moving over to look at Jon. Even on a good day the man weighed upwards of one-eighty. The muscle and his structure probably meant usually it was closer to 200. "You can't just pick up someone like that and carry them out like a carpet. It would take two people."

Steven shrugged. "Even a hedgemage, if they are willing to offer enough could make the body light enough to carry. It's an advance skill that usually wizards or archmages learn in college, but the knowledge is available if you know how to research or experiment."

George started to say something, and snapped his mouth shut, spinning away. "Body from yesterday is with Chow. Let's finish up here and you can see if his tat is any different."

I nodded and let Jon slide back into his protective space, at least here no one else would hurt him.

George scanned the labels and pulled out the last victim. I crouched to see her as she was on the bottom row. Layla. In her late twenties, with half her face scarred with what I thought looked like acid burns. Pulling open her eyes to see her mismatched colors seemed too intrusive. Instead, I set my hand down on her shoulder and asked.

Walking, the scarf fluttering against my lips, then it stops moving. I pause under the shadow of a tree, trying to breathe. Nothing. I yank the scarf away, my lungs gasping for oxygen. A woman approaches me, leads to me a bench further into the shadows. She says something, I can't hear it, all I can do is struggle for air and fight my rage. I need to breathe. Air. I feel my consciousness slipping away and the pretty blonde woman smiles at me.

"What the!" I fell back onto my ass, my heart pounding,

gasping for breath as my lungs thought I needed the air. The room spun as I hyperventilated, unable to convince my body that the need for oxygen wasn't real.

"Cori? You okay? What's wrong?" Steven crouched next to me and reached out to touch me.

I jerked away and shook my head.

~Cori, hold your breath. Do it,~ Carelian said in my head. I closed my eyes and concentrated on his voice. ~Hold. One, two, three,~ he said, his voice calm as I fought to follow his commands. ~Now release.~

I let loose a shuddering breath and this time managed to breathe in slowly. "I think she saw the killer. She was killed in a park area. Trees, a bench, a walking path." I tried to focus on what Layla had seen, but I couldn't, the clawing need for air driving me to distraction.

"Did she regularly wear a scarf?" I asked more to focus myself than anything.

"Yes. She was Muslim and wore a hijab, but friends said she wore it more to hide her scars than for religious reasons." George had moved over to me, a worried look on his face, but I focused on breathing and trying to separate out the memory of her death from her physical need.

"Did you find the scarf?" I fought not to gasp as I spoke and held my breath again. Carelian moved behind me, his warmth radiating through my clothes onto my back. It helped.

"No."

"I need to look again."

"Cori, are you sure?" Steven asked as I clambered to my feet, still shaking. "The others didn't hit you as hard. What was different?"

"Yes, I'm sure. And I don't know. She was so strong, her terror so bright, and she was so mad. I think maybe she knew, as opposed to the other two. They were confused, unsure and focused more on the lack of breath. I think she knew it was being caused and it pissed her off." I gazed down at the dead woman, so ugly and twisted, but you could see she should have been beautiful. "How was she scarred?" I touched her scars without calling up memories, not yet. I needed to see her first.

"Arranged marriage. She refused after he slapped her on their second meeting for not wearing a full hijab. He threw acid in her face when she broke the arrangement with her parents support."

I glanced at George as he spoke—this time he hadn't needed to use a notebook. He knew all this.

"She had someone hurt her before," I said as I stared at the girl. There were days I hated people. "I need a Coke after this," I muttered laying my hands on her again and asking.

It hit me again, hard like a fastball to the stomach, but I was ready this time. I pushed the physical sensations to the side, then managed to sidestep the emotions, though I could feel them battering at me. Terror, sorrow, confusion, anger, rage, all tiny knives cutting at my barriers. I gritted my teeth and focused on what she saw. The woman came from the side and I watched her lips, guessing at what she was saying.

Are you alright?

Here, sit down.

It's okay.

A touch of a smile, not sad or sympathetic, but gleeful was seen from the corner of her vision. But as Layla turned, it was gone, and her vision started to tunnel. All that filled her vision were hazel eyes framed by stubby lashes, then darkness.

I pulled my hand away and stood, breathing harshly. "It's a cruel way to die. You're suffocating and can't see why or how. Terror fills you as you fight to do something you need to live, that you've done without fail every minute of your life, and there is nothing there. Your own instincts driving you to fight to breathe." I wanted to escape this room of death, to go find the sun and drink something hot and spicy, to remind myself I wasn't dead. That wasn't how I would die. "Let me finish," I said before either of them could speak.

The tattoo was almost a letdown. Nothing but bitter disappointment and irritation. It was sloppier than the later ones, but still there.

"I think the killer is a woman or female. Long blonde hair, past the shoulders, and hazel eyes. " I placed everyone in relation to Layla as I worked through what I had experienced. "She's about two inches taller than Layla. Thin, like forget to eat thin, white, narrow face. Hair is natural color, no roots. Ragged ends. Like some chunks an inch shorter than others, no bangs." I struggled to pulled up what Layla had seen. She'd glanced at the woman, but her own need to breath meant she hadn't paid much attention, but she had focused on the woman's eyes.

"Hazel eyes. Dark brown rim." I fell silent trying to figure out how to describe what I could see.

"If I got Pavel back in here could you describe her?" George asked his body leaning towards me.

A spark leapt through me and I looked at Carelian. "Would you help with an image push?"

His ears perked up and he bared his canines. ~Excellent idea.~

Steven and George both looked confused, but I shook my head. "I'll explain later, but I can do better. First let's visit Carl." My depression was gone and I headed to the door, finally feeling like I might be able to help do something.

I headed into the hall and stopped, waiting for George and Steven. My body jiggled with contained energy. We'd found something, there was a clue.

He led me to an autopsy room. Carl lay there, pieces of the pipes still in his arms. The image of him hanging on the wall compared to the reality of him laying here clashed in my brain. He looked so broken and sad now compared to the almost holy image of him previously. I shook my head, cautiously touching his tattoo. Fierce joy, completion, orgasmic pleasure, and a sense of finality. That sent a weird shudder through me and I gagged.

"What was that?" Steven asked even as I tried to wash the feeling away. It felt odd and didn't make sense. Carelian laughed in my mind at the same time.

"I..." I swallowed needing the Coke or vodka even more now. "I think she had an orgasm because of her finished work?" I wasn't sure, but I couldn't think of anything else that might match. Even masturbating didn't really excite me, and the few times I had an orgasm, it didn't seem worth the effort. But that feeling, what the killer felt, matched all the descriptions of physical ecstasy I'd ever read, and now I felt like anything approaching that might be forever sullied.

I didn't even bother looking at either of the men, just headed out, my buoyant mood tainted.

TWENTY-FIVE

The Draft board inhabits an odd position in the government. It is not an agency, or at least not one with general law enforcement capabilities. But it is the defining authority on how to regulate and punish mages who have crossed the line without committing a legal crime. While some of their members have overstepped their authority, few are censured as no one wants an insane mage or ruthless one loose in society. ~ Magic Explained Online

---

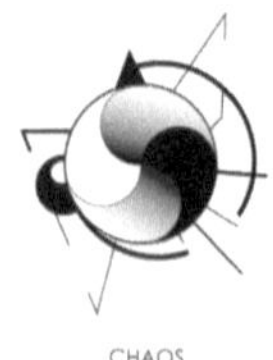

CHAOS

I headed to the parking area without waiting for either of them, going right to the soda machine in the lobby. Standing outside in the hot sun, the sounds of the city hitting me with the same ferocity as the rays of the sun helped to push out what was left of my irritation. The sun and Coke went far to cleanse my mind and body of the feeling. I needed to talk to Jo.

Huh, I haven't heard from her or Sable since yesterday.

I pulled out my phone and texted her in our group text. *how goes? Had something weird happen I need to talk to you two about when I get back. Carelian's still laughing at me. Ugh. Everything good?*

I waited a minute, but didn't see a response being typed, so I slipped the phone back in my pocket. I'd have to talk to them later.

Steven and George came out and I followed them to the car. I said nothing on the ride back, still fighting with my excitement at a real clue and the horror at the pleasure the killer had felt. Feeling that orgasmic flush wash through me and settle in disturbed me more than feeling someone struggle for air. It made me nauseous. If anything, it should have been the opposite, but all I could do was focus on how twisted you had to be to take something that should have been shining and bright and make it into something dark and tainted. Even the sounds of Chaos in my mind again would have been preferable.

"You need Pavel?" George asked as we walked back into One Police Plaza.

"Yes. I'm not going to swear I have the answers for you. But I think I have a pretty big clue."

He cast me a doubtful look, but rather than argue he led us back to the conference room. A minute later Pavel showed up, sketchbook in hand. He settled into the chair, crossing his legs and pulling at the line of his slacks before talking.

"You need me again? Another artistic puzzle?" He sounded interested and his eyes sparkled as he canvassed the room.

After Pavel sat down Carelian jumped up into the chair next to him, his body angled towards the man.

"Not exactly. I think I saw the killer and I need you to sketch her," I said still a bit excited, still aware that it may have just been a random stranger. I couldn't leap to conclusions when all I had was one memory from someone dying as she witnessed the woman.

"Excellent." He put his sketch pad on the table and pulled out a case of pencils, laying them open. "Shall we begin? What was the shape of her face?" He started looking at me, expectant, but the light of excitement had died away. This had gone back to being just work, and I knew how boring that could be some days.

"I have a better idea if you are willing to try," I said hesitantly. Sending images and mini movies to Baneyarl or Carelian was one thing. I needed to be very careful sending it to another person.

"Try what exactly?"

"Are you a hedgemage?" I asked this because I didn't know if him being a mage, even a low level one would help or not.

"No." The word was short and clipped. I sensed a story behind it. One best left alone.

"Okay. What I'd like to do is take an image of the woman we are looking for and push it to you. You should receive it like a picture in your head. It might be a bit fuzzy, but we can do it a few times from different angles if you need. Carelian is going to help me. Think of it as picture telepathy."

His eyes narrowed. "Are you going to read my mind?"

"Nope," I said, shaking my head for emphasis. "All I'm going to do is push a picture to your mind. I've only done this a few times, so you might need to be patient."

He gave me a long look, and I appreciated him not looking to the other men in the room for verification.

"Sure. Why not? I mean, even if you read my mind, the worst you'd see is thoughts about my date tonight. So, what do we do?" His hands were flat on the table, tips of his nail beds white from the pressure he exerted, but his voice remained calm.

"Go Carelian," I instructed and pulled the sharpest clearest picture I could of the woman I'd seen. I had prepared a series of three: standing, sitting, and that smile right before everything went dark for Layla.

~I am going to create a conduit between the two of you. It will not hurt, but it will let the communication happen.~ Carelian spoke in both of our minds, the strange reverberation informing me Pavel also heard his voice.

Pavel started looking around. After a hard swallow he nodded in a jerky motion.

~Go Cori,~ Carelian said in a soothing tone. I quirked my mouth at his consideration. I gathered up the pictures I'd created in my head pushing along the pipe Carelian had created.

While sending things to Baneyarl was like throwing a softball, knowing he would catch it, this felt like pushing my foot into a compression sock. It took wiggling and tugging, all while watching Pavel to make sure I wasn't hurting him. Then it slipped out of my grasp, leaving me mentally stumbling as the pressure released.

"Oh," Pavel said, blinking rapidly. "That is odd. Very very odd. But," he paused eyes closed, tongue licking dry lips. "But woman late twenties, blonde?"

"Yessss," I hissed clenching my fists in excitement. "That's her."

"Well, drawing this one will be easier than most. You sent me three pictures?" He didn't sound sure.

"That is what I tried to do." I wondered what I'd actually sent.

"Huh. One of them is like a movie clip. Interesting. Okay give me a bit, but honestly this will be the fastest I've ever been able to create a sketch." With that he picked up his pad and selected a pencil, then all his attention was on his sketchpad.

"What was that, Cori?" Steven asked, watching me intently.

I opened my mouth, then snapped it shut. I couldn't lie to him; he'd sense it if he was paying attention and I knew from the expression he was paying attention.

So I won't lie.

Instead, I smiled at him. "It's kinda cool. I can push images. I didn't know if I could do it for anyone that wasn't like Carelian. I knew I could push images to him. Like what NOT to eat in the refrigerator. But he said he'd help me push. I wonder if I can do it alone to you as you're a mage." I glanced over at Carelian, who was grooming his paw, ignoring me. "Do I need your help to send to Steven."

~Doubtful. Try~ Was all he said, and I figured he was trying not to laugh at my mental gymnastics.

I smirked in Steven's direction. "Do you want to try?"

"Absolutely." He didn't take his gaze off me while I tried to ignore his intensity, still aware of George lurking, almost dancing with impatience.

I took the images I'd prepared for Pavel and pushed them toward Steven's mind. It still felt odd to feel another person with my mind, like reaching out to touch someone and feeling a cloud instead of skin. This time there wasn't a pipe, just a string

I sent the pictures down. I still had to push a little, but not hard, before they started to slide and were gone.

"Huh, that is odd. Feels strange." His eyes were closed, brows drawn together. "It feels like remembering a movie you saw—an old movie or maybe an old home movie. But I can see her." His eyes popped back open and his gray eyes latched back onto me.

I just smiled, not saying a thing. There were days when the promise Baneyarl had made us swear was a pain in the ass. But his training and friendship were more than worth it.

"That's an interesting trick. How did you figure that out?"

I shrugged. "Carelian can send images to me. So why shouldn't I be able to send them also?" It didn't answer his question, but it wasn't a lie.

"He can?"

I just nodded. While Baneyarl had brought up the idea, the first time Carelian had done that scared me half to death. There'd suddenly been an image of a tomahawk steak in my mind and his demand that he wanted that for dinner. I'd convinced him to take hamburger.

"Can all familiars?"

I shrugged and pointed at mine, currently peering at the drawing Pavel was creating with colored pencils. "Ask the familiar."

~Yes. Many focuses don't conceptualize words as well as I do. Images leave little doubt.~

That clicked into place things that Charles Wainscot, a student and friend who also had a familiar, had said about Arachena, his familiar.

"Ah, yes. That makes sense." He sounded doubtful, but I rose to go look at the image Pavel sketched. I sucked in a sharp breath when I saw the picture. It was still a bit soft, the memory itself had been slightly fuzzy, but there was no doubt as to it being her.

"Three more minutes," he muttered. His hands flew across the page, shaping and filling in details I hadn't noticed, but as soon as they were there they matched up.

"That's a handy trick. Is this something all mages can do?" George asked as he stood near the back of the room, his hands behind his back as if trying to prevent himself from grabbing things.

"I don't know," I admitted. "It might be more figuring out you can do it." Steven coughed a low warning and I sighed. "Possibly just those with familiars, and that is pretty rare."

It sounded liked bullshit to me, but familiars were still something most people didn't understand, and it seemed to work. I shot Steven a glare out of the corner of my eye. If he didn't want people to ask questions, he shouldn't be asking me in public settings.

Steven gave me a soft nod, and I took it as the apology it was.

We waited; me hoping it worked, meaning they could find her, the others anxious for information. Carelian had settled back into his chair, ears forward in a smug manner. How that cat could imply smug with his ears I didn't know, but he managed without any issue.

"Got it. I need to do one more, a full body version while I can see it." Even as he spoke Pavel pulled a sheet off his pad and held it up in the air, other hand already starting to sketch a woman standing.

I stood and looked and there she was, more fleshed out and real than what I'd been able to see in the memories. I knew he had to have filled in stuff or that he saw more in those few moments than I, without an artist's eye, would see.

A woman in her thirties, too thin, with the choppy blonde

hair I'd noted, circles under her eyes, and a sneer on her face that felt real. Looking at that, it struck me her sympathy had been the false note, the glee had been truth.

"This is who we are looking for?" George asked the paper in his hands, eyes scouring it as if he would find answers.

"As best I can tell. Until you get me another victim, which I would really prefer you don't, I don't think I can tell you any more than I have." I shrugged. My elation had faded. Even if this wasn't what they wanted I was done and tired of death. Being a doctor would be more fun, surely for them there were occasional wins, right?

"Okay, I'll take it from here. Don't leave for a day or so, I'm still scouring the missing persons database and waiting on the results from the forensics on the tattoos but that might take another day or two." He paused and regarded me with a hard look in his eyes. "Thanks. This might be what we needed. If we capture her, you'll have to testify and maybe even explain how you could see this."

"Oh," I said and swallowed. I'd forgotten about this part of it. I might have to testify. "I can do that, or at least do my best."

"Good. Go. Enjoy my city. Don't get any tickets." George called out as he texted on his phone.

I shifted my attention to Steven. "Now what?"

Ile gave me a bittersweet smile. "Now we wait."

CHAPTER
TWENTY-SIX

Everyone swears the Statue of Liberty was made with the help of mages. But it was constructed long before magic rippled across the world, making that unlikely. She of all the great works seems untouched by time or the world changing around her. May she ever be a testament to what just men can do. ~ Freedom from Magic

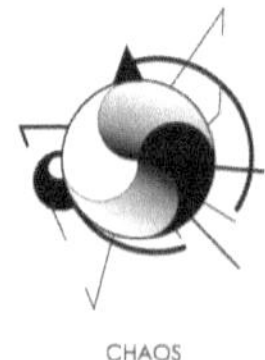

CHAOS

He hailed down a cab and the three of us rode back to the apartment. It was after four, the time at the morgue having taken longer than I'd thought. We arrived to an empty apartment and Steven sighed. I think he'd hoped Indira would be there. It was cute.

"I've got some calls to make, and Indira said she'd bring back dinner. Go explore if you want." He tossed me a smile and headed to their bedroom.

"What would you like to do, Carelian?" I asked staring out the window at the city.

~I do not think we have time to see this lady of liberty you speak of, but I think I would like to explore the city from the ground level.~

"We can do that." I changed my clothes, grabbing a key and heading out after letting Steven know. The next few hours we spent just wandering around Long Island. When it got too dark, we hoofed it back to the apartment building, where Indira was unpacking dinners for us.

"Good timing. I hear you're free tomorrow?"

I shrugged. "As far as I know. Hurry up and wait."

"Excellent. If you have nothing else to do, you and I are going to explore the stores of New York."

"But the Statue of Liberty?" I protested, visions of hours of tedious traipsing around stores flashing through my head.

"Tomorrow, I promise. And I doubt you'll find this as much of a drag as you think. In fact, given what I heard about today you might enjoy it," Indira said, that normal amused tilt of her lips telling me I was losing this battle.

"Why not, but you're feeding us."

"As I expected.

The next morning, I got my coffee fix on, and we headed out. Me in jeans and a decent top, Indira, as always, looking like she was ready to walk onto a photo shoot. She wore dark gray palazzo pants, a loose daffodil yellow blouse, and her hair in a snood. Yes, history had made sure I knew that word. She looked stunning, and I looked like me.

"Those will do for now," she commented after giving me a once over. I got a bad feeling.

"Carelian, you may stay here. This will annoy you and you will distract people where we are going. I wish to have their attention on me, not on you."

~But I am where their attention should be,~ he replied as he peered out the window onto the city below. ~However, I do not feel like dealing with that today. I do however want to see the statue Cori speaks of.~

"Of course. Come on, Cori, we'll visit a gallery or two first, then get lunch." I waved at Alixant, who smirked at me as Indira headed out the door and I trailed in her wake.

The galleries were interesting, but I kept comparing the art to what the murderer had done to Carl. It made it an odd disconnect.

When our stomachs told us food was required, the restaurant she chose was not where I would have expected. I'd figured lunch at some café, not a restaurant in the middle of the fanciest department store I'd ever been in. We were ushered in, treated like royalty, and settled down. I felt decidedly underdressed.

"Why are we here in Bergdorf's?" I asked, my voice a whisper as I looked around.

"Because I needed food, and they have an excellent menu."

"Yeah, but what are you getting here?" I persisted, even as I looked at the menu and realized I wanted all their offerings.

"I am getting you clothes to make sure you know how to impress people," she said as she set down her menu.

"Wait, what?" My voice squeaked upwards to an embarrassingly high pitch and I shrank back as people looked at me.

Indira raised a finger and I snapped my mouth shut. The waiter took our orders and returned with Coke for me, and a champagne glass and pitcher of red colored mimosas for Indira. She let him pour and then he left to fill our lunch orders.

When he left, she smiled at me. "Remember the conversation we had, about you deciding you wanted to make them choke on you as opposed to treading on you? This is the first step. Assuming you still wish to follow that path? It is not an easy one." She picked up the champagne glass and admired it before taking a sip.

That wasn't the way I would have phrased it, but my desire to be a dragon instead of a timid mouse could be boiled down to that. She had a way of phrasing things that always sounded so different than in my own mind, while being essentially the same thing.

"Yes," I said slowly, not sure what that desire had to do with taking me shopping.

"The first way to get anyone treat you as a power in your own right is to convince them you are someone they need to take seriously." She paused, taking another sip of her mimosa and smiling a bit. "There are ways to forge your own way with your own style, and to force them to meet you on your own terms, but it takes a lot of energy and time, not to mention scars. People tend to beat you down, hoping one of these times you won't get back up."

I looked around at the men and women sitting in the restaurant. They all looked much more important than I did, and it clicked. I was slow at times, but not completely stupid. "You're saying if I look like someone they should respect, it will help when I'm proving I won't let them push me around."

"Oh, it won't do miracles—assholes will still be assholes.

But it will make people stop and think. First impressions sink into your hindbrain and people don't always realize it. You need to wear clothes that scream you know how to use what is tattooed on your temple. Make them think about who they are dealing with. Right now, you look like a young impressionable woman and that is not something you can afford for anyone to think." She focused on her drink and I thought about her words.

She was right. I couldn't afford to have people assume I was young and naïve, even if I was.

"I don't like dresses particularly. And the stuff you wear is way too fancy and flowy," I said, but I wasn't disagreeing with her.

"I figured as much. That and you are much younger than me. It would make you look like you were playing dress up. Instead, I'm thinking about the rock stars and young divas that scream power when they walk into a room. We can make it so you enjoy wearing the clothes, though you do need better support garments." The way she said that made me shift in my chair. I liked my cotton. It was comfortable and absorbed sweat.

"Trust me, Cori. I know you have multiple valid reasons to have doubts about me. But if you can break their hold on us, get them to treat mages a bit better, it is worth everything."

I stared at her, not sure what to say. From everything I'd read, mages were treated well. I for sure would make much more as a mage than I would have without being one. What else didn't I see or know?

The waiter returned and we fell back to normal talk, well, clothing talk. She quizzed me about colors, laundry habits, styles, what I liked and why. By the time we were done, I almost understood my own desires when it came to clothes. I needed to be able to move, have things that for everyday wear could handle blood, but I liked soft and drapey for fancy or business stuff. While realizing my constant magic was burning calories and addressing that had increased my bra size, I'd never be Jo or Sable. I was perfectly happy with full B cups. But it meant I still needed a bra and I liked being more active than not. Having a big bag to carry around that occupied my hands annoyed me, hence backpacks. It turned out to be an interesting conversation and made me realize how very much we don't know about ourselves.

We finished lunch, which was excellent, and Indira paid to my internal wince. "Come on. I have an idea about your style. Let's go meet the shopper who's waiting for us."

"The what?" Shopper? That term made no sense at the moment, though I did follow her.

She laughed, and I watched with amusement the men and women who turned to follow her with their eyes. What was even funnier was about half flinched when they saw her Merlin status, and the other half got even more interested. All were reactions I could live without.

We were ushered into nice room with a small raised area surrounded by mirrors, a curtained dressing room off to the right, and an empty rack next to another archway. It was done in neutral beige and the lighting was almost a perfect match for the brightness of a sunny day. Four nice club chairs in white and grey stripes, each with a little tea table next to them were on the wall facing the mirrors.

Standing in the center of the room a young man waited for us. He was dressed in a sharp suit, his hair in a tasteful pouf, and he could have had GAY in neon letters above his head. I don't think, outside of a drag show Jo and Sable talked me into —it was excellent—, I'd never seen someone so obvious about their sexual orientation.

"Ladies, I am so glad to meet you. My name is Gar, short for Garfield, and your appointment is with me. It will be my pleasure to make all your apparel dreams come true." He waved his hand and all but blinded us with his smile as he welcomed us into what was obviously his domain. His over-the-top dramatics made me fight giggles.

"Thank you Gar. I'm Indira Humbert, and this is Cori Munroe. The appointment for a dresser is for her." She smirked at me and I resisted the desire to roll my eyes.

"Ah, I get the privilege of dressing a merlin? How exquisite. This will be a fantastic journey." He positively gushed and I just stared at him.

I really wanted Jo to be there so I could ask her a question, but she wasn't, though I vowed to sneak a picture of the man. But since she wasn't here, I needed to ask him the question.

"Are you for real? I mean my best friend is gay, but..." I was cut off as Indira slapped her hand over my mouth.

"Cori!" she gasped.

I narrowed my eyes and licked her palm.

"Ewwww." She ripped her hand away, glaring at me. "I apologize for my uncouth friend. Do you have a towel I can wipe my hand on?"

Gar for his part was standing there, hand over his mouth, and I couldn't figure out if he was outraged or not. But I didn't get the shouting one's sexual orientation. It made no sense to me.

He stepped over, pulled a tissue out of a box, and handed it to Indira who looked mortified. I was still curious.

"So? Real or over the top for tourists?"

At this point he started to giggle, the sound slipping out from behind his hand, filling the room. He dropped his hand, a smile on his face. "Yes. More accurately, in New York I get to be the me-est me there is. And yes, the tourists enjoy it."

"Cori," Indira moaned and I gave her a sideways glance. She had her head bowed, fingers touching her brow, a look of pain on her face.

I shrugged. "Okay. I was just checking because it struck me as a bit too much theater."

"Of course, this is New York!" He said and waved his hands around the room. "Where else should theater happen?" He grinned and winked at me. "So now, how may I dress you two lovely ladies?"

At that I pointed to Indira. "All her. She has some idea about how to make me look impressive, or at least not young and naïve."

He ran his gaze down my body and back up. There was nothing sexual about it, but I suspected he knew my bra and pants size by the time he was done. "I see. I doubt you are naïve. Maybe overly optimistic about people?"

"She wears rose colored glasses all the time and is way to internally focused to see the world around her as it is. Thus, I'm looking for clothes that make people see her as powerful and smart, not young and malleable." Indira had lifted her head and was staring at me exasperated. I just shrugged. It had been a performance, one I wanted to verify.

"Hmmm. I think I know a way to do this. But you'll need to teach her better hair styles also." His eyes narrowed, he walked around me, not touching but inspecting my hair intently. "Chignon, twist, and even a tight bun will all be improvements. For field work, learn to do a fishbone weave. It will look effortlessly elegant but keep your hair out of your face. Remember to always offer from the bottom up, not these random strands. Your cosmetology magic class should have taught you that."

I fingered my ponytail, a bit self-conscious at them talking about me like I wasn't here. "It did, just random is easier. And I know how to do a basic French braid."

He nodded sharply. "Good. Take the time to learn some fancier ones. You said you had a female friend? She a mage too?"

"Yes, both her and her girlfriend," I admitted, not sure where this was going.

"Excellent, then I will make sure to add a book on braiding to your bag. Learning how to do plaits and other braids will be both a time saver and give you multiple hair styles you can choose from without taking too much time or effort once you get practiced. You can practice on your friends. Learn to do it on them first, then switch to doing it on yourself. You can never tell when the ability to whip up a fancy braid will be a life saver." He spoke with brisk efficiency.

"Make it two books please. I could stand learning," Indira interjected as I felt like a firehose of information had been pointed at me.

"Of course, Merlin Humbert. Now, Merlin Munroe, where are you in your career? Draft or still in college?"

Indira arched an eyebrow at me as she sank into one of the waiting club chairs. Watching. Judging my performance.

"It's just Cori," I said, still tugging on my ponytail. "And college. Master's then doctorate."

Gar paused and glanced at Indira, then back at me. "Do you want to learn how to make people take you seriously? How to be treated like a merlin? With a bit of trepidation and fear?" His voice was serious, and I felt like I'd stepped into another world, one that made no sense to me. I started to shake my head.

"Yes, she does," Indira said with a sigh of exasperation. "She doesn't know it yet, but she does."

Gar smiled, it was amused and proud at the same time. "Then we'll start now. I've been doing this for a long time, and I've dealt with people from all walks of life. It's interesting what you see when you work in service, especially for Bergdorf's. Never allow someone to use your first name unless you want to seem to grant them a favor. If possible, make them call you by your full title, either Miss, Ms., or Merlin. Merlin is the best option in any situation where you are there because of your magic. It reminds them every time you are someone they need to take seriously because you have real demonstratable power."

"But I don't want to hurt people," I protested, but I couldn't deny what he said.

"I am ecstatic to hear that," he said, a quirk to his lips. "But that won't always be the case. Formality has a power all its own. Use it. So, Merlin Munroe, you are still working on your master's. Will you be working with the OMO or government prior to starting your draft?"

I nodded. "Yes. It's why I'm in New York. They pulled me in." I watched him and processed everything he said. I suspected if Indira had said it I'd have resisted more, but he stated everything as fact rather than like he was trying to make me into his idea of what I should be.

"Hmmm," he murmured and walked over to a small desk in the corner to pick up a printout. "Merlin Humbert, you sent this?"

Indira nodded. "We talked over lunch and I pulled it out of her. She is very opinionated, but you often have to dig to pull out the opinions."

Gar looked at the list and nodded. "This is doable, and I will make a list of pieces she should look for to add to her wardrobe." He shifted his gaze to me. "Remember, impressions are a type of power and you want people to treat you like a very expensive, very dangerous weapon. Don't ever let them forget or think you don't have your own agenda. Unless, of course, you want them to think of you as naive and impressionable." He smirked a bit at that last sentence.

"A dragon." The comment slipped out and he nodded. I heard Indira muffle a laugh.

"That is an excellent analogy. We shall make you into an emerging dragon. If you will give me a while, this should be fun.

I'll have someone bring you some more mimosas." He disappeared in a whirl of pale blue linen and I turned to stare at Indira.

"Why?"

"Because I damn well want to see the dragon shove people in their place. Remember the death rate Steven told you about?" She had no amusement on her face.

I nodded, all too aware of how many mages died in the draft because they weren't willing to toe the line.

"They are going to be looking for reasons to eliminate you. You are dangerous. I want to give you every weapon possible to make sure they think twice before doing anything."

TWENTY-SEVEN

Alice in Order is still beloved even though most believe Charles Dodgson was a Pattern Merlin who avoided being registered. The story of Alice in a world full of denizens that match much of what we know now about those that inhabit the realms makes it almost a certainty that he had visited there. The question then becomes how much of the story was created for children and how much was what happened. But it also raises the question, did Charles visit or was it actually his daughter who made it into the realm and back, and what happened to her afterwards? ~ Magic Explained Online

---

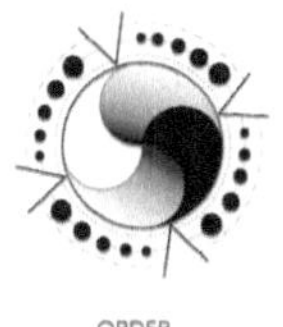

I sat down next to her, all the information tumbling about in my mind. "Spirit Mages are rare, but they aren't that rare." I took a deep breath. "Indira, why am I really here? For this case? Now?" Indira examined her hands very carefully, but I didn't move or let myself get distracted. "Indira?"

She huffed out a sigh and stood, pacing across the room. Yes. There are other Spirit mages who have been brought in. No Spirit merlins though."

"And? Soul isn't that rare. There are others who would have a strong Soul as their extra branch." I kept prodding. Something had felt off about this the entire time.

She didn't look at me, instead stared at her reflection. I watched her face, wondering what she saw in her own eyes.

"No. They were pretty sure it was a mage. They had gotten that much out of the bodies. But the women aspect, art, and especially her image were new things that you discovered. The mages they were working with couldn't break past the sensation of suffocating. One had a heart attack in the middle of It, leaving the police stuck. That much is all true. You, however, were able to push past it and not go into immediate panic attacks at the thought." Indira turned, locking eyes with me. "That impressed everyone. The other mages refused after the first immersion."

"Oh." I considered that. It had been scary, but I knew it wasn't really happening, therefore I could overcome it. Something else to think about later. "But they knew about the tattoo being odd and already had information about it?" I prodded. It made no sense for them not to.

"Yes," she started then broke off as a young woman brought in a mimosa. "I should have asked for whiskey," she muttered as she accepted the glass. The woman left and I just stared at Indira while she took a drink.

Finally she looked at me. "You really should be asking Steven. I only know what I've gleaned from his comments. But yes, they had ideas, though I don't believe any of the other mages ever tried to get anything from the tattoos, so that was new. But mostly the draft board ordered a trial for you, to see if you could work with others or if you were too arrogant, too full of yourself." She drained half the mimosa and slumped down. "The tales of your exploits have been widely repeated. I just figured maybe I could be a buffer or at least make it a bit more fun for you." She looked oddly defeated.

"Why would they think I'm arrogant?" I protested.

Am I arrogant?

She snorted. "You teleported to Japan. You're powerful, very. And most merlins are arrogant. They can do things most mages only dream of. Then add in your familiar. They are basing their expectations of you on other merlins. You've met a few now. How would you characterize most of us?" She pointed to herself with that.

"Arrogant," I sighed, seeing her point. "How much more of this should I expect?"

She gave me a bitter smile. "More than you want, hence why we are here. This will help start level setting and maybe keep you alive."

Just then Gar bustled in, his arms filled with a riot of colors. "Ladies, I believe I have items that will satisfy all your needs. Shall we?" He hung the clothes on the rack as he spoke, glee on his face. I got ready to be embarrassed and made into a dress-up doll.

It turned out to not be as bad as I thought, though Gar was amused that I didn't care if I stood there in the underwear and bra he'd found for me. I just shrugged. It covered more than the swimsuits Jo wore, and the amount of time I would have spent going back and forth behind the curtains was stupid.

By the end of the afternoon, I had what he called a capsule wardrobe along with explicit—written— instructions on how to build on it. And I had to admit I looked more the powerful young political figure than a college student.

I'd taken pictures as we went sending them to Jo and Sable, frowning more each time when they didn't reply. But if they were busy exploring, they might not have phones with them.

Two pairs of jean slacks—which I loved, they fit like slacks but were heavy and felt like denim—one in dark gray, the other black, plus two pairs of designer jeans. Three short-sleeved silk shells in blue, burgundy, and green, that draped at the neck. But they didn't pull or tug, plus they were stain-resistant and he swore I could wash them in the sink with little effort. Three soft knit V-neck T-shirts in grey, burgundy, and green. Five sets of bra, panties, and camisole sets that cost more than my laptop, but I had to admit they made a difference when I wore them. Each of the sets included three panties all slightly different yet still matching the bra and camisole. A simple black jumpsuit in a brocade silk with flecks of burgundy and green. That one needed to be dry cleaned, but as it was my special occasion outfit, I could tolerate it. Two light suit jackets in something he called a Chanel style, but they weren't bad, one in black, the other in a silvery gray. A knee length cardigan in a blue/green geometric that still looked elegant. He proved it would go with everything without an issue, and it brought out the colors in my tattoos.

"I admit you are lucky in that you have a body shape well suited to the current styles, though I'd like you to find a few burgundy pieces as you explore the world. Here are the last two pieces you need. Two pairs of low-heeled boots and this silk over vest." He pointed to the blast of color left on the rack. It was one of those I hadn't tried on yet, both attracted and repelled by the brightness. It had green, red, yellow, silver, gold, burgundy, and blue splashed through it in an abstract pattern that draped to mid-thigh. It looked like something you would wear to a renaissance fair, but it was too nice, too elegant. It went with and over everything, even the jumpsuit. I couldn't decide if I wanted to wear it always, or never put it on because I didn't know if I could be that woman.

"You sure?"

"Put it on. Or I'm stealing it," vowed Indira, looking at it. "And you don't have another version of this?"

While she argued with Gar, I took a pic of it and sent to Jo and Sable. *Yay or nay?*

"Here, put it on." Gar handed it to me. I sighed and set my phone down, then slipped it on, still dressed in the dark grey slacks and the blue shell. "Now look at yourself."

I'd become way too familiar with those mirrors over the last few hours, and I pivoted and froze. A woman, elegant in a riot of colors over her slacks, hair twisted back into a chignon, stared back at me, her gaze surprised.

"Wow," I whispered then slowly smiled. "You're right. This is the perfect addition." I turned to look at the pile of keep clothes and swallowed. "So how much do I owe?"

Gar arched a brow then shot a puzzled glance over to Indira.

"You don't owe anything, Cori." Indira said, her arms wrapped around her stomach. "Call this a graduation present. You pulled off something an awful lot of people never thought you could do. And something people tried very hard to make sure you couldn't. Think of it as penance from those of us who doubted you."

"Including you?" I carefully took the vest off, wanting to wear it.

"I didn't think you'd make it out alive. I'm still not sure how you did. Magic must have been looking out for you, it's the only explanation I have. So, yes. This is penance and a gift. You deserve both."

I started to protest but Gar clapped his hands. "Excellent. Now that's settled, Merlin Munroe would you like to wear that out?"

I froze and looked at the woman in the mirror. The confident, powerful woman with her tattoo on display for the world to see and the colors of the clothes she wore making it pop.

"Yes, she would." This time Indira was smiling, and I gave in. I reached for my phone, and took a picture, sending it to Jo.

The new me. Thoughts?

I stared at the phone waiting for a reply, but instead a chime from someone else made me jump and almost drop it. I flipped back and pulled up a text from Steven.

Have suspect in custody. Want to see her? Could use truth forcing.

I wanted to see her but grimaced at the truth forcing. I could do it. Forcing truth always felt slimy in my mind and it took a lot of out of me. The Soul teacher thought no one would be able to resist me if I ever really tried. Or they would break.

Breaking people didn't sound like fun, and I avoided it. There was something slimy about pressing my magic against someone's mind like that. Usually just telling someone you knew they were lying was enough. But if she was only a hedgemage, maybe it would be easy.

"Indira?" I showed her my text and she nodded.

"Excellent. You can wear that and see if you notice a difference in how people respond." Her smile was positively evil.

I looked in the mirror again and smiled at the woman staring back at me. "Okay."

Gar heaved a heavy sigh. "I so love transformations. Best of luck, Merlin Munroe." He gave me a warm smile and a bow of his head. "I'll get everything else ready."

"Can you have them sent to this address please?" Indira scribbled on a piece of paper. "It's where we're staying while in town. And add in a garment bag. She doesn't have anything to pack those in."

"Of course." He handed her another piece of paper and she scribbled on that while I kept sneaking glances of myself in the mirror. I didn't know the woman I saw there—she looked like a dragon, full of color and strength.

I wish Jo and Sable could have been here.

That thought prompted me to take out my phone and snap another picture, sending it to them.

So? I attached it and sent the image and the text. They were going to get so much teasing from me when I got back and found they'd been having so much fun they forgot to charge their phones. A niggle of worry hit at the back of my mind, but Indira called my name.

"Ready, Cori?"

I took one last glance at the mirror, straightening, the low heels on the boots giving me an extra inch of height. "I think so."

Her smile warmed me all the way down. "You look wonderful, Cori. Are you sure you enjoy wearing these clothes? Trust me, it doesn't matter how wonderful you look in them, if you don't feel wonderful wearing them, you never will."

I shook my head as we strode out of the little oasis of fashion and self-confidence. "No. I like this, it isn't what I would have chosen, but I feel..." I couldn't figure out what I felt like. "Not me" wasn't correct, neither was "someone else." I felt like a dragon, or at least like I could be a dragon.

"I get it. While I had many issues with my parents, my mother taught me how clothes could be as much a weapon and armor as anything else." Her voice was sad and a bit wistful.

I glanced at her, but I caught a reflection of us and what I saw there redialed my thoughts. Two elegant Merlins were standing there, looking like the world should move out of our way. I'd almost gotten used to how the new image in reflections, and Indira always looked amazing. What threw me were the people watching us. I stumbled, causing Indira to grab my arm to keep me from face planting.

"Cori?" she asked, concern in her voice.

I shook my head, breaking the image. "I'm fine. Just got distracted." And I still was. The looks of admiration and hunger for both of us seared down into my soul and I didn't know if I could live with looks like that.

But then again, dragons are either feared or admired. If I was going to be a dragon, I'd better get used to it.

TWENTY-EIGHT

More and more people are adopting long hair styles and nails to appear to be a mage. Have pride in yourself. Magic is not what you should aspire to. Aspire to be the best person you can be. Mages are slaves to their own powers. ~Freedom from Magic

SPIRIT

A taxi was waiting for us as we exited Bergdorf's. Paying more attention to the quality of the seats than ever before I was relieved to think I might make it into One Police Plaza without damaging or staining my new clothes. Our ride was quick and quiet as I wrestled with my inner thoughts. The occasional glance back from the cabbie didn't help my equilibrium. The lust and fear in his eyes made my skin crawl. Something else I'd need to talk to Indira about later. How did she deal with it, and much less seem to thrive off of it?

We stepped out, Indira paying, and headed up the sidewalk.

"Steven, over here," Indira called out as we approached the visitor's entrance. He turned and went stock still, his stare burning into me. With slow precision his eyes traveled up and down my body, but I just made myself stand straighter and give him a slow smile back.

"I don't know what I expected, but I'm impressed. You look... dangerous," he said slowly, still staring at me. "No one would doubt you are a merlin."

That made me blink and I tapped my temple with the tattoo blaring out for everyone to see. "And they would have doubted before?"

"No, but before you looked like a college student playing dress up. Now you look powerful, strong, like you have the knowledge to use what that tat implies." He shook his head. "Come on. Here's your pass." He handed us new passes with the current date on them. "Here Indira, you might as well come also."

We put them on and trailed into the building. Steven had his FBI jacket on and with his badge around his neck which made me wonder what else was going on. But I didn't ask, instead watching how people reacted to us. It was eye opening. The cops who before had glanced at me and dismissed me, something I thought I'd preferred, now looked at me and stood a bit straighter, moving out of our way. My throat was tight by the time we hit the elevators.

This could be dangerous. Do I want this?

"They have her in holding. You sure you're up to this?" he

asked as the elevator doors started closing and he pressed a button.

"Not even remotely. I don't like truth forcing. It makes me feel like I'm coated in slime," I answered, bluntly honest. This spell they only taught as needed and from what I'd heard from the other two Psychic archmages in my class, everyone felt or did it differently. Some did it by reaching in and grabbing the information from their subject. Others forced the victim to talk. Some were subtle and smooth, others like sledgehammers. And none of them, not the professor or even Baneyarl, could reach into my mind or make me talk. Carelian had smirked and refused to explain why. But I could pull information out of the other students with an ease that made me nauseous. Unlike my human teachers, Baneyarl had made me practice forcing out the truth. Jo and Sable were easy, Baneyarl was difficult. Esmere, well let's just say if I ever did it in reality on her, she'd kill me.

"Tough shit. We need to know if she took the two missing people. We think they meet her criteria," Steven said, no sympathy in his voice.

"You know if she does, they are probably already dead," I pointed out and cringed as the doors slid open and that word came out, echoing down the corridor.

"Probably, but their families are hoping." He strode down to a guarded secure door. I sighed and followed him, working hard to not trudge. Gar had insisted that people of power didn't trudge.

Faster than I liked I was standing at a one-way window in a claustrophobic room, looking at the person I'd seen in Layla's last moments. Thin enough her skin looked like canvas pulled over her bones, ashy, frizzy hair with lopsided chunks missing from the bottom, and glasses that magnified wide eyes that stared straight ahead ignoring Detective Farlane as if he wasn't there.

"He's been in there about an hour. She hasn't said one word," a man monitoring the electronics said. Through the speaker I could hear George haranguing her, but she didn't even pay attention to him. There was a Mona Lisa smile at the corner of her lips.

"They have any proof it is her? I mean besides the pictures?" I asked even though I knew it was her.

"Forensics is still going through her place. But they identified her by hitting a few tattoo shops. Apparently, she went around there a lot, asking them about customers. Most didn't talk, but they said they'd see her hanging around, listening even though they swore she was too far away to hear what they were talking about."

"Air," I sighed. Eavesdropping was a common habit among Air mages.

George slammed his hand down and she barely flinched. He stood up and stormed out the door, slamming it behind him. A moment later he yanked open the door to the room we were in and shut it much more sedately behind him.

"Nothing. Merlin, I'm not even sure she is there." He looked at me, eyes hard. "Go in there and get the answers to these questions out of her." He shoved a folder towards me.

"Excuse me?" I was thrown off by his change in behavior and he just snarled.

"You heard me—go do your job."

I bristled and my reflection in the one-way mirror added steel to my spine. "My job, as you call it, is going to college to get my degree. I don't work for you, and technically I haven't started the draft."

"Cori," Steven said warningly. I held my hand up to him.

"No. I don't have to be here and if he keeps up acting like you did, I will walk."

George gritted his teeth and took a look at me, a hard look and sighed.

"I apologize, Merlin Munroe. Would you please see if you can get the answers to these questions?" He handed me the file again, without the anger.

I nodded after a moment. "I will try." I took the folder and walked out of the room, shaking with delayed annoyance. I was so tired of people telling me what to do and not even bothering to ask. You didn't yell at dragons, they tended to eat you.

I stepped into the room and the woman didn't even look up. I pulled the chair all the way to the wall. There was no way I was risking her touching me. I had a very good idea that I had no desire to sense her thoughts or feelings. This was going to be bad enough.

The form had nothing but questions. I didn't even know her name. Fine, I'd do it my way. The questions were all stupid ones, not the important stuff. Instead, I'd ask the important stuff.

"Are Jasmine Bell and Scott Lord still alive?"

She didn't even look at me, just stared at the wall rocking slightly. I reached out with my magic, feeling the millimeters of hair vaporize. "Answer me." I upped the magic in my command.

Her mouth opened. "I don't know who that is."

Truth

It rang through me and I tilted my head. A nausea started to form in my belly but I changed the question. "Did you take any art equipment after the supplies for the crucifix in the subway?"

Energy washed over her face, but she still didn't look at me. "Yes. Two. This is my best piece yet. I can't wait for critics to see it."

I swallowed hard. "Is the art completed?" I didn't even need to put magic into the question, she was nodding with a huge smile, but her eyes wouldn't meet mine and she kept tapping out patterns on the table.

"Yes. It is stunning. The world will know my vision."

"Where is it?"

"Secret, can't tell. Soon it will be found." She was still not looking at anything but the wall.

I put magic into it. "Tell me where."

She frowned. "It's not time. Time must be right. It isn't time."

"Tell. Me." I put magic and power into each word. Her head shook back and forth in a rapid staccato, but I didn't let go and I pulled the information from her. I wish it had been harder, but it took barely any offering, mostly focus.

"40.79 by -73.95," she stuttered, and an image came with the word. Green, lush, water falling and an array of leaves, already dying, shielding something.

"Where is your studio at?" That would be what they needed, where she did her art, where she broke and moved bodies.

Sobbing she gave an address and I rose and walked out the door. As it shut behind me, I could hear her muttering, "It's not ready yet, can't see it yet."

George was on his phone as I walked in. "What do you mean you have no idea how to find a place based on coordinates? Figure it out."

"It's someplace green with water and leaves if that helps," I offered. George nodded sharply relaying that info.

"So now what?" I asked.

"She'll be drugged until trial, then executed. We verified she's a high hedgemage, but while her pales were borderline non-existent, she was almost strong enough just in air to qualify as a magician." George had hung up and handed me a file folder with papers and the woman's picture. "Her name is Kelly Warren."

I nodded. The penalty for killing with magic was death. The penalty for most felonies if you were a mage was death. There was a good reason for that.

"We might need help to get her sedated. She is resisting."

"Actually, I think she's a high functioning autistic. Watch her, she's stimming. She doesn't see the victims as people, just art supplies," I said as I watched the woman who had already signed her own death warrant, though there would still be a full trial. You didn't want to miss accomplices or have the wrong person, it had happened before. There were no appeals for mages—ever.

"Not my problem. She killed with magic," George said. "I'll need you to go back in. We will have more questions, but we need the prosecutors to get here and a defense attorney." He called someone else on his phone before I could respond.

I glared at Indira and Steven, both of whom just shrugged. My phone rang before I could say anything, and I answered it without looking.

"Yes?"

"Cori?" Marisol's familiar voice came through the line and I felt my anger fizzle out before it could flare into a bonfire. I moved over to the opposite corner, pressing the phone tighter to my ear. I loved Marisol, but she rarely called, usually I called her.

"Marisol. Is everything okay?" The dread that had been building in my stomach for the last two days started to swell.

"I don't know. Is Jo with you?"

I shook my head, then remembered to answer. "No. She's at the house with Sable. Why?"

I heard an exasperated huff. "I can't get a hold of her. She was supposed to call yesterday with some information about a job Henri is working on and she didn't call. I called yesterday evening, and then five times this morning and it just goes to voice mail. I thought maybe she was with you."

"Let me see if I can reach her. One minute." I put the phone against my chest, eyes closed as I sent a message to Carelian.

~Carelian, are you there?~

~Sleeping, warm,~ his drowsy voice came back, and I could hear a hint of a whine at my disturbing him.

~Can you reach Jo or Sable?~ I put a bit of urgency into that thought as I waited.

~You have phone. Call,~ he said, but I could hear a more alert tone in his voice.

~Marisol has been calling. I've been texting but no reply. Can you please?~ I could talk to them if I could see them, but he could talk to them from other places, just like he could to me.

~Moment,~ he fell silent and I waited, aware of Marisol on the other end of the phone call. ~Cori? I can't get to them. In fact, I don't know where they are.~

~What do you mean?~ I was glad we were talking via mind-speak—I didn't know if my voice would be steady with real words.

~They aren't here. I can't find them anywhere on this planet.~

CHAPTER
TWENTY-NINE

Trials for mages are mandatory and must be done quickly. The use of drugs to keep a mage disoriented tends to be essential to prevent collateral damage. A mage with Truth Sensing must be there to verify the validity of anything spoken by the defendant. It is one job where even a pale in Soul can be warmly welcomed. Trials are quick and to the point. Lawyers lay out the charges and evidence, there are usually only witnesses to review the information. If the mages are found guilty of breaking any laws, they are executed within a few hours of the sentence being passed. There is never any need for character witnesses or pleas for leniency, there is only one verdict for felony-level or higher crimes. ~Magic Explained

The words hit me, and I fought to remember to breathe even as I heard Kelly starting to scream in the other room. I lifted the phone back to my ear, my hand shaking.

"Marisol, I don't know where she is. Where they are. But I'll find them. As soon as I do, I'll call you. Promise."

"Cori? Is something wrong? Do I hear someone screaming?" I could hear the stress in her voice.

"Yes, but that has nothing to do with Jo. I'm here in the city, and she's back at the house. I'll get her, I promise. Let me go and I'll go find her."

"Okay. Cori?" Her voice quavered and I thought my soul did too.

"Yes?" I needed to run to find Jo, but I wouldn't risk hurting Marisol for anything.

"Remember, I love all my girls. You be careful. Call if you need us."

I swallowed. "I will. Talk to you soon. "

I disconnected the call and looked at the people in the room, all of whom were looking at me with various levels of curiosity. Taking a deep breath, I sent a text to Jo and Sable via our group text, then to each one individually.

call me asap - 911

Answer!

I stared at my phone waiting for something to rekindle the spark of hope in my heart.

"Cori?" Indira asked, starting to move towards me. "What is wrong?"

~Are they with Baneyarl?~ I sent to Carelian ignoring Indira standing in front of me and the bustle of officers all yelling to enact Mage Protocols. I'd reviewed those in class but hadn't paid that much attention to them.

~No. I asked. Esmere cannot reach them either.~ His response was almost instant and I could sense his stress as the information solidified my worry into full blown panic.

~Would they be able to find them in Chaos or Order?~ I asked as I robotically put the phone away.

~No.~ His voice a whisper.

"Cori?" Indira touched my arm. "What happened? What's wrong?"

I turned to look through the mirror, watching the chaos. Wind blew at the officers as Kelly shrieked something about her art and it wasn't time. I felt a prickle on my skin as I tried to grab my fear and turn it into something usable. "We can't get ahold of Jo or Sable. They aren't reachable. Or they aren't responding to any calls."

"I'm sure they are just out having fun or something." She tried to reassure me and I could see Steven torn between helping with the Air mage and coming over to us.

"No, something's wrong," I murmured, not looking away from the two police mages struggling to get through the door. Wind kept pushing them back, and Kelly was screaming. Her hair was vaporizing as the officers, armed with syringes, tried to get close enough to her to sedate her.

"Shit. Get in there, help them!" George snapped looking at Alixant and me. "We can't let her get away. Why didn't she fight before now?" Indira just lifted her hands stepping back into the corner leaving me there. I instantly became the focus of George's ire.

"I'll try. Killing her is easier," Steven pointed out as he stared through the glass window.

"No killing. I need her alive for trial. Those families need closure," George said, putting his own phone away and glaring at everyone.

My mind swirled with worry and I tried to convince myself they just forgot to charge their phones. "I have to go. Now." The world seemed distant and unreal. All the commotion came from a great distance as Jo being in danger filtered through my soul. All I could think was I needed to get to Jo. To Sable. To my family. I turned around, the elevators to the garage were down the hall.

"Yeah, sorry. Need you here. We will need you to testify as to what you saw. The trial should be tomorrow," George spoke, his voice horrified as he stared at the officers collapsing on the ground. "Shit, do something Alixant."

The glass broke with an explosion of sound. Glass covered my back, but it sliced into others.

"Do something, Alixant," George roared as the men in the room were clawing for air.

"I'm trying, quit distracting me," Steven snapped as he focused on the woman, but she ducked behind the table breaking his line of sight.

"I don't have time for this, I have to go." I said the words numbly. I couldn't take the time to deal with all this. Jo and Sable were more important than anything else. I gave myself a hard shake to get my mind and body moving, and turned towards the door.

"You can't go, we have to stop her!" This time George was yelling, and I was so tired of people yelling. If taking care of her gave me room to think, to figure out how to get to the house, I'd take care of her.

~Carelian, can you come to me?~ I asked as I changed

directions in the hall, going into the next room instead. Part of me registered that Steven was pulling magic in, trying to disrupt Kelly's pull on the air in the room. Air fighting Air, but she already had it listening to her, so he had to offer more. It was getting hard to breathe as the air moved away from my face.

It didn't matter. Getting to Jo and Sable did. Power I had in spades and Baneyarl didn't believe in any of us being helpless, but I needed to be able to focus to get to them. With all this going on I couldn't focus. Even with the mages attacking me I hadn't felt so terrified. All they could have done was kill me. If someone had Jo or Sable, they might kill them. That was unacceptable.

I walked directly towards Kelly.

"You traitor, don't you understand? I had to create art. I needed those supplies to create my masterpiece. There were no other options, and everyone knows you need to do trial runs to create what matters." Her eyes were wide and the feel of offerings being given to Air registered to my magic sense, but it didn't matter. All that mattered was shutting her down and getting to Jo.

They have to be okay. Please let them be okay.

The need to breathe started to sink its claws into my lungs as she backed away from me into the corner. But the previous experiences, the memories, let me push it to the side and continue forward.

"No. I must see my masterpiece be revealed, " she begged as the chair lifted up and flew towards me. I stepped to the side and it sailed into the viewing room.

"I don't care," I said. With no air in my lungs, though my hair whipped around my head, there was no sound. I made a distant note that she had excellent control of Air in general, if overly basic. The need to breathe pounded on me, but it didn't matter as much as getting to Jo. I reached out and laid a hand on her arm.

"No! Don't touch me," she screamed. I almost possessed a shred of sympathy for her. She was either severely deranged or had some other sort of disorder. But the penalty for using magic to kill was death. I sent a Knock Out pulse through her.

None of my college classes covered this, but I'd used it the first time I'd met Special Agent Steven "I'm being an Asshole" Alixant, though I hadn't known it at the time. This aspect of Psychic sent a bolt of electrical energy into a person, specifically targeted at disrupting their neural processes. It would knock out anything with electrical impulses to the brain. Baneyarl had made me practice over and over, convincing Jo and Sable to let me zap them. The headache you got afterward he compensated for with honey and fruits we couldn't get in our world meaning I knew how to knock you out, hard.

I pumped power into my touch, I needed her down and fast. The electrical charge broke past my skin and into hers and I could breathe, I heard things around me even as she arched backwards, hair flying up for a brief second, then she collapsed in a pile. I spun, leaving her crumpled in the corner as people freaked out around me, more than one officer looking at me with fear. I reached the door to the hall as George and Steven got there.

George's eyes were wide, but I swear Steven had the slightest smirk on his face.

"Problem taken care of. I'll let you know if I can come back for the trial. I need to go," I stated as I moved around them heading to the elevator, calculating the time it would take me to get back there, time Jo might not have. Could I get on the subway? A cab? I could rent a car. Take Steven's?

~Carelian?~

~I'm here,~ he said, and the warmth of his body soaked through my slacks and as he leaned against me.

"Munroe, you can't leave," George barked at me and I paused in my beeline to the elevators.

"Yes, I can."

"Actually, he's right. You're required by law to stay in within fifty miles until sentencing and be available to testify if necessary." Steven sounded serious as he kept glancing back into the room and the woman lying there being drugged by the recovered police mages.

"Too bad. I need to leave now. Give me your car keys." My imagination played pictures of them dying due to carbon monoxide or something collapsed in the house and they were trapped or food poisoning. The ways to die filled my head. It was an old house; it could be anything. Weird diseases starting coming up in my mind, or magical mishaps, and every detailed picture of them dying ramped my stress up higher. I didn't know if I could handle Jo dying on me.

I can't lose her like this. I have to be there.

"Cori, literally, I can't. I'm required as an officer of the law to keep you here. I'm sorry," Steve said sounding truly remorseful. Indira stuck her head out of the room looking at me. She had the strangest expression on her face.

"I'll call, have some officers check on your friends, but I need you to come with me, give your full statement and get it filed so we can start processing her. I want her in front of a judge before the drugs wear off, and I want you in the court room if she burns them out of her. It's happened before."

I looked at them and weighed their demands, the law's requirement, against my need to see Jo and Sable. The argument came out on the law's side. But then I weighed it against a house that might be magical. Against the possibilities they might be hurt or dying. Against Jo needing me. The law lost.

"Your problem, not mine. I'm leaving." I continued towards the elevator.

"No you're not! Merlin Alixant, stop her!" George ordered and I saw Steven sigh.

"Sorry Cori, you have to stay." He moved towards me, regret in his eyes.

I made my decision and my stress vanished. I reached down and petted Carelian and felt him purr. He rose up and put one paw on my arm.

"I'm sorry too," I said. Steven's expression changed to alarm, and as he reached for me, I side-stepped taking Carelian with me.

CHAPTER

THIRTY

One of the classic children's books is the Wizard of Chaos, where young Dorothy, an unrealized merlin falls through a rip into the Chaos plane. There she meets a mage who escaped to Chaos from prosecution decades ago. Even with the help of the friends she makes along the way, Dorothy will need all of her magic to get home. But will it be soon enough to register for the draft before her family loses everything. ~ House of Emrys book review

ORDER

The feeling of reality rushing through me lasted only a fraction of a second, and I found myself facing the house. The car sitting in the driveway, untouched. This both worried and relieved me.

~Your ability is improving,~ Carelian mentioned as he bounded up the steps.

"Uh huh," I muttered, shaking my head then racing after him. I grabbed the door, unconsciously bracing myself to be shocked, but it turned in my hand and swung in.

"Jo? Sable?" I yelled out as I crossed into the house, listening for anything, creaks, moans, groans. The house sounded and felt empty. "Carelian can you hear anything?"

~No,~ he muttered into my mind, worry coating the edges of his words.

"Then we search bottom up." I'd only been carrying the small purse, more for show because my phone was in my pocket. I dropped it on the entry table and headed to the basement stairs. I pulled open the door, calling for them as I flipped on the light and clomped down the stairs, Carelian moving much faster and quieter ahead of me.

The basement had nothing besides some dirty clothes and a few spiders, as always it felt like I was missing something, but I couldn't see anything. We headed to the back of the house, stepping out on the porch, empty too. "Where are they?" Part of me knew that if they were in the house, Carelian would have heard them. But I turned and raced up the stairs, only to come to a screeching halt as I reached the landing. The door to the memento room was shut, but the door to the third level, the one I'd tried to get into only to be told no, was wide open. It swung slowly back and forth, actively taunting.

"Carelian?"

His head lifted, lips drawn back as he scented the air. ~They were here. I smell them up the stairs, but it ends.~ He moved a step or two in, but like me, he wasn't eager to go rushing up the stairs. ~I cannot scent them now. I should be able to, this house is not that large and scents linger.~

Eyes narrowed, I headed up the stairs and looked into the room. My awareness narrowed down to a single sandal laying on the floor. Blue with green beads, the ones Sable had been wearing when we drove up here.

I wanted to rush in there, to find them, but if I disappeared here too, Marisol would never know. Fighting my own inclinations, I took a big step back and pulled out my phone. "I'm going to let Indira and Steven know where I am. There will be consequences for what I pulled, but they need to know I'm still in the state. And maybe by the time they get here, I'll know something. "

I hit Indira's name, the phone dialed, but then just disconnected with a No Service message. I frowned and looked at the phone. No signal at all.

"That's odd. I had a signal the other day." I headed to the balcony, figuring I'd step outside and try again. The door was locked. I looked closer at the knob, maybe the lock had been flipped. All I could see was the deadbolt up above, but the knob wouldn't even turn in my hand.

Any calmness that might have settled in my soul started to boil off. I turned and raced down the stairs, almost falling twice in the new boots. I grabbed the handle of the front door and twisted, but it wouldn't open either.

One last chance. I hit the back door and sighed in relief as it opened. I stepped onto the porch, Carelian at my heels, and I froze. Where not ten minutes earlier there had been a grassy lawn, an orchard, and some empty space that would make a great garden, now there was grayness. A color and thickness that I recognized.

"Carelian, can you reach Baneyarl or your mother?" While I could, I needed to concentrate and think, while for Carelian it was second nature. He'd be much faster at it than me.

His ears laid back against his skull, eyes closed while his tail lashed. Just when I was starting to get my hope up, he replied. ~No. There is something blocking me. I have never been unable to contact my *malkin*. Ever.~

I sagged back against the door frame, staring at the gray. I could sense magic, it felt like a damp wet blanket all around us and even in the Spirit realm I never sensed this much magic.

"I guess it's just us then." I wasn't sure of the swirl of emotions coursing through me, but I grabbed onto the one I could use. Anger. "So be it. If Magic wants a dragon, Magic is going to get a dragon." I looked down at my familiar, my friend, my family. "You good with that?"

Carelian purred and rubbed against me. ~My powerful quean. You will show her.~

Yes, I would.

"First things first, let's leave a message for my mentors. And I'm not going on a rescue mission in this." I waved at my new clothes. "If I'm going hunting for magical jerks, I'm doing it in clothes that I'm not going to freak out at every stain. Besides, I want my boots." I headed for the master bedroom. While I hadn't planned on working as a paramedic while here, habit meant I'd packed my boots, and a medium med kit. I'd go prepared to rescue my friends.

At this point they'd been missing for almost two days, so me being properly prepared wasn't going to make it worse and it might just make it better.

It took me about an hour. I made sure I ate a huge meal, both of us, almost stuffing myself, but I had a feeling this wouldn't be quick and I needed to make sure I had energy. I didn't know when I'd get to eat next.

I packed my backpack full as I could get it, but still carry it comfortably. Merlin knew what I'd be facing, and I wanted to leave as many clues as I could. When I was ready a letter lay on the entry way table and I'd taped a "PROP OPEN DOOR" message facing the outer door. In theory they should see it before they opened the door, but who knew what would actually happen or if they'd be able to open the door at all. I'd done what I could.

Carelian and I stood at the base of the stairs peering up to the door at the top. I had changed into cargo pants, tank top, long sleeve shirt, and my boots. I had filled the backpack with food, water, bowls, med kit, and some extra clothes for everyone. I'd packed a lot of food. If I had to be in there for days, I wanted to make sure hunger didn't make me weak, and it was possible Jo and Sable needed food too. Then there was food for Carelian, who had graciously agreed to eat tuna or salmon in packets due to the difficulty of packing fresh fish. The only electronics I'd packed had been a flashlight, and I'd tossed in a lighter. You never knew when a bit of flame would come in handy.

Plus, I'd crammed in a pair of flip flops and extra socks just in case. I left my phone on the desk in the study. It wasn't going to work where I was going anyhow. I suspected I'd need to use a lot of magic, so I'd taken the time to create twenty tiny braids around my head, each with a different colored band. This way I could just offer sections of the braid as needed. My hair might be horribly choppy later, but I wouldn't have to think or focus on my offering. I still had to focus to make my offering cosmetically pleasing. Getting too used to offering up blood wasn't wise, no matter how much magic liked that offering.

"We ready?" I couldn't take my eyes off the stairs, but I knew Carelian sat next to me, his tail stroking my legs.

~On to adventure. I knew I picked the right queans.~

I snorted. "You need your fuzzy scalp examined if you think this is something I want."

~Perhaps. But it is the life you will lead.~

Starting to climb the stairs, I groaned. Part of me was running around screaming like I'd just had a millipede climb up my pants while the rest of me bubbled with a level of excitement and anticipation that surprised me. Either way, I was doing this.

I stepped over the threshold and looked around, Carelian next to me. I peered into the shadowy space, then an offended meow and a thump made me jump. I turned. Carelian was giving the closed door an angry glare.

~It pushed me. Almost closed on my tail.~ His outrage filtered through as I stared at the door. But the fact that his tail had not been cut off reassured me. Powerful, but not cruel. That was a good sign. I turned back to face the room and froze.

I would have sworn not a moment before there had been walls, windows that pointed out to the front of the yard, and a wooden floor that needed some attention. Now it was all gone. The floor looked more like packed dirt and the shadows flickered to gray moving shapes.

"I don't think we're in Kansas anymore," I muttered. I looked around, but the only thing I could see was the door standing behind me, no longer attached to a wall. "Like that isn't creepy and weird." I looked at the seemingly endless nothingness around me and sighed. "Any idea which way?"

Carelian had his ears laid back, and the gray light made him look browner than his shiny red. ~No. This place has no smell and that is wrong.~

I used my nose as much as any human, which is to say little, so I couldn't address that. "Then forward it is." I took two steps and reached down to pick up Sable's sandal. In the gray light I turned it over and it looked like it had just been dropped there.

No damage that I could see. I slipped open one of my cargo pockets and slid it in. I contemplated pulling out the flashlight, but the light was just enough that I didn't think the flashlight would help.

I glanced behind me and the door still stood there, alone and creepy in the grayness. "Do you hear anything?"

Carelian shook his head as he circled me.

"Huh." I turned and walked back to the door. "Hey, would you sit on this side please?"

He flicked an ear at me but sat there while I walked around it. It just stood there, looking like a normal brown house door. I tried the doorknob from the side we'd come in on, where Carelian sat, and it didn't turn. Acting on a hunch I went around to the other side and tried. It turned. I pushed it open, and a wooded glade filled the frame of the door. Carelian eeped in my head.

~That is impressive magic—I see the door opening, but you are not on the other side.~ He stuck his head around and peered at me, then the other side. ~Whoever has created this is powerful and anchored.~

"What does anchored mean?"

~I don't know how to explain it. Ask Baneyarl when you can.~

I glared at him, but he didn't seem to be avoiding, just more like I would have told someone to ask Jo how an engine worked. I knew it was internal combustion but more than that I'd sound like an idiot.

"We go in?"

~Only place that I can see.~

I took a deep breath. "Ready?" He moved next to me and together we stepped into a realm.

THIRTY-ONE

The increase in familiars for archmages is interesting. No one has any hard evidence as to what is driving this, but the stats show a 15% increase in familiars. The next few years of draft may prove very interesting as mages with familiars are always powerhouses. It greatly expands what a mage can accomplish. ~ Magic Explained Online

SPIRIT

The familiar feeling of crossing into a realm washed through me, and I paused. Focusing, I tried to reach for Baneyarl, but I couldn't find him, or even leave a message. I turned to inspect the realm we were in. It took me a bit to see it, but there was a pattern to everything. I'd had enough biology classes to recognize the Fermi pattern in how the trees were placed.

"We're in Order, aren't we?" The sound of my voice was almost discordant among the harmony of the leaves, but it felt good to throw a bit of disorder into this place. Even the leaves rustled in patterns.

~Yes,~ he hissed in my mind. ~Too rigid.~ He stopped mid tail lash and jerked his head to the left. ~I scent them. This way.~

I wanted him to run, but both of us walked slowly, looking for traps or danger lurking. The air smelled like fresh pine, but I winced at the crunch of grass under my feet. I did everything possible to make sure we didn't damage anything that could be avoided, even to dropping to my hands and knees and crawling under some low hanging branches. I didn't want to do anything to make whoever was doing all this any more annoyed than they obviously were.

Because it was Order, getting on my hands and knees even with the backpack kept me from doing anything more than disturbing the leaves on the ground, it was just that neat. I followed Carelian, trying to ignore the occasional sharp poke in my knees.

~There, I see my queans,~ Carelian murmured.

I wanted to ask why he was whispering in my mind, but I didn't, I just finished inching through the gap under the trees and stopped next to him. He crouched, peering at another clearing. It looked very much like the one we had just left, orderly, neat, and somehow cold. But in this clearing, I could see the figures of Jo and Sable floating in a column of light, Sable missing her left sandal.

No matter how badly I wanted to rush out there and grab them, I didn't. I looked around trying to figure out why I was here. All I saw was a glade with two bodies floating in it.

My heart was clamped in a vise. ~Carelian, are they alive?~ I whispered it in his mind, mainly because to hear those words out loud might destroy me.

~I... believe so. I smell no decay, and there are two very slow heart beats.~ It wasn't the instant reassurance I wanted, but it would have to do.

I crawled the rest of the way until I was clear of the branches, then stood up and walked towards them. I scanned the area as I walked trying to figure out what else I might be missing. No matter how carefully I sorted through the sounds, I heard nothing but the harmonious leaves, which started to sound even more creepy. My BFF hung suspended in light looking for all the world like she floated in peaceful sleep. I reached out to touch Jo, needing to make sure she was okay. Her hair floated around her like silken tentacles as she hung there, a look of peace on her face. My hand slid off whatever had them hanging there suspended.

I can't even touch her.

I stepped back and looked again, but I had no idea how or what was holding them there, much less how to break them out. I walked around again, trying to see if I could sense anything, but all my magic sense told me was magic surrounded us. Not exactly helpful. I stepped back pondering.

"Any idea?" I asked Carelian softly. It still felt unwise to be tramping around here.

~No, but my quean will figure it out.~ He settled down facing their floating bodies, but his ears flicked at every noise, tail and whiskers twitching. I resumed inspecting what held my friends.

"What? No rage or casting magic to get them free? No showing how powerful you are?" That voice I'd been hearing in my nightmares filled the clearing and I pulled myself up a bit straighter. As I didn't see anything by my friends, I pivoted in a slow circle and stopped at about 270 degrees. There stood a form, humanoid but swathed in so much swirling gray I couldn't define anything else. Even the voice didn't give me an idea, though assigning gender to realm denizens could get you in trouble.

"I take it they are bait?"

"Of course. You left. You must pass or fail the tests, but you left rather than facing them. That could not be tolerated."

I blinked. The being sounded almost petulant, as if I hadn't followed the plan. I looked around at the symmetry surrounding us and felt an odd spurt of hope.

"Yes, I was called away. But I'm here now." I settled down on the ground, and pulled out some the snacks I'd packed, cheese and nuts. Offering meat when I had no idea what it was might be unwise. "Would you like something to eat? Walking through all this beauty has stirred a hunger." I held out the container of nuts and cheese and then set it on the ground. My stomach was clenched up so tightly that the idea of food made me want to be sick, not to mention I was still stuffed, but I picked up an almond and popped it in my mouth.

The being froze then glided over towards me. "You are strange. I have your friends, why do you not threaten me and prove your strength?"

"Are you planning on hurting them right now?" I fought to keep my voice level, but my fists clenched as I waited.

"That depends on you." The being leaned closer, inspecting the nuts. "What else is in there?"

"Dried fruit," I said and reached out to take another dried cranberry and pop it in my mouth. The tartness helped to center me as I bluffed. "Do you really want me to attack?"

"Why won't you follow the plan?" There was a whine in its voice this time and the being stomped a foot, the movement full of exasperation. "So be it." It waved its hand and the three statues from the memento room appeared. "See the folly of those who went before you. Can you be what they were not?"

I shrugged and tried to keep the shivers of terror under control. "Since I don't know what they wanted, I can't answer that. I just would like my friends back, safe." I tacked on that last word hurriedly. The last thing I could handle was them coming back hurt because of me.

"Heralds, I thought they were supposed to be the best she had to offer. But no, I get the dense one. Are you the herald magic wants?"

How do I answer this?

I'd always figured honesty was the best policy, plus I had no idea what lie would be the right lie for this situation. Besides, you never knew who could truth sense.

"Probably not. I don't want to be a herald. I don't even really want to be a mage." I carefully packed away the food. Stalling for time. "But it seems I don't really get to choose what I want." I sealed up my backpack and stood. "What do I need to do to rescue my friends? And what do you want?"

The figure froze and I got the sensation of being exposed from the soul on out. I stood there feeling more on display than when I was trying on clothes dressed only in lingerie. Carelian rose and brushed against me and I sank my fingers into his fur, letting his existence center me.

"You are most strange. I want to know my owner is a worthy one. Magic wants to know if you are worthy to wield the power you do. Those with powers like you can destroy as easy as they can create. It is a balance, one that must be kept."

That actually made much more sense and would explain why so few re-emerged mages were being found. If magic wanted to keep a balance, and those people before me were uber powerful, magic eliminated them when they didn't pass whatever requirements she had. I struggled to swallow past the lump in my throat, but I didn't move or run. I would never abandon Jo or Sable.

"Okay, so what now?" I was proud that my voice didn't shake as I spoke.

Behind each of the figures a rip appeared then widened into a full portal. "There are three challenges you must pass. Arrogance, Wrath, and Avarice."

All the emotions I'd seen encapsulated in their statues. Even now I could almost feel them radiating those emotions. I let out a shaky breath.

"Okay. What do I do?"

The figure tilted its head and waved a limb at the rips. "Face the challenges, of course. Is that not what heroes do?"

I laughed. "I'm not a hero. I'm just Cori." Even as I said the words the comments that Gar had told me—had it only been four or five hours ago?—came flashing back in my mind.

~You are a paramedic. You save people. If that is not a hero, I do not know what is,~ Carelian whispered in my mind.

"Just Cori that has a gryphon teaching her? Just Cori that has Tirsane's favor on her neck? Just Cori that has a kit of one of the Chaos lords?" The voice mocked me as she talked.

"Wait? Esmere is a lord? What does that mean?" I blurted. "And who are you? Who are you to do Magic's bidding? And why is Baneyarl teaching me, teaching us, so important?"

The being stared at Carelian, who found his paw of great

interest and was cleaning it, showing off the razor-sharp claws on each finger.

"Because you amuse me, and because you are so woefully uninformed, I may answer some of your questions after you successfully defeat the first challenge."

I glared at both of them. If acting like a dragon or a merlin would stop people from NOT telling me stuff, it was completely worth it. I pulled myself up to my full height, oddly missing those low-heeled boots, and gave it a hard look.

"Swear you will answer all my questions when I complete the first challenge."

Laughter, familiar from the first time, filled the cleaning. "You are amusing. I will answer some of your questions. Some are not mine to answer." Even though it didn't have eyes that I could see, the meaningful stare at my familiar was obvious.

"Three questions," I countered. Even I knew specifics were very important.

"Very well. Three, though refusing to answer a specific question is possible."

I narrowed my eyes at the creature then nodded. "Agreed."

"Excellent, now please go and don't fail. Because you will not turn into a statue. They thought failure meant they would not be beholden to magic, but they would keep what they earned. For you, you will keep what you want, but your friends will die. Remember that. Their lives are in your hands." It paused and looked at the three statues. "Besides, you are not as well dressed as they were. You would be an awful addition to my collection."

I sputtered at the insult, then straightened. "I am wearing appropriate clothes for adventuring. Pockets are important." Then it dawned what she was saying. "And I have no intention of failing. Spending the rest of eternity as a not dead statue has no appeal." I looked at the mages and shuddered. "None at all."

"Then you must defeat the challenge." The creature just stood there, and I wasn't a hundred percent sure it was even standing on the ground.

"I will," I said my smile shaking at the edges. This entire scenario was insane, but for Jo and Sable, I'd do what I must. "Come on, Carelian. Let's go explore the crazy tests."

He rose and moved towards me.

"No. You must fail or succeed on your own. The focus may not assist you."

Carelian hissed and I clenched my hands to control the shaking. Go in there alone? Without him by my side.

~I am her focus; I must go with.~

"Magic says not. She is the one being tested, not you. Your nature is not in doubt."

He growled, tail lashing, and sank back down. ~I will wait here for her to return triumphant. My quean is powerful and will defeat your challenges.~

"We shall see. Choose, Cori Munroe. What do you fear the most?"

THIRTY-TWO

The OMO released a study on telepathy aka mindspeech last week. While familiars have always been able to talk to their mage, most of the time they never talk to anyone else. However, more and more evidence is coming out that this is by choice, not by a bonding connection as originally suggested. It raises concerns that there is a cultural reason behind the familiar's actions which means they have a society in those other realms. A society that doesn't match ours. ~ Magic Explained Online

I wasn't about to tell this being that my greatest fear was the two people it had captured being hurt. Instead, I secured my pack and strode towards the portal of Wrath. If I was going to fight anyone I might as well get it over with now.

I ignored the weight of the being's regard while Carelian's gaze draped over me like a protective blanket. With false bravado I walked into the portal. The ground between one step and the next was at least six inches lower. I stumbled, falling to one knee, just managing to stop myself from tumbling to the ground.

Kneeling there, I looked around the area I'd found myself. Trees and bushes overhung a path that led deeper into the forest. I rose rubbing the bruises on my knee and looked behind me. The entrance was gone, instead an impenetrable wall of trees stood behind me, judging me.

You're losing it. Trees don't judge.

~Carelian?~ I tried. We'd talked across realms before, but there was no answer this time. That didn't surprise me, though it lowered my already low mood. I shook myself and started down the path to my trial. Whatever that would be. I moved along the path and I swear every branch, root, and cobweb grabbed at me or tried to trip me, and we won't talk about how many wispy bits of webbing ended up in my mouth. By the time I reached a clearing, I was tired, annoyed, trying very hard to not think about spiders in my hair, and more than a bit frazzled.

Center. Figure out what the challenge is and get it done and out of here.

I looked around the area and realized it wasn't a clearing, but a small town. If you were talking fairy tales or medieval times small town. The houses were all huts with thatched roofs and simple walls. Their windows, where there were any, looked like they had blankets stretched across them. I turned around, not sure what I was looking for, but wanting to get an idea. Six houses, all about the size of my bedroom, one bigger house with a stable next to it, and a well in the center. That was it.

Where the hell am I? And more importantly what am I supposed to do?

An old woman stepped out of the bigger house, a bucket in each hand, headed towards the well. I angled my trajectory to intersect with her.

She looked up as I approached, her eyes narrowing, but she didn't stop until she reached the well.

"Excuse me, ma'am. Do you know what I'm supposed to do?"

She looked up at me and I blinked, realizing she couldn't be much older than thirty-five or so, but her hair was gray and she had wrinkles that made me cringe.

"Stupid one, ain't cha," she spat and started to lower the bucket into the well via the hand crank.

I sighed and forced a smile. "Probably. But if you wouldn't mind explaining it?"

She spat to one side, then the bucket splashed into the water below. With a heave of effort, she started to crank it back up.

"Let me help?" I said. "In exchange for the information?"

Stepping back, she gave me an evil look, but let me crank. "Thoughts you heroes were all smarty. Knows how to save the princess. Why you asking serving wenches for aid?" Her tone and expression a sneer.

I grunted—the bucket was heavier than I'd thought—but I kept cranking. "I'm supposed to save a princess? And I'm not a hero. Just trying to... save my friends." I heaved the bucket out of the well and set it down for her.

"That I doubt. All the same you are. Gets out of here, we've nothing for the likes of you." She grabbed the full bucket and started to lug it back to the building she'd come from.

"Please?" I called. She just made a sign at me that I suspected was somewhere between being flipped off and warded against. Which didn't help.

"Now where?" I muttered, looking around the oddly quiet village.

"Kiss me and maybe your question will be answered. You will gain power beyond belief."

I spun, trying to figure out who had spoken. Movement grabbed my attention and I saw a large frog on the edge of the well.

"Did you just talk?" I asked cautiously. I wouldn't be surprised but acting out fairy tales step for step seemed a bit surreal.

"See anyone else around or are you just too stupid to realize it," it responded.

I thought about getting annoyed, but since I had a talking cat, I couldn't really blame it.

"Sorry. So, if I kiss you, you'll tell me what I need to know?" I clarified.

"Only one way to find out." It puckered huge wet, green lips at me. I almost started laughing but a simple kiss wasn't that big of a deal. I leaned down and pressed my lips on the frog's lips. They were sticky and cold, and rather reminded me of a pickle.

"Wow, you really are a moron. The guys will never believe I got you to kiss me." With a huge leap, it sprung away and splashed down into the well, leaving me there with wet slimy lips.

I wiped my lips clean, then rubbed my temples, trying to keep my frustration under control. All I wanted to do was figure out what needed to be done. Letting out a frustrated sigh I turned to see a man leaning against a tree at the edge of the village watching me.

He wore only leggings, I think they were called trews, and boots. Shirtless, his musculature was struck by a ray of light making him all but glow with health and vitality. I summoned up a smile and moved towards him.

"Hi. I was wondering if you could tell me where I'm supposed to go?" Though if I'd been dumped in some random town and not a true scenario I was going to be here for ages.

"Are you so desperate you would kiss the creatures of the water to gain their favor?" he asked once I got closer and I was surprised by how beautiful he was. I'd seen movie stars that didn't have his beauty. But his leer as he took me in did nothing to make him more attractive.

"It was a kiss, worst case, my lips got wet. It was a frog after all."

"Ah, but everything here is not as it seems," he drawled pushing himself up off the tree and striding toward me. It was a Hollywood textbook perfect stride, and I couldn't figure out how come his balls didn't catch as he swaggered my direction.

"Then what is it?" I asked, missing Carelian and his claws very much at that moment.

"You never know when a frog is really a prince in disguise."

Shrugging, I resisted the urge to turn around when I heard movement behind me, though I did pull up a thin line of dirt ready to act as a shield if I needed it. "I wasn't so lucky. Do you know what I'm supposed to do or go?"

He stood about an arm's length from me, any closer and he'd be in my personal space. As it was, he leaned closer to me and leered—it wasn't a good look on him. "Give me a kiss and maybe I'll tell you."

The instant nausea made no sense. Kissing a frog hadn't even made me blink, but the idea of kissing him did. "Sure," I said with a bright, and completely fake smile. I moved forward, grabbed his jaw with my left hand, hard, and turned his head. I dropped a quick peck on his cheek and stepped back. The entire thing had taken less than ten seconds. I felt a desire to scrub my lips again.

"There's your kiss. Now which way do I head?" I kept a quirk of a smile on my face as I watched him.

"Very amusing. Now I think I want more." He growled out the words. I suppose it was meant to sound sexy, mostly he sounded like he had a thorn somewhere. He moved into my space, but I snapped my arm out, palm braced on his chest, blocking him from coming in any further.

"No. You can tell me or not, but no." I didn't flinch as he sneered at me, just kept a calm steady gaze, the same one I used on drunks during emergency calls.

"It wasn't enough. Aren't your friends worth my attentions? I don't normally have to force myself on women." He managed to sneer the words and I fought back a shudder.

"They are worth everything, but I'm not touching you." My own dichotomy made no sense in my brain, I'd die for either one of them, but letting this thing touch me wasn't an option. Maybe it was because I knew they would never want that. There were other ways to get the information.

"Who says you'll have a choice?" He lunged at me, grabbing my arms and leering at me. "I haven't had any satisfaction in a long time."

"And you'll get none today. At least from me." I hit him with a low KO, enough to shock badly but not knock out.

He yelped and ripped his hands away from me, then stepped back glaring. "How dare you! You should be willing to do anything to save your friends. Apparently, you don't care about them."

The entire time I'd been walking down the path to wherever

I'd end up, I'd been coming up with plans. I figured at the end I probably had to fight a monster, maybe a flaming demon or something, so that meant I had to figure out ways to disable, even kill. I had ideas, but a simple man didn't require any of the more ruthless ones.

I hoped.

"I do care, but why do something I find repugnant when I have other options. What do I need to do?" I asked the question and steeled myself as I reached for his mind, determined to pull the thoughts out as smoothly as I could.

"Do? You have to fight me!" He roared springing up from the ground. I sidestepped to the other side of the small village as he charged where I had been. He had nothing in his mind but anger and a desire to hurt me. He knew nothing about my quest, or if he did, he wasn't thinking about it right now.

"No thanks. I think I'll be leaving now." I turned and headed out the other side of town. I already knew where I'd come from, but I needed to find where I should go.

"What, are you too good for our Stevie?" I flinched at the name and turned to see the same woman I'd talked to at the well glaring at me. "Too high and mighty for the likes of our Stevie?"

I stared at her, barely remembering to keep my words civil. "No. I just am not in the mood to be raped. Especially by someone who has nothing to do with what I'm looking for. Now if you'll excuse me, I'm going to go see if I can find a castle or a dragon or something." I kept walking and something pinged my shoulder.

I looked down to see a rock and another clod of dirt hit me. "Slut."

"Whore."

"Monster."

"Ugly wench."

I turned to find the source of the cacophony of voices behind me. Standing next to their creep of a village playboy was what looked like most of the people I would have expected to see in a village like this. Men and women, mostly older than thirty, wearing raw, ugly clothes, their faces lined with wrinkles and dirt. They had dirt and rocks, and maybe a vegetable or two in their hands. I had no doubt they were getting ready to throw them at me. Along with the epithets.

"What's your problem? I don't want anything to do with him. I don't like him. I just want to find the monster I need to fight and get this over with."

"Selfish woman. All you care about is yourself. Too proud to spread your legs to save a friend, or maybe you think you're above that."

I wanted to scream at them. I'd do anything to save Jo and Sable, but why waste time and energy having sex when it was stupid. When he was stupid? When they were all stupid?

"Are you going to tell me what I need to do?" Their only reply was more stones and dirt thrown at me. I dodged or ignored most of them. "Fine." I offered way more than I needed to, angry and frustrated, and yanked up a wall of dirt. Their contributions hit it and made it stronger as I turned and stalked out of the village. I'd figure it out. I wasn't sure they weren't just there to delay me, but why? I didn't think I was under a time constraint.

Worry scratched at the back of my mind and I stepped up the pace, the dark path leading me out of the town with people still yelling at me. The trees grabbed my hair, pulling and tangling, and my frustration rode at the top of my mind. As I tried to move forward, it seemed like the path got narrower and narrower.

"Ready to change your mind?" A voice I thought I'd left in the village said ahead of me on the path.

I looked up from focusing on my feet—the roots would appear out of nowhere—to see him leering at me. He leaned against another tree, his manly chest on display.

"No. Either help me or don't, but I won't have sex with you, or more accurately, let you use me." I spat the words out and resisted the temptation to just zap him, hard. But I didn't resist the temptation to try and pull more information out of him with truth forcing. "What am I supposed to do?"

"How should I know? Wow, with a friend like you, who needs enemies." He sneered at me. "They'll die and you'll look back on this and regret your choice. If I keep you here long enough, I get rewarded. I just can't kill you. So why not make it fun? I can make you scream, one way or the other." The words tumbled out, forced by a Truth spell.

My spirits sagged at the words I pulled from him, along with a feeling of guilt for affecting his free well, but his obvious enjoyment of his task tempered it.

"Go away. I need to get going." His aim to delay me ramped up my anxiety and I wanted to be gone. I kept moving forward until he stepped in front of me.

"What if I don't want you to go?" He loomed over me and my temper snapped.

"Then I make you. And if you really want to lay here unconscious in the woods where who knows what could come eat you, be my guest."

"You can't hurt me. Your little lightning trick won't stop me this time."

"Oh, for Merlin's sake," I groused and nailed him with a full KO. He dropped like a sack of potatoes on the path. I looked at his limp body and the dark woods surrounding us and groaned. "I can't just leave him here. Stupid morality."

I offered up a bit more to Earth, it found all this amusing, and asked for help. While Earth smoothed the path just enough so I wouldn't scrape his hide off on the rough path, I dragged him back to the village. Oddly, the path was much more forgiving this time, and my hair only got snagged once. The villagers, about fifteen of them, stood staring at me as I dragged him in and dropped him on the ground in the middle of the road.

"I don't have time for this. Do you know what I need to fight?"

"You killed him!" the well woman screeched.

"I didn't kill him. If I had, I'd just have left him lying there for animals to eat. So here he is. You might teach him some manners," I retorted my patience about gone and the fear that there was a clock counting down creating even more stress.

"You'll never rescue them. You aren't worthy," she spat out the words, then literally spat at me. It hit my face and slid down.

"Eww! Do you know how filthy human saliva is?" I wiped it off with my sleeve and debated digging in my pack for the alcohol wipes, but I figured that would take too much time. "What is wrong with you people? Just leave me alone, I'll figure it out myself."

"Witch!"

"Monster!"

They started screaming more things at me and the rocks and dirt clods accelerated. "ENOUGH," I screamed and let loose a widespread KO thinking yellow as I did it. A full two inches of the braid with a yellow band vaporized and they all collapsed to the ground.

I rubbed my temples, beyond exasperated and verging on angry. "What is it with people? Are people in the realms just not normal? Argh, I have got to get the monster. The trees better let me through or this time there might be some fire making my way."

With a final huff, and a quick double check that no one had seriously hurt themselves crumpling to the ground, I trudged back to the forest path. Interestingly, the branches seemed to leave me alone, which was good as I was fully ready to offer up a lot more hair if it got grabby again. The path seemed wide, and while not welcoming, it didn't have the claustrophobic closeness it had previously.

"Realm geography I swear," I muttered as I headed down the path. After what felt like forever walking, up ahead I saw a cave looming off to one side of the road. "Yes, monster. I can do this." My frustration had faded and now I was worried again about facing a monster.

It doesn't matter, I got this.

I straightened up, brought my various spells to the forefront, and headed towards the shadowy entrance. I cast Lady Luck on myself. I had Break, KO, Murphy, Open, Shake, and Volcano ready. Using Volcano wasn't anything I wanted to do. I'd never used it before, but I would if I faced something I didn't think I could just subdue. The word monster disturbed me more and more as I met creatures from other realms. Baneyarl would be a monster. Tirsane? Definitely. She still freaked me out, but I didn't think I could call her a monster. Not anymore. So what was a monster? Frankly, the people back there had struck me as more monstrous than any of the creatures I had met yet.

Granted none of them have tried to kill me yet. That might change my mind.

Taking one more moment to tighten the straps on my pack, I stepped into the cave with slow careful steps as I moved in. Ahead was a bit of light and as I didn't see any other passages, I walked towards it. At the last step I caught my foot on something and tumbled into the light.

THIRTY-THREE

The mage laws are in place for a reason. We have the 28th amendment to make sure mages never get in control of the country. But unless they are enforced strictly you risk a mage becoming a villain from horror stories: evil, ruthless, unstoppable. Use the laws, weed them out, and make very sure those who remain are on the right side for freedom of this country, even at the cost of themselves. ~Draft board internal memo.

ORDER

T scrambled to my feet, expecting an attack any second. I saw Carelian sitting there looking at me, his head tilted to one side. I turned to see the being, arms crossed, and it felt like it glared at me.

"What? Where is the monster? I can go back. I can defeat it. I just couldn't find it," I protested, turning, ready to sprint back into the portal. But the area behind the man was empty, only grass and trees where I had entered.

"Please? I'll try again." I would have begged if I thought it would do any good. I saw Carelian's tail start to lash back and forth, but I couldn't take the time to focus on him. I had to defeat Wrath.

"I don't know if I like you or really dislike you. You never act the way others have." The tone was petulant, and it floated over to me. "Do you know what he did in that situation?" Its arm lifted up to point at the statue of the male.

My shoulders slumped. "Did he defeat it?" I didn't know anything anymore. Was he wrath? Should I have met up with him? How long had I been here or there? I felt dizzy and so tired that crying seemed like a good idea. That made no sense, why should I be so tired?

"He skinned the seducer alive, though in his test it was a woman. Then he rounded up all the townsfolk and showed them exactly why he was feared. When they didn't give him the answers he wanted, taunting him with his failure to perform, he burned them and the entire town alive." It threw both hands up in the air, the gesture so evocative of its frustration I almost laughed.

"Wait, the town was the test?" I blinked at it, then felt like a complete idiot.

"Yes! And you were nice, took care of them—even when they tried to hurt you, you just put them to sleep. You even pulled the man to a safe place. Are you sure you're a mage? You don't act like one."

Relief made me giddy, and I went over to Carelian and dropped down next to him. I put my head on his shoulder. His deep purr helped calm my emotions. I dug food out of my pack and ate. My stomach informed me it was happy with this addition. I wondered how bad my time sense was here. Had hours or days passed in my world?

"Fine. You defeated wrath, or more accurately, you did not give in to it. Are you ready to face the next one? Avarice?"

I shrugged. "If they are all the same it would be easy to avoid. This one caught me because I wasn't ready for it. But I'm not greedy or anything." At least I didn't think I was.

"They are never the same. Wrath is the only one that follows the same lines. But they are your trials not mine. Pick your next trial." It waved at the two remaining portals, the women standing like guardians and warnings of what my fate might be.

I shoved more food in my face, chewing hurriedly before swallowing. "You owe me the answer to three questions first." That was partly because I wanted to know, and partly because I wanted a chance to eat some more.

It huffed at me, then floated over. "Very well. Ask."

"Who are you?"

It rotated in a circle, the tips of its feet barely touching the ground. "You still do not know? I would have thought Wells would have told you."

"I never met him. He died before I ever knew he existed or that I was a mage, or anything really."

"Ah. As you will either become an immortal statue or my owner, I do not see any risk in revealing myself." It spun faster and faster, the grey peeling away like strips of tissue, to reveal a feminine figure. It was shorter than me, maybe five-three, with arms and legs too long and lanky to ever be human. Though nut brown, her skin looked hard and scratchy. Her head was elongated, and a sharp chin and nose created a profile that reminded me of an almond. Instead of hair she had leaves that twisted and waved in the breeze.

"Wow," I murmured, having no idea what stood before me.

"Is that all you can say, human? Wells was the one who saved me, trapped me, geased me. And all you can murmur is a word."

"Well, I know you look wonderful," I said slowly. Flattery was always a better option that anything else. "But I still don't know who you are." I bit back all the questions I wanted to ask. I only had two left and I didn't want to waste them on something stupid.

"Are all humans this stupid?" her voice full of exasperation again. At this point, if her challenge was to not lose her patience with the mortal, she'd lose.

~Careful. She has never seen your kind, and even I have only seen one once.~ Carelian's warning rang clear in my mind and I focused on putting food away. Eating it all now would be stupid and risky.

"Ah. I forget how blindfolded and sheltered humans are. I am a dryad, my name is Hamiada," she said with a bow. "You should be honored."

"Oh I am. I just don't understand how a mage, even a merlin, could bind and geas a dryad." I crossed my fingers in Carelian's fur.

"Is that your second question?" it asked instead. I sighed. My trick hadn't worked. Oh well.

"No. My second question is, what does being Magic's Herald mean?"

Hamiada shook her head. "I cannot answer that. It is up to Magic what she asks of her heralds. Ask again. "

I chewed on my lip, then asked the question that mattered the most. "If I fail, what happens to Jo, Sable, and Carelian?"

Hamiada turned to me, brows creased. "Happens to your focus? That is up to him. He may stay, though I cannot see a creature of Chaos happy here, or go home or to Earth. That is his call. As for my bait?" She shrugged. "They will wake up in their bed, knowledge of this and the fact that they cannot get you back firm in their minds." She gave me another hard look then her eyes widened. "Did you think I would kill them?" She huffed. "I am not a human to kill indiscriminately. As if I was a crazy human. Last question?" That was snapped at me more than asked, but I pondered what to ask as I tried to mentally prepare for the next test.

"Why are you the house?" It came out a bit plaintive and I suspected I'd wasted a question, but right this moment my mind was in a whirl of other worries.

"Did you not notice something odd in the basement?" Hamiada countered, looking smug.

"No," I replied.

~Yes,~ Carelian said in contradiction.

I glared at the back of his head. "Why didn't you tell me you noticed something weird? What was weird?"

~All human residences are weird. Not bad but weird and I had no way of knowing what was bad weird versus good weird,~ he said, his tail slapping me on the back of the head.

I sighed and looked at the dryad. "Weird doesn't tell me much."

"It is a long story. Maybe if you live, doubtful that, I will share it. But Wells rescued me long ago, and my sapling grew into the house. My branches are in the walls, my roots protect the pipes, my leaves are the shingles on the roof. I am in a very real sense the house."

"I live in a tree house. Neat, I guess. Do we need to do

anything to take care of you?" I asked even as I had horrid images of trying to change something in the house and cutting into a branch or root.

"Take care of me?" Her voice sounded odd, stilted almost.

"Well, I figured you're getting sun and water—but do you need fertilizer or..." I fumbled. I knew nothing about plants. "I don't know, anything else? I mean you're part of the house, so what else do I need to do to keep you healthy too?"

She just looked at me. When I had started to shift, uncomfortable at the unwavering stare—dryads were worse than cats —she moved. "This will be thought about. Now onto the next challenge."

Then I remembered the next thing I was supposed to ask. How much time was passing? I growled at myself. Why did I never remember things when I needed to? I shook my head and stood up.

"I'm ready."

"You need to go and get this gem." She held out her hand and an image appeared there. A large octagonal faceted gem, reflecting red with hints of blue and purple, sat in her hand. "Get this, and only this, and bring it back to me."

I stared at the gem and the image of Aladdin's cave, filled with precious gems, pearls, carpets, and vases appeared in my mind. "Just bring you that and I pass?"

"Yes. You may not bring out anything else at all." Hamiada's voice was firm. She dropped her hand and the image disappeared.

I almost sagged in relief. This I could do. I had no desire for gold or gems, and while a flying carpet might be nice, definitely not worth Jo and Sable's lives. "Not a problem." I turned to look at Carelian who had stilled, his ears canted back. "Watch over them. I'll be back quickly."

I headed to the portal, laying it out in my mind. Find the

path, head on it up it, grab the stone—it looked small enough to slip into a pocket in my pants—and then get back here.

"Wait. Can I get three more questions when I get back?"

Hamiada tilted her head, only the tips of her toes touching the grass. It made her look like she floated. Even the green clothes that hung on her seemed perfect and even. She fit here and my disheveled existence seemed to annoy her.

"Why? You will fail. Caught by the treasures there," she said airily.

I opened my mouth, caught sight of the other statue and snapped it close. I reconsidered what I was going to say. "I think that Jo and Sable are important enough to me to make sure I pass."

"Hmmm. If you survive, I will give you two. Only because I do not believe you will. And if you do the last one, well if you pass that one, then you will own me, and I will answer any question I can."

"I get you as a servant?" That seemed way too much like slavery.

"That is a question. Survive the challenge and you may ask it if you like."

Her smugness bugged me, but I just nodded. If anything, being here made me watch my temper very closely. What had the others risked? Or had they done the challenges for the reward? I didn't think they had been vying for the house. What had their reward been?

The more I thought the more questions I had. Better questions than what I had asked.

Someday I'm going to act and think like a real adult. Not like a stupid kid.

I huffed at myself and spun back to the portal. It swirled in golds, greens, reds, and silvers. It was beautiful and rather intimidating. Compared to the dark opening of the other, this one both attracted and repelled me.

Get the gem Cori. You got this.

I repeated that over and over through my mind as I stepped into the portal.

CHAPTER

THIRTY-FOUR

There have been three investigations into the deaths of people in the draft. However, all cases have been proven to both the Draft board and the OMO investigator to be either reckless endangerment or training accidents. ~ House of Emrys report

---

SPIRIT

I stumbled a bit stepping through and paused to get my balance. When my eyes adjusted to the low light, a shriek forced its way past my frozen lips. I swallowed as I looked at the cliff that dropped away to nothing not one step from me. I didn't have any problem with heights as a general rule but to find myself on the edge of a cliff where I couldn't even see the bottom? Well, that was worth a scream.

It took me a minute to get my trembling under control before turning to look both ways. To my left about fifteen feet away was a rickety rope and wood bridge. With one last glance at the edge of the cliff I carefully made my way to it, casting Lady Luck as I did so. I was going to need all the help I could get.

The bridge looked in one piece, but it also looked hand tied and old. Old dirty ropes as thick as my wrist ran the length of the gap. Each piece of wood looked like it had been hacked out of a table by a toddler with a butter knife. And the posts? Well, they were nice solid stone, old and weathered, cracked, and the home for more species of lichen than I could count. I checked again, but as far as I could see this was the only way across. I triple secured my backpack, making sure even the chest straps were locked and cinched tight. With a deep breath I gave the rope a good yank. Nothing happened. No fraying or ominous creaking or even cracks of wood.

Jo and Sable.

I held that in my mind as a mantra. My foot touched the first rung and with one hand tightly wrapped on either side, I shifted my weight. There was a long groan and I tensed, ready to throw myself back onto land. But nothing else happened. Step by step, my hands aching from how tightly I held the scratchy rope, I crossed the bridge.

Time slowed to step, wait, step. Never letting more than one hand off the side at a time.

Three more steps and the end of the bridge taunted me. I forced myself to continue my slow measured steps, but I wanted to run, to sprint, so badly. One more step. My foot touched the ground and there was a tremendous creaking and shuddering behind me. My heart jammed itself in my throat as I threw myself to the ground and rolled away. After two rolls across the dusty ground, I sat up and looked back expecting to see the bridge in pieces, my only way back lost.

"Are you kidding me?" I shouted. Where the bridge had hung, rickety, dangerous, and something out of a Merlin Blasted Wisconsin Jones Magical Relic Hunter movie, now a gleaming marble bridge, solid and massive enough to support a tank, spanned the chasm. I could all but feel Magic laughing at me, as I figured it would have if the bridge gave and I plummeted to my death.

With my eyes closed I tried to get control of my racing heart. Near death experiences were not anything I enjoyed. Once my heart slowed, I pushed myself to my feet and took in my side of the Try to Kill Cori chasm.

A huge building, grey stone, pillars, hulking gargoyles, the stereotypical temple of doom awaited me. Frowning, I looked back at the other side to the thin ledge. I should have been able to see portal from there, but I couldn't.

Ugh. Magic. Magical Realm.

Exasperation was becoming my default state. Taking a deep breath, I headed into the building. It looked like a cross between a library and a temple. Stepping in, all my previous preconceptions were dashed to the ground. There were no piles of jewels or mounds of gold or even rolls of carpets. And definitely no talking genie.

It was worse.

I swallowed as I moved into the building. Where my imagination had chaotic piles of things, treasures to sift through and hidden objects at every turn, this was like a museum. Collections of jewels laid out on black velvet sparkled at me. Vases and lamps, clearly labeled with their origin and value, sat on pedestals, glowing with beauty.

"Okay, Order. Got it." I swallowed and kept walking. It

reminded me of a Scandinavian furniture store in that the path lead me through and around, with new treasures at every turn. Laid out and presented in ways that called to you, made you want to see them, see how they would look on you. Convenient mirrors sat next to the necklaces and tiaras, and three-way mirrors next to dresses that called to be fondled and tried on.

"I don't need any of this," I repeated and kept walking. The jewels and jewelry petered out as the clothes became more exotic and stunning, though some of them I'd never go anywhere they would be appropriate, so other than the desire to play dress up, I kept walking. An arch appeared and I moved through into a second gallery that reminded me of a library like the National Archives. The books, documents, and pictures were laid out along the path close enough to touch, and so close I couldn't help but read the placards declaring their identity.

True history of Atlantis by Mera.

Magic Explained by Morgana Le Fey – that book was at least eight inches thick.

All known causes of Death by Death.

I stopped in my tracks. That couldn't be what it meant. It had to be a joke. I shook my head and kept walking, but I couldn't stop myself from reading the placards.

Deaths and their Causes by Death

It was open and the day my brother died was written at the top of the page. I froze in my tracks.

Could this be real? Could I find out how my brother died?

I swallowed hard. It would be so easy to lean over. Read the book. Get the answer. I wouldn't take it. The book could stay.

But I would take out the knowledge. I stood there, just far enough I couldn't make out the words.

Get the gem and leave.

I forced myself to turn and continue walking. The next

placard all but grabbed my eyes: How to Cure Anything and Anyone by Asclepius.

My mouth went dry. With that I could save people. They would never have to die again. Surely knowledge wouldn't be taking something. I could figure out how I could have prevented Stevie's from dying. No one else would ever have to suffer. Bobby, the boy in the car. The one who I touched as he died. I could have saved him.

My hand reached out toward the book. I could just read a few pages. Maybe find out how to cure cancer. All the people that alone could save.

I yanked my hand back down. "I'll ask. If she says I can come back and read. I'll ask." I rushed down the path trying so hard not to see. But still things jumped out at me.

A mirror of communication, talk to anyone anywhere.

A bracelet of unification, heal divisions between people.

A necklace of languages, understand and speak every language.

I wanted so much. I could do so much with these things/ I could make so many people's lives better. I could help people.

My vision grew blurry and I realized I was crying as I walked. So many things here that could change so many people's lives. Save children. Were Jo and Sable more important than all the lives I could save? Would they forgive me if they knew what I gave up to save them?

The world fuzzed around me as I stopped. Weighing the consequences. I would get what I took, but they would die. I started to pivot, I wouldn't get the book on Death, but on Curing. I could cure anyone. Maybe even...

I jerked to a halt, remembering what Hamiada had said; "They were told they would not be magic's herald if they failed, but they would get what they took."

It had been a lie. Everything had been a lie. If I took anything from here, I would fail and Jo and Sable would die.

I wanted to scream, to rage; instead I forged ahead, the path suddenly short. It seemed only a minute before I stopped in front of a pedestal with the red gem sitting there, looking dowdy compared to other things I had seen. As if to reinforce my goal, it too had a placard.

Return to Hamiada.

I picked it up and dropped it in my pocket, then spun, anger driving my steps, and headed out of the hall of temptation.

As I rushed back through the displays seemed brighter, catchier, they called for me to look, to explore. The image of the statues remained focused in my mind. If I stole from here not only would Jo and Sable die, but I would be a statue, unable to do anything with the knowledge.

What if she lied?

I slowed. What if she lied about the consequences? I had no idea when those people turned into statues. Heck, I didn't know if anything she told me was true. She might kill Jo and Sable even if I passed the test. The books about Death and Curing lay ahead, bright and seductive. I'd never wanted anything as much as I wanted them. I'd even give up the house if I could have that knowledge. The lives I could save.

The lives it might cost.

I stood between the books. Close enough I could almost read the words. The Cure Anything book had opened and in bold type on the page Types of Cancer was easily readable. The other still lay opened to the day my brother died. A quick look wouldn't hurt. Just to know. Once and for all.

Is that knowledge worth their lives?

The answer was a resounding no. But then the book of cures lay there. How to cure cancer? I'd be willing to die for that. But—

My mind locked on the ethical ramifications. What was the difference between choosing to let Jo die and killing her myself? It was one thing if she was here and said yes. But to take that choice away? To take her life because I thought I knew better, that I knew the value of her life.

Something deep in me recoiled in horror at the thought. That would make me no better than the killer Kelly. Killing for art. Was I willing to kill for knowledge?

Never.

I turned and strode out, the temptation withered and tarnished. When I reached the chasm, I stopped and looked at the bridge. It was stone and solid. I narrowed my eyes and strode out onto it. Three steps in it shivered and began to change.

No. I am tired of being scared. Magic wants me? Well, she's going to get a Merlin blasted dragon.

I stood rocksteady as the bridge shifted. But rather than the rickety rope and wood that I expected, it became a wondrous thing of gold and silver. Filigree work graced the railings, the arch constructed of fleur-de-lises and swirls. The base a solid shining metal that led in a graceful swoop to the land on the other side.

"Is this your way of saying I passed?" I asked, looking around. I still couldn't see much more than a cliff and a temple, but it felt warmer and less oppressive than it had. There wasn't any answer that I noticed, and I walked across the bridge as if it was as steady as one human built. No matter how much I expected it to crumble underneath me.

My wariness remained until I stepped back through the portal into the glade.

CHAPTER
THIRTY-FIVE

The monsters that were reportedly at the SEC game in Atlanta should be of great concern to humans. They are examples of what happens when magic runs amok. Do you want your child changing into a snake creature or being eaten by a blob? For the sake of all humanity, we need to walk away from magic now before it is too late. ~ Freedom from Magic

"You passed. I—" Hamiada broke off staring at me. "I did not expect you to succeed."

I placed the stone in her hand and walked over to look at Jo and Sable hanging in the air. If they were aware and with me, I'd be talking this over with them. As it was, I still had one more trial to pass. That last one had been closer than I liked.

"Did you lie?" The question slipped out and I snarled—that wasn't what I wanted to waste one of my questions on.

"That is a broad question. About what?" She looked curious not smug, and I didn't know if that was better or not.

"About me getting to keep what I found. The knowledge. Them turning to statues because they failed. All of it."

"Oh, that." She smiled a tiny bit, but it was sad almost. "I will answer that question after the final trial. So that question does not count. What else did you want to ask?"

I clenched my fists and turned to look at my friends. Carelian came over and rubbed against me, the heat from his body sinking into my leg. Letting myself pet him, I tried to calm down and focus on the question I needed to ask.

"Time. How much of it is passing here?"

Hamiada furrowed her brows together. "As much time as it takes."

"No. I mean, if I spend an hour here, how much time is passing on Earth? In my realm."

"This is not the Underhill domain, simply a pocket next to your house. Time flows double there, I think." She smiled as she said that, revealing round green teeth, reminding me she was not even remotely human.

I pulled my eyes away from her teeth and glanced at my watch. I'd been here about six hours. Which meant twelve hours had passed. By the time I got back I'd probably have people banging on my door, demanding my surrender.

Good thing I didn't grab that info, I probably wouldn't be free long enough to use it.

I pushed all that away. Nothing mattered now but getting Sable and Jo home.

"Is there not more?"

Hamiada's voice pulled me out of my own thoughts, and I frowned at her inquisitive look.

Oh yeah, I get one more question.

My brain felt like a wet fog had fallen on it and I struggled to push everything away and focus.

~Cori?~ Carelian asked, his tone worried. I didn't respond but scratched his ears. The need for caffeine clammed into me so I sat, pulling out one of the mini cokes I'd stashed in my pack. It was a bit dented, but the can opened. I spent a tiny fraction of offering to cool it down. More than worth it. Warm Coke sucked.

The icy cold carbonation poured down my throat, washing away some of the film from my throat and my spirit. I took a deep breath and let the air from the glade flow down my throat and forced my shoulders to relax. I could do this. I needed to do it.

"Second question, does Salistra know you're doing this?" I was mostly curious to see how autonomous her actions were. If it was her and Magic or if there was something or someone else involved. I touched my necklace, but the idea of bringing Tirsane into this scared me more than almost anything.

A huge smile crossed her face, and she leaned closer to me, her teeth bright green beads. "Who do you think has been helping with all this?"

I suddenly needed to pee. I was so scared my body

contracted every muscle. My throat wouldn't work, and my lungs wouldn't inhale.

Oh Merlin, I'm going to die.

~See powerful quean,~ murmured Carelian. That shocked me into movement as I whipped my head to stare at him, the braids lashing at my face.

"Are you insane?" I sputtered at him. "I don't need the gods of the realms taking any interest in my life."

Hamiada snorted. "They are not gods, not exactly, and I do not think I am insane. But then, by your definitions maybe I am. Are you ready for the final test?" She watched me with unblinking green eyes.

I didn't bother to correct her assumption I'd been talking to her. The rush of fear-driven adrenaline cleared up any remaining exhaustion or mental fog.

"Yes. Let's get it over with."

"I shall watch this with great curiosity."

I sighed as I carefully drained the Coke can and put it away. "What is the trial?"

"Survive and do what you think is the best thing to do until the portal reappears."

"That's it? Just survive? Not get something or defeat something?"

"Do you really wish it to be more difficult?" Hamiada didn't quite laugh at me, but I could sense it.

"No, just checking. I want to make sure I get this done. Get my friends out of there." I gazed at the pillars of light. At least they didn't have to wait, wondering if they would live or die.

"Then you had better succeed, hadn't you?" She waved at the remaining portal.

I gave her a look I hoped was confident. "Yes, I will."

I headed towards the portal, this one an opaque silver gray

that told me nothing, but it had an odd elegance I rather enjoyed.

"Once more into the breach," I whispered and stepped through. This time it felt like walking through a fog rather than pulling ice through a membrane. I don't know how long I walked. My watch had gone wonky, and I just put one foot in front of the other. Boredom set in as I walked, but I didn't dare stop. My eyes fought to stay open as I plodded through the gray tunnel.

One step after another. I covered my mouth as I yawned. If this was the trial, I might fail 'cause I'd fall asleep with this slow nonstop walking. Trying to keep focused wasn't happening, my mind drifted to items in that place of temptation, and a pang of what might have been slashed through me. It grew stronger and hotter, and my eyes flew open—I shrieked as flames washed over me.

I made a desperate offering, giving away more than I ever would have normally to Fire, asking it to not burn me. The heat seared across my skin, then vanished as Fire accepted with a laugh. I panted for a moment as I tried to figure out where I was. Flames washed around me, flicking across my skin and clothes, but not burning. The hot air rushing into my lungs didn't help me to calm down as I turned, frantic to find a way out.

There to the left, the flames were thinner, and I thought I saw blue sky. With a gasp of relief, I jogged that direction. The fire faded and I stepped out onto a wide stone plaza. The cool air eased my lungs and skin as I gazed out at what stared back at me.

It was a triangle plaza with walls at least fifteen feet high. From where I stood at one tip it was at least fifty yards to the opposing wall. There was with a large round raised section in the middle. Large gates stood in the walls from my tip, leading to elsewhere. But what made me stand there like a deer with an oncoming semi was everything else. The other two points of the triangle were stadium seating for at least a thousand and they were packed with beings.

Not humans, beings.

I saw feathers, scales, beaks, wings, hide, skin, hair, talons, claws, and more things than I could put names to. I didn't even have names for all the beings I saw.

And they all stared at me.

I glanced behind me, just on the off hope that maybe there was something behind me. What I saw didn't help my panic levels at all. Where the other two points of the triangle had banners hanging from them, I had an archway of flames leading to where I'd come from.

Why me?

I rotated back to look at everyone looking at me.

What by Merlin's balls do I do?

My feet felt like they'd been encased in mud and I didn't know where to go. Even the flames were starting to seem attractive. Movement at the raised dais grabbed my attention. It looked round or oblong and had another stone structure on top of it that went up about three or four feet. But what caught my attention was the movement. On either side of the raised stone structure were two statues. One of a hippogriff and one of a Cerberus. I knew it was a hippogriff because instead of lion-like front paws, it had eagle-like legs and claws.

It was a beautiful gold and cream color, the only breaks in the color scheme being the black talons and the bright yellow beak. Which is why I had assumed it was a statue.

~Are you the challenger from Magic here to test our worthiness and our offerings?~

The voice rang in my head, deep and mellow, like a brass bell in a monastery.

"Huh?" was my super intelligent answer. I coughed to clear out the phlegm caused by the heat of the fire and my own panic. "I'm sorry. What?"

~You entered via the realms gate. Therefore, you were sent by Magic. Is this not true?~ There was a warning tone in his voice and my heart rate, which had just started to level out, sped back up.

Don't lie. Never lie. Tell the truth.

"I was sent here for a trial. Magic is involved in why I am here." That was the truth. It just ignored all the complications of my life. But that made me look around. How was this a test of my arrogance? Which I still didn't think I was. Before I had time to focus too much on that another voice spoke.

~Then we shall assume Magic sent you. We are the guardians of the offerings. We shall defeat you to prove our offerings are worthy of Magic.~

Huh? What did that mean?

I must have looked like an idiot blinking at them but that vanished as the hippogriff threw a spear at me. Reflexively I dove to one side, pulling Lady Luck to me. I rolled just in time to miss the attack from the Cerberus. Three jaws snapped at me as the hippogriff charged me.

"Merlin!" I yelled and grabbed Earth and begged. A bit of braid vaporized as stone burst upward blocking the Cerberus and I scrambled to my feet. My mind scattered and I fell back on my reliable spells. I reached and pulled the spirit from the hippogriff then let it snap back in.

A screech of pain and shock cut through the roars of the crowd, then it echoed back even louder. The crowd filled the arena with their stomping and clacking. My heart beat with the rhythm they set.

Hot breath on my neck had me dropping and rolling. I really

needed to get some martial arts training at this rate. Teeth snapped as I fell, close enough that saliva splattered me.

"What is it with you people and saliva? Ewww."

I readied a KO and reached out to touch the Cerberus, but it jumped back barking. The bark slammed into me with the force of a sonic wave and I snarled. A matching screech came from above as a shadow flickered above me.

One of the spells I'd only read about came to mind, and with a fast offering to Entropy I cast Disrupt straight up. It wasn't a KO spell, in that it would knock someone out, but it had correlations. Disrupt jumbled the targets thoughts and they lost track of their focus.

As I sent it up, I spied a heavy chain around the dog's neck and grinned. With another offering to both Earth and the oddness of Non-Organic, I increased the magnetic attraction between his collar and the metal in the earth.

Groaning, he fell to the ground, neck laying stretched out where the collar held him down.

I stood and looked around. The hippogriff lay shaking its head trying to remember what had been going on while the Cerberus panted, unable to move. I'd ripped up stonework and managed to tear my shirt at the elbow, raw bleeding flesh stinging at my awareness. The stadium fell silent as I stood there shaking with adrenaline and rage.

~Pax. We are defeated. Magic's Herald is mighty indeed. Do you deem us worthy of the offerings?~ The voice, the hippogriff's I thought, rang in my mind.

"Sure. You're worthy." I had no idea what I was talking about and just wanted this over with.

~Then release us, Herald, and we shall finish the offering.~

With a wary swallow, I cancelled the magic holding the dog down. The Disrupt had been fading anyhow. They both rose to the cheers of the beings watching. This entire thing made no sense, but I'd try to roll with it.

They walked towards me. I tensed, ready to sidestep or something, but they bowed to me. Which was almost worse than attacking me.

~Follow us, Herald, and we will complete the offering.~

They turned and walked to the dais, bounding up. I followed a bit slower and had to heave myself up—it was almost two feet high.

They stood next to the raised cylinder and the hippogriff had one foreclaw high in the air above the raised section.

~We have witnessed the acceptance from Magic's Herald. Now we offer up those that are ours to the will of magic. By blood and spirit, we renew our fealty to that which we are.~

I moved over to the raised area and looked down. Rage and horror flooded through me.

"By Merlin's magic, what is wrong with you!" I screamed and pulled on Earth, offering my own blood as the talon swept down.

CHAPTER

THIRTY-SIX

House of Emrys is looking for some mages interested in investigating the deaths of seventy percent of the BAM (Bad Ass Mages) gang a few weeks ago. Contact Scott Randolph for information. There is a reward for any conclusive evidence as to the cause of the deaths. Security protocols enacted. ~ House of Emrys job notice

---

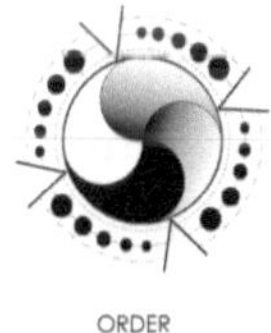

ORDER

Earth flowed up and the wickedly sharp talons bounced off it. The two I had just fought spun and glared at me. This time I could feel their rage. I didn't care. My rage burned just as hot.

My hand waved to the dome I had created to protect the three creatures laying there. In the few seconds I had to look their existence had seared into my mind with clarity that only terror brings. Something I knew too well. I could still remember every inch of the emperor of Japan's inner chambers when I dragged his assassin there.

"You were going to offer these babies to Magic?" I demanded as I let the dome crumble and stared at the three babies.

Even though I'd never had much of a maternal instinct it was all I could do not to reach down and sweep them up in my arms. Except that I couldn't carry three of them. One was a Cath kit, its fur a chocolate brown, with amber eyes and white tufts on its ears. It looked up at me mewing, the bowl too deep and smooth for it to climb out. The other looked like a baby gorgon, it even had its shell with it. Coiled and hissing as the baby snakes on its head twisted and lunged at nothing. Even with dark black scales on its lower body and a human baby face except for the slitted eyes it still managed to look cute. The third was a Chittarian like Charles' Arachena. Chittarians were creatures with too many legs. The tiny baby crouched in a cage, green and gray colors flashing as its legs moved up and down as if typing.

"How could you do this?" I demanded, wanting to cry.

"You are interfering, Herald. Step back and allow the ritual to continue," the Cerberus bellowed, hot breath and spittle flying at me.

I snarled back. "Never." If I stood by and allowed these children to come to harm it would be the same as sacrificing Jo assuming she wanted to be sacrificed. I pulled a dome over the kids again, and tried to think of what to do.

But in the few seconds that took, the stands had emptied of beings and they were all charging me. While reading emotions on beings that were not human was not my forte, it didn't take any stretch of the imagination to decide they were extremely unhappy with me.

"Crap." I panicked, trying to balance out protecting the kids and staying alive. I scrambled up on top of what I now realized was an altar and wasn't that creepy, and created a time bubble. The altar and I with the kids jumped five minutes ahead in the time line. Five minutes seemed to be my default if I didn't have time to concentrate.

"Crap, crap, crap. I'll get you out of here. Promise," I muttered as I spun trying to think. To my horror and astonishment, the hippogriff snarled and blurred, then he was in the time bubble with me.

"Ack!" I croaked and fell off the raised altar. The bubble stretched, but not enough. Desperate I pushed it out so it encompassed the raised dais, but that pulled in three other creatures. A Cath, with a midnight black coat, ears laid back hissing at me, a centaur, and what looked like a larger version of Elsba, the flying snake.

"Oh shit," I muttered as I hit them with a Disrupt. Maybe if I did that I could get them with a KO. I had never practiced wide casts like what I'd seen at the fairgrounds. Another thing to remember to do at a later point.

If I survived.

It hit the snake thing, but the Cath, Centaur, and hippogriff knocked it aside. Worse, I felt something coming at me. I pulled the dust from the dome into a shield around me so the magic hit it instead of me, dispersing to my relief. Before I could come up with another attack, the ground under my feet began to tremble.

I offered a huge amount, feeling another chunk of braid vanish as I begged the Earth to not do whatever was being asked. It became a clash of wills between the Centaur and me. I had no idea how I knew it was him, but I did.

The snake rose back up, hissing in obvious fury and shooting a stream of liquid from its mouth. My dust shield stopped it, but the materials started to dissolve. A spear flew towards my throat. Squeaking, I sidestepped out of the time bubble, figuring they needed the ritual to hurt the kids, and right now everyone was very focused on me.

I collapsed to my knees as time slammed into me.

Note to self, don't sidestep out of a time bubble.

I shook myself and pushed to my feet. The mass of furious beings had shifted, turning to face me. Nothing in my life had ever prepared me for the amount of fear that pumped through me. I was looking at my death and I knew it. I could see fireballs being readied, whirlwinds spinning up, teeth and claws bared, all with the intent of killing me.

The sound. If I lived long enough that sound would haunt me forever. Claws on stone, the rustle of wings, the growl from too many throats. I'd never realized that leather versus scaled versus feather wings all sounded different. I knew now. I also knew what rage smelled like. The odor mugged my senses, so thick it felt like a coating of musk, smoke, and regret. If I'd had anywhere to flee, I might have. If I could have taken the kids with me.

I clenched my hands. So be it, but I would go down fighting. I wouldn't let anyone murder kids. Being attacked by hordes of realm beings is an excellent motivator to extend your abilities. I knew the theory of wave KO; I'd even seen it done. I now had about three seconds to figure out how to cast it.

"Screw it," I muttered and offered a solid inch from the bottom of my hairline and mixed in the blood from the abrasion on my arm. And I thrust. There was an odd reluctance, but it was accepted, and I threw out the KO.

To my joy and horror half of them dropped unconscious as I disrupted the electrical impulses to their brains. The rest kept coming. And that was more than enough to kill me.

I'm sorry, Jo.

I grabbed Earth and pulled, shooting me straight up and almost knocking me off balance. That barely slowed the mob as half of them began to fly or climb straight towards me. Plus, the lovely fact that I'd gone up high enough that falling would result in significant injuries.

I didn't know what else to do.

I'm going to fail everything, and those kids are still going to die.

~HALT!~

A voice like a crystal knife cut through the plaza and my brain. I sagged as a spike of pain made me go blind for a moment. Teetering on the top of my earth spike I looked down at the ruin of the plaza, feeling a flash of guilt for the amount of damage. It took me a minute to register all the beings bowing and backing away from me. I turned and found myself, facing ... a huge unicorn. A unicorn that was snarling up at me revealing a great many sharp fangs.

~Cori Munroe, get down here.~ Every word shards of obsidian glass cutting through my mind. I wanted to weep from the pain it hurt so bad, but the rage embedded in every syllable didn't allow any disobedience.

My shoulders slumped as I asked Earth to lower me down. It did with alacrity and I got the unsettling impression Salistra scared it as much as me. As I lowered down the assembled crowd stepped back and formed a gauntlet for me to walk down.

Their hot angry breaths seared across my face as I plodded down the path that was much, much too short. Salistra stood there, beautiful and deadly, her head slightly turned as she kept an eye on me. Her hoof tapped the ground sending up sparks, and I swallowed.

Be a blasted dragon. If you're about to get eaten, be a dragon about it, for Merlin's sake.

I stood up straighter and marched up to her.

"Yes?"

She faced me directly, lids narrowed over eyes with too much depth in them.

~Why are you interfering with our ritual?~ she demanded and I fought not to flinch at each word.

I channeled my anger and fear and snarled back. "Why are you offering children? How could you?"

~What else would we offer? The entire process is giving magic what we find most precious. There is NOTHING more precious than our children.~

I couldn't suppress the gasp of pain as her words sliced into my brain. A trickle of liquid ran from my nose.

"And you call us barbarians? We don't offer up children!" I was shouting back at her. Around us the assembled beings watched, so quiet it felt like I stood inside a crypt with the dead watching me.

She spat at me, but this time I ignored the saliva hitting me as I bared my teeth. "I won't stand by idly by while you kill children."

~Humans!~ I hadn't realized it was possible to turn the word into a cuss word. ~And you wonder why I break my toys. So arrogant thinking they know what is best. That they can set the morals for everyone else, and Americans are the worst.~

The words hit me like a kidney punch hard and fast and all my bravado collapsed.

"Arrogant?" I whispered and I turned to look at the altar.

~Yes,~ she hissed. ~You come into our world and tell us how to live. This is why it is easier to kill you than deal with your kind. Why Tirsane favors you I will never know.~

I looked around at the beings, the people staring at me. Me who had just shattered their religious ceremony because I thought I was doing the right thing.

By my morals.

Each thought hammered into my heart as I closed my eyes. I had been arrogant. I'd expected magic, or knowledge, or medicine. But this was arrogance about being human. About thinking human ways were better than theirs. About counting their wants as less.

I looked at the unicorn, thinking how quickly those teeth could shred me and how much I had just earned it. I felt like a ball of snot that needed to be flicked off a finger, but wouldn't fall off.

"I apologize." I slowly knelt and bowed my head to Salistra. "I was... am a fool and I..." I swallowed as I forced myself to say the bitter words. "I assumed my culture and morals were more important than yours. How may I make up for my"—I paused glancing to either side, cringing at the damage I'd done to their plaza or holy place or whatever it was—"actions?"

A wave of low sounds rippled out through the crowd, a mix of clacks and rustles, slithers and growls. I stayed where I was, head bowed, and thanked everything I could think of that I hadn't killed anyone.

The shuffling silence continued, and I swore I could feel Salistra's breath on my exposed nape. But I remained on my knees. If I died, at least Jo and Sable would be okay. Carelian might never forgive me though.

~I begin to see. Stand mortal. I want to see your face.~

I winced at each word but stood, feeling disheveled and off

balance. I shifted my backpack; Merlin only knew how much had been broken in there with my rolling around on it. Luckily, I'd used mostly baggies and soft packaging for the food and water.

The weight of gazes from all the beings made me want to crumble in a ball, but I channeled what remained of my inner dragon and accepted it. I met her gaze and waited for judgement.

~You are going to repair every inch of this plaza. And you will witness the offering. If you manage to do both of those with a modicum of integrity, I may not take you as a toy. Chaos got the last one.~ She said that with an annoyed tone, while I still felt the true anger in her mental words. I didn't wipe the trickle of blood running from my nose. The odds were I'd need the offering.

~Now hear me all,~ she called out, and my eyes closed to try to protect myself from the pain. ~Corisande Munroe will bear witness to the offering of your children and she will owe a debt for the interruption. My debt will be paid by her repairing the damage done. Each of the others will choose their repayment and as long as she lives, she will fulfill that request.~ She turned eyes that had the darkness of space on me. ~Is that clear?~

Blood ran down from both nostrils now, but I stood straight and nodded my head. "Yes, Salistra."

~Excellent. Officiants, resume.~ It didn't have the word please, but this sounded more like a request than an order, and it didn't hurt as much.

The witnesses to this travesty spread out, encircling the dais and me this time. I walked over to it, climbing up dully as they took their places. I felt tears welling in my eyes. The hippogriff said a sentence, in a langue I didn't recognize but I understood in my head.

~Once again, we join here to offer up these children to the

realms. May they be accepted in the manner in which they are given,~ he glared at me at this part, ~freely and without doubt.~

His clawed hand swept down, and I locked my body to prevent myself from leaping forward, from stopping this sacrifice. Three talons touched the tops of their heads and drew a single drop of blood each. He flicked it up and the drops flew into the air—micro rips appeared and the drops flew into them.

~They are accepted. These children offered by their parents and chosen by the realms will be accepted as focuses for new mages in the Earth realm.~

Wait. What?

THIRTY-SEVEN

Support for the laws is mandatory as a mage. It is these laws that keep our world civilized. If the laws did not exist, our world would be ruled by many feudal merlins, using their powers to keep the populace under control. All you need to do is look at North Korea or some of the African countries to see the reality of this. All mages must make an effort to stay on the right side of the law, the alternative is unthinkable.~ OMO Statement.

SPIRIT

As I stood there shocked, beings came rushing up, parents I assumed, and swept up the three babies in their arms or mandibles. They all shot me looks that should have killed me on the spot.

For my part I just stood there stunned as the wave of beings swept around me.

"I... but... you, I mean..." I stuttered out unable to form a coherent sentence as the magnitude of my error slicked through me.

~You what?~ Salistra hissed right behind me, her heated breath searing my skin.

I slowly turned and fought the urge to kneel again. The attention of everyone else on me was enough to make my skin crawl, but I didn't take my eyes off the very deadly, very powerful unicorn. "When I heard offered"—I choked out the next phrase—"I assumed you meant sacrificed."

Salistra turned her head, eying me with an eye that seemed to expose eternity. I had to resist leaning forward to see into the depths better.

~They were sacrificed. Their lives were pledged to magic. They will become foci for other unworthy mortals like you.~

I shook my head, my face on fire from the sheer depths of my stupidity. "No. I assumed they were to be killed."

A sound rippled through the gathered beings. It wasn't a sharp gasp or a screech or claws and talons scraping along stone, it was all of them and it sounded like the very world crying out in shock.

~What?~ Her voice made me gasp and fall to one knee, both nostrils now trickling blood. ~Why would you think that? What could ever make you think we would kill our own children? Kill those that are rare and precious? Out of all of us, only the Chittarians give birth in large numbers, but they are also eaten in vast quantities. To have one set as a focus from this age? Not as choice after adulthood? What greater evidence of respect and power could there be?~

I was crying now, the pain in my mind feeling like someone had sliced it with glass shards coated with salt. But I lifted my head to face her. There was no choice. These were actions I had done of my own free will.

"My—human—history, and even how we phrase things in magic, we call them offerings or sacrifices. It always means to kill or destroy. When I heard those words, I thought you were about to kill those children." I faced her, tears running down my face and mixing with the blood from my nose.

The silence that fell disturbed me and I wanted to turn to see what these beings were doing, but I didn't dare take my eyes off the unicorn. We stood there, staring at each other long enough the blood quit running and started to dry.

~I have had enough of yours as toys, I should have remembered how incalculably cruel humans can be. And they call us animal and monsters.~ Salistra leaned forward, her head angled so her features filled most of my vision. ~We may kill each other; we may eat the child of another. Life is hard and cruel. We may even kill the weakest of our children in times of famine so the others may feed. There is little room for sentiment and coddling in the realms. But never would we kill a child to appease or gain honor. Any being that would ask that is not worth the favor it would grant. I sorrow to think your people still have those that believe life is spent for so little.~

The image of Carl appeared bright and stark in my mind with all his horrific beauty. Salistra hissed and reared back, silver cloven hooves pawing the air. The creatures around her, not that anyone had dared to crowd her, backed away even further.

~That, that is what you do to each other?~

I didn't know if she'd sought the image or if I had broadcast it. But either way her outraged scream had me on my knees sobbing, blood running from my ears and nose now. If she wasn't careful her voice alone would kill me. I heard a slither of scales and part of me waited to die, I was about ready to beg for it. My brain was bleeding from the inside out, or at least that was what it felt like. Only the thought of Jo and Sable kept me trying to stand back up. I had to get back. I had to.

~Enough Salistra. Your voice is too pure for the chaos of human thoughts. You know this. Look at her.~

I knew that voice, but I didn't care. Tirsane's words coated the wounds in my mind, and I sobbed in relief as the pain ebbed. I remained laying on the warm stone.

I heard a snort and assumed it was Salistra, but I didn't look up to verify, the lack of pain had me almost high as my body yo-yoed.

~Rise up, Cori Munroe.~

I pushed myself to my feet even if it felt like I weighed eight hundred pounds. Standing there swaying I took in the presence of Tirsane. Half the creatures there were bowing, and she waved her hand. In much less time than I would have expected most of the creatures cleared out. Leaving me, the Cerberus, Hippogriff, and the families—I assumed, which I knew could be very very wrong—of the children.

Tirsane dropped to speaking aloud and I sighed in relief. My brain ached with remembered pain and all I wanted to do was sleep for a week. "You displayed arrogance, fortitude, compassion, and humility. Rarely have I seen that in a mage. Asking questions sooner might be a wise habit to nurture. For now, we must finish the ritual. A drop of their blood was given to Magic. You, as her herald, owe them a matching drop."

Twenty minutes ago, I might have protested. Ten minutes ago, I might have argued that I never wanted to be Magic's

Herald. Now all I wanted to do was try and fix my seismic error. Literally. I took her words to heart.

"How?"

A smile flittered across her face. "Let Arlik nick your finger and grant a drop of blood in each mouth." I looked around, unsure who Arlik was, but the hippogriff stepped forward near the children.

I walked over and held out my left hand. I would not have blamed him if he gashed me, but the claw swept down with almost surgical precision and punctured my ring finger. I moved over to where each of the families stood. The Gorgons were easy enough as a woman, half the size of Tirsane, held out the cute little thing and it stuck out its tongue for me to drop blood on it.

A simple squeeze and a ruby drop fell. The baby smiled at me and swallowed. The mother—it had obvious breasts, so again I was assuming—pulled it close, smiling with pride.

The Cath kitten toddled up to me and started to crawl up my pants. The action so familiar to what Carelian had done once upon a time I fought not to cry with wanting him here. Glancing at the Cath with him, almost as large as Esmere but with a cream coat and dark markings in burgundy, she almost looked like a Burmese, I picked up the kitten and squeezed a drop of blood. The chocolate brown kitten caught it with its tongue mid fall, purring. The second the blood was swallowed squirming commenced and I set it on the ground in front of the adult Cath.

~You may yet have some redeeming qualities.~

I didn't know who spoke. The Cath was busy grooming the kitten, but it sounded catlike, which made no sense even in my own head.

I turned to the Chittarian. The one from the ceremony sat on its head, while the back of the large or adult Chittarian was covered with what were probably the brothers and sisters of the one offered to magic. It waved one of its many legs at me and I stepped over to the huge one, trying very hard not to think about the fact that it probably hunted things my size as prey. The baby rose up on hind legs and tilted its body back so its head was facing up. Trusting its choice, I squeezed the drop of blood. It landed on a mandible and in seconds was gone.

"Well done. Come. I believe you have a penance to pay." Tirsane was next to me and I hadn't noticed. There had been something strangely sacred about the entire ceremony making me even more ashamed of my action. I looked around the plaza cringing again at the destruction I'd caused. I didn't have any reason to trust Salistra or the other creatures, but at the exact same time I had no reason at all to distrust them. The only times I'd been hurt had been by the actions of humans.

I'm a moron.

I kept that thought to myself, but somehow I suspected Tirsane had sensed it. Whatever. I kind of deserved it.

"You didn't kill anyone, and they would have killed you." Her voice was mild with an odd sibilance to it. Probably her forked tongue. It flickered occasionally as she spoke, giving her words an unearthly accent.

"I was lucky." I talked to the ground not her. She still had a presence that even dragons were wary of.

"Oh please. You could have suffocated them, broken apart their blood, stopped their hearts. I suspect if you tried you could have ripped their life out of their bodies." She didn't sound horrified, just vaguely amused.

The idea made my blood pressure drop and I went pale and clammy as how horrible I could have been struck me. I forced past it. "It didn't occur to me."

"That is part of what makes you so unique. You think of it when calm and logical, but when under pressure or attack you delay and avoid. You might want to learn more offensive reactions."

I glanced at her from under my lashes. Her snakes, still pretty and way too intelligent to just be strands of hair, waved, danced, and winked at me. I dropped my gaze back to my boots, a much safer thing to pay attention to.

"I don't want to hurt people. I'd prefer to help them."

"But you are not, what is the word humans use – ah, pacifist?" She said it the way Mrs. Harman at my high school said shit, like saying it contaminated you.

"No. I just don't get any joy from hurting others and would rather not."

"Good enough. Now how are you going to fix all the damage you did to Salistra's ordination piazza?"

I looked around at the damage. Chunks of earth, claw marks, off kilter pillars, and scattered feathers and drops of blood where beings had fallen.

In through your nose, out through your mouth.

Focusing on breathing fully, I mentally chanted the mantra as I looked around. It was nowhere near as bad as what had happened to the campus building when the assassins from Japan attacked me. Here there had been no roof to collapse. And no one had died. Both plusses from my point of view. But the inlaid stone, the tile work, the pretty mosaics, had all been damaged.

Because I didn't keep my mouth shut thinking I knew better.

My mouth opened and I snapped it shut. Rethinking exactly what she said. Arrogance caused this, let's see if I could avoid complicating it. "Do you have any suggestions?"

She chuckled and I dared to look up at her. Inhumanely beautiful, I knew she could become something petrifying in the blink of an eye. "I might have one or two. Talk nicely to the Earth. It helped build this area." With that she turned and slithered away. I watched her go and she stopped next to Salistra, the two of them heads together, obviously chatting, but they kept me in their view the entire time.

Part of me wanted to sprint to the portal, return to Jo and Sable, try to get back the world I thought I understood. But that would destroy everything I had accomplished, and it was not the person, the dragon, I wanted to be.

The blood in runnels from my nose was still fresh. With a sincere solemnness, I offered it to Earth.

Please? I need assistance to return this to the beauty it was.

CHAPTER
THIRTY-EIGHT

Most of the branches have seven spells that work within the magic. Intention and amount of offering can change what any spell is capable of. However, it is still the same basic spell. Psychic only has four defined spells: Truth, Telepathy, KO, and Memory. There has always been a sense of absolute balance between the branches, yet this one is lacking three spells. What are they and when or how will they be discovered? ~ Magic Explained Online

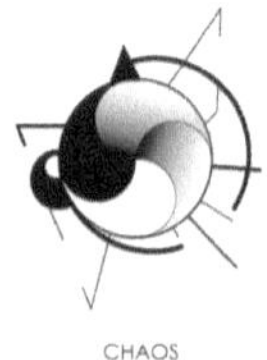

Earth responded to my request with alacrity and joy. It knew what needed to be repaired and mostly I just needed to get out of its way. The elementals weren't just dumb creatures, or spirits, or essences but actual beings. Or was this because of where we were? Either way, I let them have their way and didn't try to override it, no matter how sure I it was it might make things worse.

I spent a solid two inches of hair, all the blood from my nose and ears, and had to stop twice for food. The sun never moved, if it was a sun that lit up the area. Tirsane and Salistra moved as we worked towards them and I didn't bug them until I was pretty sure we were done. I sweet talked Air into sweeping the area clean. If there was something that had been missed, I couldn't see it.

Hot and sweaty, I made my way over to the two of them. At least if they killed me, I'd die knowing I'd repaired the damage I had caused. They looked up as I got close enough, and I could tell they quit speaking to each other, even if it was something I couldn't hear as they mindspoke. I couldn't exactly overhear that, yet I could tell.

"You have completed?" Tirsane asked looking around the area.

"I think so. If I missed anything, please let me know," I offered looking around.

~It is well done. Better than I expected. These here know me, this is my place. I am pleased at all of their work. Yours too,~ Salistra admitted as she surveyed the area.

Her words hurt, but not like before. This was a scratch, not a knife. I nodded, not sure what to say. Before I could figure out anything else, she spoke again.

~You have cleared away my wrath, but you still owe me for the stress you caused my associates. As Tirsane gave you a scale that you may ask a boon, I require the opposite and you owe the families you distressed.~

All my 'oh shit' sensors kicked into high gear and running for my life seemed like a very good idea. Though I had no doubt I'd barely make it two steps.

"You do know I don't have a way to know if you need me, correct?"

~Currently that is true. I will mark you. And I will summon you at the point and time that I am in need of your services and the families will have the same access.~

Oh shit. Shit. SHIT!

~Provide your arm. The one Tirsane marked.~ The imperious voice allowed no room for refusal or avoidance. I held out my left arm to her, the green puncture marks bright and almost glowing. She turned her body and lay the tip of her horn down beneath the green marks. I hissed in pain and surprise as it seared into me, but it was gone before I could rip my arm away.

~That is well done. Marks you as mine. Each section is for the debt you owe. When that debt is fulfilled the spaces will fill in. It has more panache than yours does, don't you think Tirsane?~ Salistra's voice was teasing with a bite of malice in it. Anyone who thought unicorns were pure and sweet had never met one.

I stared at the mark on my wrist, both stunned and horrified. Where Tirsane's mark had been two green pin pricks, Salistra had placed a miniature horn to the right of the punctures. It glared a painful red, though the pain was already fading. As I watched it faded and went to a silvery outline of a unicorn horn with four sections. It ended up looking like a high-end tattoo or scarification. I really wanted to growl, but again I knew I'd earned this.

"Indeed, it is a beautiful mark. I think I should make mine match." Those words had barely registered before Tirsane had my wrist in an iron grip with her left hand while her right drew a waving line the same length as Salistra's horn.

"What are you—" I started, then hissed out as pain and pleasure bubbled up under my skin where her finger traced. Before I could breathe in again a brilliant green serpent, spade shaped head and all, appeared over the two green dots. It looked like a real snake about to move, its tail curving around my forearm.

"That looks much better," she purred smirking at Salistra. Her fingers let go of my arm and I stared at the new designs. They were like looking at two different pieces of art side by side. One a snake that looked like the ones on Tirsane's head, the other a miniature unicorn horn that even sparkled.

At least they are pretty.

Getting more tattoos hadn't been on my list, but I wasn't stupid enough to complain. Instead, I stood and watched both of them preen a bit.

"Am I good to head back?" I still didn't even know if I'd passed or failed, but since Salistra wanted a future favor I hoped it meant I had passed. Even by my own estimation, however, it was only by a whisker.

Tirsane and Salistra ended their smirk off and changed their focus to me. Maybe I should have let them keep up with their one-upmanship, except I was afraid I was becoming their doodle pad.

~Ah yes, the mageling's challenge. ~ She turned her horsey, well unicorny head, one way then the other looking at me. ~She did what I requested, and she allowed the ceremony to proceed.~ I only had to grit my teeth while she spoke. Either she was being nice, or I was getting used to her brand of agony. I had no idea which option was better.

"It is rather well done I think, Salistra. And she did it in much less time than the last offender. She set aside her own ideas. Most can't. Their egos demand that they are correct, much like others we know." Again, that teasing. I couldn't decide if their relationship reminded me of a married couple or sisters. But there was a long relationship with a history there. My mind shut off before I could follow that path any further. Some possibilities did not need to be thought about. At all.

~True. But she still owes me for the travesty—~

"Excitement."

~—she brought to the ritual.~ Salistra continued, but now her words were almost like too hard scratches. Not comfortable, but not really painful. I needed to go before their teasing got violent. I didn't think I could survive violent.

"And you marked her." I shot a sharp look at Tirsane, there was something behind the words I didn't understand and that worried me. A lot.

Salistra snorted and scraped the ground with one hoof. ~Cori Munroe. Marks go both ways. If you believe you are in serious risk of dying before you have filled your debts, that mark will call me. Do not think I will let you leave this plane of existence without clearing our debts.~

"Yes...?—" I floundered for a second.What, by Merlin's beard, did I call her?—"Salistra." I couldn't figure out any other word. Not and keep my heart in my body.

~Humans. I hope this is the right thing. Why did she not choose someone sensible like Baneyarl?~

I blinked at the grousing from Salistra. I don't know why but it sounded like pouting. Why would a super powerful unicorn-like creature pout?

"You know why. The same reason it is neither of us, or Esmere, or even"—my mind spasmed as she said a name I didn't recognize, but I recognized the pain. The thing from Chaos. Assuming I had followed their conversation correctly, they were talking about any of them being heralds of Magic.

While I would be totally fine with Baneyarl, the idea of Esmere or that thing that was Chaos being the herald suddenly made me a much better choice.

I loved Esmere. But she had no qualms about anything she wanted. A squirrel, she'd kill and eat it, even if it spoke to her. If her claws needed sharpened, she'd use whatever she wanted. The damage was the item's problem not hers. Carelian at least understood ownership and didn't actively damage things, but Esmere would destroy cities just to see what happened. Thankfully, she didn't seem to be that powerful.

Or I'm completely wrong and she's a demigod like the rest. I mean what is a Chaos Lord?

On that thought my mind locked up and decided leaving was the best option. "I am so grateful for what you have taught me. Perhaps it is a good time for me to leave? Back through the fire portal?" I asked waving at the only end of the triangle without built in seating. The fire still flickered merrily along it and at this point offering more to Fire to get out of there was more than worth it.

Tirsane turned her perfect visage to me. For a second of sheer terror, I thought I was going to experience her other expression. The one that created statues.

"Yes. Go. I am sure we will be talking soon."

"Oh Merlin, I hope not," I blurted, then slapped my hand over my mouth, eyes wide as I stared at her.

I'm dead, she's going to kill me. Oh Merlin.

Salistra started laughing, the shards of laughter cutting into my mind, and several of Tirsane's snakes were bouncing in what looked like hysterics.

~Even your favorites worry about your looks,~ Salistra jabbed and I forgot my mortification at the flash of pain I saw flicker across Tirsane's face.

"Hey! That is not nice. Tirsane is gorgeous," I blurted out, horrified that she thought I didn't like her because of her statue look. "I'm not worried about her looks, or even the fact that she could turn me to stone. I'm terrified 'cause she is powerful, gorgeous, a fracking demigod, and seems to be intrigued by me. Mortals don't live long when powers are interested in them. And I'd like to die of old age in my bed thank you very much. But don't you think for a second that I have an issue with how she looks. My only issue with her is she so damn intimidating."

Even the leaves quit rustling and I felt every being, spirit, every creature shift their attention to me as I realized what I had done. I just told off a demigod.

For a moment, a long multiple rapid heartbeat moment, I thought about running, about ripping open the earth and fading into it, or even just willing myself dead. Then I thought about being a dragon and decided to tell everyone to take a flying leap.

I glared at Salistra. "You're being mean. I don't know why everyone thinks unicorns are so nice, cause frankly you're being a snotty bitch and I think you know your mindspeak causes actual brain damage and you don't care. I didn't like girls like you in high school and just 'cause you're a unicorn demigod, you're still a bitch."

The silence remained, and I stood there, hands on my hips glaring at the unicorn.

Silken white eyelids blinked once, then twice over eyes that held eternity. Then Salistra turned to Tirsane who had the strangest expression on her face.

~I see why you like her. At this rate she might grow on me too. It's been a very long time since there has been anything but sycophants.~

"Aye. Since we were kidlings," Tirsane said, but she didn't take her eyes off me, and neither did any of her snakes.

~Keep her. And I won't break her. Begone both of you. I have things to do.~ Without another glance our way, Salistra pivoted on her hind hooves and trotted out of the area, leaving a few strands of hair behind.

"I would collect those. Unicorn hair is handy for many things, and she never sheds without a purpose." Tirsane's voice was mild but she still had a funny expression.

Embarrassed and still a bit offended on her behalf, I bent and snapped up the hairs, stuffing them in a pocket and sealing the Velcro.

"I'll walk you back," she said as she slithered to the portal. I had to walk briskly to keep up and for some reason I felt like she wanted to ask me something, but we got to the portal and she stopped. "Enter and walk back. You should find the path home shorter than to get here."

"Thanks." I turned then stopped. I'd been teased about my clumsiness, my parents, for Jo, even my name Cori Castrophe said what people thought. I'd grown past it, but as a kid, it had hurt. Jo still flinched at some words. Gorgeous she might be now, but middle school had been a hell of acne, weight, body changes, and dealing with brothers.

"I don't know what your people regard as pretty. Lots of humans find snakes scary. But even with the snakes, which I think are cute, you're stunning and men and women would fall over themselves to be with you. But we're humans. We are cruel and stupid. Don't judge yourself on anything we say." I sighed, no longer sure where I was going with this. "Just, I think you're really pretty, and scary, and powerful, and you make a great role model."

I spun and walked into the fire refusing to look back at the demigod standing there watching me.

CHAPTER

THIRTY-NINE

The unicorn that was captured over a year ago, has escaped captivity. The handlers swore it just stepped to the side and was gone. But no rips into either realm have been detected and the holding pen was layered with sensitive equipment. The question is, did the unicorn truly escape and we will need to deal with another rampage of men being killed or has it gone back to its realm? ~ Atlanta News.

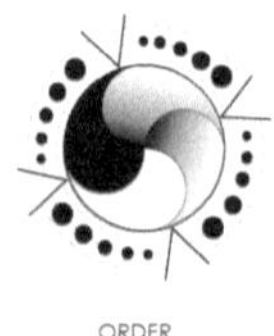

ORDER

I headed through the arch and prepared myself for the long plod back to where the others waited for me, but three steps in and I hit the grass and the orderly chimes. A quick look around convinced me I was in the right place and I headed straight to where Carelian sat watching or guarding Jo and Sable.

"Carelian!" It came out as a shout of glee and I dropped to my knees yanking him into my arms.

~Cori? What is wrong?~ Worry was clear in his tone and I realized I was shaking.

Breathe, find out what happens next.

I shook my head, buried in his fur. "Later." I gathered myself back together and lifted my head looking for Hamiada. She stood by the statues glaring, and for a moment I thought she was talking to someone. Confused and a bit worried I watched her. Two-foot stomps later she flowed over to me, her feet not really walking, more skating across the grass.

"They said you made it. They weren't sure about you originally, but they admire your conviction of purpose and willingness to see the error in your ways."

"They?" I had a very good idea, but as I had so very recently learned, assuming could get me and others dead.

"Salistra and Tirsane and the families. Though even"—she said the Chaos creature's name and I flinched. How could you pronounce something like that?—"weighed in on what the verdict was." She pouted. "You passed."

The tension that dropped out of me made my entire body feel boneless. I slumped back against Carelian. "I did?"

"I just said that, didn't I?" She sounded offended and exasperated and I didn't care. At all.

"Then release them, now." I stood, my body quivering with

the need to have Jo and Sable free. I pulled off my pack and dropped it on the ground, sighing as the weight dropped off me.

If she had been a teenager, a huff and sigh would have followed her slogging over to the two pillars of light. Hamiada placed each hand on the pillars and closed her eyes.

I watched trying to see both of them at the same time. They lowered to the ground still looking like they were perfectly asleep. The light disappeared and I rushed to Jo.

"Check Sable, Carelian," I snapped. I needed to make sure they were both okay, but I couldn't check on both of them at the same time. He was moving before I'd hit the ground with my knees. My hand on her throat. A strong steady pulse met my touch, and I felt half the stress vaporize. But was she still Jo?

"Hey, Jo, can you hear me? I need you to wake up. Please?" I didn't even try to cover up my stress or quavering voice. My breath held as I gently touched her face. "Jo?" The word was an exhalation of hope and need.

She groaned a bit and turned her head. I remembered to breathe as she moved her shoulders and lifted her hand to her temple, rubbing. "Cori? What are you doing back?" She muttered the words, her eyes squeezed shut tight. "And why does it feel like Jose Cuervo beat the daylights out of me?"

My self-control fled and I yanked her into my arms and started crying. Moments later I heard Sable's voice and then I felt her arms wrap around me. Warmth and safety surrounded me as I let the tears flow and I held them tight. My family. They just held me and let me cry out the stress and fear. Carelian pushed his way into the circle of arms purring like Jo's motorcycle when it was out of sync.

It took a bit until my tears dried up and the arms loosened. I looked up through puffy eyes and smiled at Jo and Sable. "I am so glad to see you two. I've missed you both."

Jo and Sable glanced at each other, then back at me. "I get

the feeling something major happened?" Jo finally said, her eyes sweeping across the clearing and lingering on the form of Hamiada still pouting over by the statues.

"What is the last thing you remember?" I asked as I pulled my bag over. "And are you hungry?"

Jo opened her mouth, then paused frowning. "Starving actually. Now I'm more confused."

I just nodded and pulled out the salami, nuts, and dried fruit, handing it to them. Jo tossed some almonds in her mouth, frowning in thought. "We had just eaten dinner and were sitting on the back porch."

Sable nodded as she grabbed some of the dried cranberries. "Yeah, it had been a nice day. We were talking about going to bed then exploring more tomorrow." She paused and frowned. "And then..." Her words broke off as the furrow between her brows got deeper.

Jo nodded. "Right. And then," She chewed on some salami and her brows creased. "And then I don't know. The next thing I remember is you and here."

"Same. I don't remember anything," Sable admitted. "So, what happened?"

I turned and stared lasers into Hamiada. "I don't know. What happened?"

The dryad quit pretending to be ignoring us and glided back over. "Nuts," she demanded, imperiously holding out her hand. I blinked at her tone but shrugged and handed over more almonds. The smoked kind, they were the best.

She tossed one in her mouth. "Mmm. This is tasty." With a movement that implied she had no bones she dropped into a lotus pose, vivid green eyes staring at us. I realized she had no pupils, and I didn't know if that creeped me out or if I wanted to ask a lot more questions.

"Cori! What happened and who are you?" Jo asked, her body tense, eyes locked on Hamiada.

"Jo, Sable, meet Hamiada. Your kidnapper and the house. Who is now going to tell us what happened?" I asked, eyes narrowed as I focused on her.

"The house?" Sable asked, her voice unsure.

"Please, like you've never seen a house hosting an entity before. You make flat moving stories about them," Hamiada protested, reaching for more nuts.

"Those aren't real. And usually those houses tend to kill people," Jo pointed out.

"Humans are confusing. How do you know what is real or not when it plays in that box? There is no person there to truth sense. So is it all real or all not?" She looked frustrated and unsure.

That way lay long discussions and I didn't want to deal with it right now. "Hamiada, I'll try to explain later. Right now, what did you do to them?"

Hamiada looked away, the first sign of shame or discomfort I'd seen in her. "I entranced them. It is easy with a few spores I released, and I called them up the stairs. Then they just walked into my realm via the portal in the top floor. They were set in a stasis and then I waited."

"Waited for what?" Jo demanded.

"For Cori Munroe to show up and attempt the trials."

The two women looked at each other, then me, then back at Hamiada. "Are you saying we were bait?" demanded Jo.

"Yes. And the reward and punishment. She needed to be properly motivated. Which is unusual as most leap at the chance to be ingratiated with Magic. She did not. Hence motivation."

She said all of this like I would have said, "put on a coat to prevent getting cold." It chilled me.

Jo nailed me with her stare and her eyes slowly traveled over me, noting every scratch, bump, torn bit of clothing and the random vaporization of hair.

"Cori, what by Merlin's name happened to you?"

Carelian all but crawled into my lap, hard when he weighed almost as much as I did, his purring sending vibrations through my body. I took a deep breath and then started to talk. Jo and Sable and even Hamiada listened with rapt attention.

Even though I wanted to gloss over or completely avoid certain aspects of the tests, I didn't. I was honest about the temptation to trade in their lives for those books. About my indignation and rage at the sacrifice of children. But most of all about my fear that I would fail and that Jo and Sable wouldn't be set free unharmed.

"Oh, I would have set them free. They wouldn't have remembered anything about the time they lost, but I wouldn't have hurt them," assured Hamiada. It didn't help. "Though it seems the wrong test for wrath was chosen. You don't care about yourself enough to exact vengeance, but for others, for children, what would you have done?" Her head was tilted and she was curious.

Should I answer her? I was very certain Tirsane and Salistra were listening. But all of this might be yet another test. I was so tired of people testing me. Honesty, never lie, just be selective with the truth.

"I would have rescued them, and got them to people who would protect them," I admitted.

"But would you have come back and punished the offenders?" she prodded, watching me, and the skin on the back of my neck crawled.

"Not the way you mean. If I had needed to kill to rescue the kids I probably would have, but I doubt I would have come back just to kill them. And torture is just tacky."

"And if you knew they would do it again, or to different children?"

I opened my mouth, shut it. Sat there for a moment and sighed. "I don't know. In my world I'd go to the authorities, tell them, and let them deal with it. Let justice work. But here? I never know if I'm making the right choices and some of them I don't think I could live with. Standing there when I thought the kids were about to be killed was one of the hardest things I've ever done. If they had actually been killed, I don't know if I could have handled it." I shrugged. "I'd probably ask Esmere or Baneyarl, or..." I touched my necklace and the scale from Tirsane. "The problem is, I don't know if I'd like the answer."

"Do you really think so little of us?" Tirsane's voice from behind me didn't surprise me at all. In some ways it was almost a relief.

"No. But Esmere and Baneyarl and Carelian have always made it clear that life here has different rules and expectations than on Earth. That test reinforced it beyond a doubt." I turned as I spoke to watch her slither towards us. I held out some salami as she curled up near our little group.

Jo and Sable nodded at her, wary, but she'd dropped in occasionally at Baneyarl's teaching. Kind of like having the president stop by. You were honored but concerned about why he would be there.

"Did Salistra come?" I asked, scanning the area.

"No. She has damaged you enough for one day. Human minds are not made to withstand how her thoughts are formed. You are too fragile for sustained conversations. What is this? It is most delightful." She held up the piece of meat she was delicately chewing on.

"That's salami." I glanced between her and Hamiada, who had scooted over a bit, giving her space. "You helped with all this. These tests, didn't you?" It was almost an accusation, but I kept it at a question.

"Of course. I marked you. I would have been offended if I was not invited to participate," she said as she picked up a smoked almond and inspected it.

"But Cori passed, right? She's safe? There are no more testes?" Jo asked, her hand on my knee tightening.

Tirsane popped the last almond in her mouth, eyes closed as she chewed. I could feel the anxiety radiating off of Jo and Sable, but I was almost calm. I'd done my best. At this point, if I failed they were safe.

"Yes. We are satisfied with where she is, there will be no more tests from us. She is acknowledged as a Herald by Magic. Many times those watching thought you would fail. I never did however. Those I choose rarely fail." Her snakes swerved to look at me. "Have you not looked at your wrist?"

I looked at my wrist with the snake and the unicorn horn. "These mean I'm a herald?" That made no sense—I thought they were just proofs of more hooks into my soul.

"You do have two wrists, do you not?"

I held up my right arm, yanked up the long sleeve, and stared. There, encircling my wrist were the magical symbols repeated three times. Spirit, Order, Chaos, in a bracket around my wrist. All the branches that I was strong in were filled with a vivid rainbow of colors shifting from one to another. While all my pale branches had the pastel version filling them. My nulls reflected only my skin with the faintest of an opalescence sheen.

"How the... ?" Even as I spoke, it pulsed once and faded, becoming a tattoo on my skin only visible by careful inspection.

"Magic marks her own. Any denizen of the realms will see it and react accordingly." Her voice bland as she nibbled on a piece of pepperoni this time, her slitted pupils dilating.

"What exactly does that mean?" Jo asked. I was still staring at my wrist. The symbols brightened and became clearly visible when I ran my finger over them but faded away in seconds.

"It means what it means. Much depends on Cori Munroe and the choices she makes. Magic has made hers."

With that ominous statement Tirsane rose to her full height and slithered away, disappearing between one slither and the next.

"I like her better than Salistra, but anyone that can drink your magic dry on a whim is not a comfortable person to have in your home." Hamiada sat up straighter, grinning. "Are you ready to go back to your realm?"

"What do you mean, drain you dry? Like a vampire? I didn't think they were real," Sable managed, torn between horrified and curious. I was about the same. Tirsane was a vampire?

Hamiada shook her head. "Vampires do not exist unless someone created them recently. All of the exalted have the right to drain others. How do you think they rose to exalted?"

I just stared at her. I had no idea how to even process that information and trying to figure out realm politics when I was still struggling with Earth politics sounded like an excuse for a headache.

"I'm ready. Are you?" I looked at the two women whose lives I valued more than my own.

"Very. We've been here too long," Jo said and Sable nodded in agreement.

"Hamiada, can you take us home? And maybe tomorrow show us how to help take care you? It is your home also."

I caught the confused looks from Jo and Sable, but I let it go. I'd explain later.

"Of course. I am linked." She flowed upward and looked over to where the statues had been. Now there was a simple door with a frame standing as if grown from the grass.

I pulled myself up, packed up the food stuff, and pulled my pack on. We headed for the door, so anxious to be out of this place. I paused at the edge, hand almost reaching for the knob. "You're sure? Home? No tricks?"

Hamiada stood up straight then bowed. "Home. You have been here long enough. It is time for you to return to your own realm."

My hand wrapped around the doorknob. "How long have I been here?" I pulled it towards me and smiled as a familiar room appeared.

"I believe thirty-eight of your hours."

I shivered. "No wonder I'm exhausted."

"Why aren't I? Hungry but I feel energized almost," Jo protested as we walked into the third floor of the house.

"Because you've been in the dandy pillar of light, sleeping the sleep of the innocent? Must be nice." I didn't grouse, just added sarcasm. A lot of sarcasm.

"Are you coming too, Hamiada?" I asked as we tramped into the room. Carelian slunk in behind us while Jo and Sable headed to the stairs.

Hamiada paused on the threshold her head tilted. "Why is there pounding on my door?"

"Huh?"

"CORISANDE MUNROE, COME OUT WITH YOUR HANDS UP. THIS IS YOUR LAST WARNING!" The sound of an amplified voice echoed through the room.

FORTY

An effort is being made to retrace the voyage of Odysseus. As Troy was found, it has been suggested that maybe his stay with Circe and encounters with the two monsters, Charybdis and Scylla, may have actually been guardians at semi-permanent portals into the other realms. If they could be found, it would give scientists two points of entry as the odds are the portals would be in international waters. ~ Magic Explained Online

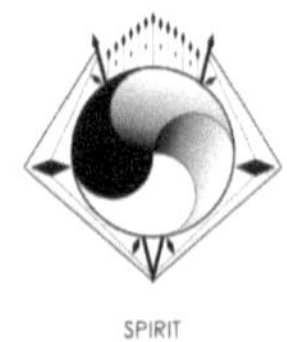

SPIRIT

"Merlin's balls, what now?" I was so tired I wanted to cry. My entire body ached from hitting the ground so many times, and I still didn't know how to deal with all the world changing information I'd received today.

"What is it?" Jo moved over and looked out the window with me. "Merlin, what did you do Cori?"

My stomach sank. We'd been gone over thirty hours. A whole day had passed. A day where I hadn't answered the phone or the door or been reachable by anyone.

"Hamiada. Did anyone come in while I was gone? Or in your realm?" I asked. Maybe Steven and Indira had gotten my note.

"No. The house was sealed as soon as you stepped into my realm. No one could get in or out."

Each word made me shrink down a bit more. It just solidified, especially when I spied Steven and Indira in the crowd, was well as Detective George Farlane.

"Oh, this is going to suck," I muttered and headed to the stairs.

"Cori? What's going on?" Jo followed right behind me."

"So, I was working with the police when Marisol called and let me know you'd missed talking to her."

"Oh shit. That's right. Ugh, Mami is going to strangle me," Jo groaned, trotting down the steps with me.

"Yeah well, I headed back here asap. I'd already been a bit worried about the two of you not responding, but I kept telling myself it was because you were having sex or exploring."

"We don't have that much sex," Sable protested but I saw Jo blush a little.

"Uh huh," I murmured. "Well, they said something about it being illegal for me to leave, but I kinda left anyhow. I guess they are a bit overanxious because I left." I dropped my bag on the entryway floor and quickly pulled my hair into a ponytail with a scrunchie from the table. When three women all have long hair, scrunchies are everywhere. I approached and peered out the door, sucking in a sharp breath as I saw everything that was laid out front on my lawn.

Not only were Steven and Indira there standing by their car across the street, but Detective Farlane was there, a bunch of people with the letters OMO on their jackets, FBI, Draft Dept, reporters, soldiers, and there were mages.

What in the world is going on?

"Ummm, Cori?" Sable said, her voice worried. "All this is because you left?"

"I guess they were more serious than I thought about me not leaving. Stay here and I'll deal with it," I said as I set my hand on the door handle.

"Oh, I don't think so. This is our fault. Well, we were the ones taken, so we're going with you." Jo had her "I am not bending" expression and Sable just nodded, her arms across her chest. I glanced at Hamiada.

"You coming too?"

Her face had darkened, becoming woodier. She closed her eyes and I felt like she was seeing more than we did. "No, but I shall watch. This is my body and I do not wish it harmed. They have machines and weapons that imply structural damage. I will be wrothful if that should occur." With one more glare towards the front yard she faded into the wall with a single backwards step.

"Huh. Nice trick," I muttered and pulled on the door. To my relief it opened up easily—I'd almost been scared we would still be trapped inside. I stepped out onto the porch and froze as multiple guns were lifted up and aimed at me. "Ummm... hi?"

I couldn't manage any more than that. The intimidation factor of having soldiers point guns at you, cop cars surrounding your house like you were a drug runner for some cartel, and the sheer number of federal agencies here, now all staring at me, made my mind go blank.

A tall thin man in a dark windbreaker that said DRAFT in the corner lifted up the bullhorn and started to speak. "CORISANDE MUNROE YOU ARE ORDERED TO GIVE YOUR-SELF UP FOR VIOLATION OF –"

I put my hand up in a stop gesture. "You're ten feet away from me. I can hear you just fine. What is going on?"

There was a snicker behind me and I glanced over my shoulder to see Jo on one side of me. I took a quick peek over the other shoulder and Sable stood there, both of them with their arms crossed looking impressive and powerful.

I should have changed back into my new clothes. Oh well.

The agent lowered his bullhorn, but he didn't look amused. "You are under arrest for violation of section 32.3 of the Mage Draft Treaty. If you are found guilty of violation, you can be sentenced to twenty years of draft or if you are regarded as unrepentant and dangerous, the penalty is death."

His hard voice sent shivers down my spine. But I had taken time to double check the law before I'd stepped into Hamiada's domain. "That is not accurate," I said, pretending I was a dragon, unconcerned about mortals. It didn't really work, but the image helped to keep me from freaking out. "The wording of that section says the mage may not leave the state or be unreachable for trial pending extreme extenuating circum-stances. I am reachable now, and the trial should be tomor-row?" I offered hopefully. It looked like it was mid-morning, and if I'd been gone thirty or so hours, assuming Hamiada was right about the time difference, the trial should be tomorrow. I hoped the trial was tomorrow.

Steven had moved up next to the agent and was speaking in low whispers. I watched all this more than a bit worried inside.

Agent dude brushed Steven off, and another OMO person pulled him away. My worry spiked.

The man all but spat his reply at me. "The trial was this morning and you have been out of communication for over forty-eight hours. The rogue mage was put to death this morning, even without your witness testimony. You are being held in violation of Mage Draft Treaty." His tone brooked no compromise and annoyance started to battle with worry.

"I'm sorry. But I had an extenuating circumstances issue and had to come here. A place that is within the state, and my liaison with the NYPD knew where I was coming back to." I made sure my voice carried and kept my hands still, not that it mattered much, but most mages made funny gestures when doing magic. Baneyarl thought that was ridiculous.

"You have violated the draft terms and conditions. Surrender now," he barked and I bristled.

"I have not entered the draft. So I haven't violated anything," I snapped back and Alixant tried to talk to him again, but was shaken off. I'd never seen anyone blow off Steven Alixant like that, and I saw him getting both angry—and what chilled me more—worried.

"Immaterial. You will surrender now and be taken into custody. All of you." His order made me tense more.

"Jo and Sable have nothing to do with this. Leave them out of it." Now I was starting to get freaked out too. This entire thing was ridiculous. I had no desire to go against the might of the draft board or the OMO. No one won those fights. It was a death sentence.

"They are charged with aiding and abetting," he started.

I interrupted him. "WHAT? They were ... they were... " I faltered looking at them. What was I supposed to say? A dryad that was or is my house kidnapped them to pull me here? "They were in distress and I needed to assist them," I finally managed.

He ran his eyes over them, then flicked them back to me. "They are uninjured. Charges stand."

"Why won't you listen? I had to go. They are fine now. But there wasn't an option."

I don't think. But then I might not have been rational.

The guns pointed at me didn't lower and I could see the mages in the back dressed in military uniforms, the colors on their temples dead giveaways that they were mages. In fact, the more I looked I saw most of them out there had tattoos, except bullhorn guy. This was very not good.

"Immaterial. That will be decided by a judge. Surrender!" His voice harsh. Alixant pulled away from the others and grabbed bullhorn guy, talking fast and urgent.

I gave in. ~Jo, can you ask Air to pull sound to us, I need to hear what he's saying.~

Out of my peripheral view I saw her nod her head and a split second, words were carried to my ears on the breeze.

Alixant hissed out the words. "Quit threatening her. She's very powerful and young. She might overreact. The government wants her skill set intact. She owes them a decade and they'd rather have a willing and enthusiastic mage in their service, rather than a resentful one or worse, a dead one." Air brought his words in a rush around my head.

"For the last time, get out of here. Otherwise, I'll have you arrested for obstruction. I know how to deal with power hungry mages. Bullets work wonders. If she won't listen, I'll take care of the matter personally. What your masters want doesn't matter, only making sure order is maintained does. Rogue mages are dangerous to everyone. You are obviously compromised." I would have felt better—still shocked and upset but better—if he'd had any emotion at all in his voice. My phone had more personality.

"Lefoin!" Alixant whispered, but this time he was all but

dragged away by more people with flashy windbreakers and the cold in my stomach turned into a snowball. A huge one rolling into my soul.

"I don't have an issue with coming with you. Just let everyone else go." I knew Carelian could flee where they could never catch him, but Jo and Sable? Maybe I had destroyed their lives.

Keeping my hands in the air, I started down the steps. My heart raced as I tried to figure out not only what I should do, but how in the hell had it come to this. It wasn't like I'd run away from my duties, but rescuing Jo and Sable wasn't negotiable.

"Cori, no! We aren't letting them take you." Jo lunged forward and grabbed my right forearm. "This can't be legal," she protested, her face a sickly pale.

"Take them out, resisting arrest. All of them. We can't afford to have rogue mages," the agent ordered into his earpiece. I heard the breath of the sniper, Air rushing around like crazy to inform me of what was happening and something inside me broke. Maybe it was the desire to play by the rules, maybe it was my faith that if I did the right thing others would, or maybe it was just my ability to give a fuck.

I yanked on Earth hard, offering blood, and I shook the earth in the immediate vicinity, knocking everyone off their feet. As that threw up earth and dust into the air, I grabbed it and created a shield around the house, at least three feet thick.

"Tell me," I whispered, "if anything tries to come through. Then stop it." I offered hair and blood which Earth inhaled like a fine whiskey.

"Trying to kill me or my friends is a bad idea. I'll talk to a magistrate, but you have just proven you can't be trusted. Leave now. Come back when someone who can negotiate is willing to." I spoke the words loud and clear still hoping they'd see sense and back down.

"Rogue mage protocol, activate," was snapped out instead.

"Oh, what is wrong with people?" I muttered even as guilt assaulted me. I could see Alixant talking frantically on his phone and Indira, paler than the clouds, leaning against the car.

"Carelian," I said, my voice low. "Tell Indira and Steve to shield please?"

I had been thinking about what Tirsane said. They never taught us how to really use magic offensively in our magic classes. It was all science, measurement, offerings, and exact results. But Tirsane had kick started thoughts in my mind. Baneyarl had been more interested in making sure we understood that magic wasn't all weights and measures. That magic was magic, not the science that humans tried to make it.

And I knew all the things you could do to the body to heal with magic. Or to harm.

~They're ready,~ he said. ~My queans will show them they are not to be messed with.~ I knew Jo and Sable could hear him, their pale faces proof.

"Hold on, this is going to get rocky. I'm sorry." I felt tears starting to well up in my eyes. I was too young to die. And definitely not over this stupid stuff.

"We aren't going anywhere. Tell us what to do," Jo said, her voice strong and almost gleeful. I glanced back at her and saw a warrior, hands full of fire and death in her eyes. On my other side stood wrath incarnate. Sable's ebony eyes glittered with rage with water summoned from the air.

"They won't know what hit them."

Terrified glee bubbled up and I sent out the strongest wide KO I could. It washed through the assembled forces, decimating them. One in ten still stood, swaying a bit, and terror had leached through them.

"Jo, ignite the powder in the bullets. Sable water in all their electronics. See if you can spare Alixant and Indira, but fry everything," I snapped. "Carelian prepare us escapes. If we have to flee, take us to Spirit. Ask Baneyarl if he'll shelter us, otherwise I pull the entire damn house out of time. We won't leave her behind for them to hurt."

~You would protect Hamiada?~ he asked.

Bullets started to fizzle and poof, making everyone drop weapons and jump back. Jo was good and she knew her mechanics, which mean there wasn't shrapnel flying everywhere but little puffs as she controlled the burn.

Meanwhile sparks were starting to fly out of phones and radios, even some of the cars. Sable had a wicked grin as she concentrated.

Unfortunately bullhorn guy didn't go down. "Take out the threat now," he bellowed, spinning to stare at the line of mages near the back. They had blocked more of my KO than the rest.

"Merlin's piss," I swore under my breath. There had been eight mages back there, and from here I could see that five of them were merlins, all Order or Chaos. Only one had dropped from my KO. Fine. I'd go to the next step, though it completely would blow away the idea that I couldn't effectively use my Null branches.

They brought up hands and I felt magic flying at me. As it hit my Earthen shield, I identified it. Entropy, fire—narrow like a laser, a water dehydration spell, and a Disrupt. There were two more I didn't recognize, but I doubled up on my shield and yanked on the Earth again. I was working really hard to not destabilize the tectonic plates. I just wanted, needed, localized earth movement, but there was a huge chance I'd cause a sinkhole.

A wisp of some sort of magic blew through my shield and slammed into me. I screamed and hit my knees. I had thought Salistra's words hurt, this felt like my mind was having a flaming needle rammed through it.

"Stroke attack," Jo snapped. "Remember Baneyarl told us about that. You know what to do, Sable. Find the clot and dry it out so small it crumbles into individual cells her body can handle. We practiced this."

"Got it," I heard her say. I kept my eyes closed, breathing through the pain. But I felt others getting ready to attack. My magic sense bubbled up all over the place and I could tell we would crumble.

"Hurry. Only chance, time bubble. Huge, big." I knew how to do it in theory. But the offering would be huge, and I'd have to make it way out of sync, like a year or more. It might kill me, but it would take them years to find the match, if they ever did, if I set the bubble far enough out of sync.

"Shush, give me a second." Sable said the words soothingly, but her hands on either side of my head were clammy and cold.

"Fire incoming. I got it." Jo reached out and took over the fire, something most mages didn't know was possible. If you asked the elemental in it, they loved bouncing to someone who would talk to them, not just order them around. She let it hang in the air, creating yet another layer of shielding.

"Shit, more incoming," Sable muttered. "They're working with entropy, trying to break down the shield and the house."

"No!" I jerked up and swayed but pushed past it. I had to believe Sable had done enough to lct my body heal on its own. Magic could do that if it needed to. "Carelian, get us those escapes. I'll try to get the time bubble to be big enough for us."

I didn't mention I also needed it long enough for them to not get to us easily. And that if I wasn't careful the time sync would kill me.

FORTY-ONE

Stare not too long into the depths of your worst thoughts, for then you will see them come alive in the actions of others. ~ Qin Lin Proverb

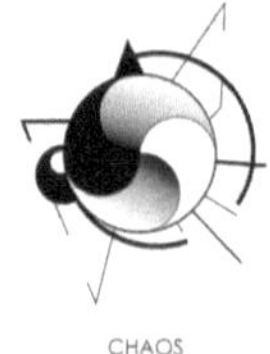

CHAOS

I felt a slash of pain as Carelian opened a portal. I shook it off as I tried to create a bubble. I needed it big enough to grab the house, the back yard and throw us at least a year out of sync. I'd never done anything that big before. My default was five minutes, and it only took the beings in the Order realm a few seconds to sync up and find the time displacement. But a year? A year would take forever. And when I was ready to end it,

I'd age a year and then some. I could live with that. If I could cast it. I could feel magic building—whatever they were about to hit us with would be devastating. I should never have let Jo and Sable come out here with me.

I reached for the magic and pulled, offering anything it wanted, and it failed. I sat there stunned. Magic had never failed for me; I hadn't known it could. And I didn't have time to figure out why it failed, but I suspected it had something to do with the house, or maybe the open portals Carelian was talking through. Either way it had failed.

"All of you, step to the other realms. I'll give myself up and see if I can protect the house and you." I had a crazy idea to throw them forward in time. It might kill me, but I'd read a story where a mage put their children ten years forward in time to protect them. They could go anywhere then, Baneyarl would help right? I wasn't sure it was even more than a theory.

There were so many things I should be doing, could be doing but I needed to delay to give everyone time to calm down. Jo and Sable were hapless victims, and I'd make sure everyone knew that.

My shield crumbled. Air whispered words to me, a spell I'd forgotten was running, carrying bullhorn's voice to my ear. "Take out the two women, I want them to be examples."

I jerked my head up and screamed, "No!" Images of Jo bleeding out in my arms but this time she wouldn't be okay. Sable's head exploding as a bullet exploded out of her. Panic and the last vestiges of caring about looking mild turned to dust. Power flew out of me in a wave of electricity at hurricane force that slammed into people like a million zaps of static and cars lit up as they were hit.

"You will not hurt my friends." I swallowed and prepared to cross a line I never wanted to cross. I couldn't torture people and there were lots of options that would leave people blind or maimed, but that seemed worse than killing them outright. When you learn how to save people, you also learn how to kill them. I closed my eyes, focusing on what I needed to do.

The best offensive mages were always elementalists. Fire, Water, Air, they all could kill without an issue. I only had a strong Earth and that tended to damage everything rather than just the person or persons trying to kill you. I was strong in Soul, Relativity, Time, and Psychic. Of those, only Soul could kill. The others just weren't meant to be used that way.

Pale in Entropy meant I had access to Age. It wasn't one they talked about much in school, but I'd read it in the Magic Explained books Marisol got me for an emergence gift. I'd only thought about using it for making bacteria or viruses grow faster in mediums for experiments. But now I'd use it to kill people to protect my family.

All I had to do was age out the heart values until they crumbled away. Fast, relatively tiny, and even with Entropy as pale, with Carelian helping I had the power. "I'm sorry," I whispered and pulled up my offering.

Three hard slashes of pain disrupted my concentration and I scrambled to get it again. I didn't have time! They would kill Jo and Sable at any moment.

~STOP!~

The word locked down my body as it rolled across the lawn as if it was thunder rolling across the sky. All of the people out there, the ones trying to destroy me and my family, locked up, some falling to the ground if they had been in motion when the word hit.

The slashes of pain faded, becoming sensitive areas in my mind and it registered that three portals had opened. Three huge portals.

Oh crap.

I couldn't speak, I couldn't move, I couldn't even mindspeak, yet Carelian brushed past me, his tail tracing a velvet path across my face. He trotted down the stairs to the lawn. I could move my eyes and I followed his path as he stopped and took the Egyptian pose at the base of the stairs.

~You humans are more than a bit annoying. Why you have been given the gift of Magic I will never understand.~ The crystal shard voice of Salistra cut through my mind, and I had a tiny bit of sympathy for the people out there who had never felt the pain of her mind voice before. ~Sit and listen, or I swear I will remove the edicts that constrain access to this world.~

The force that held me in place relaxed and I could sit up, but it wouldn't let me stand and I saw numerous people being forced to sit. I could see Indira and Steven on the ground near each other. She was as pale as an eggnog latte, while Steven was wary. I could see the whites of his eyes.

A few soldiers tried to lift guns, but they seemed unable to even pull them out of holsters or aim them up. The best they could do was move them so they could sit comfortably.

They probably forgot Jo destroyed all their bullets, or maybe they didn't even realize she did.

I searched for the mages and saw them all crumbled, holding their heads as if in the midst of the world's worst headache.

Huh, wonder if mages hurt more from her voice?

I heard, or more accurately felt, movement from around the side of the house, approaching from the lawn. The ground shook, not like a mage was moving it but more from the vibration of something very big stepping on it. As it came around the side of the house I tasted or smelled something awful. It felt like castor oil coating the inside of my brain and I gagged a bit.

I noticed others having the same reaction and this time Steven had paled to a flat white coffee shade. Turning my head, I saw Salistra walk by the edge of the porch. Where not an hour before she had been the size of a large horse, the ones that pull the beer trucks in commercials, now she made an elephant look petite and with each step the ground shook.

Behind her slithered Tirsane, her scales catching the light and creating tiny rainbows that bounced off every reflective surface. When she came around the porch my breathing stuttered. She wore her inhumanely beautiful face, and the number of men that were all but drooling over her would have made me want to giggle if fear hadn't locked everything else out.

A subtle shift of my head let me check on Jo and she just looked terrified but determined, her jaw locked as she stared ahead.

~Who is in charge here?~ Salistra's voice cut through my mind like an obsidian blade and I whimpered because this time there was fury behind those crystal tones.

Mister bullhorn guy spoke through a clenched jaw. "I am. You are interfering in an Earth legal matter. This doesn't concern you." He spat out the words and my eyes widened.

Is he insane?

Salistra didn't say anything but looked towards the other side of the house, and everyone followed her gaze, including me. Some thing slithered and crawled and bubbled around the edge of my house, leaving the lawn and pavement behind it melted and rotted. I gagged again, fighting to keep the food in my stomach while more than a few people lost that battle, though Jo and Sable didn't, and to my displeasure neither did bullhorn guy.

It had no shape and all shapes, it was black and all colors and no colors, and it made me want to scream, cry, laugh, and beg all at the same time. I didn't even have to ask; I knew this was the representative of Chaos and I wanted nothing more than to never have it in this realm again.

~The representatives of magic think otherwise. There have

been concerns for a while regarding your treatment of mages. But it is mostly your world. Now we have an issue with your current actions against a Herald of Magic.~ More than one person was bleeding from the nose at this point, including bullhorn guy.

I thought about saying something, but I had no idea what to say. I wasn't even sure why they were here.

"That is not your business. Cori Munroe broke the law. She is to be arrested."

~Point of fact, she did not.~ The razor-sharp words cut into my mind. ~By your own laws, they are requested to stay in the area. She remained in your state physically, though she had to step to another realm.~

"Which meant she wasn't reachable," the man snarled. I wondered about his sanity. Salistra's speech cut into your brain and he was going to challenge her? Did he have a death wish?

~To rescue those that are like unto family for her. Which is grounds for leaving, is it not?~ Salistra had leaned even closer to the man, her needle tipped horn less than a foot from his chest. Her voice calm, logical, and so cold I expected the temperature to drop.

Bullhorn guy cast a glance at the three of us on the porch and sneered. "I have no proof they were ever in danger. Wanting to try on clothes or have a girl's night, or just get naked with your lovers does not constitute extenuating circumstances."

I ground my teeth, frustrated and amazed at the man's stubbornness.

~Oh, I can guarantee you, they were in real danger. If Merlin Munroe had not come and rescued them, both girls would have died. I would have ensured it.~ Her crystal sharp voice cut me to the heart as I realized if I had not come they would have died because of me. Rage began to build again, pushing at my bindings.

~They were promised to me if she did not show. I would have had fun with them for a long time.~

I didn't need to know who spoke, the pain and discordant notes made it clear the thing from Chaos had replied. I really wanted it to never speak again. More than one person on the lawn was laying there retching, blood oozing from nose and ears.

Even bullhorn looked a bit shaken by that.

"Humans, trust me, the two women would have died, a long slow painful death if Cori had not rescued them. But I do not think you understand the full nature of what we want to make very, very clear to you." Tirsane had moved forward. Towering over all the humans, she had to be at least twelve feet tall, and when she turned to look at me, I swallowed at the expression of a stranger wearing a face I knew. This was the face of a demigod, not the Tirsane who sat and ate smoked nuts with us. Part of me wondered if this really would cost me everything.

And when did I start considering her my friend?

The agent struggled to his feet. I was impressed. I didn't want to move, and he was standing. The guy didn't lack for willpower. Most everyone else was sitting, though a few were curled up in the fetal position.

"And what is that nature? She is a mage, she is under our rules and controls." Bullhorn spat staring at her.

I had the petty thought of really, really wanting her to turn him to stone. Maybe it would help.

"Yes. And we acknowledge those rules, to an extent. Look," Tirsane said and waved at the porch where I sat, Carelian at the bottom steps. A rip formed, the slash of pain almost unnoticeable with the pain from all the other stuff rippling through my mind, and Esmere stepped out. Her coat gleamed like emeralds in the sun, making the grass seem pale and sickly. Another slash of pain and another rip, and Baneyarl stepped out, taking a seat on the other side of Carelian. Along my porch steps a head then a body materialized out of them and Hamiada formed sitting on the top step with a bonelessness that made my body ache even as I tried to remember to close my mouth. A flash of pain came from above me and I jerked my head up to see Jeorgaz fly from nowhere and land on the banister, his feathers so rich in color they didn't look real.

What is going on?

I shot Jo and Sable a wide-eyed glance, but they looked as confused as I did. It didn't make me feel any better.

"To make sure you understand Cori Munroe is protected, watched over, favorited, and even loved. She is special to Magic and to us. While we agree she must abide by your rules, within reason"—that last part was said with a level of menace that made my skin crawl—"if she is hurt, abused, or killed because you think your petty need for control is more important, the realms themselves will turn against you. Make very sure anything that befalls her is due to her willing actions to break your laws."

"This is blackmail? Treat her as a god or we'll punish you?" He spat and the level of spite in his gaze as it lingered on me made me want to step into another realm myself. Whatever else happened here, he was my enemy.

How is this my life that I have an enemy like this?

"Not at all. We could have removed the edicts at any time. We decided not to. Your world is rather," Tirsane paused looked around, her lips forming a perfect moue, "...boring. This is simply us telling you the consequences of your actions should you continue forward with them. She has a purpose for us, and we would like to see her achieve it."

~Or don't let her move forward with her purpose. This

world has much I would like to remake,~ the thing from Chaos said.

"Yes, Bob would enjoy that, though we all have denizens of our realms that would enjoy free access."

Bob? That thing's name is Bob now?

~But I will most definitely come for you,~ Salistra all but drawled in a honey coated tone that cut like a knife as her horn touched the agent's chest. ~For you would have deprived me of a debt that I am owed.~

For the first time, bullhorn looked shaken. "I will review the charges and if you swear the women would have been killed without her presence, then her departure may be deemed acceptable."

"Excellent. Then I am sure you shall be old and grey before we ever need to step back into this realm. Sal? Bob?" Tirsane turned in a way that no human body could ever have managed and moved to face me. "I trust, Cori Munroe, you will continue your studies with Mage Elder Baneyarl and accept guidance as always from Chaos Lord Esmere. Do remember to call upon Jeorgaz as needed for advice and research, especially regarding his late master's work." She winked at me, which did nothing to allay the wholesale panic waiting at the back of my mind. But what was also there was the knowledge that I could take them all if I wanted. That I was a dragon, I just needed to grow into my scales.

Each of them preened or lifted wings or did something to drive home that they were magical creatures as she called their name. And now she wanted me to speak and be semi coherent?

I kept my focus on her and forced myself to my feet. If that jerk could do it, so could I. Forcing a smile to my face I performed a shallow bow. "I would be honored to continue our associations. My training with Mage Elder Baneyarl has been informative so far."

From the flicker of a smile on her lips I knew that was the right thing to say, even if these were politics I never had planned on playing in.

"And I know your coven members will continue also," she said, turning that inhuman gaze onto Sable and Jo.

They had also managed to stagger to their feet. They both bowed, agreeing.

"We shall be watching. Remember your rules do not apply to our realms." Tirsane's words were cryptic but I sensed they were meant more for me than anyone else.

"Understood," the man with the bullhorn ground out.

The three beings turned and swept towards the back of the house. Bob left a trail of destruction I knew would take me weeks to restore, and then they were gone. People slowly sat up and guns were raised and pointed my way. I didn't react, I just stood there like a dragon surveying my realms and stared at the interlopers on my lawn, Baneyarl, Carelian, Esmere, Jeorgaz, and Hamiada arrayed at my feet.

CHAPTER

FORTY-TWO

While familiars amplify the power of their mage, there is no quantitative data on how or if the type of familiar makes a difference. While the occasional familiar will mention being from a specific realm, they don't always match the class of a mage, or the primary class of a merlin. And no two offerings are ever the same cost, even if two mages have the same power scheme and the same type of familiar. ~ Magic Explained.

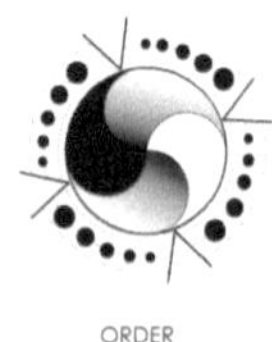

ORDER

"Put the guns down, and help the people still having reactions, and someone check on our mages. They took a pretty big hit." He didn't take his eyes off me, but he dropped the bullhorn and headed my direction.

Bullhorn looked at me, his lips pressed in a thin line, and I was very glad I had three if not four predators between me and him. Carelian, Esmere, and Baneyarl sat in front like an honor guard, while Jeorgaz and Hamiada had taken up spots on either side of the steps, flanking me.

"Miss Munroe," he ground out, stopping about three feet in front of my friends. I didn't bother to inform him I knew for a fact any of them could cross those three feet before he had time to blink, much less react.

"Merlin Munroe, if you please," I replied, trying to channel Indira's cool competence. "Would you explain what all of this was actually about?"

"You fled the scene of an active murder investigation." Each word sounded like he wanted to spit it at me. I pretended I was Esmere and didn't care.

"No," I corrected, while wishing I was dressed in my new clothes, not beat up and worn down from the trials. I felt disheveled and exhausted, which meant I probably looked worse. "I left a police station where the suspect was already in custody and had all but admitted to her actions. The merlin who was my liaison knew where I was going and had an idea as to why. All they needed from me was redundant testimony as there was more than enough evidence." I tried to stay cool and calm, but I made a silent vow to memorize every single law regarding mages on the books.

His eyes narrowed. "You were told not to leave. The law requires you to stay."

"I was told not to leave by someone who had no authority over me as I have not entered the draft and I was present only as a courtesy to my mentor. It was a trial run. There was no real difference between me coming here and going back to the apartment in the city."

~Cori,~ Carelian's voice purred in my mind. ~Steven says the law only applies to mages in the draft or formally contracted by the police department. You weren't. You weren't contracted to anyone except the FBI, and this wasn't an official assignment. The fact that they want to try you means they are trying to prove something, and it also means you aren't liable, because otherwise it would be a law you broke, not a trial to try and say you broke a law.~

I wanted to dance in joy and relief. I was definitely memorizing every single law and I would make Carelian memorize them too.

"I haven't entered the draft yet. As the police did not contract with me and this was not an official assignment, while I may have been ethically obligated to stay, I was not legally required. All the laws have clauses for need and the ability to be contacted. I was still in the state, and my location was known." I hoped that would shut him down hard. If anything, he just seemed to get more annoyed.

"You were not reachable here and didn't answer your phone." His eyes tried to drill holes into me. Behind him, Indira and Steven were slowly approaching and other people were looking decidedly freaked out. More than a few were still gagging or bleeding from Salistra and Bob's mind speech.

I clenched my fists so tight my nails cut into my palms, giving me something to focus on besides the complete meltdown I wanted to have. I didn't understand why no one else realized the equivalent of gods had just walked onto my front lawn and said —"We like her, be nice to her or else."

With a smile pasted on my face, and focusing on the pain from my nails, I responded. "I did not know that when I arrived. All I knew was that my friends and roommates were unreachable and had been for days. When Mrs. Guzman called me, I became aware it was more serious than a dead battery or phone. As my ability to assist with the investigation was done, I traveled here. I fully expected to find them with dead phones and goofing off."

A mage had crept up behind bullhorn man, the Soul symbol emblazoned on his temple. "You're lying," he said in a flat voice. Bullhorn's eyes narrowed.

I heaved an overly exasperated sigh. Jo's muffled laugh told me I'd gone a bit too dramatic. "Fine. I was afraid that they were dead. I'd hoped they had just had their phones die and were too busy having sex to think about me."

Both girls choked behind me, and I cast them silent apologies.

"Now. Would you like to explain exactly why, when the mage admitted to her crimes, and you had various other mages that could testify how the victims were killed, you felt you needed to show up here?" I knew the answer, but it was time to be a dragon. "And maybe you should tell me your name?"

He flushed an ugly red orange that clashed with his sandy red hair. "I am Director Harold Lefoin of the Draft Board. I make all the recommendations as to how further policies should be developed to control the abilities of mages and make sure our country is assisted by them, not harmed. When it was reported to me that you had teleported for something so frivolous as to check on friends, the board became concerned. Especially when your mentors swore you would contact us shortly. After twenty-four hours passed, we had reason to believe either you had fractured from your exposure to the insanity of Kelly Morris or were fleeing for some reason."

My mind shouted lie at the last part and I almost called him out on it, but instead I shut my mouth, thinking fast about how to lie without lying.

"This house is special and there are things here that could hurt anyone. I was frantic over my friends' inability to be reached and I might have over-reacted. As it was, they were in danger, but I should have been more politic about my departure."

Lefoin glanced at the mage next to him who nodded. "Why were you not answering your phone?" His tone told me clearly he still thought I was lying.

"Because I left it here as I knew I was probably going to be in another realm." I paused as the mage sucked in air through his teeth.

"You went to another realm?" the mage blurted, looking at me. Lefoin looked annoyed at the derailment of his accusations.

I gave both of them my best flat dragon stare. "You did just see what came and flattened my yard, right?" I jerked a finger to the grass that was black and mushy. "Where did you think they came from? They wanted me there and ensured it by taking my friends. It wasn't like I had cell phone service there."

The mage flushed, then paled and snapped his eyes to the various beings surrounding me.

"Why were they in danger?" Lefoin demanded.

I tilted my head staring at him. "Why does it matter?"

"Because I need to know if something is affecting my mages' ability to do their service," he snapped back.

"I haven't started my draft. None of us have. So until day one, it is none of your business," I responded, barely managing to not snap back. "Is there anything else?"

Lefoin sneered at my allies, and moved closer, eyes not leaving my face. "I don't like having ultimatums handed down to me by animals from another realm. Be assured we will be watching you very closely and if you so much as set a toe over the line, I will be there to make sure you pay the price."

I wanted to laugh and cry at the same time. The arrogance of this man astounded me, and I suspected he really did think they were animals.

"And you can be assured that anything that happens to me will be investigated to the fullest. I can only imagine Bob would be the one doing the questioning." It felt so wrong referring to that thing as Bob, and frankly there wasn't any other adjective or pronoun to use, but the resulting paling of the mage and Lefoin made me feel better. Though why Bob would do anything on my behalf made no sense.

Esmere stood and Lefoin took a step back as her size registered. With a flick of her tail, she walked up the steps to me and took a seat next to me.

~Cori, hold out your arm.~ It wasn't a request, and I knew exactly which arm she meant. With a muffled sigh, I pulled up the sleeve of my left arm and exposed the snake and the unicorn horn. ~Ah, I see. Well Bob,~ the emphasis she made on his "name" was so sarcastic I almost choked on the laugh that burbled up inside me, ~is annoyed no mark represents Chaos. Especially as your focus is of Chaos.~

Lefoin and the other mages had the blood drain from their faces, their eyes wide as they stared at her. The rest of the people in the area came to a standstill, watching us with sudden interest.

Great, she's broadcasting this to everyone.

~I cannot say that emotion is inaccurate. Let me fix it.~ She moved her head towards my arm, and I tried not to flinch, expecting another bite. At this rate my arm was going to look like a full sleeve of tattoos.

But instead of biting me, she placed her nose and whiskers against my arm, the dampness of her nose cool against my warm skin. A flash of electrical heat centered at that spot and raced out a few inches, then faded.

She pulled back her muzzle and peered at my arm. ~Yes, appropriate I feel, even if it is not what Bob might have wanted.~

Bracing myself, because Merlin only knew what a Cath would think was appropriate even if I was sure I'd be happier with her choice than with what Bob might have wanted, I looked at my arm. A smile was surprised out of me by what I saw. With the snake from Tirsane in the middle, and the mini horn from Salistra on my inner side, the outside now held a perfect nose and whiskers etched in a rainbow of colors. It was both pretty and chaotic, and oh so Cath.

I lifted my eyes to Esmere watching, an inscrutable look on her Cath face. "I love it."

~I rather thought you might. Very appropriate for the mage my kit chose.~ Esmere, as if she was all too aware of the audience she had gathered, turned to look at the people on the lawn. ~I shall see you later, Merlin Munroe. We have much to discuss about your new role as the Herald.~ With that she leapt up, deadly power personified, right toward Director Lefoin and disappeared. There wasn't even a ripple to indicate whether she'd sidestepped or went into another realm.

The man flinched back, arms blocking an attack to his head. He straightened when nothing impacted him and snarled at me. "You told her to do that," he accused.

I laughed. As did Carelian, Baneyarl, and Jeorgaz.

"She's a Cath. I don't tell her to do anything," I pointed out at the same time as Carelian, still with an undertone of amusement in his mind voice, spoke.

~No one tells my malkin what to do. The last one that tried ended up feeding her for a month.~

Lefoin stared at everyone, grinding his jaw.

"Be careful. Dental repairs are expensive," I said, my voice coated with sugar. Okay I probably shouldn't have said that, but dammit I was teetering on exhaustion as I'd been up for a long time and my body was complaining.

His hands clenched and I just knew he wanted to be looming over me, trying to make me see how insignificant I was. But I had allies and I knew I had a dangerous game to play, and I couldn't start out seeming weak.

"Watch yourself, Munroe. Just because you think your animal friends will help you, don't think that means you can flout the rules. I can't wait for you to screw up and I'll be the one to cut off your head." If he'd been any closer to me, I'm sure I would have had his spittle on my face.

Please let him be gone by the time my draft starts.

"Don't worry. I plan on making sure I follow every single rule, and then some. Now please do find someplace else to be." I added a bit of anger to that and looked at the tire tracks in the lawn, the trash they'd dumped, and the huge hoof marks from Salistra.

One last glare raked across the three of us, pretending Baneyarl and Jeorgaz didn't exist, then he spun on his heel and stalked across my lawn, each step an extra hard stomp.

"Jerk," I muttered. I watched the crowd of people pick up and go, though the mages lingered the longest, looking at Baneyarl and Jeorgaz with strange expressions of lust and curiosity. Everyone, except the power-mad director, had a freaked out look and kept jumping at every sound or sudden movement. Baneyarl had way too much fun flapping open his wings and scaring them.

Indira and Steven waited until the majority of the people

had packed up before making their way up to the porch, both still a bit pale. They looked at Baneyarl, Jeorgaz, Hamiada, and then at me.

"Maybe we should talk?" Steven said, his voice more polite than I'd ever heard.

CHAPTER

FORTY-THREE

Covens are interesting legal entities. They are not marriages or corporations, yet they fall in between. While US law requires two adults for marriage, covens are governed by the OMO and only require all members be mages. While there are no minimum or maximums for a coven, generally they act like a family group and are treated as a small company. They file a declaration very similar to an LLC and any children are legally children of all partners of the LLC. While communal living is not required, it is common. ~ History of Magic

---

SPIRIT

S able and Jo went to drag chairs out back, Baneyarl was a bit too big to comfortably fit through the doors. I knew I was past exhausted, but this couldn't be put off until later.

Jeorgaz still hadn't said much to me, and I walked over to him while the others were headed around back and asked, "Everything okay?"

He gave me a long look, his tail rustling in the breeze. ~James said once there was an ancient Babylonian curse: May your life never have boredom, and always challenge you. I fear you have been cursed in such a way. The avalanche has started and neither you nor I have the power to stop it. I wonder if either of us will live to see it come to fruition. Call if you need me, Cori.~

He vanished in a flash of fire and air, his departing words leaving me even more worried. I went through the house, grabbing a cold Coke from the fridge. I needed the sugar and the caffeine. I knew when I laid down I'd be out, but I couldn't do it quite yet.

The chairs were arranged in a semi-circle with Baneyarl, Hamiada, and Carelian closing the circle. I sank down into the empty chair and just looked at all of them.

"Well?" Dragon I might be, but right now I was a tired dragon and liable to bite someone's head off. I wondered if heads were tasty with ketchup while trying to focus on staying awake for this.

Indira licked her lips. "Would you mind telling us what happened?"

The wrist with the mark of Magic on it pulsed once and I sighed. I stalled, taking another slow sip of Coke, and tried to speak to Hamiada.

~Hamiada?~

~Yes, Master?~ Her voice sounded like wind in the trees, and I closed my eyes wanting to sleep so bad.

~Ugh, no, don't call me master. Just Cori. I'm going to blame you for the tests— Magic doesn't want me to share the herald stuff. Is that okay?~

~Of course. I am yours now.~

~Okay we will have a very long talk about that later. ~ Hamiada just looked away and didn't say anything.

"Apparently you need to be worthy to own this house. I blame James. So, there were a series of trials that Hamiada here administered." It wasn't a lie, quite. And Steven didn't call me on it. I explained what happened and Salistra's annoyance with me, hence the marks. Then Tirsane's one-upmanship.

Everyone, even Baneyarl and Jeorgaz listened as if I was telling the greatest story of all time. I didn't go as in-depth with the challenges as I had with Jo, Sable, and Carelian. Just skimming them and focusing more on the outcome.

"Then we show up here and that idiot is outside yelling." I swallowed and looked at them. "Did I really mess up that much? Thanks for the info by the way."

Steven held Indira's hand tight, he looked older for some reason. "Yes. You skated by, barely, because I stayed and the city had contracted me, not you. But Cori," he hesitated, looking at Baneyarl and Jeorgaz. "I don't know if bringing them here was a brilliant move or if you just shot yourself."

I started to laugh, as did Baneyarl and Jeorgaz. I was about to fall out of my chair with exhaustion amplified giggles.

~As powerful as Cori is, I believe you give her too much credit.~ Baneyarl spoke, his voice rich as always. ~Tirsane requested that I consider showing myself to mortals and establish that I was her teacher. I have been aware of the plans in motion for a very long time and deemed it worthy of the attention. Though when I agreed, I had not been aware that Esmere or Jeorgaz would be on display also.~ He ruffled out his wings a little before settling back down.

I fought a smile. Baneyarl disliked having the attention pulled away from him, and few could compete with a phoenix. And Esmere had her own level of fascination for humans.

"Wait, you're really her teacher? For how long?" I almost started laughing again at the spluttering astonishment from Steven.

~Since the day I took both of you to my home after eliminating the humans that were hunting you.~ Baneyarl had a level of smugness to his voice that sounded too much like Carelian.

"And how long have you been waiting to tell him that?" I asked as I tried to crush the last of my giggles.

~At least a year,~ Baneyarl admitted. ~There were many things your instructors passed on that contained so many levels of inaccuracy it was painful.~

"You killed the sniper on the roof," Indira hissed her eyes wide. "But I looked, I couldn't see you."

~You mean like this?~ Baneyarl shimmered and vanished.

"Okay, he makes it look so much cooler than when I do it," Jo said, staring at the dented grass. "Though doing it on grass is a giveaway."

"Wait, you can do that too?" Steven's head rotated to stare at Jo.

"Kinda. I still am there if you know to look." She tilted her head and the air shimmered around her and she disappeared. But if you stared really hard you could see a vague distortion and her outline, like a heat haze. A minute later she shimmered back into view. "See, he's much better at it."

~I have also been practicing for a century or more,~ Baneyarl said.

"He's been teaching all of you?" Indira's voice cracked and I had to admit part of me enjoyed seeing her calm composure fractured. It wasn't a nice part of me.

"I swore not to tell anyone. But apparently Tirsane decided I didn't need to keep it quiet?"

Baneyarl re-appeared, his wings shifting. ~The need for covert actions is gone.~ He shifted and settled in giving me a sideways look. ~It was better use of resources to declare.~

"I'm both jealous and in awe. You had actual other realm denizens acting as teachers?" Indira just looked stunned.

"We all have. It's kinda cool everything Earth doesn't understand," Sable said, laughing softly as Water came up from her glass and swirled around her.

"So why did they come?" Steven asked. "You know they will pin me down as soon as they can and ask."

"Other than to prevent me and my friends from being killed? I don't know. I don't know what their plans are, I don't know why Tirsane seems to think I'm a friend, I don't know why Salistra hasn't killed me, and as for Bob?" I glared at Carelian. "Bob?"

~Well every time we said~— a spike of pain slammed down through my eyes and out my ears and I whimpered——~everyone reacted like that,~ Carelian said, exasperation in his voice.

I pried my eyes open to see the rest of the humans also reacting like someone had shoved a flaming dagger into their brain.

"Bob works," I muttered. I cleared my throat. "When I figure it out and I think it is safe to tell you, I will. For now?" I looked at everyone and sighed. "I know I've made an enemy, but I still have three or four years before I'm done with my degree, so maybe he'll be gone. I need to learn every single law and have it memorized. I need to learn how to use my magic offensively. Falling back on Earth every time causes way too much collateral damage." I felt a twinge of guilt at the memory of Daniela Morris' death, but it faded quickly. I hadn't meant for her to die.

~That sounds like fun. It has been a while since I have dug out my war spells. But I did not think humans used them?~ Baneyarl had both enthusiasm and curiosity in his voice.

I just shrugged.

"We don't know of any, or at least none are freely talked about. I provided a list of some to Cori, but they are a shadow of what you know." Steven looked at Jeorgaz, who had done little but listen. He just shook his head. "And to think we prided ourselves as mentors when you had these people in your court. And when did you get on a first name basis with Tirsane?"

"Um, my birthday probably. She showed up. Said she likes cake." I shrugged. "And I don't know that she has more than one name. You know like Cher?"

"And Bob and Salistra?" Steven asked.

I just shrugged. "You'd have to ask them." I held up my arm. "The snake is to show Tirsane is aware of or intrigued by me. The horn is 'cause I pissed Salistra off and she says I owe her.

We all sat in silence for a few minutes, then Indira started giggling. I looked at her funny. "What?"

"Cori, you just intimidated and forced one of the more powerful men in the US to back down." Indira shook her head, still smiling. "I know the OMO is going to be taking notes and you can expect constant requests for information about the beings that showed up. You've made an enemy in him; he doesn't tolerate losing well. Yet you have more power behind you and in you than any mage I've ever heard of. And we thought we were mentoring you. Cori, you've so far surpassed what we hoped we could do. Merlin, I'm about ready to ask you to mentor me. List you as one of my sponsors and maybe see if that gets people off my back."

"Oh," I murmured, concentrating on my feet, not sure how

to answer that. I'd just wanted to quit being the timid mouse, but I was starting to realize that maybe I'd gone too far.

"All of you will need to watch your step. Jo and Sable that includes you two. They will try to get you to make a mistake in order get their claws into Cori, so be very careful as you'll start the draft before Cori does," Steven said, his voice serious. "I'd follow her lead in memorizing the laws. You're going to need to know how fine those lines are at times." He shrugged. "But I'm wondering what the three of you are going to change."

Everyone looked at us, and we looked at each other and shrugged. I jerked up straight.

"Hamiada!" She flinched as did half the people in the yard. I ignored them. "The books. Were the books real?"

Jo and Sable knew what I meant though I hadn't described the books when I reviewed what happened.

"Books?" Steven asked, but I ignored him, focused only on Hamiada.

She shifted. "Yes and no. The death book is real, it is a list of all deaths and why, but it only shows you either people you know or someone you are seeking," her voice slow. "It is written by magic as every being dies."

I pushed that down—someday I would figure out why Stevie died, it wasn't worth Jo or Sable's life. "But the others?"

"Yes, if a cure is known it is listed there. But until a cure to a disease has been discovered it is never listed."

"So only diseases we already know how to treat would be there?"

Hamida looked up at the sky. "Mostly. There are some things you have forgotten, or the necessary ingredients have disappeared. But yes."

I sagged. "And the magic items?" Disappointment pulling at me hard enough that sleep surged back up as priority.

"Oh real. But then replicating those only takes a-"

~Cori, didn't you mention forming a coven? Are the three of you going to bond, then?~ Baneyarl's question distracted me and Hamiada faded a bit into the grass, looking greener than before.

"A coven? Are you going to officially form one?" Indira asked seemingly delighted.

That gave me a jolt of worry. I looked at Baneyarl and Jeorgaz, then shifted to Carelian, who was licking his paw and washing his face.

"We're still discussing it."

Jo and Sable gave me startled looks then smiled, their hands clasped.

Someday we would talk about it. Just not today. I had no idea what I'd started or what it would involve by the time it was done, but I was Magic's herald now and I'd make sure I was enough of a dragon to protect my friends and family. And with Jo and Sable on my side, plus Carelian, a griffon, a phoenix, and maybe a Chaos lord—whatever that meant—I might just end up being a very scary dragon.

Here's to being a dragon. And finally getting some sleep.

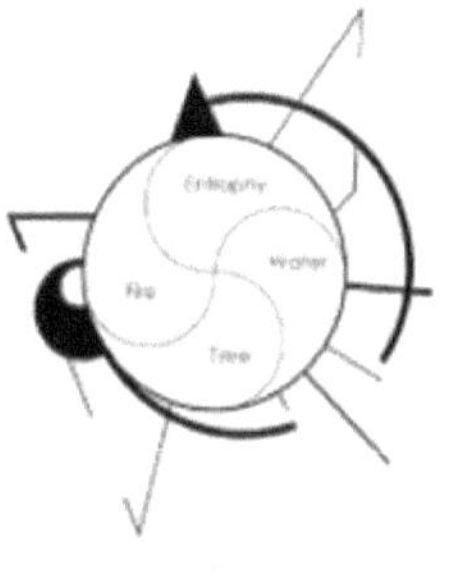

Chaos:
- Entropy
- Fire
- Water
- Time

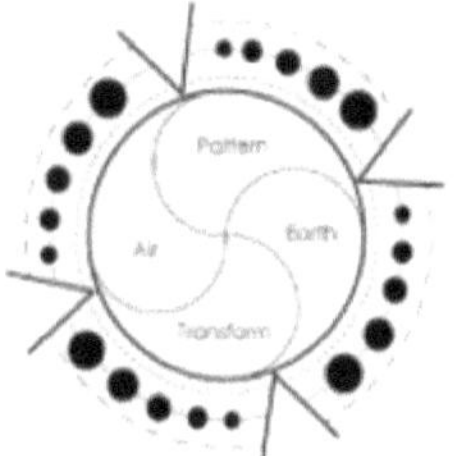

Order:
- Pattern
- Air
- Earth
- Transform

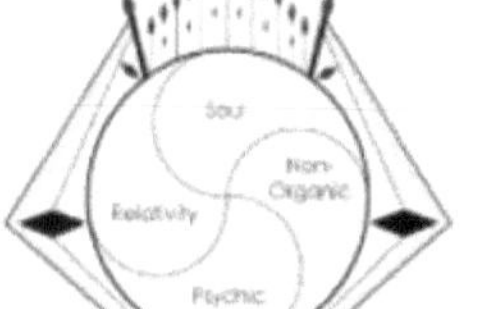

Spirit:
- Soul
- Relativity
- Non-Organic
- Psychic

AUTHOR NOTES

This is book 4 in Twisted Luck, based in the Ternion universe. This series is just the first stories in what is a complicated and fascinating world. If you enjoyed Cori getting a taste of what life holds in store for her, wait until you see where she ends up. This is a long series and I hope you enjoy this world as much as I do.

If you loved this novel, please take the time to leave a review, you will be amazed at the difference it makes.

Book 5, Drafted Luck, is available now.

If you'd like to stay in touch, you can follow me on social media at the following places:

Website: https://badashpublishing.com/
Facebook: https://www.facebook.com/badashbooks/
Twitter: https://twitter.com/badashbooks
Instagram: https://www.instagram.com/badashbooks/
Bookbub: https://www.bookbub.com/profile/mel-todd

There is a Twisted Luck Fan Group. I can't wait to see you there - https://www.facebook.com/groups/1500124503671599

If you're interested in free books, keeping up with what is going on in my life, as well as sales and launch announcements, you can sign up for my newsletter at my website. You never know what freebies might be in it.

Take care!

Mel Todd

About the Author

Mel Todd has over 20 stories out, her urban science fiction Kaylid Chronicles, the Blood War series, and the new Twisted Luck series. Owner of Bad Ash Publishing, she is working to create a place for excellent stories and great authors. With over a million words published, she is aiming for another million in the next two years. Bad Ash Publishing specializes in stories that will grab you and make you hunger for more. With one co-author and more books in the works, her stories can be found on Amazon and other retailers.

facebook.com/MelTodd.Author

x.com/BadAshBooks

instagram.com/BadAshBooks

www.ingramcontent.com/pod-product-compliance
Lightning Source LLC
Chambersburg PA
CBHW051201190726
48288CB00006B/1748